Resounding praise for
New York Times bestselling author
ELIZABETH PETERS
and her
AMELIA PEABODY
mysteries

"No one is better at juggling torches while dancing on a high wire than Elizabeth Peters."
Chicago Tribune

"The Amelia Peabody books [are] a delightful series filled with Egyptology, crime, murder, mystery, and intrigue."
Pittsburgh Post-Gazette

"Amelia is rather like Indiana Jones, Sherlock Holmes, and Miss Marple all rolled into one."
Washingto...

"Pete... ... derring-do... ... eems a bit ner... ... r pleasure ... ... volved in these archaeological mysteries."
New York Times Book Review

"This author never fails to entertain."
Cleveland Plain Dealer

"Peters's wily cast of characters keeps the reader coming back for more."
San Francisco Chronicle

Books by Elizabeth Peters

The Amelia Peabody Series
A River in the Sky • Tomb of the Golden Bird
The Serpent on the Crown
Guardian of the Horizon • Children of the Storm
The Golden One • Lord of the Silent
He Shall Thunder in the Sky
The Falcon at the Portal
The Ape Who Guards the Balance
Seeing a Large Cat • The Hippopotamus Pool
The Snake, the Crocodile and the Dog
The Last Camel Died at Noon
The Deeds of the Disturber • Lion in the Valley
The Mummy Case • The Curse of the Pharaohs
Crocodile on the Sandbank
and
Amelia Peabody's Egypt *(edited with Kristen Whitbread)*

The Vicky Bliss Series
The Laughter of Dead Kings
Night Train to Memphis • Trojan Gold
Silhouette in Scarlet • Street of the Five Moons
Borrower of the Night

The Jacqueline Kirby Series
Naked Once More • Die for Love
The Murders of Richard III • The Seventh Sinner

and
The Copenhagen Connection • The Love Talker
Summer of the Dragon • Devil-May-Care
Legend in Green Velvet
The Night of Four Hundred Rabbits
The Dead Sea Cipher • The Camelot Caper
The Jackal's Head

ELIZABETH PETERS

THE DEEDS
OF THE
DISTURBER

HARPER

An Imprint of HarperCollinsPublishers

HARPER

An Imprint of HarperCollins*Publishers*
10 East 53rd Street
New York, New York 10022-5299

Copyright © 1988 by Elizabeth Peters
ISBN 978-0-06-199922-2

First Harper premium printing: March 2011
First Avon Books paperback printing: April 2001
First Avon Twilight printing: April 2000

HarperCollins® and Harper® are registered trademarks of Harper-
Collins Publishers.

Printed in the United States of America

Visit Harper paperbacks on the World Wide Web at
www.harpercollins.com

10   9   8   7   6   5   4   3   2

To Charlotte MacLeod
My favorite mystery writer
and dainty little lady

His sister was his protector,
She who drives off the foe,
Who foils the deeds of the disturber
By the power of her utterance.

The clever-tongued, whose speech fails not,
Admirable in the words of command.
Mighty Isis!

—*"Hymn to Osiris,"*
Eighteenth Dynasty

ONE

In a great many respects I count myself among the most fortunate of women. To be sure, a cynic might point out that this was no great distinction in the nineteenth century of the Christian era, when women were deprived of most of the "inalienable rights" claimed by men. This period of history is often known by the name of the sovereign; and although no one respects the Crown more than Amelia Peabody Emerson, honesty compels me to note that her gracious Majesty's ignorant remarks about the sex she adorned did nothing to raise it from the low esteem in which it was held.

I digress. I am unable to refrain from doing so, for the wrongs of my oppressed sisters must always waken a flame of indignation in my bosom. How far are we, even now, from the emancipation we deserve? When, oh when will justice and reason prevail, and Woman descend from the pedestal on which Man has placed her (in order to prevent her from doing anything except standing perfectly still) and take her rightful place beside him?

Heaven only knows. But as I was saying, or was

about to say, I was fortunate enough to o'erleap (or, some might say, burst through) the social and educational barriers to female progress erected by jealous persons of the opposite sex. Having inherited from my father both financial independence and a thorough classical education, I set out to see the world.

I never saw the world; I stayed my steps in Egypt; for in the antique land of the pharaohs I found my destiny. Since that time I have pursued the profession of archaeology, and though modesty prevents me from claiming more than is my due, I may say that my contributions to that profession have not been inconsiderable.

In those endeavors I have been assisted by the greatest Egyptologist of this or any other century, Radcliffe Emerson, my devoted and distinguished spouse. When I give thanks to the benevolent Creator (as I frequently do), the name of Emerson figures prominently in my conversation. For, though industry and intelligence play no small part in worldly success, I cannot claim any of the credit for Emerson being *what* he is, or where he *was*, at the time of our first meeting. Surely it was not chance, or an idle vagary of fortune that prompted the cataclysmic event. No! Fate, destiny, call it what you will—it was meant to be. Perchance (as oft I ponder when in vacant or in pensive mood) the old pagan philosophers were right in believing that we have all lived other lives in other ages of the world. Perchance that encounter in the dusty halls of the old Boulaq Museum was *not* our first meeting; for there was a compelling familiarity about those blazing sapphirine orbs, those steady lips and dented chin (though to be sure at the time it was hidden by a bushy beard which I later persuaded Emerson to remove). Still in vacant and in pensive mood, I allowed my fancy to wander—as we perchance had wandered, among the mighty pillars of ancient Karnak, his strong sun-brown hand clasping mine, his muscular frame attired in the short kilt and beaded collar that would have displayed his splendid physique to best advantage . . .

I perceive I have been swept away by emotion, as I so often am when I contemplate Emerson's remarkable attributes. Allow me to return to my narrative.

No mere mortal should expect to attain perfect bliss in this imperfect world. I am a rational individual; I did not expect it. However, there are limits to the degree of aggravation a woman may endure, and in the spring of 18—, when we were about to leave Egypt after another season of excavation, I had reached that limit.

Thoughtless persons have sometimes accused me of holding an unjust prejudice against the male sex. Even Emerson has hinted at it—and Emerson, of all people, should know better. When I assert that most of the aggravation I have endured has been caused by members of that sex, it is not prejudice, but a simple statement of fact. Beginning with my estimable but maddeningly absent-minded father and five despicable brothers, continuing through assorted murderers, burglars, and villains, the list even includes my own son. In fact, if I kept a ledger, Walter Peabody Emerson, known to friends and foes alike as Ramses, would win the prize for the constancy and the degree of aggravation caused me.

One must know Ramses to appreciate him. (I use the verb in its secondary meaning, "to be fully sensible of, through personal experience," rather than "to approve warmly or esteem highly.") I cannot complain of his appearance, for I am not so narrow-minded as to believe that Anglo-Saxon coloring is superior to the olive skin and jetty curls of the eastern Mediterranean races Ramses strongly (and unaccountably) resembles. His intelligence, as such, is not a source of dissatisfaction. I had taken it for granted that any child of Emerson's and mine would exhibit superior intelligence; but I confess I had not anticipated it would take such an extraordinary form. Linguistically Ramses was a juvenile genius. He had mastered the hieroglyphic language of ancient Egypt before his eighth birthday; he spoke Arabic with appalling fluency (the adjective refers to certain elements of his vocabulary); and even his command of his native tongue was marked at an early age by a ponderous pomposity of style more suitable to a venerable scholar than a small boy.

People were often misled by this talent into believing Ramses must be equally precocious in other areas. ("Catastrophically precocious" was a term sometimes applied by those who came upon Ramses unawares.) Yet, like the young Mozart, he had one supreme gift—an ear for languages as remarkable as was Mozart's for music—and was, if anything, rather below the average in other ways. (I need not remind the cultured reader of Mozart's unfortunate marriage and miserable death.)

Ramses was not without amiable qualities. He was fond of animals—often to extremes, as when he took it upon himself to liberate caged birds or chained dogs from what he considered to be cruel and unusual punishment. He was always being nipped and scratched (once by a young lion), and the owners of the animals in question frequently objected to what they viewed as a form of burglary.

As I was saying, Ramses had a few amiable qualities. He was completely free of class snobbery. In fact, the little wretch preferred to sit around the sûk exchanging vulgar stories with lower-class Egyptians, instead of playing nice games with little English girls and boys. He was much happier in bare feet and a ragged galabeeyah than when wearing his nice black velvet suit with the lace collar.

The amiable qualities of Ramses . . . He did not often disobey a direct command, providing, of course, that higher moral considerations did not take precedence (the definition being that of Ramses himself), and the order was couched in terms specific enough to allow no possible loophole through which Ramses could squirm. It would have required the talents of a lord chief justice and a director general of the Jesuit order to compose such a command.

The amiable qualities of Ramses? I believe he had a few others, but I cannot call them to mind at the moment.

However, for once it was not Ramses who caused me aggravation that spring. No. My adored, my admired, my distinguished spouse was the guilty party.

Emerson had some legitimate reasons for being in an evil humor. We had been excavating at Dahshoor, a site near Cairo that contains some of the noblest pyramids in all Egypt. The firman (permit, from the Department of Antiquities, giving us permission to excavate) had not been easy to secure, for the Director of the Department, M. de Morgan, had intended to keep the site for himself. I had never asked him why he gave it up. Ramses was involved in some manner; and when Ramses was involved, I preferred not to inquire into details.

Knowing my particular passion for pyramids, Emerson had been naïvely pleased at being able to provide them. He had even given me a little pyramid of my very own to explore—one of the small subsidiary pyramids which were intended, as some believe, for the burials of the pharaoh's wives.

Though I had greatly enjoyed exploring the dank, bat-infested passageways of the miniature monument, I had discovered absolutely nothing of interest, only an empty burial chamber and a few scraps of basketry. Our efforts to ascertain the cause of the sudden, inexplicable winds that occasionally swept through the passages of the Bent Pyramid had proved futile. If there were concealed openings and unknown passageways, we had not found them. Even the Black Pyramid, in whose sunken burial chamber we had once been imprisoned, proved a disappointment; owing to an unusually high Nile, the lower passages were flooded, and Emerson was unable to procure the hydraulic pump he had hoped to use.

I will tell you a little secret about archaeologists, dear Reader. They all pretend to be very high-minded. They claim that their sole aim in excavation is to uncover the mysteries of the past and add to the store of human knowledge. They lie. What they really want is a spectacular discovery, so they can get their names in the newspapers and inspire envy and hatred in the hearts of their rivals. At Dahshoor M. de Morgan had attained his dream by discovering (how, I refused to ask) the jewels of a princess of the Middle Kingdom. The glamour of gold and precious stones casts a mystic spell; de Morgan's discovery (I do not and never will inquire how he made it) won him the fame he desired, including a fulsome article and a flattering engraving in the *Illustrated London News*.

One so-called scholar who excelled at getting his name into print was Mr. Wallis Budge, the representative of the British Museum, who had supplied that institution with some of its finest exhibits. Everyone knew that Budge had acquired his prizes, not from excavation but from illegal antiquities dealings, and had smuggled them out of the country in direct contravention of the laws governing such exports. Emerson would have scorned to follow Budge's example, but he would have settled for a stele like the one his chief rival, Petrie, had found the year before. The world of Biblical scholarship was abuzz about it, for it contained the first and thus far the only mention in Egyptian records of the word "Israel." This was a genuine scholarly achievement, and my dear Emerson would have sold his soul to the Devil (in whom he did not believe anyway) for a similar prize. Flinders Petrie was one of the few Egyptologists whom Emerson respected, albeit grudgingly, and I am sure Petrie reciprocated the sentiment. That mutual respect was probably the reason for the intense rivalry between them—though both would rather have died than admit they were jealous of one another.

Being a man (however superior to his peers), Emerson could not admit this wholly natural and reasonable desire. He tried to blame his disappointment on ME. It is true that a slight detectival interlude had interrupted our excavations for a time, but Emerson was quite accustomed to that sort of thing; it happened almost every season, and in spite of his incessant complaints he enjoyed our criminous activities as much as I did.

However, this latest diversion had had one unusual feature. Once again, as in the past, our adversary had been the mysterious Master Criminal known only by his soubriquet of Sethos. Once again, though we had foiled his dastardly schemes, he had eluded our vengeance—but not before he had proclaimed a sudden and (to some) inexplicable attachment to my humble self. For several memorable hours I had been his captive. It was Emerson who freed me, fortunately before anything of unusual interest had occurred. Over and over I had assured Emerson that my devotion had never weakened; that the sight of him bursting through the doorway with a scimitar in either hand, ready to do battle on my behalf, was a vision enshrined in my heart of hearts. He believed me. He doubted me not . . . in his head. Yet a dark suspicion lingered, a canker in the bud of connubial affection, that would not be dispelled.

I did all I could to dispel it. In word and especially in deed I spared no effort to assure Emerson of my unalterable regard. He appreciated my words (and especially my deeds) but the vile doubt lingered. How long, I wondered sadly, would this situation endure? How often must I renew my efforts to reassure him? They were beginning to wear on us both, to such an extent that Ramses commented on the dark circles under his father's eyes and asked what prevented him from getting his proper rest.

Never one to falter when duty (as well as affection) calls, I determinedly pursued my efforts until sheer exhaustion forced Emerson to concede that I had proved my case. The discovery of an inscribed block enabling us to identify the hitherto unknown owner of the Bent Pyramid allowed him to end the season with a triumph of sorts. But I knew he was still brooding; I knew his vaulting ambition had not been satisfied. It was with considerable relief that I finished the task of packing our possessions and bade a fond though (I hoped) temporary farewell to the sandy wastes of Dahshoor.

Any woman can imagine the pleasure with which I contemplated our rooms at Shepheard's, that most elegant of Cairene hotels. I was looking forward to a real bath, in a genuine tub—to hot water, scented soap, and soft towels—to the services of a hairdresser and laundress—to shops, newspapers, and the society of persons of refinement. We had reserved berths on the mail steamer from Port Said, which went directly to London in eleven days. It would have been quicker to take a ship to Marseilles, but rail travel from that city to London, via Paris and Boulogne, was uncomfortable and inconvenient, especially for travelers with a great deal of luggage to transfer. We were in no especial hurry and looked forward to a leisurely voyage; but before embarking I felt I was entitled to a few days of luxury. I doubt that any woman could accept with more equanimity than I the difficulties of housekeeping in a tent or an abandoned tomb or a deserted, haunted monastery—all of which I had encountered—or relish more the beauties of desert life. But when comfort is at hand, I believe in being comfortable. Emerson does not share this view. He is happier in a tent than in a fine hotel, and he loathes the company of persons of refinement. However, we were only to be in Cairo for two days, so he endured his fate with resignation.

The afternoon of our arrival in the city found me splashing merrily in my tub, enjoying a rare moment of freedom from care. Ramses had gone off with Abdullah, our excellent reis, on some expedition or other. The cat Bastet, who rarely left the boy's side, had refused to accompany him, which confirmed my suspicion that the trip, concerning which both Abdullah and Ramses had been vague, involved something of which I would not approve. No matter; Ramses was as safe in the company of Abdullah as he was in that of any man or woman. (That is to say, relatively safe.) He would return in due time, reeking and filthy and gorged with food that would have rendered any other child desperately ill, but that would not affect the cast-iron internal organs of my son. I would deal with Ramses in due time. In the interval, his absence could only add to my pleasure.

The cat Bastet sat perched on the rim of the tub, watching me through slitted golden eyes. She was fascinated by baths. I suppose total immersion in water must have seemed to her a peculiar method of cleansing oneself.

Though Dahshoor is not far from Cairo, we had not visited the city in the past few weeks. A sizable pile of letters and periodicals awaited us; at my request, Emerson left the door to the bathroom ajar and read the mail to me. There were several letters from Emerson's brother Walter and his wife, my dear friend Evelyn. They congratulated us on our imminent return, and gave us news of our nieces and nephews.

The remainder of the mail was inconsequential. Emerson laid it aside and turned to the newspapers, of which there were several weeks' accumulation. I listened with lazy amusement to the snippets he chose to read aloud, for his notion of what I might find interesting was rather curious. The progress of our forces in the Sudan—yes, I did take an interest in that, since it was so close to home (our home of the spirit, Egypt). But advertisements for Daimler Wagonettes (a novel vehicle propelled by an internal combustion engine of two cylinders) and the Lambeth Patent Pedestal Combination Water Closet failed to inspire me. I did not protest; Emerson's deep baritone fell pleasantly on my ears and his pungent comments on "modern inconveniences" added spice to the news itself. Dreamily contemplating my toes, as they floated on the surface of the scented water, I fell into a kind of waking doze, from which I was rudely awakened by Emerson's scream of rage.

"Of all the infernal nonsense!" he cried.

I deduced that Emerson had turned from *The Times* to another periodical—most probably the *Daily Yell*, whose columns often provoked such a reaction.

"What is infernal nonsense, my dear?" I inquired.

A great rattling of pages followed. Then Emerson exclaimed, "Just as I suspected. I might have known. Your dear friend O'Connell is the author of this rubbish!"

I was about to reply that Mr. Kevin O'Connell was no particular friend of mine; but that would not have been strictly true. I had not seen a great deal of him in recent years, but during our investigation of the bizarre murder of Lord Baskerville I had become quite fond of the young journalist. Brash and impertinent in the pursuit of his profession he may have been; but he had proved a staunch ally in the time of our desperate need, and he had been quite good-natured about Emerson's having kicked him down the main staircase at Shepheard's.

"What has Mr. O'Connell done now?" I asked.

The newspaper rattled noisily. "He is up to his old tricks, Peabody. More cursed mummies, more cursed—er—confounded curses."

"Really?" I sat up, splashing water on the paws of Bastet, who grumbled low in her throat and fixed a golden glare upon me. "I beg your pardon," I said.

"What for?" Emerson shouted.

"I was speaking to the cat Bastet. Pray go on, Emerson. Read me what he writes."

"I think not," Emerson said.

"I beg your pardon, Emerson?"

"I beg yours, Amelia," my husband replied, in tones of freezing dignity. "I will not read you this article. In fact, I intend to destroy the newspaper and all others that contain the slightest reference to a subject that has, for reasons I cannot explain, the most extraordinary effect on your ordinarily competent brain."

"Competent, Emerson? Competent, did you say?"

Emerson's reply, if any, was drowned by the sound of paper being ripped, crumpled, torn and trampled upon. I waited until the tornado had subsided before calling out, "Really, Emerson! You cannot destroy every copy of that newspaper in Cairo, and your actions must inevitably intensify my curiosity."

Emerson began mumbling to himself. He does that at times. I caught a few words—"forlorn hope . . . damnable persistence . . . ought to know better . . . after all these years . . ." I proceeded to soap my foot without further comment; marriage had taught me the useful fact that silence is sometimes more effective than prolonged discussion. Finally—tacitly acknowledging the force of my argument—he began to read. His voice was so distorted by sarcasm as to be positively falsetto.

"Latest example of the curse. The royal mummy strikes again. Where will it end? On Tuesday last, at three in the afternoon, a distinguished lady visitor sprained her ankle after slipping upon an apple core . . ."

I laughed aloud. "Very good, Emerson. Very humorous, upon my word. Now read me the story."

"I am reading it," Emerson replied. "It is impossible, Amelia, for me to satirize the literary style of your friend O'Connell. Those are his exact words."

His voice had dropped in pitch, but I knew, from his use of my first name, that he was still annoyed with me. Since the halcyon days of our courtship, in an abandoned tomb in Middle Egypt, Emerson has referred to me by my maiden name of Peabody when feeling affectionate. For my part, I never succumb to the childish trick of employing his given name of Radcliffe, which he detests. Emerson he was to me then, and Emerson he will always be—the name hallowed by memories as tender as they are thrilling.

However, he was eventually persuaded to relate to me what he had read of the case. The malignant mummy did not reside in Egypt, as I had supposed, but in the dusty halls of that venerable institution, the British Museum. The sprained ankle was a rather labored device of Mr. O'Connell's, but the initiating incident had been a good deal more serious—fatal, in fact.

Going to his post in the Egyptian Room one morning, a guard had discovered the body of one Albert Gore, a night watchman, sprawled on the floor in front of one of the exhibits. The poor fellow had apparently suffered a stroke or heart attack, and if he had collapsed by a black-figured vase or a medieval manuscript, his passing would have attracted no interest—except, one presumes, to his friends and family. However, the exhibit happened to be a mummy case, complete with mummy, and that had aroused O'Connell's journalistic instincts. He could be regarded, I suppose, as something of an authority on ancient Egyptian curses.

"Brain seizure—but why?" was his first headline. Emerson's reply: "Curse it, the chap was sixty-four years of age!"

"What caused the look of frozen horror on the dead man's face?" O'Connell demanded. Emerson: "The lunatic imagination of Mr. Kevin O'Connell."

"Can fear kill?" Kevin inquired, and Emerson replied, to me: "Balderdash!"

The mummy had been presented to the museum the preceding year, by an anonymous donor. Kevin had displayed the enterprise I would have expected of him in tracking down the name of this individual, and his discovery only served to intensify interest in what was otherwise a fragile tissue of imaginative fiction. Nothing fascinates the British public so much as royalty, and a hint of royal scandal is even better.

I deem it advisable to conceal the true names and titles of the individuals concerned, even in the pages of this private journal, for if at some future time the archaeological notes contained herein should be deemed worthy of publication (which they unquestionably will), I would be the last one to wish to recall a long-forgotten stain upon the Monarchy which, despite its failings, must command the loyalty of any true Englishwoman. Suffice it to say that the donor—whom I shall henceforth designate as the Earl of Liverpool—was related by blood to a most distinguished Lady. As Emerson would say—and in fact did say fairly often—she had altogether too many descendants, direct and collateral, bumbling around the world and getting into trouble.

If the Earl hoped to save himself from the malignant influence of his Egyptian souvenir, he delayed too long. Shortly after giving it up, he met with a fatal hunting accident.

"Served the villain right," commented Emerson, who shared my aversion to blood sports. "Sensible mummy; intelligent cadaver. His son did not get off scot-free either. He seems to be a thoroughly disgusting young reprobate, who suffers from a thoroughly disgusting degenerative disease. Perfect case of poetic justice. Excellent mummy!"

"What disease is that, Emerson?"

Emerson had turned to another issue of the newspaper. He rattled it loudly. "A modest woman would not ask such a question, Peabody."

"Oh," I said. "*That* thoroughly disgusting disease. But surely even a newspaper like the *Yell* would not name it."

"There are euphemisms, Peabody, there are euphemisms," Emerson replied austerely. "And anyone who knows the young man and his set could conjecture correctly."

"So that is the extent of the mummy's baneful influence? A hunting accident, a case of—er—disease, and a natural death from heart failure?"

"The usual number of weak-minded ladies have felt faint in its presence," Emerson replied caustically. "And the usual psychic investigators have received messages from the Beyond. Humph. I suppose one can hardly blame the gullible public, when our distinguished Keeper of Egyptian and Assyrian Antiquities feeds their folly."

"Wallis Budge? Oh, come, Emerson, not even Budge would—"

"He would. He has. That fellow will stop at nothing to get his name in print. How such a ranting imbecile could attain that position . . . DAMNATION!"

No device of the printer's art, not even capital letters, can indicate the intensity of that shriek of rage. Emerson is known to his Egyptian workers by the admiring soubriquet of Father of Curses. The volume as well as the content of his remarks earned him the title; but this shout was extraordinary even by Emerson's standards, so much so that the cat Bastet, who had become more or less accustomed to him, started violently, and fell with a splash into the bathtub.

The scene that followed is best not described in detail. My efforts to rescue the thrashing feline were met with hysterical resistance; water surged over the edge of the tub and onto the floor; Emerson rushed to the rescue; Bastet emerged in one mighty leap, like a whale broaching, and fled—cursing, spitting, and streaming water. She and Emerson met in the doorway of the bathroom.

The ensuing silence was broken by the quavering voice of the safragi, the servant on duty outside our room, inquiring if we required his assistance. Emerson, seated on the floor in a puddle of soapy water, took a long breath. Two of the buttons popped off his shirt and splashed into the water. In a voice of exquisite calm he reassured the servant, and then transferred his bulging stare to me.

"I trust you are not injured, Peabody. Those scratches . . ."

"The bleeding has almost stopped, Emerson. It was not Bastet's fault."

"It was mine, I suppose," Emerson said mildly.

"Now, my dear, I did not say that. Are you going to get up from the floor?"

"No," said Emerson.

He was still holding the newspaper. Slowly and deliberately he separated the soggy pages, searching for the item that had occasioned his outburst. In the silence I heard Bastet, who had retreated under the bed, carrying on a mumbling, profane monologue. (If you ask how I knew it was profane, I presume you have never owned a cat.)

Studying my husband as he sat on the bathroom floor in a puddle of water, carefully separating the soaking pages of the newspaper, I was overcome by renewed admiration and affection. How cruelly was that man maligned by those who did not share the intimacy of his acquaintance! His explosions of temper were as brief as they were noisy; afterward he immediately reverted to his customary affability, and I believe few men could appear so cool and dignified in such a position. Bastet's considerable bulk had struck him full in the chest. His wet shirt molded the splendid musculature of that area of his body; and though the water in which he sat was slowly darkening the fabric of his trousers, producing a considerable degree of discomfort, he remained unperturbed.

At last he cleared his throat. "Here it is. I beg, Amelia, that you will refrain from commenting until I have finished reading.

"Hem. 'Stop press. Startling new developments in British Museum Mystery. Your correspondent has learned that within a few weeks a team of expert investigators will attempt to solve the case of the malignant mummy. Professor Radcliffe Emerson and his spouse, Amelia Peabody Emerson, whose daring exploits are well known to readers of the *Daily Yell*—'"

It was impossible for flesh and blood to remain unmoved. Rising impetuously to my feet, I cried, "Good Gad!"

Emerson peered at me over the sagging rim of the soggy wad of newspaper. His eyes blazed a brilliant blue—a sign of ire with which I was well acquainted. Waving my loofah to emphasize my words, I went on, "Surely, Emerson, you do not suppose I am responsible for initiating that preposterous story? Even if I cared to investigate the case—and I agree with you that it is stuff and nonsense—there would not have been time enough for me to communicate with Mr. O'Connell. The paper you are holding must be several weeks old—"

"Fifteen days, to be precise," said Emerson.

He tossed the newspaper aside and rose to his feet. His gaze remained fixed on me, and the brilliance of his eyes had, if anything, intensified.

"Don't you believe me, Emerson?"

"Certainly, Peabody. Certainly." Having unfastened his wet trousers, he stepped out of them and fumbled with the buttons of his shirt.

"Do please hang your trousers over the chair," I exclaimed. "I sent most of your clothing out to be laundered and I don't know when . . . Emerson! What are you doing?"

The dampened fabric resisted his effort to free the buttons from the buttonholes. Biceps bulging, Emerson ripped it apart, and the remaining buttons flew about the room like bullets. "Aphrodite," said Emerson in a hoarse voice. "Rising from the foam."

I realized I was still standing, with water dripping off me and the big sponge I held. I burst out laughing. "Emerson, you are too absurd. If you will hand me that towel—"

In a single bound Emerson crossed the room and clasped me to his breast.

I attempted to expostulate, pointing out the open window, the time of day, the slippery condition of my person (and his), the possibility of interruption by the safragi, Ramses, and/or the cat. Emerson's only intelligible reply was a reference to a certain volume of Arabic verse which recommends a number of notions which would never ordinarily occur even to the most devoted of married persons. I soon realized he was beyond appeals of a rational nature and abandoned the argument; and indeed, at a somewhat later time, I readily agreed with his suggestion that the volume in question might open up a number of new and interesting possibilities.

It was with heavy hearts that we bade farewell to our faithful friend Abdullah and his extremely extended family at the railway station in Cairo. Abdullah had wanted to escort us to Port Said (at our expense), but I had persuaded him otherwise. Though the beard which had been grizzled when we first met was now snowy white, Abdullah was as fit as a fellow half his age, but in moments of depression or high drama he was inclined to make mournful references to his increasing years and the possibility that we might never meet again. The more prolonged the parting, the more painful it would be—for me, not for Abdullah, who relished drama of all sorts.

Hence our departure was less painful than it might have been. The men, including Emerson and Ramses, squatted on the platform laughing and joking and recalling the events of the past season. When the time for the departure of the train was imminent, our devoted fellows cleared a path through the crowd and carried us on their shoulders to the door of our compartment. So great is the affectionate respect felt by all Egyptians for my famous husband that few of the people who were accidentally toppled over voiced complaints; and as the train chugged away, a hundred voices blended in the cries of farewell. "Allah preserve thee, Father of Curses! The blessings of God be upon thee and thy honored chief wife, the Sitt Hakim! Ma'es-salâmeh—peace be with thee!" It was an affecting moment; and tears blurred my vision as I watched young Selim, Ramses' particular friend, running along the platform to keep us in sight as long as possible.

I had felt some degree of apprehension with regard to the voyage, since we had been unable to provide an attendant for Ramses. The young man who had performed that function had left the position through no fault of his own; he had been placed under arrest for murder in the first degree, a charge from which we were happily instrumental in freeing him. He had returned to England with his bride—another of the romantic successes for which I understand I am becoming known—and although I am always pleased to assist young persons in affairs of the heart, Mr. Fraser's departure had left us in a difficult position, past experience having proven that Ramses, unattended and on board a ship, constituted a serious threat to shipping and navigation, not to mention the nerves of his parents. Emerson flatly refused to allow him to share our cabin. He was utterly devoted to the lad, mistake me not; but, as he expressed it, "not between the hours of midnight and eight A.M."

For once Ramses caused no trouble. He was fully occupied with some nasty experiments having to do with his study of mummification, and, I am sorry to say, with the book of Arabic poetry which Emerson, in the fatigue following the application of one of the suggested procedures, had neglected to conceal under the mattress, as was his usual custom. Fortunately, or unfortunately, depending on one's viewpoint, we did not discover this latter interest until we had almost reached London, since Ramses always put the book neatly back where he had last found it.

As soon as we had settled ourselves on board ship, I hastened to the salon in search of newspapers more recent than the ones I had perused before leaving Cairo. I took the precaution of clipping out articles of interest, which was fortunate, since as soon as he discovered what I was doing, Emerson threw every one of the newspapers overboard, to the extreme annoyance of the other passengers. Armed with my clippings, I found a comfortable deck chair and brought myself up to date on the case of the malicious mummy.

Emerson's remarks in the bathroom had been both uninformative and misleading. It was not entirely his fault; one had to read carefully between the lines in order to obtain the facts, which had been distorted, mangled, and misquoted in the normal process of reporting.

Though popularly referred to as a mummy case, the object that had aroused such a furor was more properly termed a wooden inner coffin. If I were asked why this distinction should be made, I could do no better than refer the dedicated student to Emerson's monumental work, *The Development of the Egyptian Coffin from Predynastic Times to the End of the Twenty-sixth Dynasty, with Particular Reference to Its Reflection of Religious, Social, and Artistic Conventions*, Oxford University Press. Knowing, however, that the majority of readers are not dedicated students, I venture to supply a brief synopsis.

The earliest coffins were simple wooden boxes, more nearly square than rectangular, since the bodies they contained had been folded into a crouching or fetal position. As time went on, the wooden surfaces, inside and out, were painted and/or carved with magical spells and religious symbols. By the Middle Kingdom (about 2000–1580 B.C.), the coffins had become elongated and there were usually two of them. The so-called anthropoid coffin, shaped like the mummified form it enclosed, did not appear until the Empire Period (approximately 1580–1090 B.C.). A well-to-do person might possess as many as three such coffins, each smaller than the last, fitting inside one another like a set of Chinese boxes; and the nest of coffins was sometimes enclosed as well within a stone sarcophagus. Such was the vain pre-occupation of these amiable but misguided pagans with the survival of the flesh! (In which aim, a moralist might add, they defeated their own purpose, for a body so swathed and boxed up was more susceptible to decay than one exposed to the hot, dry air and baking sands of the desert.)

From the engravings reproduced in the newspapers and from my familiarity with the seminal work of my distinguished spouse, I was able to deduce that the coffin in question dated from the Nineteenth Dynasty. The artist had sentimentalized the face into simpering prettiness, but the details were characteristic of the period—the heavy, ornate wig, the arms folded across the quiet breast, the conventional religious symbols and bands of hieroglyphic inscriptions. The engraving did not show these clearly, but one reporter—an enterprising rival of Mr. O'Connell's—had made a copy of them. I recognized the standard mortuary formula, addressed to the God of the Dead: "Invocation to Osiris, Lord of Busiris, et cetera, et cetera, by the Chantress of Isis, Henutmehit . . ."

So the lady (she was female, at any rate) was not a princess or the priestess of a dark and sinister cult. I had suspected as much from the form of the coffin;

her titles made it clear, for although she had held a minor temple appointment, she was no more out of the ordinary than the wife or sister of a modern clergyman. Why should this undistinguished, if handsome, coffin have been singled out as a source of death and peril?

The answer, as Emerson had already suggested, had to be found in the fertile brains of the reporters. O'Connell was not the only one to fall on the story like a vulture on a corpse; in the vivacity of his inventiveness and the lurid tone of his prose he was equaled, if not surpassed, by at least one rival, a certain M. M. Minton, who wrote for the *Morning Mirror.* Minton had had the ingenuity to trace and interview a young person who had been (so she claimed) in the employ of the late Earl. Led by Mr. Minton, she had recalled how she "used to come all over queer" when requested to dust in the room where the mummy reposed. Vases and bric-a-brac had been found smashed to bits in that same room; on the night of the full moon, eerie cries and moans issued from it.

This was nonsense, of course, as were the tales of accidents befalling visitors to the museum. Much more interesting to a student of human nature like myself was the effect the story had had on weak-minded individuals. Some had placed flowers before the exhibit or sent money to the museum for the same purpose. Others had written, recounting similar occult experiences. A notorious medium had claimed to be in communication with the spirit of Princess (*sic*) Henemut (*sic* again), who explained that the officials and trustees of the museum had offended her modesty by exposing her to public view. (An unjust accusation, to say the least, for between the coffin and the wrappings she was more modestly covered than some of the ladies who came to look at her.) She demanded to be returned to her tomb. Since its location was unknown this request was not susceptible of fulfillment even if the museum authorities had been mad enough to consider it.

The most entertaining of the mummy's admirers was a lunatic (he could be nothing else) who visited her from time to time dressed in the costume of a *sem* priest. The distinguishing feature of this ensemble was the leopard-skin cloak the priest wore over his shoulders. In wearing this skin and in imitating the priest, whose duty it was to officiate at funerals, the lunatic showed his familiarity with ancient Egyptian customs, but when interviewed, Mr. Budge jeered at the suggestion that the madman might be a scholar. "The fellow wears a wig. As Herodotus tells us, priests always shaved their heads and *all other parts of their bodies.*" (The italics are not mine. I hoped they were not those of Mr. Budge.)

Budge had never actually said he supported the insane theories of the reporters; in fact, he had rejected them in formal terms. It was perhaps not entirely his fault that his answer to some of the questions asked him did not go quite far enough in denying superstition. "But did not the ancient Egyptians believe in the power of curses, Mr. Budge?" "Why, yes, certainly; we have a number of examples of such things." "And the priests had magical powers, did they not?" "One would not wish to deny the authenticity of Scripture; we read in Exodus how the priests turned their rods into serpents . . ."

"Idiot," I said aloud. The elderly gentleman in the deck chair next to mine gave me a startled look.

Through haste or (more likely) a deliberate attempt at deception, Emerson had omitted one interesting aspect of the night watchman's death. Like many of the people who hold such posts, Albert Gore had been elderly, uneducated, and given to the excessive consumption of spirituous liquors. None of these failings detracted from his ability to carry out his tasks, or so it was supposed; he was only required to make the rounds of certain sections of the museum several times during the night and doze in his cubicle near the door the rest of the time. It was most unlikely that a thief would have the temerity to enter the museum; apart from other difficulties, such as the impossibility of selling the unique objects on the open market, the building was always locked up tightly and the surrounding streets were constantly patrolled by constables.

It was probable, then, that poor Albert Gore had suffered a cerebral hemorrhage while patrolling the Egyptian Galleries, for overindulgence in food and drink not uncommonly leads to such a result. I discounted Kevin's reference to "the look of frozen horror imprinted on the dead features" as a typical journalistic excess.

But there was one odd thing. Clustering around and under the body, and more widely dispersed through the room, were a number of unusual objects—broken bits of glass, scraps of paper and cloth, dried splashes of some dark liquid substance and—most peculiar of all—a few crushed, withered flowers.

After I had finished reading, I followed Emerson's example and tossed the clippings overboard. He had been quite right; the whole affair was humbug, unworthy of the attention of a sensible person. We had not seen the end of it, though. Our names had been mentioned, our authority appealed to; we owed it to ourselves and our scholarly reputations to deny the allegations as vigorously as possible.

Humbug it was, unquestionably. And yet there were those withered flowers . . .

TWO

More recently than in Spenser's day the "sweete Themmes" ran "softly," through green banks whereon "the Violet pallid grew; The little Dazie that at evening closes, The virgin Lillie and the Primrose trew." I have spoken with Londoners who could still remember summer trips to the pastoral beauties of Greenwich as delights of their childhood. But long before the time of which I write the trees on the Isle of Dogs had given way to ugly factories belching black smoke into the filthy cloud that hung over London like a funeral pall. The river, lined with mean houses and coaling docks and warehouses, flowed sullen and slow, befouled by unspeakable and unthinkable refuse. Standing on the deck as our steamer headed for the Royal Albert Dock, I observed it was raining. It always seemed to rain the day we returned to England.

Yet though I thought with fond nostalgia of the hot blue skies of Egypt, I could not help but be stimulated by my proximity to the greatest of cities—center of Empire, home of intellectual and artistic prowess, land of the free, and home of true British grit.

I remarked as much to Emerson. "My dear Emerson, there is something stimulating about returning to the center of Empire, the home of intellectual and artistic—"

"Don't talk such blood—er—blooming nonsense, Amelia," Emerson growled, applying his handkerchief to my cheek and displaying a grimy smudge. "The very air is black."

Ramses stood between us—I held him by one arm, Emerson by the other—and of course he had to add his opinion. "Anatomical studies on the cadavers of Londoners prove that prolonged breathing of this atmosphere turns the lungs quite black. However, I believe Mama was not referring to the physical environment, but to the intellectual—"

"Be still, Ramses," I said automatically.

"I am quite aware of what your mama meant," Emerson said, scowling. "What are you up to, Amelia? I will probably be obliged to spend more time than I would like in this filthy town if I am to finish my book—"

"You will *unquestionably* be obliged to spend a *great deal* of time in London if you are to finish it before we return to Egypt next autumn. Considering that the Oxford University Press announced its imminent publication a year ago—"

"Don't nag, Amelia!"

I shot a reproachful glance at Emerson and a meaningful glance at Ramses, who was listening with owl-eyed interest. Emerson put on a sugary-sweet smile. "Ha, ha. Your mama and I are joking, Ramses. She never nags; and I would not be so rude as to mention it even if she did."

"Ha, ha," said Ramses.

"As I was saying," Emerson resumed—turning his head away so Ramses would not see him scowl, "I cannot help but wonder, Amelia, if you are suddenly enamored of this pestilential ant heap of human misery because you—"

"Dear me," I said. "We are all becoming a trifle smutty. Ramses, your nose . . . There, that is better. Where is the cat Bastet?"

"In the cabin, of course," said Emerson. "She has better sense than to expose herself to this pernicious atmosphere."

"Then let us retire and complete our preparations for disembarking," I suggested. "Ramses, you have Bastet's collar? Remember, tie the lead to your wrist and do not allow her . . ." But Ramses had departed, wriggling from my grasp with eellike agility.

The sullen skies were just as dark when we again stood on the deck, but for me they were brightened by the sight of those who awaited us on the dock: Emerson's dear brother Walter, his wife Evelyn, my sister in affection as well as in law; our faithful parlormaid Rose, and our devoted footman John. As soon as they saw us they began to wave and smile and call out greetings. I was particularly touched at Evelyn's braving the filthy weather. She hated London, and her fragile blond beauty looked quite out of place on the grimy dock.

As was so often the case, my dear Emerson's thoughts were the reflection of my own, though he did not express them quite as delicately as I would have done. Squinting narrowly at his sister-in-law, he demanded, "She is not pregnant again, surely? It is unnatural, Peabody. I cannot conceive why a woman—"

"Hush, Emerson," I said, poking him gently with my parasol.

Emerson looked warily at Ramses. He had never fully recovered from a conversation the previous winter, during which he had been obliged to discuss with Ramses certain matters which do not ordinarily interest an English gentleman until he has reached the age of twenty-five or thirty.

Ramses stood stooped under the weight of the cat, who was lying across his narrow shoulders; but Ramses had been known to talk—at length—under even more adverse conditions. "I am eager to question Aunt Evelyn concerning that," he remarked. "The information you gave me, Papa, was inadequate to explain why any sensible individual would place himself—or, particularly, herself—in positions that are at best unnatural and at worst—"

"Be still, Ramses," Emerson shouted, crimsoning. "I told you never to discuss—"

"You are not to ask your Aunt Evelyn anything of the kind," I exclaimed.

Ramses said nothing. His silence suggested that he was working on ways to get around my prohibition. I had no doubt he would succeed.

Thanks to Emerson's imposing physical presence and loud voice we were among the first to disembark, and I rushed toward Evelyn with outstretched arms. Conceive of my surprise when, just as I was about to enter her fond embrace, I was seized by a tall, portly individual in a black frock coat and silk hat, who pressed me to his enormous stomach and planted a whiskery kiss on my forehead. Extricating myself instantly from his embrace, I was about to retaliate with a shrewd blow from my handy parasol when the man exclaimed, "My dear sister!"

I *was* his sister. That is to say, he was my brother—my brother James, whom I had not seen for several years (because I had taken considerable pains to avoid him).

It was no wonder I had not recognized him immediately. Once he had been stout. Now the only words that could begin to do justice to his size were words such as corpulent, obese, and elephantine. Limp whiskers framed a face as round and red as a hunting moon. Instead of retreating into a normal neck, his chins advanced, roll upon roll, until they met a swelling corporation uninterrupted by any hint of a waistline. When he smiled, as he was smiling now, his cheeks swelled up and squeezed his eyes into slits.

"What the devil are you doing here, James?" I demanded.

From my dear Evelyn, standing to one side, came a gentle cough of remonstrance. I directed a nod of apology to her, but I did not feel obliged to apologize to James for my blunt but understandable language.

"Why, I am here to welcome you, of course," was James's smooth reply. "It has been too long, dearest of sisters; the time has come for familial affection to mend the rents of misunderstanding."

Emerson had wasted no time in clasping his brother's hand and pumping it with the hearty force that is the Englishman's manner of displaying affection in public. Placing a brotherly arm around Evelyn's slim shoulders, he remarked, "Is that James? Good Gad, Peabody, how fat he has become. So much for the roast beef of old England, eh? And the port and the Madeira and the claret! Why doesn't he go away?"

"He says he has come to welcome us home," I explained.

"Nonsense, Peabody. He must want something from you; he never comes to see us unless he wants something. Find out what it is, tell him 'no,' and let us be off."

James's forced smile trembled in the balance, but he managed to hold on to it. "Ha, ha! My dear Radcliffe, your sense of humor . . . Upon my word, it is the most . . ." He offered his hand.

Emerson eyed it for a moment, lips pursed, then seized it in a grasp that brought a squeal of pain from my brother. "Soft as a baby's," said Emerson, flinging the member aside. "Come along, Peabody."

However, we were not to be rid of James so easily. He stood his ground, smiling and nodding, while the rest of us exchanged those charmingly inconsequential bits of domestic news that mark the meeting of friends after a long absence.

Rose continued to hold Ramses (and the cat) in a close embrace. She had a quite unaccountable attachment to the boy and was one of the few people who defended him on all occasions. Such cases are not unknown, I believe; Rose had no children of her own. Though her official position was that of parlormaid, she was the mainstay of our household and

cheerfully performed any service requested of her.
She had come up to London for the express purpose
of watching over Ramses for the few days we intended to remain in town. Not that she was really
capable of controlling him; but then, as Emerson
said, no one was.

John—who could not control Ramses either—had
been out to Egypt with us one winter, and he was full
of questions about his friends Abdullah and Selim
and the rest. The look of surprise and contempt on
James's face at seeing us so friendly with a mere footman was very amusing; but at last a slight cough from
Evelyn reminded me of the damp weather, and we
took an affectionate leave of John, who was returning
immediately to Kent with our baggage.

There were too many of us for the carriage, so
Walter suggested the ladies make use of it, while he
and his brother followed in a cab. I did not hear him
mention *my* brother; that did not prevent James
from joining them. Emerson was already inside the
cab, so I was spared seeing his reaction.

Ramses and Rose went with us in the carriage.
He immediately launched into one of his interminable monologues, describing his winter's activities,
to which Rose listened with a fatuous smile. I turned
to Evelyn, who was seated beside me.

"How long do you mean to stay in London, my
dear?"

"Only long enough to welcome you, dearest Amelia, and persuade you to spend the summer with me in
Yorkshire, at Chalfont Castle. I have missed you and
dear little Ramses so much; his cousins constantly ask
for him—"

"Ha," I said skeptically.

Ramses interrupted his speech long enough to give me a long, direct stare; before he could comment, I continued, "I am not certain of Emerson's plans, Evelyn, but I expect he will have to be in London a great deal of the time. I am trying to help him finish the first volume of his *History of Ancient Egypt*; the Oxford University Press has become quite insistent, and no wonder, since he promised them the manuscript a year ago. Then there is our excavation report to prepare for the printer—"

"That is what Walter said," Evelyn remarked. "So I have concocted a little scheme I hope will please you. We mean to keep the town house open, so that Radcliffe can stay there instead of at a hotel. But I had hoped you—"

"Oh, Emerson cannot get on without my help," I said. "Much as I would prefer to rusticate in the tranquillity of the country, and greatly as I enjoy your companionship, my dear, I cannot—I never will—abandon my dear Emerson at such a time. Without my assistance and my little reminders he will never finish that book."

"Of course." A smile played about the corners of Evelyn's delicate lips. "I understand."

"Aunt Evelyn." Ramses leaned forward. "Aunt Evelyn, I am in particular need of information, so I beg you will excuse me for interrupting you and Mama—"

"Ramses, I forbade you to discuss the subject," I said firmly.

"But, Mama—"

"You heard me, Ramses."

"Yes, Mama. But—"

"Not under any circumstances, Ramses."

"Now, Amelia, do let the dear child speak," Evelyn said with a smile. "I cannot imagine that he could say anything that would distress me."

Before I could refute this absurdly naïve remark, Ramses took quick advantage. In a rush he cried, "Uncle James is staying at Chalfont House."

"Ramses, if I have told you once, I have told you a hundred—What was that?"

"Rose says that he came there with his valet and his luggage, and is staying. I thought you would want to know that, Mama, having observed the decided lack of cordiality with which you and Papa greeted—"

"Ah. Without admitting the necessity of a prolonged explanation of your reasons for introducing the subject, Ramses, I confess that I am grateful for the information and for the opportunity to discuss its implications without your father's being present. I am afraid he will not be at all pleased."

"You mustn't blame me, Amelia," Evelyn began, her hands twisting in her lap.

"My dearest girl! How can I possibly blame you for a weakness so engaging as a kind heart? Knowing James, I am sure he simply moved in, bag and baggage, presuming upon a relationship which is as distant as the affection he purports to feel for me." Across from me I saw Rose nodding like a marionette, her lips primped and her cheeks pink. I gave her a kindly nod. "The question is, what is James up to? For, as Emerson so wisely remarked, he must want something."

"You are very cynical, Amelia," Evelyn said reproachfully. "Mr. Peabody has been open with me; he regrets the sad estrangement between his family and yours and yearns to restore loving relations—"

"Restore, bah," I said. "There never were loving relations between me and James, much less James and Emerson. However, you are far too unworldly to recognize a hypocrite when you see one, and too well-bred to treat him as he deserves. Never mind, I will get rid of him—if Emerson has not already done so."

However, as it turned out, Emerson had not been informed of James's presence in the house, probably because he had talked the whole time without allowing Walter or James to get a word in. Indeed I was somewhat relieved to see James descend from the cab (with what huffings and puffings I will not attempt to describe), for Emerson was perfectly capable of throwing him bodily out of it if displeased. Jumping lithely to the ground after him, Emerson seized his hand, wrung it fiercely, dropped it, and turned away. Seizing Evelyn in one hand and me in the other, he escorted us rapidly through the gate and along the path toward the house.

Before Emerson bustled me indoors I saw something that took my mind off my brother's machinations. It had begun to rain harder, and there were not many people abroad. Only one head was uncovered to the elements. It belonged to an individual standing by the park railings across the street, and it was crowned by a mop of fiery red hair.

Catching my eye, the individual in question stood on tiptoe and went through a series of extraordinary gesticulations, first raising a hand with the thumb folded under, then bringing an invisible vessel to his lips, as if drinking, then pointing, holding up his forefinger, and pointing again. These gestures were performed with great vigor and intensity, before he clapped a shabby cap on his head and glided rapidly away.

With a tact I had not expected from him, James absented himself from the luncheon table. Afterward Emerson and Walter retired to the library to revel in conversation of an Egyptological nature until teatime. I persuaded Evelyn to lie down for a little rest (Emerson's random surmise as to her delicate condition having been verified by no less an authority than Evelyn herself); and, having left Ramses lecturing Rose on various subjects that did not interest her in the slightest, I was able to concentrate on the peculiar behavior of Mr. Kevin O'Connell.

Why he had not left a written message instead of following us from the dock and carrying on like a maniacal mime, I could not imagine. Possibly—I speculated—he feared Emerson might intercept or inquire about such a letter. Well, I was no more anxious than he to involve Emerson, but I was very anxious indeed to talk with Mr. O'Connell. I had a few things to say to him.

Since four o'clock was the hour he had indicated, I had a little time to spare before leaving to keep the appointment, and I occupied it in reviewing the past week's newspapers. They had been tidied away, but at my request one of the footmen retrieved them and brought them to my room.

By the time I had finished reading, my amused tolerance for Mr. O'Connell had completely evaporated. His cool and unfounded statement that we had consented to investigate a fictitious criminal case was bad enough. His most recent references to us were positively infuriating.

Since the so-called mystery was no mystery at all, only a string of meaningless coincidences, it would have died a natural death had not O'Connell and his co-conspirators of the press kept it alive by various doubtful stratagems. Especially useful to them were the activities of certain members of the lunatic public, including the *sem* priest who had been mentioned in an earlier article. This individual had become a regular visitor to the exhibit where, attired in flowing white robes and moth-eaten leopard skin, he prostrated himself and performed mysterious rituals with the intention, one presumes, of propitiating the mummy.

Emerson and I had been Mr. O'Connell's principal victims. There were several stories about our past activities, including a picture of Emerson that would assuredly drive him to homicide when he saw it. The artist had depicted an incident that had occurred the summer before, on the steps of the British Museum. Emerson had only waved his fist under Mr. Budge's nose, he had never actually struck the man; but the drawing might have served as an illustration to a sensational novel—"Take that, you dastardly cur!" Budge's bulging eyes and look of abject terror were very cleverly portrayed. (The dispute, a mere tempest in a teapot, had arisen after Budge had the effrontery to write to *The Times* objecting to Emerson's valid criticisms of an Egyptian pottery exhibition. In the course of the letter he had used language no gentleman should use of another.)

Mr. O'Connell had not even scrupled to exploit an innocent child in his pursuit of a journalistic sensation. The paragraphs mentioning Ramses were in the worst possible taste. There was no need to mention the fact that Ramses was regarded by certain Egyptians (the most ignorant and superstitious) as a kind of juvenile jinni, a demon in youthful shape. I also deeply resented O'Connell's implication that only negligent, uncaring parents would expose a child so young and so "delicate" (his word, not mine) to the unhealthy climate and manifold perils of an archaeological excavation. Compared to London, Egypt is a veritable health resort, and I had certainly done all any human female could do to prevent Ramses from exploring abandoned pyramids, being buried alive in the sand, and carried off by Master Criminals.

So it was in a frame of mind almost as homicidal as Emerson's would have been that I prepared myself for the assignation. I had of course meant to take my parasol. I never go abroad, in London or in Egypt, without it. It is the most useful object imaginable, serving not only as a protection against sun or rain, but, when need calls, as a defensive weapon. At the last minute I turned back to the bureau and removed from it another article of attire. Emerson is always making fun of my belt, even though the implements attached to it, in the manner of an old-fashioned chatelaine, have more than once saved us from a horrible and lingering death. Matches in a waterproof box, a little flask of pure water, notebook and pencil, scissors, knife—these examples are sufficient to explain why my belt was an indispensable aid in all climes and countries—including certain parts of London. The belt itself was of stiff leather, two inches wide, and on one memorable occasion it had served me well—to fend off (for a brief but vital interval) a threat more perilous than death.

I managed to leave the house unobserved by any of the occupants except Gargery the butler. He was new to the post, having been hired since I last was in England: a sandy-haired, youngish man of medium height and build, with an ingenuous face that had not quite mastered the perfect imperturbability the office requires. He stared at my belt and its jingling accoutrements as if he had never seen such a thing before (which in fact I suppose he had not).

St. James's Square is not far from Pall Mall and the bustling traffic of Regent Street; but on that dismal spring afternoon it might have been a thousand miles from the city. Fog muffled the clatter of wheels and horse's hooves and gave a ghostly air to the budding trees that surrounded the pool in the center of the square.

Following the direction O'Connell had indicated, I turned into York Street and then into the first street opening off to the left. I hoped I was going the right way; I wished he had not been so cursedly vague and theatrical. His gesture of drinking left open the question of whether he referred to a restaurant, or a teashop, or a coffee stall; the only thing I could do was walk on until I found an establishment in which liquid refreshment was purveyed, or until I saw O'Connell himself.

Before long I found myself in a neighborhood quite unlike the aristocratic purlieus of St. James's Square. It was respectable enough, I suppose, but the houses were cramped close together and the people hurrying by had a shabby, harried look. There were not many umbrellas in evidence; I held mine high, peering keenly from side to side in search of a familiar face and form.

It was not his face or form I made out first, but the flaming Titian locks not even a London pea-souper could mute. He stood peering out from the recessed doorway of an establishment bearing the extraordinary name of The Green Man; seeing me approach, he waved his cap and a broad smile spread across his freckled face.

I furled my umbrella and joined him in the shelter of the recess. Keeping a wary eye on the umbrella, he began, "Sure and you brighten the gloomy day, Mrs. Emerson. Indeed and the Fountain of Youth must be in Egypt, for you gain in youth and beauty each time—"

I shook the umbrella at him. "Spare me the brogue and the empty compliments, Mr. O'Connell. I am seriously annoyed with you."

"Empty, is it? Sure an' I spoke from the deepest depths . . . Please, ma'am, won't you open that infernal parasol and accompany me to a place where we can talk?"

"This will do nicely," I said, indicating the door.

O'Connell's eyes popped. "My dear Mrs. Emerson, this is hardly—"

"It is a public house, is it not? Very interesting. I have never patronized such an establishment. Emerson, though in general the most obliging of men, has always refused to visit one with me. Come, Mr. O'Connell; I am exceedingly short of time and I have a great deal to say to you."

"Sure an' I'll wager that's the truth," muttered O'Connell. With a shrug he followed me inside.

Our entrance caused something of a stir, though I cannot imagine why; I was certainly not the only woman present. In fact, there was a female behind the bar—a fleshy young person who would have been rather pretty if she had not painted her cheeks such a garish pink.

I led the way to a table, Mr. O'Connell trailing after me, and summoned the barmaid with a flourish of my parasol. Poor thing, she seemed to be a trifle lacking. When I ordered a pot of tea, her jaw dropped and she stared blankly at me.

"I'm afraid . . ." O'Connell began.

"Oh, I see. This is an establishment in which only alcoholic beverages are served? In that case, I will just have a whiskey and soda."

O'Connell ordered, and I added in a kindly voice, "The table appears to be rather sticky, young woman. Please wipe it off." She continued to gape. Nudging her gently with my parasol I said, "Run along, run along. Time is of the essence."

Mr. O'Connell did not relax until I had stowed the parasol under my chair. Planting his elbows on the table, he leaned toward me.

"You are late, Mrs. E. Did you have trouble following my instructions?"

"Not at all, though they certainly might have been more explicit. However, I would not have troubled myself to follow them had I not been seriously annoyed with you. My only reason for being here is to demand an apology and a retraction for the things you have been saying about us in your wretched newspaper."

"But I said only the most complimentary things about you and Mr. Emerson," O'Connell protested.

"You implied I was an unfit mother."

"'Twas no such thing! My exact words were, 'She is the most affectionate of parents—'"

"'Which makes her inability to prevent the lad from engaging in hair-raising adventures all the more astonishing.'" O'Connell met my stern gaze with eyes as blue, as limpid, and as serene as the lakes of Eire. "Well," I said after a moment, "perhaps, after all, the statement is not entirely inaccurate. But what on earth was in your reputed brain, Kevin, to say Professor Emerson and I had consented to solve the mystery of the malignant mummy? That is a flat-out fabrication."

"I said no such thing. I said—"

"I have not the time to exchange quibbles with you," I said sternly. "I slipped out of the house without Emerson's knowledge; if he misses me he will raise a hullaballoo."

A shudder ran through Kevin's wiry frame. "A very descriptive word, Mrs. E."

The young person shuffled up, carrying a tray and a damp cloth. The cloth was not very clean, but

the energy with which she swabbed the table indicated a willingness to please, and so I forbore to
comment, only pointing out a few spots she had
missed. Kevin had already seized his glass and consumed a considerable amount of the contents. He
ordered another of the same, and I remarked in the
kindliest possible fashion, "Young woman, that is a
very nice frock, but with so much of your chest exposed, you run the risk of catching a severe cold.
Have you no scarf or shawl?"

The girl shook her head dumbly. "Take mine,
then," I said, removing it from about my neck. It
was a nice, thick wool plaid. "There. No, wrap it
closely—so—that is much better. Now run along and
get this gentleman his—what was it, Mr. O'Connell?
Stout? A curious name for a beverage."

But O'Connell's arms were on the table and his
head rested on his arms, and his shoulders were shaking. In response to my inquiries he assured me he
was quite all right, though his face was almost as red
as his hair and his lips were quivering.

"Now," I said, sipping my whiskey, "what were we
talking about?"

O'Connell shook his head. "I have not the slightest idea. Conversation with you has a strange effect
on my brain, Mrs. Emerson."

"Many people find it difficult to follow my mental processes," I admitted. "But really, Kevin, your
profession demands quick thinking flexibility, con-
centration. Especially the latter. You must learn to
concentrate.

"We were discussing your statement that Professor Emerson and I had consented to investigate the case of the curse."

"I did not say you had consented. I said you would be consulted."

"By whom? The *Daily Yell*?"

"Would that 'twere true," Kevin exclaimed, pressing his hand to his heart in an outrageous parody of rapture. "My editors would pay any sum—any reasonable sum, that is—to retain you and the professor as consultants. Dare I hope—"

"No, you may not. Not only would it be beneath our dignity to have our names associated in a professional capacity with a newspaper—especially a disgusting example of libelous trash like the *Daily Yell*—but there is absolutely nothing to consult about. We are not detectives, Mr. O'Connell. We are scholars!"

"But you solved the Baskerville murder—"

"That was another matter altogether. We were called into that case as Egyptologists, to carry on the work begun by Lord Baskerville, whose mysterious death was followed by other incidents of a desperate and dangerous and distracting character. This case is quite different. It is a wisp, a fiction, concocted by Mr. Kevin O'Connell."

"Now, indeed, ma'am, you wrong me. I am not the guilty party. Will you condescend to let me explain?"

"I have been waiting for you to do so."

Kevin tugged at his fiery locks. "It was not I who broke the story. It was—someone else. Such a sensation was aroused that my editors felt we had to follow it up. Since I am regarded as something of an authority on ancient Egypt and supernatural curses . . . I couldn't refuse, Mrs. E., without risking the loss of my position. What was I to do?"

"Hmmm," I said thoughtfully. "The rival to whom you refer is the M. M. Minton of the *Morning Mirror*? I recall seeing the name on several stories, and wondering that the *Mirror* would stoop to such sensationalism. You weave a touching tale, Mr. O'Connell, but the fact remains that you have exploited your acquaintance with me in a contemptible manner."

"But you are my greatest asset," O'Connell explained guilelessly. "My acquaintance—dare I say friendship? No, perhaps not . . . My acquaintance, then, with you and the professor is the only advantage I have over rival journalists. It was my personal connection with the Baskerville case that made my reputation—and yours, insofar as the reading public is concerned. You and the professor are news, Mrs. E. People are fascinated by archaeology and archaeologists. Add to that your—how shall I put it?—your panache, your disregard for convention, your remarkable talent for criminal investigation—"

"I prefer the term 'panache,'" I interrupted. "I cannot explain why Emerson and I are so often involved with violent crime; I am inclined to attribute it to a certain frame of mind, an awareness of suspicious circumstances that elude persons of duller wit."

"No doubt that is the case," Kevin said, nodding seriously. "So you understand why I was forced to mention your names."

"To understand all is not to forgive all," I replied. "This must cease, Mr. O'Connell. Our names must never again appear in your periodical."

"But I was hoping for an interview," O'Connell exclaimed. "The usual interview, concerning your archaeological excavations this past season."

His soft blue orbs met mine with a look so open, that a person unacquainted with him would instantly have offered him her confidence. I smiled ironically. "You must take me for a fool, Kevin. We read your effusions on the Fraser case.* Emerson raged for days. I feared for his health."

"I got my information from Mrs. Fraser," Kevin exclaimed. "The effusions, as you call them, were direct quotations from the young lady and her husband."

It was difficult for me to be angry with him, since I secretly agreed. Enid Fraser, nee Debenham, had spoken no more than the truth, and the word "effusions" was Emerson's, not mine.

Watching me shrewdly, O'Connell went on, "She and the others whom you have rescued from death and disgrace have sung your praises to the world. And why not? How seldom are courage and kindness given the recognition they deserve! You are an inspiration to the entire British nation, Mrs. E."

"Hmmm. Well. Since you put it that way . . ."

"Risking your life—and a commodity more precious than life—in the defense of the innocent," Kevin went on enthusiastically. "How the professor

*Lion in the Valley.

must have suffered—what anguish he must have endured—fearing that even your indomitable spirit and physical courage must falter before that desperate villain . . . What were *your* feelings, Mrs. E.?"

I had been nodding and smiling like an idiot. Then the sense of what he was saying penetrated, and I emitted a cry that made him cringe away and raise his arms in a posture of defense. "Curse you, Kevin—how dare you insinuate . . . Who told you? There is no truth whatever in . . . Wait till I speak with Enid. I will—"

"Calm yourself, Mrs. Amelia," Kevin begged. "Mrs. Fraser did not betray your confidence; indeed, she absolutely denied the story after her husband (he is not the most intelligent of men, is he?) let something slip. She threatened me with the direst consequences if I printed a word."

"Her threats will pale, I assure you, in comparison to Emerson's," I informed him. "If the slightest hint of . . ."

I did not finish the sentence; there was no need. Kevin's countenance had paled visibly. With a sincerity I could not doubt, he exclaimed, "Sure, an' don't you think I was aware of that? My high regard for you, Mrs. Emerson, would prevent me from besmirching your reputation. Besides, my editor told me it would be actionable."

This last remark was more convincing than his claim of concern for my reputation; adding to it his terror of Emerson (a terror which, in this case, was well founded), I thought I could count on his silence. "Very well," I said, finishing my whiskey and looking about, in vain, for anything resembling a serviette. "I cannot dally, Mr. O'Connell. It is quite dark and Emerson will be looking for me. I leave you to pay the tab, since it was your invitation."

He insisted on walking me back to the house, and although I felt no trepidation—after some of the areas through which I have walked after dark, London held no fears for me—I acceded to his request. As we approached the door the young woman sidled up to me and offered me my scarf. I rearranged it around her neck, tucking the ends in securely, and told her to keep it, as I had others.

I was glad of Kevin's company, if only because my hold of his arm kept me from slipping. The mixture of mud, water, and various slimy substances underfoot made walking treacherous. The fog had closed in, dimming the gaslights to ghostly globes of sickly yellow-gray and distorting monstrously the forms of passersby. Yet there was a certain grisly charm in the scene, and I was moved to remark that dear old London need not yield even to the slums of Cairo in sinister and malodorous fascination. Kevin's only response was to tighten his grip and hurry me forward.

At the spot where York Street debouched into the square, he stopped and announced his intention of leaving me. "You will be all right now, Mrs. E."

"I have never been anything other than all right, Mr. O. Thank you for entertaining me at the public house; it was a most interesting experience. But don't forget what I told you."

"No, ma'am."

"You will not use my name again."

"Certainly not, Mrs. E. Unless," Kevin added, "some incident of unusual interest occurs, and the other newspapers learn of it, and report it. You surely would not expect me to be the only journalist in London who refrained from printing the story, would you?"

"Good Gad, O'Connell, you sound just like Ramses," I said in exasperation. "No such incident will occur. I have no intention of becoming involved with the nonsensical doings at the British Museum."

"Oh, indeed?" His rather wide mouth opened, not in a smile but in a snarl of rage. "Sure an' begorra, but I might have known . . . The spalpeen! The treacherous little serpent—"

"Who? Where?"

"There." Kevin pointed. "D'ye see that big yellow umbrella?"

"The weather being inclement, a number of parasols are to be seen," I replied. "But in this dreadful fog it is impossible to make out colors with any degree of—"

"There, just there—in front of Chalfont House." Kevin growled deep in his throat. "Lying in wait, lurking like a ghoul . . . Och, the shame of the creature then!"

The umbrella he had mentioned was not difficult to distinguish after all, for unlike the others on the pavements it remained stationary, just outside the high iron fence enclosing the grounds of Chalfont House. Though there was a lamppost not far away, I could see very little more than the umbrella itself. It was a very large umbrella.

"Who is it?" I asked, squinting in an effort to see better.

"Who else but that creeping snake Minton? You had better go round to the back, Mrs. E."

"Nonsense. I will not skulk into a house as if I had no right to be there. Run along, Mr. O'Connell (and make sure you change your boots and your socks as soon as you get home). A confrontation between you and Minton could only lead to acrimony and to delay."

"But, Mrs. E.—"

"I am quite capable of dealing with impertinent journalists. As you ought to know."

"But—"

The heavy doors of Chalfont House burst open. Light spilled out onto the steps; from the form silhouetted against it came a voice weirdly distorted by the damp and the fog. "Peabody! Where are yooooooou, Peabody? Curse it!"

I could see the butler plucking at Emerson's coat-tails, trying to calm him; but 'twas of no avail. Sans hat, coat, scarf, or umbrella, Emerson plunged down the stairs and ran to the gate. In his passion he was unable to deal with the latch; he clung there, bellowing and banging on the railings. "Peeeeeea-body! Devil take it, where are yooooooou?"

"I must go," I said. But I spoke to empty air; a rapidly fading shadow was the only sign of Kevin O'Connell.

I called to my agitated spouse, but his irritable iterations drowned out my voice. By the time I reached him, the yellow umbrella had pounced. Emerson confronted it head-on, with only the gate between them. He had fallen silent; I heard another voice, high-pitched and rapid. "And what is your opinion, Professor . . ." it was asking.

"Emerson, what the—what are you doing out in this fog without a hat?" I demanded.

Emerson glanced at me. "Oh, there you are, Peabody. The most extraordinary thing . . . Only have a look."

Whereupon he seized the umbrella and spun it like a wheel. The person under it, who seemed to be attached to it in some fashion I could not make out, spun with it, and the lamplight fell full upon her face. Yes, dear Reader—*her* face! The journalist—was a woman!

"Good Gad," I exclaimed. "I was under the impression that you were a man."

"I am as capable as any man," was the fierce reply, as a notebook was brandished in my face. She had attached her umbrella to her belt in order to leave her hands free for writing, and I had to admire the ingenuity of the concept even as I deplored her forward behavior. "Tell me, Mrs. Emerson," she went on, with scarcely a pause to draw breath, "are you working with Scotland Yard on the murder case?"

"What murder case? There is no indication—"

"Amelia!" Emerson had recovered from his surprise at discovering that the assiduous reporter was female—for that was my interpretation of his mention of the word "extraordinary." Now he seized me by the arm and attempted to draw me inside the railing. Since the gate was still closed, this did not succeed. "Don't talk to that—that person," he insisted. "Don't speak a word. Even a 'yes' or 'no' will be misquoted by these vultures—excuse me, young lady—and you know your unfortunate tendency to babble—"

"I beg your pardon, Emerson!" I exclaimed. "But we will go into that at another time. I have no intention of permitting an interview; I particularly object to being waylaid and accosted at my front door. However, let me point out that I cannot enter until you open the gate."

I moved as I spoke, edging in between Emerson and Miss Minton. She was forced to retreat in order to avoid being jabbed by the spokes of my open parasol, but once out of its range she stubbornly stood her ground and repeated her question. I could make out her features more clearly now. She was younger than I had expected. One could not have called her pretty. Her features were too strongly marked, her chin positively masculine in outline, her brows heavy and forbidding. The pins and combs that attempted to confine her thick black hair had lost the struggle; jetty locks straggled damply over her ears.

Cursing (but, let me do him justice, cursing under his breath), Emerson fumbled with the latch. Miss Minton stood poised on tiptoe, as if ready to leap forward, and I verily believe she would have done so, following us to the very door of the house, if something had not happened to distract her.

It was I who first caught sight of the weird, the unbelievable vision, and my exclamation of astonished incredulity caused Miss Minton to turn and Emerson to look up. For a moment we all three stood frozen in disbelief; for the form we saw, advancing with measured strides along the pavement opposite, was that of an ancient Egyptian priest clad in long white robes and a leopard-skin cloak. Long wisps of pale fog clung to his garments like trailing mummy wrappings, and the lamplight glimmered in the ebon waves of his curled wig. He passed into the clustering mist and vanished.

THREE

Miss Minton was the first to move. With a yelp like that of a hunting dog, she went in pursuit, the umbrella bouncing up and down as she ran.

I started to follow. Emerson's fingers clamped over my shoulders and slammed me against the iron bars of the gate.

"Move on your peril, Peabody," he hissed. "Take one step—just one—and I will . . ." The gate finally yielded to his efforts, so I never heard the remainder of the threat. Firmly he drew me to him; briskly he marched me to the door of the house. He maintained an ominous silence, and discretion would have suggested I do the same; but I am proud to say discretion has never yet prevented me from doing what was right.

"Emerson," I cried, attempting to free myself from his steely grip. "Emerson, think! She has qualities I would not like to see in a daughter of mine, but she is young—impulsive—a woman! Can you abandon her to what may be grave danger? I cannot believe it—you, the most gallant of your sex!"

Emerson's steps slowed. "Er—hmmm," he remarked.

I had known my appeal would not be in vain. Emerson is himself somewhat impulsive (indeed, it is a distinctly masculine trait, unjustly attributed to women), but he is the kindest of men. He had rushed me off without stopping to consider the young woman, but once reminded he was ready, as always, to do an Englishman's duty.

"I intended to go after her as soon as I had got you indoors," he grumbled. "I cannot trust you, Amelia, indeed I cannot."

"But by then it may be too late," I exclaimed. "Who knows what that ill-omened figure portends? Once in its vile clutches—"

Emerson had come to a stop at the bottom of the steps. He shook me absent-mindedly. "Amelia, I beg you will not go on in that fashion. Certain citizens of this metropolis enjoy wandering about the streets and the museums in bizarre costumes. No doubt the climate has addled their brains. Lunatics, who ought to be confined—"

"Precisely, Emerson. Miss Minton may even now be in the power of an escaped lunatic. Let us not waste time arguing, but instantly pursue—"

Emerson's face relaxed. He turned me around. "Your concern is needless, Amelia."

Miss Minton was no longer alone; facing her was a tallish, thin young man wearing a long overcoat and a silk hat. They appeared to be arguing; two voices, one baritone, the other a piercing alto, blended in passionate duet.

Emerson called out. "Are you in need of assistance, Miss—er—or is that a friend of yours?"

The young lady abandoned her companion and darted across the pavement, splashing recklessly through puddles. Emerson had taken the precaution of closing the gate behind him; she could advance no further, but stood clutching the bars and peering between them like a prisoner in gaol.

"Please, Professor and Mrs. Emerson—a brief interview? It will only take a few moments—"

Emerson let out a roar. "Curse it, young woman, have you no sense of decency? We delayed only to make certain your rash action had not led you into difficulty, and you reward our charitable concern with—"

"Now, Emerson," I interrupted. "You have made your point and I am sure it has been taken."

"Quite," said the young man, who had joined Miss Minton at the gate. He was wearing eyeglasses; they kept slipping, perhaps because of the damp, and throughout the ensuing conversation he was perpetually adjusting them. "Good evening, Mrs. Emerson—Professor. I had the pleasure of meeting you last year in Mr. Budge's office at the Museum. My name is Wilson. I don't suppose you remember me."

"Vaguely," Emerson replied. "What the devil are you—"

"Emerson, you can be heard clear across the square," I said. "If we were to join the young people at the gate, it would not be necessary to shout."

"Not on your life, Peabody," my husband replied, taking a firmer grip on me.

"I am a friend of Miss Minton's," the young man went on. "Thank you for your concern, but you need not worry about her. I did my best to keep her from bothering you and Mrs. Emerson, but could not prevail; naturally I felt obliged to accompany her, though at her request I kept at a distance."

"Shame should have kept you at a distance," Emerson shouted. "What an outrageous thing! You, a fellow professional, aiding and abetting—"

"It was not his fault," the young lady cried, brandishing her umbrella. "He did his best to prevent me."

"Well, well," Emerson said, with surprising good humor. "I believe I understand. I presume the lunatic made good his escape?"

The young lady scowled. Her companion said timidly, "I saw no such person, Professor. It is very foggy."

"Emerson," I murmured, "that large man coming toward the house appears to be a constable."

The argument would have had no effect on Emerson, but young Mr. Wilson caught sight of the advancing form, its oilcloth coat glistening wetly in the lamplight, and with a muffled exclamation, he drew the young lady away. Emerson waved cheerfully at the constable, who had paused at the gate to examine us curiously, and we went into the house.

The entire household had gathered in the hall. Evelyn rushed to me. "Amelia, you are soaked to the skin. Had you not better change your wet clothing at once?"

"Certainly," I replied, handing my parasol and my wrap to the butler. "I hope I am not too late for tea. A cup of the genial beverage would be just the thing."

"Wouldn't you prefer a whiskey and soda?" asked my brother-in-law, his eyes twinkling. Walter is the most amiable man; he seems always to be on the verge of laughter. I was about to refuse when I realized that there might be a lingering aroma about my person, from the last whiskey I had drunk; and that Emerson, in the course of our customary predinner rituals, would be sure to detect its aroma, which would lead to questions I preferred to avoid.

"What a splendid idea," I said. "I will just take a glass upstairs with me; it is a sovereign remedy for warding off a cold."

Once we had reached the privacy of our rooms, I managed to take a sip of the whiskey before Emerson proceeded to do what I had expected he would. "At least wait until I remove my wet gown," I suggested. "You will have to change too; your shirt is already quite—"

"Mmmmm," said Emerson, more precise articulation being at that moment beyond his powers. With the agility I had come to expect and admire, he assisted me to accomplish the suggested change without interrupting what he was doing for more than a few moments.

Much as I would have liked to continue, the sound of the dressing bell compelled me to remind Emerson we would be expected downstairs, and that prolonged delay might lead to speculation.

"Humbug," Emerson replied lazily. "Walter and Evelyn never speculate, they are too well bred, and if they did, they could only approve. We are lawfully wedded, Peabody; in case that fact has slipped your mind, let me refresh your memory. Thus. And thus . . ."

"Oh, Emerson. Now, Emerson . . . Oh, my dear Emerson!"

Unfortunately at that moment we heard a scratching at the door, and with a vehement comment Emerson bolted for the dressing room. Fortunately it was Rose, not one of the servants who were unfamiliar with our habits; she had learned, through painful experience (painful particularly to poor Emerson), never to enter a room without making her presence known.

"The dressing bell has rung, ma'am," she murmured, through a tactfully narrow crack in the door.

"I heard it. Come back in ten minutes, Rose."

The door closed. Emerson emerged from the dressing room. He had assumed his trousers, but not his shirt, and the sight of his tanned and muscular body aroused the most remarkable of sensations and made me yearn to be home again in Kent, where cook was quite accustomed to putting dinner back an extra half hour on short notice.

However, the interruption had made him remember his grievances, and he was not slow to mention them.

"How dare you leave this house without telling anyone?" he demanded. "How dare you wander the streets of this city alone, unprotected—"

"I had an errand," I replied calmly. "Your evening shirt is there, Emerson, on the chair."

"I hate dressing for dinner," Emerson grumbled. "Why must I? Walter and Evelyn—"

"It is the custom. Never mind, my dear, we will soon be home and then you can be as uncouth as you like."

"It can't be too soon for me," Emerson assured me. "We haven't been in town a day and already you are being followed by lunatics dressed up in their nightshirts. How the devil did he find us? Did you send him a telegram?"

"I presume you are joking, Emerson. The newspapers have reported our activities in considerable detail. Besides, our names were on the passenger list; anyone who wanted to know the time of our arrival could have found out at the offices of the steamship company."

"That would explain the young lady," Emerson admitted. "What an extraordinary thing, Peabody."

"That a woman should be a journalist? Unusual, certainly; commendable, undoubtedly. Much as I dislike the profession, it warms my heart to see my sisters venture—"

"You don't take my meaning. What was so extraordinary was the resemblance."

"To whom, Emerson?"

"To you, Peabody. Didn't you observe it?"

"Nonsense," I replied, taking the pins from my hair. "There was not the slightest resemblance."

"Are you sure you haven't a sister?"

"Quite sure. Don't be absurd, Emerson."

Rose's reappearance ended the discussion. Emerson once again retreated to his dressing room while Rose buttoned me into my frock and tried to do something with my untidy hair. Emerson had not closed the door and I could hear him mumbling to

himself. When he came out he was fully dressed
except for his studs and links, which he can never
locate. Still muttering under his breath, he began
tumbling my toilet articles about in his search for
the missing articles.

Rose found them in the top drawer of the bureau,
where they belonged, and advanced on Emerson.
"If I may, sir—"

"Oh. Thank you, Rose. Did you happen to notice
the young lady who was at the gate earlier?"

"No, sir. I don't waste time looking out the windows when I have me duties to perform."

"Amazing resemblance to Mrs. Emerson," said
my husband, lifting his chin in response to a rather
sharp poke from Rose.

"Indeed, sir?"

Her brief, cool answers were out of character, for
Rose was normally on the best of terms with both of
us and often condescended to exchange a bit of local
gossip or a friendly jest while helping me dress.
Turning to look at her, I observed that she was subjecting Emerson to a kind of small torture, prodding and jabbing at him as she inserted the studs.

"Where is Ramses?" I inquired. "He wasn't in
the hall and he is usually the first one on the scene
when something is going on."

A loud, rather damp sniff from Rose was the only
answer I got from that quarter. Emerson scowled.
"Ramses is in disgrace. He is to stay in his room
until I give him leave to come out. You had better
get back to him, Rose; I don't trust him to . . . Ow!"

The exclamation was prompted by Rose's giving
his wrist a shrewd twist as she inserted the link.

"Yes, sir," she snapped. Wheeling, like a military person on parade, she marched out of the room.

"You have offended Rose," I said.

"She always takes his part," Emerson grumbled. "Did you see what she did, Peabody? She dug her nails into my hand—"

"I assure you it was an accident, Emerson. Rose would not be so childish. Why is Ramses in disgrace?"

"Look there," Emerson said, indicating the heap of papers on the table.

It was the manuscript of *The History of Ancient Egypt*; I had observed it earlier and had been pleased to see evidence of industry, but succeeding events had distracted me and prevented me from looking closely. Now I advanced to the desk and took up the top page. It was covered with closely written emendations, corrections, and revisions; I was about to congratulate Emerson on his industry when I realized the handwriting was not his. I knew whose handwriting it was.

"Oh no," I murmured. "Surely he would not . . . Well, on this point at least he is correct; the date of the beginning of the Fourth Dynasty—"

Emerson clapped his hand to his brow. "*Et tu*, Peabody? Bad enough that I have nourished a viper in my house, but another in my very bosom . . ."

"Oh, Emerson, don't be so theatrical. If Ramses has had the audacity to revise your manuscript—"

"Revise? The little scamp has practically rewritten it! He has corrected my dates, my analyses of historical events, my discussion of the origin of mummification!"

"And your syntax," I said, unable to repress a smile. "Really, Ramses' notions of English grammar are rather eccentric." Seeing that Emerson had turned red as a turkey cock, I obliterated the smile and said seriously. "It is too bad of Ramses, my dear. I will speak sharply to him."

"That seems inadequate punishment for the crime."

"You—you didn't strike him, Emerson?"

Emerson gave me a look of freezing reproof. "You know my views on corporal punishment, Amelia. I have never struck a child or a woman—and I never will. Though I came as close, this evening, as I ever hope to come."

I agreed with Emerson in opposing corporal punishment, though not for the same reasons; his were ethical and idealistic, mine were purely practical. A spanking would have hurt me more than it hurt Ramses, for he had extremely sharp, hard bones, and a high tolerance for pain.

I sympathized with my poor Emerson. He had had a bad day altogether, and the sight of my brother James, even more appallingly rotund in full evening kit, did not improve his temper. James seemed anxious to please; he laughed immoderately at Emerson's remarks, even those that were not meant to be humorous, and paid me extravagant compliments on my gown, my general appearance, and my qualities as a mother. As the dinner progressed, I began to get some inkling of his real purpose, but the idea seemed so incredible I could hardly credit it.

Not until after the meal did he get to the point. He kept waiting for the ladies to retire, and finally

Evelyn felt obliged to explain. "Amelia believes, dear Mr. Peabody, that the custom is outmoded and insulting to the female sex."

"Insulting?" James stared at me.

"Ordinarily the gentlemen save the intelligent conversation—if they are capable of it at all—until the time for port and cigars," I said. "I like a drop of port myself, I am agreeable to intelligent conversation, and I have no objection to the aroma of a good cigar."

"Oh," said James, looking dazed.

"We generally discuss Egyptological matters," I continued. "If you find the subject tedious, James, *you* may retire to the drawing room."

Evelyn looked as if she thought I had gone a bit too far, but James decided to take it as a joke—which it was not. With a loud guffaw, he leaned across the table and patted my hand. "Dear Amelia. You haven't changed since you were a little girl. Do you remember the time . . ."

There he stuck, probably because he could not recall any fond memories of our childhood. I certainly had none that included him. Abandoning this approach, he tried another. "Papa always said you had the best head of the lot," he said. "And he was correct. (Pass the port, please, Walter my boy.) How very well you have done for yourself, eh?"

"I have an excellent solicitor to advise me on my investments," I replied sedately.

Emerson had been studying him with the faint distaste of an anatomist confronting a new and unsavory organ; now he shrugged and, turning to Walter, continued a discussion on the Berlin Dictionary that had begun earlier. This suited James: he addressed me in a confidential tone, as he continued to help himself to port.

"I only wish I had your good sense, li'l sister. Not that it was m' fault. No. Not my fault that the cursed ships were cursed unseaworthy. Too many cargoes lost . . ."

"Are you trying to tell me you are in financial difficulty, James?" I inquired. "For if you are hoping for money, you won't get it."

"No, no. No. Not to say difficulty. I can recoup." He laid one fat finger beside his nose and winked. "Secret. Great prospects. Only thing is . . ."

"No, James. Not a penny."

James blinked. "Don' wan' money," he said in a hurt voice. "Wouldn't take it 'f you offered. Want your loving mother's heart for poor unfort'nate childr'n . . ."

"Whose?" I inquired curiously.

"Mine. Who else's would I be asking for?"

"No one's, James. The very idea of your demonstrating disinterested compassion boggles my imagination. But why do yours need mothering? You have a wife, I believe? At least you had one . . . What have you done with—with . . ."

I could not remember her name, and at first I thought James couldn't recall it either. She was the sort of woman one yearns to forget—heavyset and doughy-faced, with a mind as narrow and inflexible as her lipless mouth.

"'Lizabeth," James said. "Yes, that's the name. Poor 'Lizabeth. She suffers from a nervous complaint. Doctor's prescribed . . . course of treatment—the waters—that sort of thing. Needs complete quiet, rest, change. No kiddies. As for me, I'm off for the East. India. That private matter I spoke about. I'll come back a rich man, mark my words! So you see, dear sister, why I throw myself 'pon your mercy— not for me, but for my poor orphaned children. Will you watch over them, Amelia? Just for the summer. I'll be home in three months, and Emily—er—Elizabeth—should be back before then. Six weeks, the doctor said. Will you, Amelia? For—for old times' sake?"

"Really, James, what an extraordinary request," I exclaimed. "What about their educations? I assume Percy is attending a boarding school—"

"Tutor," said James. "No school for Percy. Won't hurt him to do without lessons for a while. I don't hold with all this education. My son's going to be a gentleman, by Gad. A gentleman don't need to be educated."

Emerson chuckled. "He's right about that, at any rate."

Evelyn had already been won over. She is a dear girl, and the best friend I have in all the world, but the hopeless sweetness of her nature makes her susceptible to any smooth-talking rascal; and when the appeal concerns children, on whom she dotes (her fondness for Ramses being sufficient indication of her absence of discrimination in this area), she is hopelessly uncritical. Tears glistened in her eyes; clasping her hands, she exclaimed, "Oh, Amelia, of course you will say yes. How could you not? The poor, dear children . . ."

In justice to myself I feel I must explain to the

reader why I did not respond with the unhesitating warmth the bonds of blood and familial affection might seem to demand. Blood is one thing; affection is quite another. The first has no claim on me. I have never believed that the accident of birth incurs any obligation on the parties concerned, not even between parent and child once the period of dependency has passed and the adult offspring, having been given every advantage of health and education, is capable of standing on his or her own two feet. Affection, in contrast to blood, must be earned. For those who have my affection I would give my life, my sacred honor, and all my worldly goods—and I take it for granted they would do the same for me.

There had never been any affection between my brothers and myself. They were all older than I, James, the eldest of them, being seven years my senior. The others ignored me altogether, but James was throughout my childhood not my defender and guardian, as sentimental tales suggest, but my tormentor and bête noire. He kidnapped my dolls and held them for ransom, the ransom consisting of the few shillings I collected from relatives on the occasions of birthdays and Christmas. When my pecuniary resources failed, he dismembered and disfigured the hostages. He was always pinching and prodding me in public places; when I protested, I was blamed for creating a disturbance. The happiest day of my youth was the day James was sent away to school.

In due time my brothers went off to pursue careers and found families, leaving me to care for Papa.

Between his vagueness and my brothers' cruelty and indifference, I had learned to have no good opinion of men, so I was deemed a soured spinster, with little hope of an advantageous marriage.

Revenge is sweet, says an old adage. Revenge is unworthy of a Christian woman, say the Scriptures. In this case the Scriptures err. How I reveled in my dear brothers' fury when it was discovered that Papa had left his entire large fortune to me! James had actually attempted to take the case to law, claiming I had exercised undue influence on a helpless, aged parent. Thanks to Mr. Fletcher, Papa's excellent man of business—and to my own excellent character—this attempt went for naught, but it can hardly be supposed that it endeared my brother to me. A kind of awkward rapprochement had been patched up; James had attended my nuptials, though his expression, as he beheld the final hope of one day inheriting my money go up in the flames of marital affection, was more suitable for a funeral than a wedding. We had met only once since—at a funeral, appropriately enough—that of my brother Henry, who had succumbed to a digestive disorder. (The rumor whispered about by her loving sisters-in-law that he had been poisoned by his long-suffering wife was probably false, though I would certainly not have blamed her if she had done it.)

These poignant memories flashed through my mind in far less time than it takes to write them out, but when I came back to myself I realized that conversation had ceased and that all eyes were upon me, including those of my dear Emerson. Undoubtedly he had heard James's request, but instead of the forceful comment I had expected he remained silent, his expression unusually enigmatic; it gave me no clue as to his feelings.

James had clasped his fat fingers round the stem of his glass and was leaning forward, elbow planted crudely upon the table. Perspiration streaked his encrimsoned cheeks; his thick lips sagged, conveying not so much the appeal he intended as habitual ill humor. "My dearest, kindest sister," he began.

I turned from him to Emerson. What a difference—what a heavenly contrast! The firm, well-modeled lips, the lean brown cheeks and piercing blue eyes, the wavy black locks that crowned his head, the jutting chin with its pronounced dimple (or cleft, as Emerson prefers to call it when he refers to it at all, which is not often). A soft yet electrical warmth penetrated my limbs. I repressed it—for the time being.

"I must consult my husband," I said. "No such decision can be made without his advice and concurrence."

Emerson's eyes widened, then narrowed with poorly suppressed amusement. "Just what I expected you would say, Peabody. We never act on important matters without consultation—do we?"

"Certainly not, Emerson. We will let you know our decision after we have discussed the situation, James."

But James, being a man, had not the sense to leave well enough alone. Lurching sideways in his chair, he spread his hands in appeal—dropping his glass in the process—and addressed Emerson. "Radcliffe—dear brother—glad to see, master in his own house.

Fine woman, my sister—bossy, though. You tell her, eh? Tell her . . . woman's duty . . . mother . . . gadding about the world . . . poor children . . ."

"Good Gad," said Emerson. "I really think we must oblige, Peabody, if only for the sake of the unfortunate offspring of this disgusting object. How did you ever come to have such a relative?"

With the help of two of the stronger footmen, James was persuaded to retire to his bed, all the more readily since he sensed, even in his inebriated condition, that he had won his case. Emerson's argument had a strong effect on me, and Evelyn's pleas could not leave me unmoved, particularly since I feared she might be foolish enough to offer to take the children herself. Walter was the only one who voiced an objection. In his mild, soft voice, he remarked, "Ramses ought to be considered, don't you think? He is not exactly . . . His habits are . . . He may not . . ."

"Speak up, Walter, and don't stutter," Emerson replied, frowning. "If you are implying that Ramses is not the most suitable companion for well-behaved children, you have a point. If you are suggesting we invite Ramses' opinion, I beg to inform you that you are out of place. He has been wretchedly indulged."

With a smile and a shrug, Walter abandoned the argument; but later, when we had retired to our room, I raised it again. "Emerson, I feel I must ask you this. I am willing to take the children, but I cannot understand your willingness to accommodate James. Are you sure you aren't doing this to pay Ramses back for rewriting your book?"

"I have never heard such an outrageous accusation in my life," Emerson exclaimed. "Pay Ramses back? Can you suppose I would stoop to revenge myself on a little child? My own little child? My sole heir, the prop of my old age, the—"

"I thought so," I said. "Shall we go and say good night to the boy?"

"He'll be asleep," Emerson said.

"No, he won't."

And of course he was not. The room was dark except for a softly glowing lamp; tender mother that she was, Evelyn believed in night lights for small children, lest they learn to fear the dark. Ramses was not afraid of the dark, or anything else that I had been able to discover, but he took advantage of the light in order to read in bed. As soon as we entered he dropped the heavy tome he had been perusing and sat up.

"Good evening, Mama, good evening, Papa. I had feared Papa's well-justified resentment might prevent you from coming to say good night; I am happy to learn I was mistaken. Though I was attempting to distract myself with this latest volume from the hand of Mr. Wallis Budge, even his absurd statements concerning the process of mummification could not wholly soothe my—"

"You should not be reading in this poor light, Ramses." I sat down on the side of his bed and took the book from him. "You should be asleep, or searching your conscience. Papa's resentment was well founded. You owe him an apology."

"I have already apologized," Ramses replied. "Several times. But, Mama—"

"No buts, Ramses."

"I thought I was helping Papa. Knowing how busy he is, and that the Oxford University Press has several times demanded the manuscript, and hearing your frequent remarks to Papa on the subject of completing the book—"

"Good Gad!" I jumped to my feet. I had been feeling sorry for Ramses; in the soft light he looked almost like an ordinary child, his small face sober and his black curls tumbling over his infantile brow. How like the little wretch it was, to blame *me* for his action! "You will do better to admit your fault and promise never to do it again," I said severely. "You are never to touch a manuscript of your father's again, Ramses. Do you understand?"

"Not even to rescue it in the eventuality of a fire, or one of the dogs happening to get hold of it, or—"

I stamped my foot. I am sorry to say that Ramses often drove me to this childish extremity. "Enough, Ramses. You know what I mean. You are not to write on your father's manuscript, amend it, correct it, or change it in any way."

"Ah," said Ramses thoughtfully. "Now that you have made your meaning clear, Mama, I will certainly obey your command."

"Good." I turned to go. A small voice behind me said, "Will you not kiss me good night, Mama?"

The rigid form of Emerson, arms folded, brow

thunderous, sagged visibly. "Don't you want Papa to kiss you, my boy?"

"That would please me more than I can say, Papa. I had not ventured to ask because I believed your anger—your well-merited anger—might inspire a refusal which would have wounded me to the quick. I might have expected you would demonstrate the quality of forgiveness which marks a noble character and is, according to the Koran—"

At this point I fell upon Ramses and gave him the kiss he had requested, though I am bound to confess I was moved as much by the desire to stop his talking as by affection. Emerson succeeded me; his embrace was as fond as any parent could provide, and after we had hastily left the room—to prevent Ramses from starting another monologue—I said, "You did not tell Ramses about the children."

"Time enough for that tomorrow," Emerson grunted, opening the door of our room and stepping back to let me precede him. He looked rather sheepish. I had expected he would; Emerson is devoted to Ramses and he usually repents harsh words as soon as they have been uttered.

"Perhaps we ought not take them, Emerson."

"I have not changed my mind, Peabody. Ramses is a good little chap—in his way—I am sure he really was trying to be helpful, and perhaps I was a trifle harsh. But he is . . . He sometimes . . . He really is a trifle *odd*, Peabody, don't you think? He has been too much in the company of adults. It will do him good to join in the innocent games of ordinary youngsters. Cricket and—er—that sort of thing."

"Did you ever play cricket, Emerson?"

"I? Good Gad, no! Can you picture ME wasting my time with what is probably the most infernally illogical and pointless activity ever conceived by the human brain?"

And when he put it in that light, I had to confess that I could not.

FOUR

Do not suppose, dear Reader, that I had forgotten or dismissed the interesting occurrences of the early evening, particularly the appearance of the eerie apparition. It was not until the morning after these events, however, that I was able to turn my attention to a consideration of their meaning.

I usually wake before Emerson does. Sometimes I take advantage of the interlude to write letters and compose articles for archaeological journals; more often I lie quietly in bed, planning my activities for the day. I daresay my mental processes are assisted by Emerson's presence at my side; the vigorous sounds of his breathing, the solidity and warmth of his person remind me that in many respects I am among the most fortunate of women.

If memory serves me correctly (which it seldom fails to do), my thoughts that morning ran along the following lines.

Imitation is not unknown in the annals of crime. Indeed, an intelligent criminal might well take advantage of a series of murders or robberies by inserting (so to speak) a single effort of his own, similar in method and appearance, thereby disguising his true motive. It was possible that a second lunatic, too limited in imagination to invent his own eccentricity, had imitated the original *sem* priest. However, that did not seem likely. I had no doubt the apparition I had seen was the same one who haunted the halls of the British Museum. He might be mad, but he was not without intelligence. In common with most of the other inhabitants of London, he could easily have ascertained where we were staying and when we would be likely to arrive there. That he should be curious about us was not surprising; the newspapers had intimated we were about to be consulted by the Museum. But, much as I would like to have hoped that I had become an object of interest to a homicidal maniac, that premise did not stand up, for the simple reason that no homicide had been committed. Emerson had been right all along, and I . . . I too had been correct, since I had never believed the malignant mummy was anything more than a journalistic faradiddle. The lunatic had no murderous designs upon us; he had not even fired a revolver in our direction.

I had reached this stage in my meditations and was struggling to control the disappointment and chagrin my conclusions provoked, when the door opened and Rose poked her head in.

"Hush," I hissed. "The professor is still asleep."

"Indeed, madam?" Her voice was not hushed; indeed, it was a trifle loud. "I came to ask whether Master Ramses may leave his room."

"I cannot say, Rose. The professor confined him to his room, it is the professor's decision as to whether he may leave it."

"Yes, madam." Rose's voice rose to a well-bred shriek. "May I inquire—"

"No, you may not. I don't want you to wake the professor."

"Of course, madam. Thank you, madam." She slammed the door. Emerson stirred irritably. "She always takes Ramses' part," he muttered, and pulled the sheet over his head.

He was obviously awake, and obviously out of temper. There was no use remaining, since he would not be in a proper frame of mind to pursue the course of action that often recommended itself to him on occasions when conditions were propitious. I therefore arose, dressed—not thinking it wise to request Rose's assistance—and went downstairs.

I wanted to get Emerson out of London as quickly as possible—in order that I might get him back to London even more quickly. Though Egypt is my spiritual home, and a nice tidy tomb is my favorite habitation, I am very fond of our house in Kent. It is a modest manor house (eight principal bedrooms, four major reception rooms, and the usual offices) built of mellow red brick and dating from the time of Queen Anne. The surrounding park and farmland comprise two hundred forty seven and one-third acres. We had purchased the estate after the birth of Ramses, and renamed it Amarna Manor in sentimental memory of the scene of our courtship; and we had lived there year-round while Emerson held his appointment at University College. It was always a pleasure to return to it, but I did not expect we would spend much time there this summer. No; foggy, dreary, dirty London would hold us—at least until Emerson finished his book. The sooner he got at it (as I had frequently remarked), the sooner we could return to the soft green fields and drowsy peace of our (English) home.

I had completed most of the arrangements for a departure the following day by the time Emerson made his appearance. He was accompanied by Ramses; from the smiles that wreathed both faces, even the saturnine countenance of my son, it was obvious they had made up.

But it was not from his father that Ramses learned of the imminent arrival of his cousins. No; he got that information, and a painful pinch on his thin cheek, from James. "Won't that be fine, young fellow?" he wheezed. "High time you had some kiddies your own age to play with. My boy Percy is a fine little chap; he'll help put some roses in those pale cheeks, toughen up those muscles of yours . . ."

Ramses endured the squeezing and prodding of his upper arm with more equanimity than I would have expected. "How old are my cousins, Uncle James, and what is their number? I am forced to confess that I have scarcely been moved by the thought of them, and am uninformed—"

"Be still, Ramses," I said. "How can your uncle answer your question if you go on talking?"

"Er—hmph," said James. "Let me see. There are two of them—Percy and little Violet. I call her 'little' Violet because she is her daddy's precious girl. Their ages? Let me see . . . Percy is nine years of age, I believe. Or perhaps ten. Yes. And dear little Violet is—er—"

Emerson's curling lip betrayed his opinion of a man who could not remember the age of his precious girl, or his heir, but he said nothing; he never addressed James directly the entire time.

Ramses rose from his chair. "I beg you will excuse me. I have finished breakfast and I must take something to Bastet. She is behaving rather oddly this morning; perhaps, Mama, you would have a look at her, for I would not want—"

"I will come in a little while, Ramses."

After he had gone James shook his head. "Never heard a child talk like that in my life. But my Percy will soon whip the little chap into shape. He's a regular boy, is my Percy. Healthy outdoor exercise, that's the ticket; soon get your boy back to health. Counter that unfortunate family tendency toward consumption, eh, Amelia?"

He returned to his gobbling of breakfast and I regarded him with silent contempt. There has never been any tendency toward consumption in my family. James had only mentioned it to imply he was doing us a favor, instead of the reverse.

After he had eaten everything on the table, James took his departure, which was a relief to all concerned. He had informed me he would bring the children to us by the end of the week. As he climbed into the cab that was to take him to the railroad station, he was smirking in a way that raised serious doubts in my mind as to the wisdom of my decision. However, the die was cast; and Amelia Peabody Emerson is not the woman to turn her shoulder from the wheel or abandon a task when it is once begun.

James being gone, Emerson's humor improved, but unfortunately it was adversely affected by the morning paper, which contained a story by Miss Minton about her encounter with us the night before. The young lady had a very brisk, entertaining style of writing, but the accuracy of her reporting left a good deal to be desired. The apparition had not gibbered and capered and made obscene threatening gestures; Emerson had not rolled up his sleeves and challenged it to an exchange of blows; and I had certainly not swooned with terror as he drew me toward the house. (My movements may have been a trifle jerky, but only because Emerson was pulling me along.)

After littering the salon with the shreds of the newspaper and jumping up and down on them, Emerson felt more himself. We then turned to discussing our arrangements for the summer months. Walter and Evelyn repeated their kindly offer of Chalfont House, and I accepted with the proper expressions of appreciation. Emerson's face fell. I aimed an admonitory kick at his shin, which he avoided, having become only too accustomed to little reminders of that nature; but fortunately the reminder was not required. Emerson's own good heart, a quality for which he receives far less credit than he deserves, conquered his bile; and he expressed himself with befitting gratitude.

In truth, Chalfont House is not the most comfortable residence for simple people like ourselves who scorn ostentation for its own sake and prefer domestic comfort to show. "The cursed catacomb"

(Emerson's amusing appellation) resembles a museum rather than a residence; it contains upwards of fifty rooms and not nearly enough windows. It is one of the oldest houses on the square, having been built at the beginning of the eighteenth century; but it was extensively remodeled in the early 1860's by Evelyn's grandfather, in a (vain) effort to keep up with the Rothschilds. The grand staircase had been inspired by one in the Palazzo Braschi in Rome, the ballroom owed its design to the Palace of Versailles; the billiard room had a vaulted ceiling and walls draped with Chinese silk. In one respect at least later residents could be grateful to the old gentleman and to Mr. Rothschild. Each bedroom possessed an adjoining bath.

It was Walter who suggested we all spend the afternoon at the British Museum. If the idea had originated with me, Emerson would have objected to it; coming from Walter, it occasioned only a good-natured grumble.

"I trust you are not planning to treat us to a visit with the notorious mummy, Walter. You know we abhor that sort of sensationalism."

Walter glanced at his wife, who was smiling to herself over some tender private thought. "My dear Radcliffe, nothing could be farther from my mind. Though I confess I am rather curious. I don't have your cool scientific detachment."

"Bah," said Emerson.

"There is a papyrus I want to examine," Walter continued. "You know I have been working on my translation of the Leyden Magical Text. A few constructions perplex me; I hope to find parallels in B.M. 29465."

"Oh, if that is the case, I will gladly accompany you," Emerson replied. "I may as well announce my arrival and make sure that idiot Budge hasn't given my study to someone else. If you can call a cubicle without windows containing only a desk and a few bookcases a study. I don't suppose you will want to go with us, Peabody."

"You suppose nothing of the kind, Emerson. I am anxious to see how Mr. Budge has displayed the pottery we gave the museum last year."

"If I know Budge, our contributions are still in the packing cases," Emerson grumbled. "The man's insane jealousy of other scholars—I name no names, Peabody—passes all bounds."

Evelyn declined the invitation, at my suggestion. I told her to take a nice little rest, at which she nodded meekly enough; but knowing her propensity to waste time with children, I agreed to Emerson's suggestion that we take Ramses along. With Ramses out of the way, the chances of Evelyn's resting were greatly increased.

Ramses was delighted to be asked. I deduced this, not from his expression, which was as blandly uninformative as usual, but from the long elaborate speech he made expressing his feelings on the subject.

Budge was not in his office. Drawn by the racket Emerson made—"Hi, there, Budge, where the devil are you?" and other expressions of similar nature— a young man emerged from a nearby doorway. It was Miss Minton's less-than-enthusiastic escort of the night before; I recognized him by his gold-rimmed eyeglasses and his air of timid indecision, for fog, darkness, and his voluminous outer garments had prevented me from seeing much more than that. In daylight, he proved to be a slender young fellow of medium height with a long, narrow face and mild dark eyes.

He greeted us with an air of reserve which I attributed to youthful modesty; but Emerson soon put him at his ease, wringing his hand and making a little pleasantry about our last meeting. The young man blushed becomingly.

"I apologize again, Professor. It was a most unfortunate—"

"Why should you apologize? You are not responsible for Miss Minton's actions. But perhaps you would like to be, eh? A handsome young lady, and very—er—high-spirited."

The blush spread from Wilson's cheeks up to his hairline and down to his chin. He adjusted his eyeglasses. "You misunderstand, Professor. I admire, I respect . . . But I would never presume . . ."

"Well, well," said Emerson, becoming bored with the subject. "So Budge is playing truant, eh? Good. I won't have to waste time with him. I will be returning to London in a week's time, Wilbur—oh yes, Wilson. Make certain my study is ready for me, will you? It is the one on the north side, at the far end."

"But that room has been assigned to . . ." The young man swallowed convulsively. "Yes, Professor. Certainly. I will attend to it."

Emerson and Walter went off to examine the papyrus, and I took Ramses—over his vehement protests—to visit the book and manuscript collection. "I know you are only interested in Egyptian antiquities," I told him. "But your general education has been sadly neglected. It is time you improved your understanding of literature and history."

Ramses, who was small for his age, could hardly get his nose (or, more pertinently, his eyes) above the top of the cases. After we had inspected the Shakespeare folio and the Gutenberg Bible, the Anglo-Saxon Chronicle and the autographs of the kings and queens of England, and I had lectured briefly on them, we examined the logbook of H.M.S. *Victory*, the flagship of the gallant Nelson. I was distressed, though not surprised, to find that Ramses had never heard of the gallant Nelson. He complained he had a crick in his neck; so, after describing the battle of Trafalgar, I conceded he had probably absorbed enough for one day and graciously permitted him to lead me to the Egyptian Galleries.

How Ramses had learned about the malevolent mummy I do not know. I had certainly taken care not to mention the subject in his hearing. However, his means of acquiring information, particularly on matters that were none of his concern, verged on the uncanny. His hearing and eyesight were preternaturally acute, and although he had reluctantly agreed to abandon the practice of eavesdropping ("except, Mama, in cases when other, stronger moral considerations prevail"), Emerson was not always careful about watching his tongue.

At any rate, he had heard of the matter and frankly admitted as much when I asked him why he passed by other exhibits that would ordinarily have

been of interest to him and headed straight for the
room where the mummies were displayed. I must
give him credit in this case for candor; instead of
pretending, as he might reasonably have done, that
he was anxious to see the mummies because he was
presently investigating that aspect of Egyptology,
he replied, "According to the newspapers, it is at
this time of day that the individual disguised as a
sem priest often appears."

"I cannot imagine why you are interested in the
aberrations of some poor lunatic, Ramses."

"If he is a lunatic," Ramses said portentously.

The same doubt had occurred to me, so I could not
reproach him for suggesting it. However, I did not
feel like discussing it—at least not with Ramses—so I
remained silent.

The so-called Mummy Room was always popular with visitors of morbid or vulgar tastes. Today
the spectators had clustered around a particular
case, and it was immediately apparent that a theatrical performance of some kind was in progress. As I
approached, I saw that the focus of attention was
not the priest, but a woman swathed in flowing and
flimsy draperies of a pre-Raphaelite character. I recognized her as a spiritualist medium whose séances
had been all the rage a few years earlier, until a representative of the Society for Psychical Research published a blistering article on her methods—which
were, according to him, even clumsier than those of
the ordinary stage magician.

One could hardly blame the woman for taking
advantage of this latest outbreak of public ignorance
to advance or restore her career, but I wished she

were more inventive. The performance was the typical tedious exchange of question and answer between the voices of the medium and her "control" or "spirit guide." Madame Blatantowski's guide had the fascinating (and linguistically impossible) nomen of Fetet-ra, and his baritone voice bore a striking resemblance to her own hoarse tones. He seemed to be urging that all those who wished to see the "princess" restored to her tomb should send contributions to Madame.

The audience listened with respectful solemnity or with broad skeptical grins, depending on their degree of gullibility. Seeing a particularly broad and skeptical grin on a face nearby, I approached it.

"I thought you were not interested in this sort of sensationalism," I remarked.

"Walter made me come," said Emerson. "Hullo, Ramses, my boy; pay close attention, you will seldom see such a striking example of human folly."

Walter greeted me with a nod and a smile, but Mr. Wilson, who was with him, did not share his amusement.

"Oh dear, oh dear," he bleated, like the sheep he rather resembled. "What will Mr. Budge say? He ordered me to discourage this sort of thing . . ."

Walter patted him on the back. "Cheer up, Wilson. This does bring visitors to the museum; some may linger and improve their minds."

Wilson wrung his thin hands. "You are kind to say so, Mr. Emerson, sir, and I will certainly put that argument to Mr. Budge; but he does not . . . He has ordered me . . ."

"For once I agree with Budge," Emerson announced. "This is a waste of time. The wretched female has no notion how to interest an audience."

"Your exorcisms are much more effective," I agreed. "But, Emerson, few people possess your dramatic talents."

"True," Emerson said. "I suppose she deserves a little something for her effort." And before I could stop him, he pulled some coins from his pocket. With a skillful toss he pitched them over the heads of the spectators, so that they fell, ringing musically on the marble, at the feet of Madame.

That put an end to the performance. Some of the watchers burst out laughing and threw more pennies. Others dived to pick them up. Emerson watched with a benevolent smile.

"How very rude, Emerson," I scolded.

"My tolerance for fools is limited," said Emerson. "If she . . . Ha! Look there, Peabody. The prologue is over and the play is about to commence."

The "priest" had timed his entrance well. All eyes had been focused on the medium; no one—certainly not I—had seen him approach. It was as if he had emerged from one of the anthropoid coffins ranged along the wall. He stood as still, arms folded on his breast. The painted faces of the coffins were no more immobile than his own.

Which was not surprising, since he was wearing a mask—not the modern sort that covers only the face, but a skillful replica of the papier-mâché constructions that were sometimes placed over the heads of mummies. The molded ringlets of the hair accurately reproduced the elaborate wigs of the late

Empire period. The features were carefully modeled, the lips tinted, the brows outlined in black paint. The eyes were empty holes.

The leopard skin was genuine. I can't say why that detail should have struck me; perhaps it was the fierceness of its snarl and the contrast of the soft, dangling paws. It had been thrown over one shoulder and fastened so that the head lay on the wearer's breast. Under it he wore a long white robe.

It would have been an understatement to say that the bizarre figure was impressive. The watchers were struck dumb with awe. When the man moved, they fell back before him as worshipers of olden times would have given way to a priest or a king. Looking neither to right nor to left, he advanced till he stood before the mummy case.

The Lady Henutmehit had a pretty taste in coffins. Instead of being covered by bright, ofttimes garish, scenes of gods and demons, hers had been painted a soft gold—leading one to speculate whether the coffins of more distinguished individuals might not have been made of the precious metal itself. (A speculation unhappily not susceptible to verification, since no royal coffins have been found, or are likely to be, the skill of ancient tomb robbers being what it was.)

More relevant, perhaps, was the obvious fact that the coffin had belonged to a person of modest means and social position. She wore no crown or uraeus or other insignia of royalty. The chaplet encircling her black hair was adorned with a simple lotus flower.

After bowing deeply, the priest stood motionless, gazing steadily into the serene face of Henutmehit.

The tableau had a certain effectiveness, but Emerson, who is not easily affected, soon became bored. Turning to young Wilson, he said loudly, "This performance is even more tedious than the last. Why don't you carry out your orders, Wilbur? Apprehend the lunatic, remove his mask, ascertain his identity and hand him over to the keepers of the asylum from which he has escaped."

But Wilson could only wring his hands and murmur distressfully. One of the guards edged up to Emerson. "The pore chap ain't doin nothing to make a disturbance, Professor, 'e's just standin' there, you see. Course, if you should ask me to clear the room—"

"No need to put yourself out, Smith," Emerson replied. "If I want a room cleared, I will clear it myself."

The masked figure turned and pointed. The movement was so startling, after his prolonged immobility, that those nearest him gasped and started back. A low husky voice murmured.

> *His sister was his protector,*
> *She who drives off the foe.*
> *Who foils the deeds of the disturber*
> *By the power of her utterance."*

"What the devil," muttered Emerson. "Peabody, is that—"

But the performer had not finished. His voice gained strength. "The clever-tongued, whose speech fails not. Admirable . . . admirable in . . ."

The voice faded, with an odd suggestion of indecision. I held my breath. What deep and solemn warning would break the silence?

The voice that broke the silence was not deep and solemn, it was small and high-pitched. "Admirable in the words of command," squeaked Ramses. "Mighty Isis, who protected—"

Emerson burst into a shout of laughter. "Mighty Isis? No, by heaven—it is you he means, Peabody! The clever-tongued . . . ha, ha, ha! Whose speech . . . fails not . . ." Mirth overcame him, and he doubled up, clutching his stomach.

I caught at Ramses. "Where are you going? Stay with Mama."

"But he is getting away," cried Ramses.

He was. Moving with astonishing speed, his sandals slapping on the stone floor, the "priest" reached the doorway and disappeared.

"Never mind," I said. "What possessed you to prompt the fellow, like a stage director with a forgetful actor?"

"It appeared to me he might have forgotten his lines," Ramses explained. "He was reciting the 'Hymn to Osiris,' and he—"

"Never mind, I said. Emerson, you are making a spectacle of yourself. The lunatic has escaped—"

"Let him," Emerson gasped. "I feel a great sympathy for the fellow. He is obviously a person of wit and refinement. Oh, good Gad! 'Whose speech fails not . . .'"

"A very pretty compliment," said Walter, whose lips were twitching in sympathy. (Emerson's laughter, however inappropriate, has so cheery a ring to it that it is very contagious.) " 'She who drives off the foe and foils the deeds of the disturber.' No truer word was ever said, dear Amelia."

"Hmm," I said. "Walter, I believe you are right. Emerson, pray control yourself. It is time we went home."

The remainder of the day passed in soothing domestic intercourse with those who were dearest to us, and I was able to reassure Ramses as to the health of the cat Bastet. She appeared to be in an odd state of excitability, but her appetite and temperature were normal, and I concluded she was a trifle disturbed by the long journey and the frustration of being kept indoors—for of course we did not let her out in London. After a refreshing night's sleep, we took our leave of one another, amid assurances of soon meeting again; the younger Emersons departed for Yorkshire and we for Kent, little dreaming how short an interlude of pastoral peace some of us were to enjoy before a horror as great as any we had ever known came upon us.

I have often wondered how old our butler Wilkins really is, but I have never had the impertinence to ask outright. When he has been asked to do something of which he disapproves (a frequent occurrence in our household), he totters and mumbles like an aged man on the verge of collapse. Yet his appearance has not changed in ten years, and on several occasions—most of them occasioned by Ramses—I have seen him move with a celerity that would do credit to a man of twenty-five. I suspect he dyes his hair to look older.

He was so glad to see us, he actually ran down the stairs and returned Emerson's hearty handclasp before he remembered that the master is not supposed to shake hands with his butler. John was the next to greet us, beaming from ear to ear and proudly reporting the successful delivery of our baggage. Maids, footmen, and gardeners followed in their turn; John's wife carried her new baby, and we had to admire him and say how much he resembled his father (though in point of fact there was little to be seen of him except plump pink cheeks and an assortment of shapeless features).

Ramses rushed off to his room to unpack his trunks. Checking on him later, I found the place in the state of chaos I had expected, and Ramses absorbed in contemplation of a small chest or coffer filled with what appeared to be sand. "You carried that back from Egypt?" I exclaimed. "There is all the dirt you may need here, Ramses; and when I think of the expense—"

"This is not dirt, nor ordinary sand, Mama," Ramses replied. "It is natron. You recall, Papa gave me permission to carry out certain experiments on mummification—"

"Well, don't spill it all over the house," I said in disgust. "Really Ramses, there are times when I wonder . . ."

"It may seem morbid, Mama, but I assure you I suffer from no such tendencies. I am convinced Mr. Budge and the earlier authorities—I am thinking primarily of Mr. Pettigrew—are in error when they describe a bath of liquid natron as the essential agent. A mistranslation of the original Greek—"

"Mistranslations are Budge's specialty," said Emerson, who had followed me into the room. "He never had an original idea in his life; he simply repeated Pettigrew's error without ever bothering to investigate on his own—"

I left them to it. Having encountered a good number of mummies in the course of my daily life, I have developed a professional indifference to them, even though some are extremely nasty. However, I do not believe it is necessary to dwell on such matters.

Somewhat to my surprise, Ramses appeared more pleased than otherwise at the prospect of having his cousins visit—particularly Violet. The gleam in his black eyes when he mentioned her made me a trifle uneasy. His questions, the previous winter, regarding the relationships between the sexes, had left his father in a state of shock from which he had not yet fully recovered, and disconcerted his mother not a little; but upon reflection I realized that such precocity was not as surprising as it seemed; Ramses had spent most of his life in the company of Egyptians, who mature at a much earlier age than Europeans, and who are often married before they reach their teens. Stern lectures had (I hoped) impressed on Ramses the advisability of repressing his curiosity in public. But I was not counting on it.

James wasted no time. We were still unpacking when he arrived with his children, and an uncharitable person might have suspected he was anxious to be rid of them, such was the haste with which he took his leave, refusing even to stay for dinner. (In

fact, no one invited him to stay.) The children duti-
fully waved "bye-bye to Papa," as I requested, but
there was a singular absence of emotion on either
young face as the carriage rolled on down the drive.

They were nice-looking children—much nicer-
looking than I would have expected, knowing their
parents. Percy had brown hair, and I fancied I saw a
certain resemblance to myself. His sister was fair,
and looked more like her mother's side of the family, with plump cheeks, a pursed little mouth, and
very big, very vacant blue eyes. These attributes are
not particularly endearing in an adult woman, but
they suit a child well enough. Certainly Ramses
found her fascinating. He stood staring in that cool
unblinking way of his until she began to giggle, and
hid behind her brother.

Except for the giggling—which I suspected would
soon get on my nerves—I had no fault to find with
their manners. Percy addressed Emerson as "sir"
(sometimes to excess, adding the word to every sentence), and me as "dear Aunt Amelia." Violet spoke
very little, which was a pleasant change from what I
was used to.

In short, the initial impression was favorable, and I
was pleased to learn, when Emerson and I discussed
the matter at dinner that evening, that he agreed.
"For a boy with the misfortune to be named Percival
Peabody, he could be worse," was his assessment of
Percy, and "a pretty little wax doll," of Violet. "She
seems a bit silly," he added amiably. "But that appears
to be the modern fashion in little girls. You'll soon
knock that out of her, Peabody."

In the days following our return I congratulated

myself on having had the foresight to provide Ramses with companionship, for the constant interruptions and escapades that had heretofore marked his behavior would have driven me wild. Emerson had locked himself in the library with dire threats of unnameable punishment to be inflicted on any person who dared disturb him, and I was bustling about from morning till night dealing with the endless details that follow a long absence and the anticipation of another. The weather was fine, so that the children could be out of doors most of the time.

Of course there were a few mishaps, as one must expect when children are enjoying jolly times together—particularly when one of the children is Ramses. He acquired a prominent purple lump on his brow, from falling down the stairs, and himself admitted he had been so absorbed in staring at little Violet, who was with him at the time, that he had not watched his footing. One incident was a little more serious, and (I may confess in the private pages of this journal) gave me quite a turn.

The sounds of cries and shouts approaching the front door of the house brought me out of my chair, where I was going over the household accounts for the past winter. I went flying into the hall in the hopes of quelling the uproar before it disturbed Emerson; but I forgot lesser concerns when I beheld the limp form of my son carried in the arms of John. Only the whites of his eyes showed, and his breath came in harsh, whooping gasps.

Violet was in scarcely better case. The volume of her shrieks was absolutely astonishing. For the first time I saw a resemblance to her father, for her red, swollen face was shiny with tears that streamed down her cheeks and soaked her frills. "Dead, dead," she kept screaming. "Oh, oh, dead, oh, dead, dead . . ." Rose came running down the stairs, cap ribbons fluttering, and I directed her to look after Violet who had flung herself on the floor, writhing and sobbing.

Percy was the only one of the group who remained sensible, and was from him that I demanded an explanation; for although hand, heart, and brain itched to assist my child, I could not apply remedies until I had ascertained the cause of his condition. Percy's distress was manfully controlled; he stood with shoulders straight and hands clenched, his eyes never leaving my face. "It was my fault, Aunt Amelia. I cannot tell a lie. Beat me, strap me, flog me—or perhaps Uncle Radcliffe should do it, he is stronger. I deserve to be punished. I am at fault, I ought to have known better . . ."

I seized him and shook him. "What did you do?"

"The cricket ball struck him square in the stomach, Aunt Amelia. I was trying to show Ramses how to bat, and—"

I turned back to Ramses. To my relief I saw his eyes had rolled back into place, though they were not yet well focused, and his breathing was less difficult. A hard blow in the solar plexus can be painful and terrifying, but it is seldom fatal, at least in the young; I well remembered having suffered such an injury in childhood, after James had hit me with a rock of considerable size. (He told Papa I had tripped and fallen.)

"He'll be all right," I said, with a long breath of

relief. "Take him upstairs to bed, John. Percy, how could you be so careless?"

Percy's lips quivered, but he answered in a low, steady voice. "I take full responsibility, Aunt Amelia. My hands slipped . . . but that is no excuse."

From behind me came a weird, wheezing murmur. "The ability . . . to direct the path . . . of a projectile hurled . . . or struck with a bat . . . is not always within the powers . . ."

"Quite right, Ramses," I said, brushing the hair from my son's perspiring brow. "It was an accident, and I was unjust to Percy. But why the devil couldn't you say so, instead of beginning a long, tedious peroration? Considering that you are still short of breath—"

"However, under some circumstances . . ." Ramses wheezed.

"Enough, Ramses! Upstairs with him, John. I will follow directly."

John obeyed, Rose led the sobbing Violet away, and I turned my attention to Percy, who stood straight as a little soldier awaiting punishment. He flinched visibly when I placed my hand on his shoulder, and I hastened to reassure him.

"No one is flogged or beaten in this house, Percy— not people, not animals, not even children. What happened was an unfortunate accident, and it was courageous of you to take all the blame on yourself."

The boy's astonished look told me he was unaccustomed to kindly, reasonable treatment from adults. It made me all the more determined to demonstrate the superiority of our methods of child-rearing over those of his parents.

Toward the end of the week I began to be less optimistic about the good effects of well-behaved children on Ramses. Percy took to moping around the house; when pressed he admitted he was lonely, not only for "dearest Mama and Papa" but for his playmates. Ramses would not play with him. Ramses—said Percy sadly—did not like him.

I took Ramses aside and gave him a little lecture about courtesy to guests. "Percy misses his Mama and Papa, Ramses, which is only natural. You must put yourself out a little; give up your own hobbies for a while and join in the things that amuse Percy."

Ramses replied that Percy's ideas of amusement were not to his taste and that, to judge by Percy's remarks about his papa, he did not at all miss him. Since I abhor gossip of all kinds, especially from the mouths of young children, I cut Ramses off rather sharply. "Percy says you don't like him."

"He is quite correct," said Ramses. "I don't."

"Perhaps you would, if you would try to know him better."

"I doubt that very much. I am busy, Mama, with my work. My study of mummification—"

Again my retort was prompt and sharp; for Ramses' study of mummification had already prompted one unpleasant incident, when he attempted to impress Violet by showing her some of his better specimens. The ensuing fit of hysterics had brought Emerson raging out of the library.

Before long I had the opportunity to discuss my concern about the children with a person whose opinion on such matters I valued. She was one of the few ladies in the neighborhood with whom I was on speaking terms—the headmistress of a girls' school nearby, who shared my views on such important matters as education for women, votes for women, sensible dress for women, and the like. I had sent her a note announcing our arrival and inviting her to call, but it was not until the end of the week that she was able to accept.

She was a Scotswoman, ruddy of face and stout of figure, with gray streaked brown hair and shrewd, deepset eyes. Observing her tweed bloomers and stout boots I asked, "Surely you didn't bicycle the whole distance?"

"Surely I did. It is scarcely ten miles—and," she added, with a laugh "the good women of the village have stopped throwing stones when I pass along the High Street."

I made Emerson's excuses, explaining that he was hard at work on his book. In fact, he was not overly fond of Helen's company, claiming that between the two of us he could not get a word in. Helen accepted the excuses with equanimity; she was not overly fond of Emerson's company either.

"All the better," she said. "We can have a woman-to-woman chat. Tell me about your latest adventures, Amelia. I read about them in the newspapers, but one cannot credit anything one learns from that source."

"You certainly should not believe what you read in the newspapers. It is true that we were able to assist Miss Debenham—now Mrs. Fraser—in a critical situation . . ."

"And uncover a murderer and free an innocent man from suspicion?"

"That, yes. But anything else you may have read—"

"Then the lurid hints of Master Criminals (excuse me, I cannot help smiling; it is such a ridiculous name, straight out of a novel), and abduction—"

"Greatly exaggerated," I assured her. "In fact, Helen, I would prefer to say no more about it."

I gave her a brief description of our excavations, concluding, "Emerson feels sure the pyramid belonged to Snefru of the Third Dynasty. We hope next season to finish the excavation of the funerary temple and perhaps begin the exploration of the interior."

Helen had listened with a slightly glazed look. She was a classical historian and was relatively uninformed about Middle Eastern archaeology. She turned the subject, asking about Ramses.

"He has now taken up the study of mummification," I said, with a grimace.

Helen laughed heartily. She found Ramses quite entertaining—no doubt because she saw very little of him. "He is a remarkable child, Amelia. Don't try to make him into a little English schoolboy, the breed is detestable."

"There is no making Ramses into anything he doesn't choose to be," I said. "To be honest, Helen, I am glad we have this chance to chat. I am concerned about the boy, and your expertise on the subject of children—"

"Girls only, Amelia. However, what little knowledge I have is, as always, at your disposal."

I told her about Ramses' antipathy toward his cousin Percy. "They fight Helen, I know they do; and it must be Ramses who starts the squabbles, for he makes no secret of disliking Percy, and Percy is pathetically anxious to be friends. I thought Ramses would profit from having other children to play with, but it seems to have made him worse."

"That only shows you know little about the breed," Helen said comfortably. "Ramses is an only child, reared in—what shall I say?—unusual surroundings. He is accustomed to the full attention of his parents. Of course he resents having to share them with other children."

"Do you really think so?"

"I know so. I have seen the same thing with my girls. The advent of a new baby into the household frequently brings about a change in behavior."

"But Percy is no baby."

"That makes it all the worse. All little boys fight, Amelia—yes, and some little girls as well, though they are usually slyer and more subtle in their means of getting back at those they dislike."

She went on to tell me some stories about her charges that made me glad I had taken up another line of work.

Some of her theories sounded outlandish to me; they certainly were not in accord with the authorities I had read, but then I had no particular respect for the said authorities anyway.

When the time came for her to go, she suggested I might like to take a spin on her new safety bicycle, whose design she strongly recommended.

But when we emerged from the house, there was no cycle to be seen. "I left it just there," Helen said, looking about with a puzzled expression.

Then I saw Violet, crouched behind one of the

tall urns that line the terrace. "What are you doing there, Violet?" I asked. "Have you seen the lady's cycle?"

"Yes, Aunt 'Melia."

"Don't cower," I said sharply. "Come out of there."

"You are frightening the child, Amelia," Helen said.

"I? Frightening a child? How can you suppose—"

"Let me speak to her." She advanced, holding out her hand and smiling. "You are Violet? Your aunt has told me what a good girl you are. Come and give me a kiss."

Violet sidled forward, one finger in her mouth, her eyes rolling sideways to watch me. Anyone seeing her would have supposed I beat her daily. Helen stooped to take the child in a motherly embrace. "Tell me what has happened to my bicycle, little Violet," Helen cooed.

Violet pointed. "Ramses took it."

From the door of the house to the gates of the park is a good quarter mile. The graveled drive forms a circle before the terrace; because of plantings of trees and shrubbery, the far half of the circle and the straight stretch are hidden from sight. I now beheld, emerging from the enclosing trees, the bicycle. On the high seat perched Ramses. His legs were too short to touch the pedals except when they were at the topmost point of their circle, so he progressed in a series of rushes, wobbling erratically from one side of the drive to the other and prevented from falling—or so it seemed—by Percy, who was running alongside the machine.

Helen let out a gasp of outrage and concern, and

as the ensemble came closer I realized that instead of helping to hold the cycle, Percy was, in fact, attempting to stop it. I was assisted in this deduction by his cries of "Stop, Cousin; indeed, you must not, you didn't ask permission," and the like.

Ramses caught sight of me. His legs stopped moving, and at the same instant Percy snatched at the handlebars. The results were predictable. Cycle and rider fell to the ground with a grating crash. Percy saved himself from following them only by an agile twist of his body.

Helen ran toward the wreckage. Violet began to scream. As her cries of "Dead! Dead!" rang morbidly through the welkin, I hastened to join Helen.

At first sight Ramses appeared to be inextricably entwined with the bicycle, but we finally managed to free him. His arms and face were scraped and bleeding and his new sailor suit was a total wreck. So was the bicycle.

Having ascertained that he was unharmed, I gave him a little shake. "Whatever possessed you to do such a thing, Ramses? In addition to being foolhardy and dangerous, it was also very wrong. The bicycle was not yours and you had no right to ride it without asking permission."

"Violet told me—" Ramses began.

"Ramses, Ramses." Helen shook her head sadly. "A little gentleman does not excuse his actions by blaming them on a young lady. You were under no compulsion to do as Violet asked."

"Excuse me, ma'am—Aunt Amelia," Percy said quietly. "Violet only said she would dearly love to see Ramses ride a bicycle; he was bragging a little

about how well he could ride. I should have prevented him. I take full responsibility."

Ramses turned and kicked his cousin on the shin.
"I won't have you take responsibility for me! Who
the devil are you to take responsibility for me?"

Percy made no outcry, though his face twisted
with pain and he made haste to back away from
Ramses. The latter would have gone after him if I
had not twisted my hand in his collar.

"Ramses, stop it! I am bitterly ashamed of you.
Your language, your attack on your cousin, your
destruction of Miss McIntosh's machine . . ."

Ramses stopped squirming. "I apologize to Miss
McIntosh," he gasped, swabbing his bleeding face
with his bloody sleeve. "I will repay her as soon as is
possible. I presently possess twelve shillings sixpence ha'penny and will soon . . . Mama, your grasp
on my collar has twisted it about my windpipe in a
manner painfully suggestive of what a criminal must
experience when the hangman's noose—"

"Let him go, Amelia," Helen ordered. I complied,
all the more readily since the color of Ramses' face
had visibly darkened; I had not intended to be quite
so rough. Helen stooped to touch the boy's lacer-
ated cheek.

"I am not angry with you, Ramses, but I confess I
am disappointed. Not about the cycle; you didn't
intend to damage it. Do you know why I am disappointed in you?"

Ramses had always been fond of Helen, in his
peculiar fashion, but if he had looked at me as he
was looking at her, I would have sent for a constable.
Then his abused countenance took on its habitual

expression of phlegmatic unconcern. "You feel I am not behaving like a little gentleman?" he suggested.

"Quite right. A gentleman does not take the property of others without permission; he does not seek to excuse his behavior by referring to others; he does not use bad language; and he never, never kicks another person."

"Hmmm." Ramses thought it over. "In justice to my Mama and Papa, let me say that they have endeavored to impress such standards upon me, without, however, presenting them in such a pontifical manner, but until the present time I have never fully considered the difficulties of—"

"Go to your room, Ramses," I exclaimed.

"Yes, Mama. But I would like to say—"

"To your room!"

Ramses left. I observed he limped.

I ordered the carriage for Helen, commended Percy on his good intentions and manly behavior, spoke to Violet—who had stopped wailing as soon as she realized no one was paying any attention to her—and went wearily into the house.

I had a long, serious talk with Ramses. He condescended to let me examine his leg and apply cold compresses to the purpling bruise thereon, but to judge by his sole comment, my kindly lecture had little effect. "Being a little gentleman," he remarked, more to himself than to me, "seems hardly worth the trouble."

After the incident of the bicycle, conflict between the children lessened—perhaps because I had confined Ramses to his room for three days. I was thus able to finish my household chores and make plans to leave for London. Emerson had been locked up in the library, emerging only to take his meals and grumble at the rest of us. At first I used to hear angry cries, resulting from his discovery of another of Ramses' revisions of the manuscript; but these lessened as time went on, and at length he informed me that he had reached a point where consultation of reference materials at the British Museum was necessary. I informed him, in turn, that I was ready whenever he was.

Wishing to avoid any possible source of controversy between us, I had made no reference to the strange case of the malignant mummy; but rest assured, dear Reader, I eagerly consulted the newspapers each day to see what, if anything, had happened. The results were disappointing in the extreme. Mr. O'Connell and his rival did their best, but the only one who provided them with copy was the accommodating lunatic in the priestly vestments, who made regular calls on the mummy case. No visitor or official of the museum suffered so much as a paper cut.

I had virtually forgotten the matter when one morning—I believe it was on the Tuesday—Wilkins came to announce that I had a visitor. The young lady was unknown to him, nor had she consented to give a name; "but I believe, madam, you will wish to receive her," said Wilkins, with a most peculiar look.

"Indeed, Wilkins? And why do you believe that?"

Wilkins coughed deprecatingly. "The young lady was most insistent, madam."

His repetition of the word "lady" was emphatic and meaningful; Wilkins, snob that he is, is careful to make such distinctions.

"Show her in, then," I said, putting down my pen. "Or, no—better that I should go to her, I can excuse myself more easily. Where have you put her, Wilkins?"

He had put her in the drawing room—another indication of social status. I proceeded to that chamber.

The "young lady" was busily engaged in examining the family photographs ranged along the mantel. Though her back was turned to me, I recognized her at once from the inquisitive tilt of her head and the fact that she was scribbling in a pocketbook.

"Young *lady*, did you say, Wilkins?" I exclaimed loudly.

She let out a yelp and spun round. It was indeed Miss Minton, looking very smart in a neat blue tweed tailor-made and striped shirt. A straw sailor hat perched atop her head.

Wilkins tactfully withdrew and Miss Minton proved herself no lady. Without greeting or apology she rushed at me, brandishing her notebook. "You must hear me, Mrs. Emerson, indeed you must!"

I drew myself up. "Must, to ME, Miss Minton? You know not to whom you speak!"

"Oh, but I do—I do! Why else would I be here? Excuse me, Mrs. Emerson, I know I am behaving badly, but I haven't time to be polite, indeed I haven't. I hired the only trap at the railway station, but I don't underestimate his devilish resourcefulness, he will soon find other means of transport and follow—"

The speech ended in another small yelp or scream as a fusillade of knocking and calling broke out, clearly audible even through the closed door.

Miss Minton stamped her foot. "Devil take it! He is quicker than I would have believed possible. Mrs. Emerson, will you—"

She did not finish; the turmoil without culminated in the bursting open of the drawing-room door. On the threshold stood Kevin O'Connell. Hatless, wind-blown, his complexion matching his hair in intensity if not in precise shade, his cheeks streaked with per-spiration, he was momentarily bereft of speech by haste, exertion, and outrage.

Beyond him I saw Wilkins, seated on the floor of the hallway. Whether he had slipped, tripped, or been pushed, I did not know; but he continued to sit there without moving or blinking.

The two young people burst into speech at one and the same time. Miss Minton insisted that I do something—what, I could not ascertain. Kevin's conversation consisted solely of imprecations di-rected at Miss Minton. A recurring refrain was "Ah, begorra, if you were a man, now . . ."

Needless to say I did not permit this to continue unchecked. After considering the situation I decided that Wilkins must wait; he appeared to be unharmed, only stupefied. I first shut the door. Then I said, "Be quiet!"

I have had ample opportunity to practice that speech with Ramses. Silence instantly ensued.

"Sit down," I ordered. "You there, Miss Minton, and you, Mr. O'Connell, take that chair, on the far side of the room."

I remained standing as I continued severely, "Seldom have I beheld such an unseemly spectacle. You especially, Mr. O'Connell, should know you risk severe bodily injury by bursting into the house in this manner. I only pray the professor has not heard the ruckus. He is not in a happy frame of mind these days."

Kevin was sobered by the reminder. "Indeed, but you've the right of it, Mrs. E.," he said uneasily. "To be honest I was so beside myself with rage at the way I was outmaneuvered by this bold-faced wench—"

Miss Minton bounced up from her chair, her small fists clenched. I pushed her back into it. "Have you taken leave of your senses? Explain this intrusion at once. No, Mr. O'Connell, be silent, you will have your turn to speak."

The girl reached into her bag and took out a newspaper. She thrust it at me. Her eyes were bright with excitement. "The mummy has struck again. There has been another murder!"

FIVE

Kevin and Miss Minton continued to exchange whispered imprecations while I perused the newspaper. It was the latest edition of the *Mirror*, fresh off the press (as the ink that transferred itself to my fingers testified).

Miss Minton had been guilty of journalistic hyperbole in saying "another murder," since the death of the watchman had never been proved to be other than natural. However, the latest event must cast serious doubts upon that diagnosis, for the second death was unquestionably homicide. It is possible for a man to cut his own throat, but the severity of the wound, which had actually severed the windpipe and damaged the spinal cord, made such a conclusion extremely unlikely. Nor was the second victim a lowly workingman. (I speak in the social sense only, for a person of humble rank may be worthier in the eyes of Heaven than a peer of the realm.) He had been identified as an assistant keeper of Egyptian and Assyrian Antiquities, one Jonas Oldacre.

"The body was discovered on the Embankment," I murmured. "Not in the Museum—"

"But where on the Embankment?" Miss Minton demanded, her pencil poised. "At the foot of Cleopatra's Needle!"

"It is a pity that inaccurate name has taken hold," I remarked, continuing to peruse the newspaper. "Cleopatra had nothing to do with that monument, which is properly termed an obelisk. It was raised by, and bears the name of, King Thut-mose III. If you continue to scribble in that notebook, Miss Minton, I will be forced to take it from you."

"Yes, ma'am." The young woman closed the book and slipped it into her pocket. "Whatever you say, Mrs. Emerson. It is an Egyptian monument, though?"

"Obviously. Pray let me finish . . . This purported scrap of paper found in the hand of the dead man—do you have a copy of the message?"

"No," Miss Minton admitted.

"Then how do you know what it said? For you have quoted it here, word for word—and in English translation."

For the first time Miss Minton had no ready reply. Before she could think of a reasonable explanation, Kevin, who had been controlling himself with difficulty, burst out, "She bribed the constable! Not only with money—I tried that, and failed—but with her despicable woman's wiles—"

"How dare you!" Miss Minton cried, reddening.

"Smiles and dimples and sweet words," Kevin went on angrily. "Touching his muscles with a timid finger and telling him how brave and strong—"

Miss Minton leaped up, ran to Kevin, slapped him across the face, and returned to her chair. I had not the heart to scold her, for I would have done the same.

"Shame, Mr. O'Connell," I said severely.

Kevin rubbed his flaming cheek. The blow must have stung; it had certainly made a loud enough noise. "Och, well," he muttered.

I laid the newspaper on the table. "I won't ask you how you got the message translated, Miss Minton, for I think I know. If there was a message . . ."

"There was a message," Kevin said. "The police have admitted as much."

"Then one of you probably wrote it. I have never seen an inscription remotely resembling this one. Hmmmm. The facts of the case seem clear enough . . ."

"To a keen, incisive brain like yours, perhaps," said Kevin. "I confess that I myself am completely baffled."

I was about to enlighten him when I saw that Miss Minton had surreptitiously removed her notebook from her pocket, and that Kevin was watching me with a keenness I had good cause to remember. "Then you must remain baffled," I said shortly. "If you have come pelting all the way from London in order to obtain an interview, you are doomed to disappointment. What ghouls you are, snapping and snarling over me like dogs over a moldy bone!"

They burst into simultaneous protestations. I gathered that I had been quite mistaken; they had not come to interview me, but to offer me fame and fortune as the official consultant of their respective newspapers.

It was a most intriguing offer. Even more intriguing was the rapidity with which the fee rose, from fifty guineas to a hundred and fifty, within the space of a few minutes. Though I was tempted to remain silent, and ascertain precisely how much I was worth to the publishing industry, I feared interruption, from a source I am sure I need not name, if the racket continued.

"Quite out of the question," I said firmly. "Not under any circumstances. The discussion is terminated. I am sorry I cannot offer you refreshments before you leave, but after all, I did not invite you to come. Good day to you."

The refusal was accepted more graciously than I had expected. From the gleam in Kevin's eye I knew he had not given up, but meant to try again at another time. Miss Minton murmured, "So long as you don't accept *his* offer . . ."

I had hoped to get them out of the house without a further scene, but alas, it was not to be. Once again the abused door of my drawing room was flung open, this time by a brawnier arm than that of Kevin O'Connell.

Emerson believes that physical comfort is essential to intellectual labors (an opinion in which I heartily concur), so he was in his shirt sleeves, without cravat or vest. His hair was tousled and his face was liberally besprinkled with ink spots, unmistakable signs of a desperate (though victorious) struggle with his recalcitrant prose. His blue eyes sparkled, his brows were lowered, a flush of choler added a becoming pink to his lean brown cheeks.

"Ah," he said mildly. "I thought I recognized your voice, Mr. O'Connell."

Kevin retreated behind the sofa, a massive structure of carved rosewood and crimson plush. Nodding politely to Miss Minton, Emerson addressed me. "Amelia, why is Wilkins sitting on the floor of the hall?"

"I have no idea, Emerson. Why don't you ask Wilkins?"

"He appears incapable of speech," Emerson replied.

"I never laid a hand on him," Kevin exclaimed. "Sure an' begorra, I wouldn't touch an old soul like that—"

"You never laid a hand on him," Emerson repeated. He began to roll up his shirt sleeves.

"No, Emerson, no," I cried, attaching myself to him as he moved toward the cowering journalist. "You will only provide Mr. O'Connell with the copy he ardently desires if you descend to blows."

This argument had more effect on Emerson than my attempt at physical restraint. "You are in the right, as always, Peabody," he said. "But I beg you will get the fellow out of my house at once. I am the most reasonable of men, but even a temper as equable as mine must crack under such provocation. The effrontery of invading a man's own house to interrogate that man's wife—"

"It is not what you suppose, Emerson," I explained. "There has been another murder!"

"Another murder, Peabody?"

"Well—a murder. Mr. Oldacre, the assistant keeper of Oriental Antiquities."

"Oldacre? I knew him. A pompous idiot, as you would expect any protégé of Budge's to be . . . What happened to him?"

I explained. Emerson listened politely. "A sad tragedy. But it has nothing to do with us. Let us bid these young people good-bye and return to our work."

Moving on tiptoe and using the furniture as cover, Kevin had edged his way to the door. He knew Emerson only too well and was not at all reassured by the deceptive mildness of my impulsive husband's demeanor. Emerson watched him out of the corner of his eye; though his face remained preternaturally grave, a tiny twitch at the extremities of his well-shaped lips gave evidence of inner amusement. Having reached the doorway, Kevin stopped.

"Yes, Mr. O'Connell?" Emerson inquired.

"I—er—I was waiting to escort Miss Minton . . . that is, I had hoped she might give me a lift to the railroad station."

"Ah, yes. Miss Minton." Emerson's eyes turned to the young lady. She raised a nervous hand to her hat. "I understand how Mr. O'Connell managed to invade my house," Emerson went on. "Sheer brute force, perpetrated against a man old enough to be his grandfather. Splendid example of Hibernian manners, eh, Peabody? But you, Miss Minton; how did you persuade Wilkins to admit you? For I am certain that had he presented your card to Mrs. Emerson, she would not have consented to receive you."

"You are quite in the right, Emerson," I assured him. "Miss Minton refused to give her name. In some manner, I cannot imagine what, she convinced Wilkins that her errand was urgent."

"You cannot imagine," Emerson said musingly. "But I believe I might hazard a guess. That oh-so useful resemblance . . . What did you tell Wilkins, Miss Minton? That you were Mrs. Emerson's long-lost sister or the abandoned memento of a youthful indiscretion—"

Miss Minton's indignant rebuttal was scarcely louder than mine. "Emerson, how dare you!"

"*Very* youthful indiscretion," Emerson amended. "Well, Miss Minton?"

"I said nothing of the sort," Miss Minton replied. "If your butler chose to reach a false conclusion, that is not my fault."

"Ah, but I think it is your fault," Emerson said jovially. "Go away, Miss Minton."

The young lady's smile faded as he moved toward her. "You wouldn't strike a woman," she gasped.

"I am deeply hurt that such an idea should enter your mind," Emerson answered. "However, there is nothing to prevent me from picking you up and carrying you, gently and respectfully, out of my house."

"I'll go, I'll go" was the agitated response.

"Then do so." Emerson followed her as she backed toward the door. But there she paused. "You haven't heard the last of me, Professor," she cried, her eyes snapping. "I don't give up so easily."

Kevin caught her arm and dragged her out. Wilkins was still sitting on the floor, and I was vexed, though not at all surprised, to see that Ramses stood beside him, studying his frozen form with grave curiosity. I did not doubt that Ramses had heard every word that had been spoken—or shouted, rather—in the drawing room; as Miss Minton and

O'Connell appeared, he turned an even more curious stare on them. Emerson called, "Get up, Wilkins, and close the door. Make sure you bolt it."

He then closed the drawing-room door and turned to me. "Dear me, Peabody. Dear me," he remarked.

"Of all the absurd things," I said. "This presumed resemblance you fancy you see—"

"If it pleases you to deny it, Peabody, by all means continue to do so. The matter is entertaining, but irrelevant. I confess I rather admire the young woman's ingenuity in making use of it." Picking up the newspaper, he sank into an armchair and began reading.

"I suppose you will claim this is only an odd coincidence and has nothing to do with the death of the night watchman," I began.

"There you go jumping to conclusions again, Peabody," Emerson said mildly. "At least let me study the facts—pardon me, the newspaper story, which is not the same thing—before I make up my mind. Hmmm, hmmm. Yes. Blood-drenched corpse found at the foot of the obelisk . . . scrap of paper with a message calling down the curse of the gods on those who profaned the tomb . . . mysterious figure clad in white robes skulking along the Embankment in the curdling fog . . . Miss Minton writes with zest, does she not? Another bond between you."

"Your harmless lunatic is not so harmless, it appears," I remarked, ignoring the last comment.

"The police are as skeptical of the priest's presence as I would be, my dear. It seems the witness is not noted for his adherence to the principles of temperance. I would not be at all surprised to learn that Mr. O'Connell committed the crime himself. These journalists will stop at nothing to achieve—"

"Ridiculous, Emerson."

"Why? Oldacre was small loss to the world. An effete snob, always toadying to titles; a gambler, a lecher, an habitué of vile dens—"

"Dens of iniquity, Emerson?"

"I was thinking of opium dens and low grog shops and—er—well, yes, one might call them dens of iniquity." Emerson tossed the newspaper aside. Frowning, he fingered the dent in his chin as is his habit when deep in thought.

I considered this a hopeful sign. "Then you think the matter deserves to be investigated, Emerson?"

"It certainly requires to be investigated, and I feel certain the police are doing so."

"Oh, Emerson, you know what I mean!"

"Yes, Peabody, I know what you mean." Emerson continued to stroke his chin. "There is one aspect of this case that tempts me," he said seriously.

"The archaeological aspect," I cried. "I knew, Emerson, that you would—"

"No, Peabody. The fact that this case has not the slightest aroma of aristocracy about it. Not a lord or lady, not a sir, not even an honorable! Only a lowly night watchman, and then an assistant keeper. Almost, Peabody, I am moved to interfere."

"Emerson, there are times when your sense of humor . . ." I caught my breath. "Emerson! Do you realize what you have said? A night watchman and *then* an assistant . . . The lunatic is moving up the social ladder. Where will he strike next?"

Emerson's dour face brightened. "Budge!" he cried. "What a delightful thought, Peabody!"

"My dear Emerson, such inappropriate expressions of levity would be sadly misinterpreted if they were overheard. I know you better; you would not really like to see Mr. Budge foully murdered—"

"No," Emerson admitted. "I would prefer to see him alive and suffering."

"But what if Mr. Budge is not the next victim? There are a number of Oriental scholars in London, Emerson. Soon there will be another—the greatest, the most distinguished of them all."

Emerson, who—to judge by his smile—had been pleasurably pondering the sufferings of Mr. Budge, looked up. My suggestion seemed to strike him all of a heap. His thick dark eyebrows swooped up and down, his lips moved, as if seeking the precise, the exact word. Finally he found it.

"Lunatic," he shouted. "Of all the lunatic theories you have ever concocted—and my dear Peabody, there have been a number of them—this is the most . . . the wildest . . . the . . . But—but I must compose myself. I must exercise that stern control refined by years of bitter experience."

"You really must," I agreed. "Your face is absolutely engorged, Emerson. Either control your emotion or express it—rid yourself of it. Tear up the newspaper, Emerson. Break something. I have always disliked that vase—"

Emerson leaped from his chair. He reached for the vase, but thought better of it. He stood, rigid, fists clenched, murmuring brokenly to himself; and slowly the fiery flood of ichor that had tinted his cheeks subsided. He emitted a weak laugh. "You had me for a moment, Peabody. What a joker you are. You don't believe it either. You were only teasing me."

I said nothing. The truth could not be expressed, for fear of arousing another storm of wrath; a lie was impossible to one of my open and candid personality.

"It was an excuse," Emerson mused. "Not a very good one, either, if I may say so; usually you can come up with more sensible rationalizations for meddling in murders. You are going to meddle, aren't you, Peabody?"

"Why no, Emerson. I never meddle."

Reader, I spoke the truth. I never have and never will meddle in other people's affairs. It is a word I abhor. There are times when a gentle hint or a helpful suggestion may save unnecessary suffering, and this I would not scruple to employ. But meddle—never.

My dear Emerson was himself again. A healthy flush warmed his brown cheeks; his irresistible chuckle bubbled up in his throat and issued from lips that had parted to display strong white teeth. He threw his arms around me.

"What a cool liar you are, Peabody. You can hardly wait to begin. We won't have been in London a day before you will call on Scotland Yard, on Budge, on the mummy—"

"Emerson, I must protest the unjust, not to say frivolous—" But I was unable to continue reasoned discussion, since Emerson's actions had—as they not infrequently do—a peculiar effect on my ability to concentrate. I essayed one last protest: "Emerson. Your hands are covered with ink from the newspaper; I am sure you are leaving prints all over my blouse, and what Wilkins will think when he sees . . . Oh, my dear Emerson!"

"Who cares what Wilkins thinks?" Emerson muttered. And I was forced to confess that he had, with his customary acumen, struck straight to the heart of the matter.

"Superstitious" is not a word, I believe, that anyone would dare apply to ME. Amelia Peabody Emerson prey to degrading and irrational beliefs? A short, sharp bark of laughter is the only possible response to such an idea.

And yet, dear Reader, and yet . . . At one time in my life I had been forced to believe in the premonitory nature of dreams, when one such vision was later fulfilled to the last lurid detail. I do not insist that such is always the case. It may well be, as some authorities now claim (at the time I pen these words) that dreams reflect other, even more repugnant, elements—low, disgusting racial memories, repressed unnatural desires, and the like. I am never dogmatic; my mind is always receptive to new ideas, unlikely and unpalatable though they may be.

But enough of philosophical musings. Suffice it to say I dreamed that night: a vision of such horror that for many years thereafter the mere thought of it set me to shuddering uncontrollably.

I huddled in musty darkness, fearing I knew not what. A cold stone wall was at my back, cold stone pressed the soles of my bare feet. At first there was utter silence. Then, so dim with distance that it might have been no more than the murmur of my own pulsating blood, came a sound. Gradually it strengthened. It became a deep and solemn chanting. And then—then the aforementioned blood turned to ice in my veins, for I knew that evil music.

Light accompanied the chanting and grew with it. The lights came from torches, visible at first only as distant specks of flame moving in slow procession. They came nearer; the darkness yielded to their ghastly illumination.

I stood, or crouched, on a ledge high above a vast chamber carved from the living rock. The polished walls, smooth as satin, reflected and multiplied the lights of the torches. They were carried by figures robed in white and crowned by monstrous masks—crocodile and hawk, lion and ibis, carved with the appearance of life. The chamber brightened as the torchbearers moved to their positions, surrounding a low altar presided over by a monumental statue. It was Osiris, ruler of the dead, divine judge; his body tightly swathed in mummy wrappings, his arms crossed over his breast, his hands holding the twin scepters. His tall white crown and snowy alabaster shoulders shone pale in contrast to the flat black of face and hands (for so the pagan Egyptians depicted their divinities—an interesting and as yet unexplained phenomenon).

Pacing slowly behind the light-bearers came the

high priest. Unlike his shaven-headed subordinates he wore a great curled wig, with row upon row of ringlets. The mask that concealed his face had human features, rigid as the face of death. Beyond a gasp of horrified recognition I paid this apparition little heed; for behind him, borne aloft on a litter carried by naked slaves, was a form I knew.

They had loaded him with chains, against which his mighty sinews strove in vain. His bare arms and breast gleamed like polished bronze from the oil of anointing and the perspiration of struggle; his teeth were bared and his eyes blazed. But even courage such as his could not avail; as the deep voices rose and fell in hideous invocation, rough hands dragged him from the litter and flung him upon the altar. The high priest advanced, the sacrificial knife in his hand. And then—oh, then—my heart fails me even now when I remember—the doomed man's sapphirine eyes turned to where I stood frozen, finding me even in the darkness; and his lips shaped a word . . .

"Peabody! Peeeeea-body . . ."

"Emerson!" I shrieked.

"What the devil is the matter with you?" Emerson demanded. "You were grunting and squirming like a hungry piglet."

The soft light of a spring sunrise illumined his beloved, unshaven face and tumbled hair, his sleep-heavy eyes and familiar scowl.

"Oh, Emerson . . ." I flung my arms around him.

"Hmmmm," said Emerson in a pleased voice. "Not that I object to a warm, soft, squirming little . . ." But the remainder of the conversation has no bearing on the present narrative, and indeed I fear that I have already said too much.

I did not think it wise to describe my dream to Emerson. For one thing, it would have reminded him of that other vision whose ghastly fulfillment he had beheld with his own eyes,* and the recollection of which still had a deleterious effect on his blood pressure. For another thing, it would have provoked rude jeers and remarks about meddling. Emerson never ordered me to do, or refrain from doing, anything; he knew the futility of *that*. But he had pleaded with me to avoid involvement in yet another criminal case. He had a great deal of work to do that summer, he remarked pathetically; and he absolutely refused to be distracted again.

Of course it would end as it always did, with the two of us hand in hand, equal partners in detection as in archaeology, nose down on the trail of another vicious villain. Emerson would thus have the satisfaction of doing what he secretly yearned to do, and the even greater satisfaction of blaming it all on ME. This is a favorite trick of husbands, I have observed, and although Emerson is vastly superior to the majority of the species, he is not entirely free of masculine weaknesses.

As for me, my decision had been made. The hideous dream could not be a literal portent of things to come. Though my trained scholar's brain had

Lion in the Valley.

functioned even in sleep, sketching a reasonable
rendering of priestly costume and carved god, there
had been a number of inaccuracies in the scenario.
For one thing, human sacrifice was not practiced by
the Egyptians—at least, not at the period repre-
sented. At least . . .

I promised myself I would investigate that question at a later time. At the present time, I could
think only of Emerson. The dream had been a warning. Not that Emerson stood in any danger of being
sacrificed on a no longer extant altar of a god whose
last worshiper died several millennia ago; that was
only the symbol my dreaming mind had chosen to
warn me that peril of some sort threatened my beloved husband. Superstitious? No, not I! But I would
be the first to acknowledge—nay, to insist—that
such profound affection as binds my dear Emerson
to me with hoops of steel (to quote the Bard) consti-
tutes a profoundly mystical union; and that under
those circumstances anything is possible. I had as
yet no real proof that my theory was correct. But if it
were—oh, dear Reader, if it were . . . If some new
homicidal killer stalked the fog-ridden streets of London by night, seeking not unfortunate abandoned
women but Egyptologists . . .

To ignore that possibility would have been to fail
in my obligations as a wife and risk the destruction of
all I held dear (except, of course, for Ramses). I therefore completed my remaining tasks in short order;
and on the following morning we left for London.

The first part of the drive was pleasant, through sunken country lanes where the blossoms of wild blackberry twined among the thorny hedgerows, and along fields fresh with the green of new crops. However, the carriage was somewhat cramped for five of us, especially when three of the five were children. Ten minutes after we drove through the gates of Amarna House they began asking when we would be there. Emerson, who chafes at inactivity, was almost as bad. He had actually proposed taking the train up to London, leaving me to bring the children and the luggage. Needless to say, I promptly quashed this idea. Violet, Percy, and I occupied one seat, with Ramses and Emerson opposite. In this way I hoped to prevent the sort of rude scuffling between the boys that often occurred when they were in close proximity.

Ramses was in a glum mood, however, for he was without his constant companion. The cat Bastet had disappeared.

The cause of her strange behavior became clear after we got home. The congregating of what appeared to be every male feline within a ten-mile radius left no doubt, in my mind at least, of what was afoot; and although I am sympathetic to the expression of amatory excitability in man or beast, I must say that the advent of Bastet's admirers added considerably to my difficulties. Their passionate singing filled the night and made sleep impossible; they fought, among themselves and with the dogs. It was something of a relief when she finally chose one suitor from among the rest and eloped with him. But she had not returned by the time we left and I was forced to reject Ramses' plea that we wait for her return. I would never have been cruel enough to tell him what I feared—that this event might be indefinitely delayed. I had no fear of her survival. She was larger and stronger than most domestic cats and had grown to maturity in the inhospitable Egyptian desert. From the wild she had come, graciously consenting to share our lives for a time; and to the wild she might well return. This possibility never occurred to Ramses; he assumed the cat's devotion to him was as profound as was his to her. A touching, childish notion . . . And since it was one of the few childish notions ever expressed by Ramses, I chose not to disabuse him of it.

With Ramses sunk in brooding silence and Emerson fidgeting and Percy spouting questions like a repeater rifle, and Violet becoming increasingly sticky from the sweets she sucked (a supply of these being the only method of keeping her from whining), I cannot say I enjoyed the journey. However, all anguish must end at last; green fields gave way to suburban villas and then to the wilderness of brick and mortar that is the city. After crossing the bridge under which the gray water flowed with sluggish flood, and enduring the chaos of traffic that filled the Strand, we arrived at the relative peace of St. James's Square.

Luncheon was waiting for us, but Emerson announced he would not partake of it.

"You are going out?" I inquired. My tone was calm and pleasant as I hope it always is, but Emerson reads the innermost secrets of my heart. Twisting his hat in his hands and trying to avoid my intent look, he said, "Well, but Peabody, there is nothing I can do here. If I could assist you—"

"Oh, I have nothing to do either, Emerson. Only settling the children, and unpacking, and speaking to cook about dinner and explaining to the housemaids that on no account must they touch any of Ramses' experiments, and replying to a dozen letters and notes—"

"What letters and notes?" Emerson demanded. "Curse it, Amelia, I will not be distracted by social obligations. How did the writers of these notes and letters learn we were to be in London?"

"The news is generally known, I suppose," I replied. "Evelyn informed the staff here of the expected time of our arrival, and you know servants will gossip about the doings of persons like ourselves."

"And you wrote to everyone you know, inviting them to call on us," Emerson grumbled.

"Only those professional friends whom I knew you would want to see, Emerson. Howard Carter and Mr. Quibell, Frank Griffith, who is at University College—"

"Then read your cursed notes and letters and reply to them. Only don't expect me to be present at luncheon, tea, and what-not when you entertain. I have work to do, Peabody!"

Slapping his hat on his head, he charged out the door.

In fact, my dear Evelyn had done everything possible to make our temporary residence in London as free of care as it could be. There was always a skeleton staff at Chalfont House, on board wages when the family was not in residence. The staff was actually much larger than was required, for Evelyn, who has the kindest heart in the world, was always taking in bedraggled young girls and offering them refuge. The housekeeper, though not at all bedraggled and certainly not young, was also an object of her charity; a distant relation of Evelyn's mother, now long deceased, she had been the wife of a village clergyman and had been left destitute and without occupation upon the death of her husband. Being keenly aware of the tribulations of this class of women—gentlewomen without education, training, or resources—Evelyn had provided her not only with a refuge, but a purpose and an occupation. Mrs. Watson had responded with a grateful determination to be of use to her kind employer. The young girls she trained, some of them rescued from situations so horrible I would fear to tax the reader's sympathy by relating them, looked on her as a mother, and most of them went on to excellent positions or to marriage.

Knowing that this good lady would have matters well in hand, I had been guilty of a slight exaggeration when I complained to Emerson; even so, there were a number of things to be discussed before a smooth routine could be established, and I settled down with Mrs. Watson to discuss them.

We had not brought any of our servants with us. Rose was my second-in-command; Amarna House could not get on without her. Wilkins was—to be quite honest—more trouble than he was worth. I had considered bringing John, since he was accustomed to our ways (even Ramses' mummies) but it would have been unkind to ask John to leave his little family.

Mrs. Watson assured me there would be no difficulty. "Three of our girls have just left us, but there are plenty more where they came from."

"Unfortunately," I said, sighing.

"Yes." The housekeeper shook her head. She continued to favor the formal dress of her youth, and was never to be seen without a cap on her handsome white head. These caps betrayed an unexpected touch of frivolity, each being more extravagant than the last in the way of ribbons, lace, and bows. That day she looked as if an entire group of large lavender butterflies had settled on her head.

"I will put an advertisement in the *Post*," I said. "We want someone to watch over the children. A nurserymaid for little Violet; for the boys, someone—er—sturdier."

"A tutor?"

"A guard," I replied. "Do you think one of the footmen—"

"They are good lads," the housekeeper replied doubtfully. "But none are well educated, and their habits are not precisely what you would want your son to acquire."

"I am not so much concerned with educating Ramses as with preventing him from killing himself—or his cousin," I said. "They don't get on, Mrs. Watson. They are constantly at one another's throats."

"Boys will be boys," said Mrs. Watson with a tolerant smile.

"Humph," I said.

"One of the housemaids—Kitty or Jane—might do well enough in the nursery for the time being," Mrs. Watson mused. "And Bob is a husky young fellow—"

"I will leave it to you, Mrs. Watson. I have every confidence in your judgment." Having concluded these arrangements, I took my hat and my parasol, and left the house.

It was a fine spring day. A stiff northwest breeze had cleared away some of the smoke and an occasional glimpse of blue sky was to be seen. I set out at a brisk stride, looking with contempt and pity at the other ladies I saw; laced into tight stays and teetering on high-heeled shoes, they were almost incapable of motion, much less a good healthy walk. Poor foolish victims of society's dictates—but (I reminded myself) willing victims, like the misguided females of India who fought to fling themselves into the funeral pyres of their bigamous husbands. Enlightened British laws had put an official end to that ghastly custom; what a pity British opinion was so unenlightened with regard to the oppression of English women.

Musing thus, I was unaware of the footsteps that kept pace with my own until a breathless voice behind me remarked, "Good afternoon, Mrs. Emerson."

Without moderating my pace, I replied, "Good afternoon, Miss Minton, and good-bye. There is no sense in your following me, since I am not going to do anything that will interest your readers."

"Please, won't you stop for a moment? You walk so rapidly I can't keep up and talk at the same time. I want to apologize."

I was forced to stop, since Regent Street, which I proposed to cross, was filled from curb to curb with moving vehicles. Miss Minton said, "I behaved very badly. I am heartily ashamed of myself. Only . . . it was all his fault, Mrs. Emerson. He does irritate me so—and then I act without thinking of the consequences."

Taking advantage of a break in the traffic, I proceeded to cross the street. Miss Minton was on my heels, though an omnibus narrowly missed knocking her down.

"You refer, I presume, to Mr. O'Connell," I said.

"Well—yes. Though he is no worse than the others. It is a man's world, Mrs. Emerson, and if a woman is to make her way, she must be as rude and aggressive as they are."

"Not at the risk of losing her femininity, Miss Minton. One may succeed in any profession and still remain a lady."

"That is certainly true of you," Miss Minton said earnestly. "But you are a unique person, Mrs. Emerson. Dare I confess something to you? Ever since I first read of your adventures in Egypt, I have looked up to you. One of the reasons I have pursued this story so indefatigably is that I hoped it would give me the opportunity to meet you—my idol, my ideal."

"Hmmm. Well, Miss Minton, I certainly sympathize with your aspirations and I quite understand that the profession you have chosen makes difficult demands on a woman."

"Then you forgive me?" the young lady asked, clasping her hands.

"Forgiveness is required of Christians and I hope

I always perform my Christian duty. I hold no grudge, but that doesn't mean I have any intention of cooperating with you in your quest for a sensation."

"Of course not. Er—you aren't by chance going to Scotland Yard, are you?"

I looked sharply at her and saw that her lips had curved in a smile. "Ah," I said. "You are having a little joke at my expense. Very amusing, upon my word. In fact, I am going to insert an advertisement in the *Post*. Not one of your mysterious notices in the agony columns, but a simple request for a servant. After that I am going to meet my husband at the British Museum, where he is working—not on the mysterious mummy problem, but on his history of ancient Egypt. All very harmless and innocent, you see; you are at liberty to follow me if you like, since I can't very well prevent you, but it will be a waste of your time as well as a long, tiring walk."

Miss Minton's eyes widened. "You are going to walk to Fleet Street and then to Bloomsbury?"

"Certainly. *Mens sana in corpore sano*, Miss Minton; a *mens sana* is dependent, in my opinion, upon a *corpore sano*, and regular exercise—"

"Oh, I quite agree," Miss Minton exclaimed. "And now I understand your youthful appearance and fit, handsome figure. I hope you don't mind my saying that."

I shook my head, smiling; for really, the girl had very pretty, charming manners when she chose to display them. "And your costume," she went on, "how practical and yet how becoming. In the best of taste and yet comfortable."

"I wish I could say the same of you," I replied good-naturedly. "Not that your dress isn't very pretty. Sleeves have become even larger, I observe (though I would not have supposed it to be possible), and the width of your skirt allows you to walk freely without swaddling your limbs in excessive fabric. The color—what do they call it this year—saffron, mustard, goldenrod?—it becomes your complexion. And those scrolls of braid on the wrists and lapels . . . You had better button the coat, Miss Minton, the wind is a touch cool. Here, allow me. Yes, it is as I suspected; your stays are too tight. It is a wonder you can catch your breath." I proceeded to give her a little lecture on the iniquitous effect of tight corseting upon the internal organs, to which she listened without attempting to conceal her interest. All at once she said impulsively, "How interesting all this is. Mrs. Emerson, would you—could you—is it possible that you would consent to stop and have a cup of tea with me while we continue this discussion?"

I hesitated; for indeed I was reluctant to give up the hope of converting yet another young woman to the advantages of rational dress and perhaps saving her health, or even her life. She went on persuasively, "You won't lose any time, I promise; for if you will permit me the very great pleasure of doing a small service for you, as apology and thanks, I will be happy to insert your advertisement in the *Post*. I am going to Fleet Street in any case. That will save you a good many steps, since you can go directly to the Museum."

Waving her umbrella, she indicated a nearby shop.

I recognized the name; it was one of a line of tea-shops which catered, I had been told, to respectable ladies of the professional class, of which there were a growing number. (Though not so many as there ought to have been.)

We had a nice little talk. The conversation ranged widely, from fashions to the rights of women, from marriage (to which institution I have certain serious objections, though personally my experience has been almost entirely positive) to the profession of journalism. However, I confess (since the reader has probably suspected it already) that my chief interest was in subtly extracting from Miss Minton all she knew about the case of the malignant mummy.

Miss Minton agreed with me that the identity of the lunatic in the priestly garb was of primary importance. His elusiveness thus far verged on the supernatural; to say, as the more sensational accounts did, that he had a habit of vanishing into thin air was unquestionably an exaggeration, but metaphorically it was a reasonable description. However, Miss Minton insisted that he had thus far eluded pursuit primarily because no one had been particularly interested in following him.

"He was only one lunatic among many," she said, smiling cynically. "Now, however . . ."

"I thought the police didn't believe the witness who claimed to have seen him near the scene of the murder."

"So they say. But that may be only a device on the part of Scotland Yard, to lull him into a sense of false security. In any case, he is an object of consid-

erable interest to the press. How I would love to be
the one to apprehend and unmask him! What a
journalistic coup!" Her eyes flashed.

"You have a scheme in mind," I said shrewdly.
"Does it by chance involve your young friend at the
Museum?"

"Eustace?" The girl gave a peal of merry laughter.
"Dear me, no. Eustace would like nothing better
than to see me give up the case, and the profession of
journalism."

"But you don't scruple to make use of him," I said.
"Shame, Miss Minton. To take advantage of a young
man's affectionate feelings in order to extract information is really . . . I presume he was acquainted with
the murdered man?"

"Yes." She hesitated for a moment; but my encouraging smile and expectant air were too much
for her to resist. "I should not say it, but from what I
have heard, Mr. Oldacre was no great loss."

"Strange. Emerson said much the same."

"I had occasion to meet him while I was pursuing
my initial investigation," the girl continued. Her
soft mouth hardened in distaste. "A sleek, smooth-
talking rascal with wet hands—you know what I
mean, Mrs. Emerson—and eyes that seemed to look
through one's clothing. He was overly familiar with
equals and fawning to superiors; always trying to
imitate a way of life he could neither afford nor
appreciate—"

"Ah," I said keenly. "Was he in debt, then?"

"Constantly."

"Then perhaps it was a moneylender who killed
him."

"Moneylenders don't kill the goose that lays the golden eggs," Miss Minton said. "Nor do they continue to lend money without security. Oldacre was not independently wealthy, and his salary from the Museum was not enough to support him in the style he desired. You see what I am getting at, don't you, Mrs. Emerson?"

"Blackmail."

"Quite right. And the victims of blackmailers do sometimes turn on their tormentors."

"But that theory raises more questions than it answers," I said. "Whom was he blackmailing, and for what reason? And what does the lunatic priest have to do with the affair? You reason ingeniously, Miss Minton, but you lack my experience in these matters, and I must tell you . . ."

Which I did, at some length, concluding, "Well, my dear, I wish you luck. It would be a pleasure to see a woman succeed where arrogant males fail."

Her eyes gleamed. "If you feel that way—" she began.

"You must not count on my assistance, Miss Minton. I take no interest in the case. I have not the time to pursue it. I will be very busy this summer. Assisting the professor with his book on the history of ancient Egypt, preparing our excavation report for publication, attending the annual meeting of the Society for the Preservation of the Monuments of Ancient Egypt (where I have promised to read a paper on the flooding of the burial chamber of the Black Pyramid) . . . oh, any number of things. So I had better be on my way."

We parted with assurance of mutual regard, and I thanked her again for undertaking my errand.

I waited until her slim, trim figure was out of sight before I started walking. It would never have done for her to see the direction I took—not toward Piccadilly and Shaftesbury Avenue, the most direct route to Russell Square, but following her, to the Strand and the Embankment. I walked jauntily, swinging my parasol, for I was feeling quite pleased with myself. I had not told a single falsehood (a habit I deplore), yet I had managed to get her off the track.

Emerson would have said it served me right for being so smug. Yet who could have suspected that her pretty smiling face was capable of concealing such dark duplicity?

Certainly not an individual as forthright and honest as I.

SIX

Heretofore all my criminal investigations had occurred in the Middle East, so I had never had occasion to visit New Scotland Yard. I had, of course, observed the building with professional interest whenever I happened to pass by, and I did not agree with the aesthetes who sneered at its architecture. Red brick banded with white Portland stone gave it a picturesque charm, and the rounded turrets at each corner suggested a baronial castle. Its appearance may have been at variance with its grim function, but I see no reason why prisons, fortresses, factories, and other places of confinement should not look attractive.

Being accustomed to the vagaries of Egyptian police officials and the rudeness of their English superiors, I was pleasantly surprised by the efficiency and affability with which I was received. Having asked for the person in charge of the murder of Mr. Oldacre, I was shown at once to a (rather dreary) office with windows overlooking the Embankment. It contained two desks, three chairs, several cabinets, and two men, one a uniformed constable, the other a lean, grizzled man as emaciated as any mummy, which he rather resembled, for the skin of his face was set in a thousand wrinkles. When my name was announced, he hastened to greet me, his thin lips straining as if trying to smile.

"Mrs. Emerson! I need not ask if you are *the* Mrs. Emerson; I am familiar with your appearance, from portraits that have appeared from time to time in the newspapers. Do sit down. Will you have a cup of tea?"

I accepted, partly out of politeness and partly because I was curious to see what sort of beverage they brewed in the precincts of Scotland Yard. After dusting off the chair he offered, I sat down, and the constable hastened out to do his chief's bidding.

"I am Inspector Cuff," said the grizzled gentleman, seating himself behind his desk. "I was expecting you, Mrs. Emerson. Indeed I expected you would do me the honor of calling on me before this."

His lips had abandoned the struggle to shape a smile, but there was a friendly, not to say admiring, twinkle in his keen gray eyes. I was gratified and said so, adding, "I apologize for not coming before this, Inspector. Family and professional duties, you know."

"I quite understand, ma'am. But you also owe a duty to the citizens of England, and to the hardworking Metropolitan Police, to assist us with your famous talents in the area of crime detection."

I lowered my eyes modestly. "Oh, as to that, Inspector, I can hardly claim . . ."

"You needn't be reticent with me, Mrs. Emerson. I know all about you. We have a mutual acquaintance, who is also an admirer of yours. Mr. Blakeney Jones, who formerly advised the Cairo Police."

"Mr. Jones—of course! I remember him well. He took my statement on one occasion, when I was able to deliver to him a pair of hardened criminals who had been annoying me. Is he back in London, then?"

"Yes, and has been for over a year. He will be sorry to have missed you; he is on holiday at the moment."

"Please give him my regards when next you see him." I stripped off my gloves, folded my hands, and regarded Cuff earnestly. "But enough compliments, Inspector. Let us get down to business."

"Certainly, ma'am." The twinkle was very much in evidence. "How may I assist you? Or have you come to assist me?"

"I hope I may be able to be of use, Inspector. But at the moment I am in quest of information. Tell me all about the murder."

Mr. Cuff burst into a fit of coughing. The constable returning at that moment with two heavy white mugs containing a murky brew, I pressed one upon the Inspector.

"Thank you, ma'am. It is the confounded—excuse me—London fog. You may go, Jenkins, I won't be needing you."

After the constable had left, Cuff leaned back in his chair. "As to the murder, I fear we know little more than is known to the public. The severity of the injury and the fact that no weapon was found eliminate the possibility of suicide. The dead man's watch, purse, and other valuables were missing—"

"But surely robbery was not the motive for the killing," I interrupted.

"That is correct, Mrs. Emerson. A wandering vagabond, of the sort that prowls our streets by night, came upon the body and stripped it of the said valuables. We have the fellow in custody, in fact; he is well known to us, but we don't believe he killed Mr. Oldacre."

"So far you have told me nothing but what is public knowledge," I said. "And not even all of that. What of the strange message clutched in the stiffened fingers of the corpse?"

"How well you put it," said Inspector Cuff admiringly. "Yes, the message. I have a copy of it here."

His desk was exceeded in messiness only by that of my estimable husband; and, like Emerson, Cuff was able to put his hand instantly on the paper he wanted. Drawing it from under a heap of other such documents, he handed it to me.

"They are genuine hieroglyphs," I said. "But there is no such text in Egyptian literature. The message appears to read, 'Death shall come on swift wings to him who invades my tomb.'"

"So I have been told by other authorities, ma'am."

"Then why ask me?" I demanded, tossing the paper onto the desk.

"I thought you asked to see it," Cuff said meekly. "Besides, it never hurts to ask another expert— especially one as gifted as yourself. Perhaps you would like to take this copy and show it to the professor."

"Thank you, I believe I will. Though I must warn

you, Inspector, that if I can persuade Emerson to assist you, you will have to deal tactfully with him. He has these little prejudices against my assisting the police."

"So I have been informed," said Inspector Cuff.

I persisted in my questions, but was forced to believe that the police were—as usual—baffled. The story of the priest having been seen near the body was dismissed by the Inspector with his peculiar version of a smile. "The witness was intoxicated, Mrs. Emerson. He has a habit of seeing visions—snakes, dragons, and—er—scantily clad females."

"I see. Inspector, has it occurred to you that we may have another Jack the Ripper on our hands?"

"No," said the Inspector slowly. "No, Mrs. Emerson, I can't say that it has."

He was clearly impressed by my theory and promised he would reexamine the evidence in the light of that suggestion. "However," he added, "unless—which God forbid—there should be another killing, I don't believe we can insist on that theory . . . just yet. Wait and see; Mrs. Emerson; that will be our motto, eh? Wait and see."

Laying his finger aside of his nose like Saint Nicholas—whom he did not in any other way resemble—he winked at me.

We parted on the most agreeable terms. I could not help liking the man, he expressed himself so pleasantly; but as I left the building I permitted myself a small ironic smile. If Inspector Cuff thought he had deceived me with his compliments and his vile cup of tea, he was sadly mistaken. He knew more than he had told me. He was just like all the other aggravating policemen I had met, unwilling to admit that a woman could equal (modesty prevents me from saying "surpass") his skill in detection. Well, as the Inspector had said—we would see!

Since time was getting short—not because I was tired, for I was not—I hailed a cab and was borne, with the swiftness for which these vehicles are justly famous, to Great Russell Street. I wish I could say that the sight of the Museum filled my breast with respectful admiration for this center of learning and archaeological treasure, but in fact I cannot. The original design, imitating that of a Greek temple, was handsome enough; but in the thirty-odd years since it was completed, the filthy air of London had turned it a deep, depressing grayish-black. As for the condition of the exhibits . . . Well, to be sure, the place is overcrowded and always has been, despite the constant addition of new wings and galleries; but there is no excuse for the inaccurate labels on the exhibits and the ignorance of the so-called "guides" who repeat these inaccuracies to uninformed but honest visitors. What they need in the British Museum, as I have always said, is a female Director.

Emerson was not in the Reading Room or in his "study." I had not expected he would be, so I proceeded at once to the Egyptian Galleries on the upper floor.

The Second Egyptian Gallery was even more crowded than it had been the first time I visited it. The gathering was cosmopolitan (and even polyglot, for there were one or two turbaned Hindoos present, and the dialects of Yorkshire, Scotland, and other remote districts can hardly be considered identical with English). Fashionable ladies, gossiping and tittering behind gloved hands, rubbed elbows with stolid tradesmen and clerks nattily attired in checked unmentionables. There were a number of children, as well as a few individuals bearing the unmistakable stamp of journalists; and even a photographer, with only his legs visible under the black hood of the camera. It required very little intelligence to deduce that some special event was about to take place.

It was impossible to see, much less approach, the celebrated mummy case. I made my way through the throng until I had reached a dark-complexioned gentleman sporting a purple turban and an enormous black beard.

"Hullo, Peabody," he said. "What are you doing here?"

"I might ask you the same, Emerson."

"Why, I saw the notice in the newspaper, as I assume you did. Mr. Budge is to give a talk. How could I resist the opportunity to improve my understanding of Egyptology?"

The awful sarcasm of his voice is not to be described.

I replied, "Leaving that aside, Emerson, I might rather ask what you are doing here in that unusual costume. The beard is somewhat excessive, don't you think?"

Emerson stroked the appendage in question lovingly. He had had a beard when I first met him; he had shaved it off at my request, but I had always wondered if he missed it.

"It is a splendid beard, Peabody. I will brook no criticism of it."

"You don't want Mr. Budge to recognize you, is that it?"

"Oh, come, Peabody, let us not fence," Emerson growled. "I am here for the same reason you are. The lunatic is bound to show up; he must read the newspapers, and he won't be able to resist a confrontation like this. I intend to catch the rascal and put an end to this nonsense."

"The beard should be a great help, Emerson."

Emerson was prevented from replying by a bustle at the far end of the gallery, heralding the arrival of Mr. Budge. He was surrounded by guards, who, in a somewhat brusque manner, cleared a space between the exhibit case and the camera. Mr. Budge struck a pose; a flash and puff of smoke betokened the taking of a picture.

One could only hope it would flatter him. He was at that time in his late thirties, but he looked older. To quote an American colleague of ours (Mr. Breasted from Chicago, whom Emerson considered one of the most promising of the younger generation of Egyptologists), Budge was "pudgy, logy, and soggy-faced," and his handshake "had all the friendly warmth of a fish's tail." Narrowed, cold eyes squinted suspiciously at the world from behind his thick spectacles. His superiors at the Museum regarded him with a mixture of approval and distaste; approval because he filled the Museum halls with choice objects, distaste because his methods of acquiring them brought him into disrepute with every respectable member of the archaeological community. He had written authoritatively and inaccurately on practically every scholarly subject, in Assyriology as well as Egyptology. Tales of his dubious practices, which ranged from bribery and customs fraud to downright theft, provided tea-table gossip for the entire world of Oriental scholarship.

This, then, was the man who confronted his audience and prepared to lecture on mummification in ancient Egypt.

The lecture was Budge's usual blend of borrowed erudition and braggadocio. He kept bringing in references to the Papyrus of Ani, one of the Museum's prizes which had been acquired by Budge himself under circumstances that could only be described as questionable in the extreme. Since it is a funerary papyrus, I suppose there was some excuse for his using it to illustrate mortuary ceremonial; but the audience, who had come there to hear about princesses, curses, and the magic lore of ancient Egypt, began to grow restive. The ladies resumed their whispering and giggling and some of the listeners drifted away.

Budge droned on. "The heart of the deceased was weighed against the feather, emblematic of Right and Truth or Law. This ceremony was performed . . ."

For once Emerson did not enliven the lecture with sarcastic commentary. He kept clawing at his beard (I suppose the adhesive itched) and scanning the room. Since I had not his advantage of height I could see very little, but I recognized Kevin O'Connell despite the fact that his cap was pulled low over his brow, concealing his hair. Not far from him was a familiar saffron (or goldenrod) ensemble, and I silently commended Miss Minton for her assiduous pursuit of her profession. She had not seen fit to mention her intention of attending the lecture, but then I had not seen fit to mention my intention to her either.

A few more people left and others entered. There was no one to prevent them, though the room was becoming uncomfortably close and crowded. The guards had fallen into that state of perpendicular repose so characteristic of the breed, and in this case one could hardly blame them.

Having laboriously worked his way through the spiritual aspects of Egyptian funerary ritual, Budge launched into a discussion of embalming methods, and the audience perked up. The standard quotations from Herodotus were received with appropriate shudders and murmurs of horror. "In the first and most expensive method, the brain was extracted through the nose by means of an iron probe, and the intestines were removed entirely from the body through an incision made in the side. The intestines were cleaned and washed in palm wine . . ."

But we were not to discover on that occasion what was done with those unsavory organs thereafter. Most of the audience was intent on the lecturer, or else semicomatose; Budge was smirking at the camera. To most of those present, the form must have appeared with a suddenness that verged on the supernatural—a form swathed from throat to feet in flowing white robes and a leopard-skin cloak.

My fingers closed tightly over Emerson's arm. His muscles tensed, rigid as granite, but he did not move. I knew what was in his mind; better to wait until the lunatic was well inside the room, with several dozen bodies between him and any possible exit. There were only two, one at either end of the room.

Budge was almost the last to catch sight of the newcomer. He broke off with a high-pitched squeak of surprise, and as the stately figure advanced slowly toward him, along an aisle hastily cleared by the onlookers, he shrank back.

"Seize him!" he cried. "What are you standing there for? Don't let him come nearer!"

These words were presumably addressed to the guards, most of whom had been caught off-balance by the appearance of the apparition. Finally one of them, a little bolder and less drowsy than the rest, started toward the "priest."

"Wait!" The voice echoed in hollow resonance within the mask. Ramses would have claimed the fellow had been practicing his role; his tones were deeper and more confident than before, and he raised one hand in a solemn gesture whose dignity the great Sir Henry Irving might have envied.

"Touch me at your peril!" the deep voice droned. "He who lays impious hands on the anointed of the gods will surely die."

A breathless, motionless hush fell, broken only by the agitated attempts of the photographer to insert a new negative. Slowly and yet more solemnly, the "priest" intoned, "I come to protect, not to cause harm. I will pray for mercy and forgiveness. Without my intercession, the curse of Ancient Egypt will fall on all—ALL!—who are within this room!"

"That's done it," said Emerson, twitching his sleeve from my grasp.

Alas, he was correct. The threat, uttered in tones of eerie portentousness, sent the crowd into a panic. Everyone moved at once, some seeking one exit, some the other, some crying out in alarm, some shrieking with hysterical laughter. One lady collapsed in a faint. The braver souls (and the reporters) tried to fight their way toward the lunatic. The camera swayed and toppled over, crushing a little old lady in a rusty bonnet and a golden-haired child. Emerson, whose inspired expletives rose over the uproar, was prevented from moving by the lady, who had cannily selected his sturdy breast upon which to swoon.

Needless to say, I remained calm. I could not move; indeed, it required all my effort to remain on my feet as I was buffeted from every side by fleeing spectators. The madman darted toward the case containing the coffin—and toward Budge, who stood next to it. Budge tried frantically to turn and flee, but his figure did not lend itself to rapid movement; he slipped on the marble floor and tumbled over, emitting shrill cries of alarm and breathless demands for assistance.

The madman did not touch him. Pausing only long enough to address an unintelligible remark to the sculptured form on the coffin lid, he forced his way toward a curtain at the back of the room and disappeared behind it.

It was my gallant Emerson who prevented what might have been a nasty business. Tucking the swooning female under one arm, he made his way to Budge's side and stood over him, thereby (I feel certain) saving him from being trampled underfoot. In the voice which has earned him the proud title of Father of Curses, he addressed the frantic throng.

"Silence!" he shouted. "Stand where you are! He has gone! The danger is past!" and other remarks of a similarly encouraging nature. The crowd responded, as indeed it must have done to a presence so commanding; and Emerson then dragged the unhappy Keeper to his feet. Budge had lost his spectacles, his cravat was twisted under his left ear, and his face was crimson with fury and embarrassment. Emerson handed him the fainting lady. Budge staggered, but managed to stay on his feet.

"Take command, you nincompoop," Emerson said. "You are always bragging about your ability to bully 'the natives'; let us see you exercise a little authority here."

Without waiting for a reply, which Budge was at that time incapable of making, Emerson made his way to me. Even as he had stood at bay like a beleaguered lion, clutching the form of the lady, for to let her fall might have been to expose her to serious injury—even as he had striven to protect the helpless while he watched in stoic calm the ruination of his scheme—even then his eyes had sought me and his lips had shaped a question. Seeing me upright and calm, my parasol at the ready, he had proceeded to do his duty. That duty done, he returned to me with the tender query, "All right, Peabody? Good. The fellow is long gone, of course, but we may as well follow his trail."

The draperies behind which the priest had vanished were of heavy brown velvet, and at first glance they appeared to be all of one piece. After an interval of fumbling and cursing Emerson located the gap through which the lunatic had passed. He pulled the velvet aside. Behind it was a blank marble wall.

Emerson had known (as had I) that there was no way out of the room but for the archways at either end; but, being Emerson, he refused to believe the obvious. Vanishing in his turn, he followed the wall to where the curtain ended. A wild billowing and flapping of velvet marked his progress and raised quite a lot of dust.

Accompanied by a brace of guards, Budge bustled up to me.

"What the devil is going on here?" he demanded. "Mrs. Emerson, I insist—"

Emerson's head popped into sight from behind the draperies. He was glaring hideously. "Watch your language in the presence of my wife, Budge."

Budge waved a chubby fist. "Come out of there, Professor!"

The rest of Emerson followed his head. "Nothing but a blank wall," he muttered.

"And a vast quantity of dust," I added, brushing at Emerson's sleeve. "Really, Mr. Budge, your housekeeping—"

Budge waved both fists. "Out!" he shouted, purpling. "Out of here, all of you! This gallery is now closed to the public—"

"That makes sense," Emerson agreed. He stared at the only other people who had remained in the room—those dedicated journalists, O'Connell and

Miss Minton, and a third individual who was unfamiliar to me. "Cursed reporters," Emerson said.
"Throw them out."

Both stubbornly stood their ground, and the third
individual stepped forward, smiling self-confidently.
His close-fitting black frock coat displayed a trim,
athletic figure, but he was not in his first youth. Deep
lines scored his high forehead and sallow cheeks, and
there were pouches of sagging flesh under his eyes.
His silk hat and snowy linen were of the finest quality, and he twirled a gold-headed cane in his gloved
fingers.

"I'm sure your prohibition does not extend to me,
Mr. Budge," he drawled.

Budge's manner changed abruptly. He babbled,
he beamed, he all but groveled. "Certainly not, your
lordship. Your lordship is always welcome. If
your lordship would condescend—"

"You're a good fellow, Budge," said his lordship,
with the condescension Budge had invited. "Won't
you present me? I know this lady and gentleman by
reputation—as who does not?—but I have not had
the pleasure of meeting them."

Mr. Budge stuttered through the introductions
while his lordship studied me through his monocle.
I took a firm grip on Emerson, who has been known
to object violently to monocles, impertinent stares,
and members of the aristocracy; but he only said
mildly, "Lord St. John St. Simon. You are Canter-
bury's youngest son, I believe?"

His lordship took off his hat and bowed. Though
long strands of hair had been carefully stuck in
place with pomade, they did not conceal the bald

THE DEEDS OF THE DISTURBER 157

spot on the crown of his head. "You flatter me, Professor. I had not expected the activities of a dilettante like myself would be of interest to you."

"Your activities have been widely reported," said Emerson. "I believe you are an intimate of the young man whose father presented the famous coffin to the Museum?"

This was news to me, and I began to see why Emerson was standing there chatting when I would have expected him to be in hot pursuit of the false priest.

"Yes, yes," said Budge importantly. "Lord Liverpool is a splendid young man, and a generous patron; dare I hope he accompanied you today, your lordship?"

"He is somewhere about, I believe," Lord St. John said, hiding a yawn behind his impeccable glove.

"Indeed? Is he indeed? I must find him, then. Present my compliments . . ."

Emerson continued to stare at his lordship, and eventually even that supercilious gentleman showed signs of self-consciousness. Twirling his stick, he asked, "Well, Professor, what now? I expected you would be hot in pursuit of the priest. Tallyho, yoicks, and that sort of thing. Or do you agree with some of the reporters that he has supernatural powers and can vanish into thin air?"

"Humbug," said Emerson.

"Oh, quite, Professor. And yet he went behind this curtain and did not come out. I heard you say there is no door, no exit—"

"Surely the answer is obvious, your lordship," I said. "All he had to do was remove the mask and wig—which are all of a piece—and the robe, and join the rest of the spectators. There was such confusion—"

"In which case he must have left the room by that door," said Emerson, pointing. "Mingling with the others, he would pass through the Third Egyptian Gallery and thence to the stairs. They lead down to the Hall of Sculpture; from there he could reach the main entrance onto Great Russell Street. However, we may as well follow. One of the guards may have noticed someone carrying a large parcel or a bag."

"Containing the costume?" his lordship said. "Excellent, Professor. Mrs. Emerson, may I offer you my arm?"

"As you can see, your lordship, I already have one—or, to be quite accurate, three, since in addition to my own appendages, my husband has lent me his."

Lord St. John's smile broadened. "You have a charming wit, Mrs. Emerson. Miss Minton, then?"

"Miss Minton had better take herself off," said Emerson, scowling.

Budge was forced to agree. "Yes, yes, be off with you, young woman. And you too, O'Connell. I am always willing to speak with the press if the proper application is made, but I do not allow common journalists—"

"Miss Minton is not a common journalist," said his lordship gently. "You surely don't suppose any ordinary young woman would be employed by a newspaper unless she had extraordinary influence? Her grandmother—"

"Don't you dare tell," cried Miss Minton.

"—is the Dowager Duchess of Durham, and formerly a close—er—friend of the owner and publisher of the *Morning Mirror*. The old lady is a desperate woman's-rights advocate and fully supported the aspirations of Miss Minton—the Honorable Miss Minton—"

His speech was interrupted by a cry of "You wretch!" and by a small gloved hand that struck his lips with stinging force. Miss Minton then destroyed the superb effect of her remonstrance by bursting into tears and running from the room.

His lordship laughed. "Bless the ladies and their charming inconsistency! They demand to be treated like men, but they react like women."

"Much as I dislike doing so, I must agree with you," I said. "The young lady's tears were tears of rage, I am sure, but they were demeaning. I will have to have a little talk with Miss Minton."

"No, you will not," Emerson growled. He added vehemently, "Curse it! Curse it!" Then his eyes lit on O'Connell, who, except for a murmured "Begorra!" when Miss Minton's identity was revealed, had remained thoughtfully silent. "Well, well, Mr. O'Connell," he said affably. "Why haven't you gone after the young lady to console her?"

"Because she would strike me with her parasol," said O'Connell.

"Very possibly. Women can be the devil, can't they?"

"Yes, sir. I'm so glad you aren't angry with me, Professor. You know I was only trying to do my job—"

"Oh yes, no doubt." Emerson beamed. "And the next time my name, or that of Mrs. Emerson, appears in that rag of yours, I will come to your office and thrash you within an inch of your life. Good day, Mr. O'Connell."

O'Connell precipitately vanished.

"So much for the confounded press," said Emerson with satisfaction. "Budge, you may as well leave too; you are no help at all. Your cursed bowing and scraping and empty courtesies have already detained me too long."

Budge took himself off, sputtering and fuming. I myself felt that Emerson's accusation was a trifle unfair. Courtesies never detained him when he did not wish to be detained. The surprising tolerance he had displayed toward his lordship continued; he made no objection when the latter followed us, remarking pleasantly that he had always wanted to observe a famous detective at work.

However, our inquiries proved to be in vain. Once in the Third Egyptian Gallery, the fugitive had several routes of escape open to him: along the western galleries of the upper floor to the main stairs, or down the back stairs and along the lower floor to the exit. None of the guards had noticed anyone carrying a large parcel, or—it was my suggestion—an unusually obese individual.

His lordship said little, but he watched Emerson's every move. He seemed more alert and less supercilious, and the few suggestions he made gave evidence of a keen intelligence. Emerson always does bring out the best in all those who associate with him, however briefly.

When we reached the main entrance, with his lordship still on our heels, we found the last strag-

glers leaving and the guards preparing to close the
Museum. Emerson knew many of the guards personally; as he was conversing with them, trying to
jog their memories, a young man detached himself
from the pillar against which he had been leaning
and strolled toward us.

"So there you are," he drawled, in a faint, husky
voice. "You've been a confounded long time, Jack. I
am about to scream from boredom."

"It's your own fault, Ned, for being so lazy," his
lordship replied. "You missed the excitement."

"I did?" The young man raised his cane to his
mouth like an infant sucking a teething ring and
peered sleepily at us.

I had immediately deduced that the effeminate
young man must be the Earl of Liverpool, and so it
proved. His lordship performed the introductions
with easy grace, adding, "Professor and Mrs. Emerson are the famous archaeological detectives I told
you about, Ned. I have just had a most interesting
time watching them detect."

Emerson glowered at this remark, which certainly did seem to contain a hint of sarcasm. The
Earl gave a high-pitched giggle. " 'Pon my word, is
that so?"

Though he was dressed with a foppish elegance
even greater than that of his friend, with great diamonds blazing from his cravat and his fingers, he
had not the older man's presence, being painfully
thin and hollow-chested. His face was a pasty yellow, and when he laughed his parted lips displayed
teeth as brown and rotten as an old man's.

"We are not detectives, Lord Liverpool, but

archaeologists," I corrected. "We have been inspecting the coffin your late father gave the Museum. It was a generous gesture, though I must say the effects have been unfortunate."

"Is that so? Er—yes, I suppose they have. Pity. The poor old governor would be—er—mighty surprised . . ."

"And distressed," said Lord St. John smoothly.

"Er—yes. To be sure." The Earl sucked his cane and stared. "Mrs. Emerson . . . you're the lady who digs these—er—these mummies up, ain't you? Seems—er—an odd idea, eh?"

"What a tease you are, Ned." His lordship took his friend by the arm. "Mrs. Emerson is a very distinguished scholar. Perhaps you might like to invite her to visit Mauldy Manor and see your father's collection."

"Er—what? Ah, yes." The Earl smiled sleepily. "Lots more of them—mummies and—well, no, not mummies, that was the governor's only one—little bottles and statues and such things. Very welcome, I'm sure. Anytime."

"No time," Emerson barked, before I could express my thanks for the invitation—such as it was. "We have no time for such things. Kind of you, I suppose, but we have better things to do."

"Oh, I'm sure you and Mrs. Emerson would find objects of interest at Mauldy Manor," said his lordship.

"Quite, quite," the Earl agreed, with another feeble sputter of amusement.

But Emerson's patience had given out. With the briefest of farewells he drew me away.

A heavy bank of dark cloud had moved in over the city. Through a rent in that somber curtain a flash of crimson marked the path of the declining sun; and as we watched the two men walk westward, the slighter of them leaning on the arm of his friend, they appeared to be heading for the fiery perdition that surely awaited at least one of them.

"He is an opium eater, Emerson," I murmured. "Poor fellow; the drug has affected his brain, he scarcely makes sense."

"It is not opium but his disease that is rotting his brain, Peabody. It is almost enough to make one believe in a God of Wrath and Vengeance. Whatever the boy's sins—and they are infinite—they don't deserve a death like the one he faces." Then my dear Emerson's natural optimism triumphed; giving himself a little shake, he remarked, "Ah, well, better men and women than that pathetic sprig of the nobility meet worse fates daily. I need my tea, Peabody. Or something stronger, perhaps."

Since the hour was late, I agreed to Emerson's suggestion that we take a cab. These vehicles, with their musty smell and cracking leather seats, have an odd effect on my spouse; perhaps it is the soft music of the horse's trotting hooves, or the sense of being cozily shut up in a shadowy, private place. However that may be, we were scarcely inside when he began to make demonstrations of a distracting nature and I had some difficulty in persuading him to postpone them long enough for him to remove his beard, which was even more bristly and uncomfortable to the touch than a natural one would have been. Though his attentions were as skilled and assiduous as always, I sensed the seething frustration that boiled within him and I sought to relieve it with a friendly jest.

"It appears, my dearest Emerson, that the aristocratic element has entered the case after all."

"Yes, curse it," Emerson grumbled. "I had believed myself safe from the journalists, at least. Do your long-suffering spouse one favor, Peabody. Do not take the young lady under your wing. I have resigned myself to danger and distraction, but I cannot endure another of your sentimental rescues of young lovers."

"I doubt that the eventuality will arise, Emerson," I replied soothingly. "Miss Minton doesn't appear to have a romantic interest. Unless his lordship—"

"Good Gad, Peabody, she struck him in the face!"

"You lack experience in these matters, Emerson. Such demonstrations are not infrequently indicative of affection. If you recall some of our earlier—"

"I don't want to recall them, Peabody."

"Then there is young Wilson, who was with her the other evening," I went on. "You said you knew him—"

"He will probably turn out to be the Prince of Wales," Emerson said gloomily. "I do draw the line at members of the royal family, Peabody. The aristocracy is bad enough."

When the cab stopped before the house, Emerson helped me out and turned to pay the driver. A fine drizzle, more soot than rain, darkened the twilight; at first I took the shapeless object by the gate for a bag of trash. Then it stirred and I recognized it for one of the poor vagabonds who frequent the streets of London—their only home. Usually the constables on duty kept these unfortunates away from St. James's Square and other fashionable neighborhoods. This one had apparently eluded the law.

As we approached the gate, the figure drew itself to its feet and held out its hand in mute appeal. I said pitifully, "It is only a child, Emerson. Can't we—"

Emerson was already fumbling in his pocket. "We can't take them all in, Amelia," he grumbled—not his usual grumble, but the softer sound that expressed pity and helpless anger. "Here you are, my boy"—coins chinked heavily with the solid ring of silver—"buy yourself some dinner and a lodging for the night; the constable will be along shortly, so you had better move on."

A whine of wordless gratitude was the response as the small hand closed tightly over Emerson's bounty. Emerson cursed softly as we proceeded to the house.

"Yes," I agreed. "It is a sad world, Emerson. Let us hope there is a better one somewhere for such people."

"Humbug," snarled Emerson.

"So you say, my dear, but even you cannot be certain of that. At least one little lad will have hot food and a warm bed tonight. How late we are! Our own dear little ones will be waiting for tea; we must count our blessings and teach them to do the same."

But only two dear little ones were waiting in the drawing room. Violet's voluminous ruffles and huge sash made her look almost as wide as she was tall. Percy jumped to his feet when we entered the room. "Good evening, sir. Good evening, Aunt Amelia."

"Good evening, Percy," I replied. "I am sorry we are late. Mrs. Watson, will you send one of the maids to call Ramses?"

The housekeeper wrung her hands. "Oh, madam—"

"Ah," I said. "Gone again, is he?"

"I don't know how he could have got out," the poor woman groaned. "I kept a close eye on him—I know the dear boy's habits—"

"My dear Mrs. Watson, Ramses has eluded wilier keepers than you," I assured her. "Emerson, do sit down and stop tearing at your hair."

"I will not sit down," Emerson replied furiously. "See here, Amelia, your calm does you no credit. I know, Ramses has done this before and has never taken any harm, but there is always a first time, and this cursed city—"

"I suppose I had better go and fetch him, then," I said, rising. "Have a cucumber sandwich, Emerson, it will cool your temper."

But of course Emerson followed me into the hall, and so did the others. At my direction the butler opened the door; he tried to fetch me my coat, but I waved it away.

It was as well I acted when I did; the wretched beggar child had not escaped, but was held in the clutches of a very large constable. His shrill expostulations mingled with the growls of the police officer. "Move along, my lad, you can't stay here. Ow—oh, you would, would you, you little—"

"Constable," I called, hurrying down the walk. "Let the child go."

"But ma'am, he was lurking here, waiting to—"

"No, I fancy he was trying to get back into the house," I replied. "Ramses, did you kick the policeman?"

"I was forced to bite him, since I am not wearing shoes," Ramses replied.

"Oh dear. Emerson, would you—"

Coins chinked again. The constable touched his hat and moved away, shaking his head. I reached for my son's collar and then thought better of it, waving him inside the gate without touching him. In ominous silence we returned to the house.

In the full glow of artificial illumination the effect of Ramses' appearance was little less than breathtaking. I had to give him credit; when he did something, he did a thorough job of it. His bare feet were black and blue—black with dirt and blue with cold—for the evening had turned sharply cooler. He wore the most indescribably horrible rags I have ever seen, the great rents in shirt and pantaloons gaping wide or held precariously together by huge pins; the cloth was sodden with a vile mixture of rain, soot, and mud. He smelled as bad as he looked. Mrs. Watson backed away, pinching her nose.

Ramses snatched off his cap. (I was pleased to see that my lectures on the subject of manners had had some effect.) Reaching inside his foul shirt, he drew out a bedraggled bunch of daffodils—culled, I did not doubt, from the neatly tended beds in the park—and advanced on Violet. "I have brought you . . ." he began.

Violet backed away, hands flapping, as if she were

warding off an attack of bees or wasps. Her face was distorted. "Ugh, ugh, nasty, nasty," she screamed. "Ugh, nasty—"

Ramses' face fell, but he mastered his disappointment manfully. Turning to me, he dragged another miserable bundle (mostly stems) from inside his shirt.

"For you, Mama."

"Thank you, Ramses," I said, taking the slimy offering between my fingertips. "It was a kind thought, but I am afraid we are going to have to garnishee your pocket money to pay for the *pourboires* we are forced to offer persons you offend. It is beginning to mount up, Ramses."

Emerson had been opening and closing his mouth like a frog. "Why is he dressed like that, Peabody?" he inquired weakly.

"I am practicing my disguises," Ramses explained. "You remember, Papa, I was allowed to take the things we found in the lair of that master of disguise, the person known by his soubriquet of—"

I hastened to interrupt, for Emerson's face was as black as a thundercloud. Any reminder of that incredible episode and even more incredible man had a deplorable effect on my worthy spouse's blood pressure.

"You must never leave the house without permission, Ramses," I said—knowing full well the prohibition was fruitless, for Ramses was already considering ways of getting around it. "Go upstairs and . . . Wait a moment. What is that scrape on your forehead? And don't tell me Percy did it."

"I had no intention of doing so," said Ramses.

Percy cleared his throat and stepped forward.

"But it is my fault, sir, and Aunt Amelia—Ramses leaving the house without permission, I mean. I was teasing him to play with me; I wanted to go into the garden, to look for butterflies for my collection, you know—and when he wouldn't, I may have said something about him being afraid to go out without a nursemaid or his mama . . . It was only a joke, sir, but I take full responsi——"

Ramses rounded on his cousin with a snarl that would have done credit to his admirable sire. Emerson caught him by the collar.

"Don't shake him, Emerson," I shrieked. "For pity's sake, don't shake—"

But it was too late.

We all went upstairs to change. The only one who had avoided the spatter of unspeakable liquid was Violet. As Ramses skulked past her she pointed a plump white finger at him. "Ugh," she said. "Nasty." Ramses' disheveled head drooped lower.

Tea was rather late that evening, but I was determined to go through with the ritual since my theories of child-raising required that we all be together as a family for one hour a day, if possible. It was a sacrifice, but one I felt morally obliged to make. Emerson did not feel morally obliged to make it, but he did it anyway, because I insisted.

Violet sat playing with her favorite doll, a simpering waxen-headed thing almost as large as she, and (truth compels me to remark) bearing a striking resemblance to her in its porcelain simper and fat yellow curls. She pretended to feed it bits of sandwich and sips of tea (heavily laced with milk, as I am sure I need not mention). Observing Ramses' fixed stare, she smiled and invited him to join her and her "friend Helen," adding, "I am sorry I was rude about the flowers, Cousin Ramses. But you know, they were very, very nasty."

I expected Ramses would respond with courteous disdain, but he accepted the invitation, and went so far as to ride the doll on his knee and smooth her golden curls. No further reference was made to his misadventure; I do not hold with endless recriminations, and Ramses had already accepted his punishment—the confiscation of all the bits and pieces of disguise which, against my better judgment, he had been allowed to remove from the secret headquarters of the Master Criminal. These consisted for the most part of paints, powders, and dyes designed to change the color of hair and skin. There were also some ingenious pads which could be inserted in the mouth in order to change the shape of the face; several sets of false teeth; mustaches, beards, and wigs, all cunningly constructed of human hair. Among the wigs was one any lady of fashion might have envied: masses of golden waves and curls, soft as silk and smooth as honey. Ramses had rather cleverly altered this to fit his own head, trimming the hair and padding the interior.

Emerson manfully tried to chat with Percy, but found sensible conversation impossible with a lad who knew nothing whatever of predynastic pottery or the principles of stratification, so he soon gave it up. Picking up the evening newspaper, he turned through the pages, and I remarked, "You will not find any mention of today's adventure, Emerson; that edition must have gone to press before it happened."

"Adventure, Aunt Amelia?" Percy exclaimed. "What adventure, if I may ask, sir?"

I would have preferred to keep the children—particularly Ramses—in the dark, but Emerson, who has not my sensitive understanding of the juvenile mind, at once launched into a spirited narrative. His sarcastic comments about Mr. Budge were wasted on Percy, I fancy, but the lad listened openmouthed to Emerson's description of the lunatic priest and the near riot.

"I say, sir, how exciting!"

"Nasty," Violet murmured.

"Nasty?" Emerson repeated indignantly.

"She means the mummies, sir. You know how girls are, sir. I think you were frightfully brave, sir. What a pity you couldn't catch the fellow."

Ramses cleared his throat. "The individual in question would appear to have an excellent sense of timing and an appreciation of what might be called the habits of the mob. He anticipated a large crowd and counted on being able to make use of it in order to elude pursuit. It makes one wonder whether the word 'lunatic,' which has been carelessly applied, really suits a man as clever as that."

He continued to stroke the doll's curls as he spoke. I found the spectacle as alarming as it was ludicrous; for if Ramses would sink to such folly, his infatuation with his cousin must be greater than I had supposed.

"An interesting idea, Ramses," said his father thoughtfully. "However, so-called lunatics are not feeble-witted. They have one mental quirk or aberration, and their over-all intelligence need not be diminished thereby."

"Like that Jack the Ripper chap," suggested Percy. "They never caught him either, did they, sir?"

"Good heavens, Percy," I exclaimed. "I am surprised that your mama and papa allowed you to hear about that horrible business."

"The servants are still talking about it, Aunt Amelia. You know how servants gossip."

"Nasty," said Violet. She added pensively, "Dead."

"Good Gad!" said Emerson, contemplating the child with open horror.

"She doesn't know what she is saying, Emerson," I assured him, hoping I spoke the truth.

"Let us trust," said Ramses, "that this is not a parallel case. For if the murderer is a homicidal maniac with an obsessive hatred of one particular profession, no one connected with the Museum will be safe."

This statement raised so many hideous possibilities that I rang the bell and ordered the tea-things to be removed. I had no desire to hear Ramses explain how *he* happened to know of Jack the Ripper, and most especially how he had found out that the homicidal slaughterer of unfortunate young women had an obsessive hatred of what could only loosely be called a particular "profession."

Having observed Emerson's reaction to Ramses' mention of the phrase "homicidal maniac" (a term that affects him almost as painfully as "Master Criminal"), I decided to give him time to cool off before I raised the subject again. I waited until we were midway through dinner before I did so.

"Much as I deplore Ramses' interest in such things, he does have a certain (possibly inherited) flair for crime," I remarked. "You observed, Emerson, that he proposed the same theory I did?"

Emerson was in the act of attacking a rather tough slice of beef. The knife slipped, and the beef slid onto the floor.

"A pity the cat Bastet is not here to tidy up," he remarked, watching Gargery crawl under the table to retrieve the food. "Has there been any word of her, Peabody?"

"Not yet. I instructed Rose to send a telegram as soon as she returns. Don't try to change the subject, Emerson. I won't have it. The situation is too serious."

"You are the one who is always telling me not to discuss serious matters before the servants," Emerson retorted. "A nonsensical rule, I have always thought. Gargery here is just as interested in sensible conversation as any other man, isn't that right, Gargery?"

"Er—certainly, sir," the butler replied, retreating to the sideboard.

"I long ago abandoned any hope of converting you to correct behavior, Emerson," I said. "And under the present circumstances, rules of that sort need to be relaxed. When I consider the danger that threatens you—"

"Oh, nonsense, Peabody," Emerson shouted. "The idea of a homicidal maniac makes no more sense coming from Ramses than from you. Two deaths, one of them natural, do not constitute a crime wave!" Then he added, glancing at the butler, "Don't pay any attention to Mrs. Emerson, Gargery. She is always going on like that. I am in no danger at all."

"I am—I am relieved to hear it, sir," Gargery said earnestly. "Will you have more roast beef, sir?"

Emerson helped himself. "The priest had nothing to do with the murder of Oldacre," he announced. "A man like that must have had dozens of enemies. I didn't like him either. As for the goings-on at the Museum, they are either the product of a deranged mind, or a peculiar practical joke."

"Ah," I murmured. "So that possibility had occurred to you?"

"Now you are going to claim you thought of it first," Emerson grumbled. "You always do. But you couldn't have done, Peabody, it did not occur to me until after I realized Lord St. John was mixed up in the business. It is the sort of thing a depraved degenerate like him might find amusing. You know who he is, don't you?"

Since the question was obviously rhetorical, I did not bother to answer, and Emerson proceeded to deliver a brief biographical sketch of his lordship. Even allowing for my spouse's prejudices and circumlocutions, it was an ugly picture, and in one sense a tragic one. Gifted with good looks, ample wealth, and above-the-average intelligence, Lord St. John had been regarded as a young man of great promise. His university career had been without blemish, except for those escapades and crude practical jokes (most involving the arrangement of bathroom utensils in public places) which are considered normal for a young man of good family; and he had served with distinction in the Khartoum campaign of '84. Then he fell in with a certain group centering around that royal rapscallion Prince Albert Victor of Wales, heir apparent after his father to the throne. The premature death of the prince had brought sorrow not unmixed with relief to the nation and to his parents; for it is no secret (hence my lack of reticence on the subject) that Prince "Eddy's" behavior had aroused the gravest doubts as to his capacity to reign.

It was after the prince's death in '92 that Lord St. John had lured the young Earl (then Viscount Blackpool) into his "set." The result (said Emerson) I had seen for myself. There was no vice, natural or unnatural, to which the young man had not been exposed by his Machiavellian mentor.

"Natural or unnatural," I repeated. "To be quite honest, Emerson, I am unsure of the distinction, when applied to vice."

Emerson gave me a freezing stare. "The distinction is one that need not concern you, Peabody."

"Ah," I said. "I believe I understand. Are you suggesting, Emerson, that Lord St. John is the false priest?"

"No," Emerson said reluctantly. "He cannot be. I saw him among the spectators just before the priest made his entrance."

"Are you certain he didn't slip out and assume the disguise at the last moment?"

"Impossible, my dear Peabody. Look here." Emerson drew a pencil from his pocket (he had refused, as usual, to dress for dinner) and began drawing on the tablecloth. "The robe would cover a multitude of sins, including trousers; it was floor-length. The sleeves reached below the elbow; coat-and shirt sleeves could be rolled or pushed up under those of the robe. Those operations would take only a few seconds, but then he had to adjust the leopard skin, lower the mask over his head, remove his shoes and socks, and slip his feet into sandals."

"Yes," I agreed. "It was not a bad copy of Nineteenth Dynasty garb, in fact. Except that the original would have been of sheer fabric; and the wig is not often seen in representations of priests, who usually had shaven heads."

"The modifications were dictated by the necessity of concealment, obviously," Emerson replied impatiently. "And contrary to Budge and that over-quoted authority Herodotus—who was describing, not always accurately, customs prevalent two thousand years later than the period in question—what was I about to say?"

"That there are depictions of individuals wearing both the *sem* priest costume and an ornate wig," I replied. "Not that it matters; as you say, authenticity had to give way to practicality."

"True. Yet there is a certain suggestion of knowledge-ability in his behavior, Peabody. Did you happen to hear what he said to the mummy?"

Having observed that Gargery had given up all pretense of serving the food and was leaning over Emerson's shoulder trying to see what he had drawn on the tablecloth, I announced we would retire to the drawing room. Gargery bore the disappointment bravely.

After we were comfortably settled, I answered the question Emerson had asked earlier.

"No, I did not hear what the lunatic said to the mummy, Emerson. There was a great deal of noise."

"But I was closer," Emerson replied. "And, as you know, I am fairly adept at lip reading. This is my best recollection of his remarks."

Since there was no tablecloth at hand, and he was too impatient to search for writing materials, he scribbled on his cuff, pronouncing the hieroglyphs aloud as he wrote them.

"Hmph," I remarked. "Very good, Emerson. But why are you speaking ancient Egyptian if the priest spoke English?"

"He did not speak English, Peabody."

"Good heavens, how astonishing. But that means— that suggests—"

"I don't know what it means, Peabody, and neither do you."

"He spoke English before."

"Precisely. There is no consistency in his behavior, which is what one might expect from a madman, eh? It is obvious that he has some familiarity with Egyptology, but any intelligent amateur could acquire this much information, particularly if, as may well be the case, he has had a lifelong obsession with the subject."

"How well you express yourself, Emerson." I took his hand and turned it so that I could read the hieroglyphs again. "It is quite acceptable Egyptian."

"A memorized formula, Peabody. 'A thousand loaves of bread and a thousand jars of beer for the spirit of the Lady Henutmehit.' The standard mortuary offering formula."

His fingers twined round mine, holding them fast. This tender gesture—and his interest in a subject he had formerly sworn never to speak of again—persuaded me to share something with him.

"That is a standard formula perhaps; but this is not." I reached into my pocket and drew out the copy of the message that had been found in Oldacre's dead hand.

Emerson's eyebrows drew together. "Where did you get this, Peabody? One of your cursed newspaper friends, I suppose; curse it, Peabody, I told you . . . Hmmmm. What a bizarre hodgepodge this is, to be sure. It certainly is not a standard formula; I have never seen such an inscription."

"Nor I, Emerson. Could it possibly have been taken from the inscriptions on the coffin in question? There is no such thing on the outside, but perhaps the interior surfaces . . ."

"Now you are beginning to sound like a cursed journalist, Amelia. To the best of my knowledge, the coffin has never been opened. Are you suggesting the lunatic has second sight—or, no, here's a better plot: he is the reincarnation of the scribe who originally decorated the coffin for his beloved. Ha, ha! I wonder your intimate friend O'Connell hasn't thought of that one."

His eyes shone with amusement and his expressive lips curved in a smile to which I could not fail to respond. "Very good, Emerson. I am glad to see you in such high spirits, my dear."

"Mmmmm," said Emerson, bringing my hand to his lips and kissing each finger in turn. "I hope to be in even better spirits shortly, Peabody. Shall we . . ."

So we did. Yet to me, Emerson's attentions that evening had an even greater poignancy, for they reminded me of what I stood to lose if Ramses'— and my—theory proved to be correct. This thought led, I believe, to a response even more wholehearted than was normally the case, and Emerson expressed his approval in no uncertain terms. However, his last remark was a sleepy chuckle and a murmured "I say, Peabody, will you ever forget how idiotic Budge looked, lying on his back kicking like a dung beetle and bleating like a goat?"

SEVEN

Emerson left the house immediately after breakfast, remarking that he meant to get through a
great deal of work that day and would not be home
for luncheon. He was in an excellent mood (for reasons on which I need not elaborate), and I was careful not to spoil it by allowing him to see the morning
newspaper. It contained a spirited account of the
riot in the Mummy Room, and a picture of Emerson clutching the fainting lady that made him look
like Jack the Ripper contemplating his next victim.

I was having a second cup of tea when Mary Ann
came in with a telegram. It was from Rose, announcing Bastet's return and adding, "Tell Master
Ramses. All well and happy. Wish you were here."

I did not begrudge her the slight extravagance in
verbiage (and expense), for the news was indeed better than I had dared hope. I went upstairs at once to
carry out Rose's instructions. Ramses' door was
locked and I had to identify myself before he would
consent to open it.

"I don't like this business of locking doors, Ramses,"
I told him. "What if you were to become ill?"

"That is certainly one argument against it," said Ramses, stroking his chin in unconscious imitation of his father. "But it is unlikely, Mama, that I would be so suddenly and violently stricken that I would be unable to call for assistance; and when balanced against opposing arguments, such as my need for privacy, which you have always been good enough to recognize, and the possibility of someone disturbing my specimens—"

"Very well, Ramses. Although," I added, with a disgusted look at the specimen he was holding, by its long naked tail, "it seems to me very unlikely that any sane person would want to touch your specimens. Where did you get that one?"

"From Ben, the gardener's boy. The setting of traps, particularly in the stables, where such creatures abound, is one of his duties. Greatly as I abhor the use of traps, or the unnecessary murder of any animal, I must bow to necessity in this case, since rats eat grain and also carry fleas, which some authorities believe—"

"Enough, Ramses."

"Yes, Mama. Would you care to inspect a few of the specimens? The process of desiccation is already well advanced in several of the smaller varieties, confirming my belief that solid rather than liquid natron—"

"No, thank you." I glanced at the table near the window, where Ramses' specimens were laid out, each in its own little container. There were other things on the table, which I chose not to examine either, for knowing Ramses' thoroughly logical approach to Egyptological matters, I felt sure he had not overlooked any possible method of preparing a body for the final step in the process of mummification.

I hastened to tell Ramses the good news, adding that I would have done so at once if he had not distracted me by his lecture on mummification. He responded with one of his rare smiles. "Not that I seriously doubted she would return if she were able," he remarked. "But life, as the Koran puts it—"

"Don't tell me how the Koran puts it, Ramses. I must go now; I have a great deal to do. I only stopped for a moment to tell you about Bastet."

"I am deeply grateful, Mama. May I ask whether there have been any new developments in what one might call the British Museum mystery?"

"I believe not, Ramses."

"The theory I proposed yesterday evening was somewhat exiguous," Ramses said thoughtfully. "All the same, Mama, I would be relieved to learn that in your opinion there is not the slightest possibility of Papa being in any danger from this peculiar individual."

His voice was as cool as ever, his countenance unmoved. Patting his rumpled curls, I said reassuringly, "I am sure Papa is in no danger, Ramses. And even if he were—which, as I say, I consider unlikely—he is capable of defending himself with the utmost skill and energy. Just concentrate on your nice mummies and don't worry about your Papa."

It had rained during the night, but when I left the house the sun was trying to break through London's perpetual blanket of smoke. I was thankful for my stout boots as I splashed through puddles and darted across the muddy streets. As I proceeded eastward along the Strand, the traffic thickened and the noise rose to deafening proportions. Wagons and omnibuses rumbled, horses' hooves clattered, street vendors cried their wares. Yet the scene had a certain lively charm, and straight ahead, like a celestial commentary on the vanity of human bustle, the great dome of St. Paul's lifted against the sky, its swelling curves chastely veiled in wisps of cloud.

The offices of the *Daily Yell* were on Fleet Street. I had never had occasion to visit them, and I was not certain of the hours when Mr. O'Connell might be found there, but I thought I might as well make the attempt. His employers would certainly have his home address.

According to the clerk on duty inside the main door of the building, Mr. O'Connell was indeed within. The clerk directed me up the stairs to a large, crowded, and extremely dirty room filled with desks, most of which were occupied. The air was thick with cigar and cigarette smoke and (if I may be permitted a rude metaphor) blue with profanity, remarks of that nature being made at the top of the speaker's lungs and with no apparent malice. A great deal of the invective was aimed at the young boys who darted from desk to desk, delivering and picking up papers of one sort or another.

Most of the "gentlemen" of the fourth estate were in their shirt sleeves and several had hats perched on their heads. My arrival did not go entirely unnoticed, but no one removed a hat or assumed a coat or rose from his chair or asked how he might assist me. I was not put out. For one thing, it was a pleasure to find a group of men who had worse manners than my own son.

Peering through the clouds of blue smoke, I caught a glimpse of fiery auburn hair. It was a flash, no more; but it was enough. I called out.

"Mr. O'Connell!"

All conversation abruptly ceased. In the profound silence a sound, as of shuffling footsteps, could be heard. "I hear you, Mr. O'Connell," I cried. "Come here at once, if you please."

A man at the side of the room leaned sideways out of his chair and addressed a muttered remark to someone who was invisible to me. After a moment O'Connell rose sheepishly to his feet and the man behind whose desk he had been hiding said with a grin, "Here he is, ma'am. What's he done—got you in the family way?"

"If that is an example of journalistic humor, I don't think much of it," I replied, as Kevin gave the humorist an outraged stare. "Come here, Mr. O'Connell. Don't be such a coward, I only want to talk to you."

"Coward, is it? There's never been an O'Connell, male or female, that was afraid to face—"

"Yes, to be sure. Only make haste."

Kevin snatched his coat from the back of a chair, clapped his hat onto his head, and approached me. "Make haste indeed," he muttered. "You've ruined my reputation for a certainty, Mrs. E."

Once we were outside, Kevin blew out his breath in a long sigh. "I apologize, Mrs. Emerson. I'll be having a few words with Bob later. But really, you know, you shouldn't be coming to such places."

"I have been in worse," I replied. "And what about Miss Minton? She is employed in just such a place."

"Oh, now, you don't suppose such a fine lady would share the same room with common, low journalists."

"I don't suppose the common, low journalists would want her in the same room," I said dryly. "They cannot have lost all the instincts of gentlemen; the presence of a lady might make them uncomfortable, incredible as it might seem. Where is she, then, if not at the offices of the *Mirror*?"

"She lives with a widow lady in Godolphin Street," Kevin replied. "Sends her bit stories to the paper by messenger; the old dowager fancies herself a suffragist, but she'd not approve of the Honorable granddaughter rubbing elbows with rough, vulgar men. 'Twas pure accident that the death of the watchman turned into a cause célèbre, her editor only assigned her to the story to keep her out of harm's way, hoping, no doubt, she would soon tire of her little hobby—"

"Nonsense. She was the one who turned the story into a sensation, you said so yourself. And she writes very well—journalistically speaking."

"She's learning," Kevin said grudgingly. "But it's the family connections and her acquaintance with that prim bespectacled stick at the Museum—"

"Jealousy, Mr. O'Connell! Pure jealousy, and your masculine blindness to the superior abilities of women. I believe I will go along to her lodging and see if she is in. What is the address?"

"I'll walk with you, if I may. 'Tis a fine, bright day, and too pleasant to be indoors."

I knew his true reason; but I flatter myself he got as little out of me as—regretfully—I was able to learn from him. The only time he forgot himself and spoke without calculation was when I mentioned Lord St. John.

"That filthy spalpeen! May goats—er—sit on his grandmother's grave!"

"What do you have against his lordship?" I asked.

Mr. O'Connell had a great deal against his lordship. "We learn things we can never print, Mrs. Emerson, not even in the *Daily Yell*. 'Tis not so much a question of news fit for the eyes of ladies and children, as of legal action. If I were to tell you all I know of his lordship—"

"I doubt I would be shocked or surprised," I replied sedately. "Yet he makes a favorable impression, don't you think?"

"Oh, he's charming to the ladies! And," said Kevin grudgingly, "he's kept fairly quiet the last year or two. Says he's reformed. Maybe he's turned over a new leaf, as he claims, but I have me doubts."

Godolphin Street was in an old-fashioned neighborhood, between the river and the Abbey; it was lined on both sides with rows of houses built in the last century, including the one in which Miss Minton resided. They were tall and narrow houses, almost forbiddingly respectable in appearance, with steep steps leading up to the front door. As we approached, the door opened and out came Mr. Eustace Wilson.

He was deep in thought, frowning over a paper he held in his hand, and did not see me until we were almost face to face. "Oh," he exclaimed, removing his hat. "Is it you, Mrs. Emerson? I did not expect . . ."

"I came to call on Miss Minton."

"As did I. We were to have luncheon together. But she is not here."

"She broke an engagement with you?"

The young man's lips relaxed into a shy, rather engaging smile. "That would be nothing new, Mrs. Emerson. She . . . But you know how young ladies are. She was kind enough to leave a note for me, saying she was suddenly called away from London for an indeterminate time."

"Ah, well, in that case there is some excuse for her rudeness. Perhaps her grandmama has been taken ill."

O'Connell had remained at a distance until he heard that Miss Minton was not there. Now he joined us, hands in his pockets, cap pulled low, slouching in a manner that suggested he was trying to look as different as possible from the dapper young Wilson.

"No doubt she's run away to hide her shame," he said with a sneer. "After having the secret of her birth exposed—"

"She has nothing to be ashamed of, Mr. O'Connell," I said severely. "High rank involves no blame; she has an equal claim with those of humble name to be respected."

"Very well said, Mrs. Emerson," said Mr. Wilson, with an indignant glance at O'Connell. "Miss Minton deserves credit for refusing to use her position to derive special favors. Though I, for one, hate to see her in such a disgusting, degrading profession—"

"Degrading, is it?" O'Connell doubled his fists. "Use that word again, me fine young cockerel, and I'll be pushing it back down your scrawny throat!"

"Well, really," exclaimed Mr. Wilson, adjusting his glasses.

"Now, boys, don't fight," I said. "At least not on the public street."

"I apologize, ma'am," said Mr. Wilson politely. "May I say I am glad you took no injury yesterday. Your husband was quite the hero of the affair, I understand."

"Mr. Budge certainly was not," I replied.

Wilson smiled. "He was in a vile temper this morning. I was glad to claim my half day and escape."

"I expect his nerves are a bit on edge," I said. "And so should yours be, Mr. Wilson. The maniac appears to hold a grudge against the British Museum and its employees."

Wilson's smile faded. "What on earth do you mean, Mrs. Emerson? The fellow is harmless enough."

"Don't be too sure, Mr. Wilson. There have been two deaths already—and both of them connected, not just with the Museum, but with the Oriental Department! The priest may be harmless, or he may not; he may or may not be the killer; but it seems more than likely that the killer is a man who feels some grievance against Orientalists. A disaffected scholar, whose theories have been contemptuously dismissed, perhaps, or a student who has been passed over for promotion or recognition, or . . . But there, I am talking too freely. These are only unproved theories as yet, Mr. Wilson. I may be altogether mistaken."

"Oh dear," gasped Mr. Wilson.

"Excuse me, Mrs. E." O'Connell edged closer. "Are you saying . . . Did I hear you use the words 'homicidal maniac'?"

"No, you did not, and if you quote me to that effect . . ." I raised my parasol in a playful manner. O'Connell did not even blink. Journalistic fervor had overcome his fear of my opinion and my parasol. Mr. Wilson was fingering his eyeglasses and muttering, "Oh dear, oh dear," like the White Rabbit in *Alice*.

"What an idea," O'Connell exclaimed. "I wonder I didn't think of it myself! In fact . . . begorra, I did think of it myself! It's not quoting yourself I'll be, Mrs. E., me dear; I thank you for recalling my theory to my mind. Aha! Wait till the Honorable Miss Minton reads tomorrow's *Daily Yell*!"

Chortling fiendishly, he trotted away.

"Were you serious, Mrs. Emerson?" Wilson asked. He was rather pale.

"I prefer not to commit myself, Mr. Wilson. But I promise you this. Professor Emerson and I are on the trail, and we have never yet failed to capture . . . Well, at least we have never failed to foil a foe. Which is not a particular compliment to us, since the criminal mind is so inferior. Have no fear, Mr. Wilson. You may not be the next victim. Perhaps it will be Mr. Budge."

Mr. Wilson did not appear especially cheered by the suggestion.

As he walked away, shoulders bowed and head bent, I was tempted to call him back and offer him a friendly word of advice on dealing with young ladies of Miss Minton's sort, for it was clear to me that his feelings for her were more than those of a friend. However, I decided not to bother. He was too timid and insecure ever to succeed with such a young lady—nor, in my opinion, did he deserve to.

I spent a few hours in the shops, for my wardrobe was in sad need of refurbishing. Costumes suitable for the vigorous activities of excavation are not the thing in London. I also ordered shirts for Emerson, who had an absent-minded habit of ripping them off when he was in haste to disrobe, and several suits for Ramses, whose habits were just as destructive to clothing as were his father's, though not, I hardly need add, for the same reasons.

I returned to the house early, for I felt I needed a brief time of repose and contemplation before the teatime encounter with the children. Mrs. Watson and Gargery were both waiting for me, Mrs. Watson to inform me that she had taken the liberty of confining Ramses to his room, for knocking Percy down and jumping on him, and Gargery to announce there was a gentleman waiting to see me.

I was just as happy to postpone the inevitable visit to Ramses, so I proceeded to the green drawing room. This very formal and handsomely appointed chamber (so called from the green China silk that draped walls and ceilings) was seldom used; I deduced that the caller must be someone of distinguished rank and title to be granted such an honor by Gargery; and as it proved, I was correct.

Lord St. John was absorbed in contemplation of a fine Gainsborough portrait of the third Duke that hung over the malachite mantel. As soon as I entered he hastened to apologize for his intrusion.

"It was an unwarranted liberty on my part, Mrs. Emerson, but your butler insisted you were expected back directly and I have something important I want to say to you."

"Not at all, your lordship. Please sit down." Ringing for the housemaid, I directed her to bring tea. "But not the children," I added quickly. "Not just yet."

"Don't keep the little dears out on my account," his lordship begged. "I would deem it an honor to meet your children."

"You don't know what you are saying," I assured him. "In fact, the professor and I have only one son, but we are watching over two of my brother's children for the summer."

"How good of you. But it is only what I might have expected; your kind heart, Mrs. Emerson, is as well known as your tireless pursuit of learning."

His smile changed his entire aspect, smoothing out the lines of weariness (or, as Emerson would probably have said, of dissipation). I flatter myself that I am too much a woman of the world to be deceived by fine manners and a bland smile, however. I acknowledged his compliment with an inclination of my head; apologized for Emerson's absence; and poured the tea.

"But perhaps you would prefer something stronger, your lordship? May I offer you a whiskey and soda?"

"No, thank you." He added, with a sly little laugh, "I have reformed, Mrs. Emerson. Most people would say it was time I did."

I was a trifle put out by his refusal; I would have joined him in the cup that cheers, but I could hardly sit there swigging down spirits while he genteelly sipped tea. Accepting his cup and a watercress sandwich, he went on more seriously, "I have been a sad rascal in my time, Mrs. Emerson. Most young men have sowed their fields of wild oats—"

"And yours, I understand, would cover most of England."

His lordship laughed heartily. "Bravo, Mrs. Emerson. It is so refreshing to find a woman—or an individual of either sex—who doesn't mince words. Your blunt candor suits me. Yes, I am heartily ashamed of some episodes in my past. Time mellows us and improves us, if we are wise. It is time I settled down. I am discovering the pleasures of learning; I am looking for a good woman with whom I can glide smoothly and peacefully into middle age."

"Miss Minton, perhaps?"

"Good heavens, Mrs. Emerson! Miss Minton's path will never be smooth and peaceable. I require someone more tranquil, more aware of life's simple pleasures." He leaned forward and placed his cup and saucer on a table. "That is one of the reasons why I ventured to call, Mrs. Emerson, to explain my caddish behavior yesterday. I have known Margaret since childhood; our families come from the same part of Gloucestershire. I feel quite like a brother to her and I can't get over the habit of teasing her in a brotherly fashion. The poor little dear takes herself so seriously! But it was too bad of me to expose her secret—though it can hardly be secret from most people . . ."

"It was too bad of you. (Will you be pleased to hand me your cup, your lordship? Thank you.) But it is Miss Minton, not I, who deserves your apology. And if that is the important matter on which you wanted to consult me—"

"No, not at all. Though your good opinion, Mrs. Emerson, is important to me." His lordship smiled in a friendly way at the housemaid who had passed the tray of sandwiches. She blushed furiously; she was very young and quite pretty, and since this was the first time I had noticed her, I assumed she had just been promoted to a higher position in the household following the departure of the girls Mrs. Watson had mentioned.

Time was getting on; Emerson would soon be returning, and although I found his lordship's conversation interesting in the extreme, I was forced to indicate that he ought to be getting on with it. "Then—" I prompted.

"I wanted to consult you about the odd incidents at the Museum, of course. Is it true that you and the professor are investigating the case? I would not venture to ask, except that as a patron of the Museum and a friend of Mr. Budge—"

"You need not explain your interest. But it would be an exaggeration to claim that we are investigating anything. Like others, we are curious. The matter is very odd. However, we have not been formally approached by the authorities."

"I have reason to believe you may be, in the near future."

"Indeed?"

"Mr. Budge is . . . well, to be quite honest, he is frightened. This notion of a vendetta, or feud, against Egyptologists—"

"So I am not the only one to whom this interpretation has occurred," I exclaimed. "Ha! It is the only sensible explanation, your lordship; but has anything else happened that would support my theory? Any murderous attacks, any threatening letters?"

"Not to my knowledge," his lordship said slowly. "But the recipient of an anonymous letter might not make it known, for fear of ridicule."

"True. Yet I have every reason to believe—"

We were interrupted, at this juncture, by the last person I had expected to see—my errant offspring, Ramses. He flung the door open and stood panting, too short of breath to speak.

I sprang to my feet. "Ramses, you were told to remain in your room."

"I took it for granted . . . the usual exceptions . . . prevailed," Ramses gasped. "Mama, my room—"

"Go back upstairs at once."

"My room is on fire," Ramses said.

And indeed it was. The truth of Ramses' statement was confirmed as soon as I reached the hall, by the outcries abovestairs, and by a pervasive smell of scorched linen. Rushing up the stairs—closely followed by his lordship and Ramses—I found a gaggle of agitated servants clustered in the doorway of the boy's room, while one of the footmen, ably assisted by Percy, tore down the blackened and smoldering curtains.

A quick examination assured me that no great damage had been done, but that only quick thinking and quicker action had prevented a serious fire. I commended the footman, who replied, "It's the young gentleman who should be thanked, madam. He had the flames out when I got here."

Percy had modestly retired to the corner. His hands and face were smeared with soot, but he assured me he was not burned. "It was only a little fire, Aunt Amelia. You see, I was helping Ramses perform a chemical experiment. It was my fault, my hand struck the Bunsen lamp. I take full responsibility."

I reached for Ramses, anticipating that the phrase would have its usual effect; but he only stood staring at Percy, with an odd look of calculation. "The responsibility is mine," he said in a quiet voice. "I ought not to have allowed Percy to help me with the experiment."

"What sort of experiment? No, don't tell me, I really do not want to know. Well, Ramses, I did not forbid you to entertain a guest in your room, and since it never occurred to me you would be carrying out chemical experiments, I neglected to prohibit the Bunsen lamp; so I suppose I cannot hold you accountable. You can thank your cousin for being let off so leniently."

Ramses' lips moved; but since he did not pronounce the word aloud, I chose to take no notice of it.

His lordship, lounging in the doorway, chuckled softly. "What were we saying about wild oats, Mrs. Emerson? I feel quite an affinity with these two lads. Which is yours?"

I introduced the boys, who responded in characteristic fashion: Percy with a bow and an apology for not shaking hands—the sooty palm he displayed being sufficient excuse; and Ramses with a long impertinent inspection of his lordship, from head to toe and back again. He was about to begin one of his interminable speeches when a piercing shriek from the corridor turned all our heads in that direction. It was the familiar and haunting refrain, "Dead, dead, oh, dead . . ."

"Curse the child," I said, without stopping to watch my words. "Call to her, Percy, and assure her you are not injured, before she has another of her fits."

It was Lord St. John, however, who deftly intercepted the shrieking, ruffled bundle that rolled toward us, and scooped it up into his arms. "Hush, little darling," he said fondly. "No one is dead; it was only a small fire, and your dear brother is not harmed in the least."

Violet's shrieks stopped as if they had been cut with a knife. Watching her simper and giggle and twine her arms around Lord St. John's neck, I was tempted to snatch her from him and shake her till her curls came unhitched from the bows.

"Go back to your room at once, Violet," I said sternly. "Put her down, your lordship; I am sorry you should have beheld such a spectacle."

His lordship gave Violet a hug. She squealed with delight. "Please don't apologize, Mrs. Emerson. I love children. Especially little girls."

My dear Emerson professes to despise the works of Mr. Dickens ("next to you, Peabody, the most rampageous sentimentalist I have ever encountered"), but I notice that he often quotes him. On Sunday morning as we sat round the breakfast table, he launched into a diatribe on the English Sabbath, and although he did not mention the source, I recognized it as a passage from *Little Dorrit.*

"Everything was bolted and barred that could by possibility furnish relief to an overworked people . . . Nothing to see but streets, streets, streets. Nothing to breathe but streets, streets, streets . . . Nothing for the spent toiler to do, but to compare the monotony of his seventh day with the monotony of his six days, think what a weary life he led, and make the best of it—or the worst, according to the probabilities."

Emerson (and Mr. Dickens) had a point. The Sabbath should, of course, be dedicated to rest and reflection and the pursuit of higher ideals; but the same people who saw nothing wrong in requiring a coachman to drive them to and from church, and in returning to a hearty dinner prepared by their servants, were adamant about allowing the workingman any access to the means of edification or wholesome entertainment—including the British

Museum, which was, I suspected, the main source of Emerson's discontent.

Ramses, of course, wanted to know what Mr. Dickens meant by "the worst." On my advice, Emerson refused to answer.

Emerson never attends church services, since he is opposed to organized religion in any form. I always took Ramses when we were at home in Kent, though I did not suppose he profited from the sermons, since dear old Mr. Wentworth, who had been vicar of St. Winifred's since time immemorial, was so extremely decrepit one could not understand a word he said. However, the murmur of his soft voice was very soothing, and the members of the congregation took advantage of the time to doze or meditate, according to their habits.

That Sunday I took the children to St. Margaret's in Westminister to hear Archdeacon Frederick William Farrar, who was one of the most famous preachers in the country. It was a most edifying discourse, and I hoped the subject, "Brotherly Love," would have its effect on my contentious companions, for the process of getting them to the church had taxed all my stock of patience. Violet had been the worst offender. Her shrieks of rage had disturbed me while I was dressing; when I reached the nursery, expecting to find that Ramses had offered her a mummified mouse or ancient femur (from his collection of treasures), I found the nurserymaid cowering in a corner and Violet standing atop a heap of discarded garments, screaming that they were all too ugly, too tight, or too crumpled. They certainly were crumpled by that time, for she had stamped on them. The topic of her attire was one of the few subjects that roused her from her simpering sluggishness; even before that episode I had begun to wonder if reforming Violet was beyond my capacities.

The sermon, for all that it was clearly audible, had no noticeable effect. Violet whined all the way home about her frock and Ramses called Percy a confounded coprolite.

"Where did you learn that word?" I demanded.

"From a guide to London that is in the library," Ramses replied. "In accordance with your suggestion, I was attempting to broaden my interests, and I soon came upon a sentence that read, 'The upper stratum of the Strand soil is composed of a reddish-yellow earth containing coprolites.' Naturally I consulted the dictionary, since I am always eager to expand my vocabulary, and I was interested to discover—"

I confined Ramses to his room for the remainder of the day. After brief reflection I confined Percy and Violet to their rooms as well. This was unfair, but necessary to my sanity.

Emerson had gone out, leaving a message that he would return about half past six. I spent the afternoon in the library looking over his manuscript and making a few little corrections, and then had a nice quiet tea all by myself, in my own snug room.

Shortly after the designated hour I was pleased to hear the well-loved footsteps. The door burst open, but instead of entering, Emerson lingered on the landing, and the first sentence I heard made it clear that he was not alone.

"Now, Mrs. Watkins, I cannot imagine why you are making such a fuss. This can is much too heavy for the girl, she is no bigger than a kitten. You should have sent one of the footmen to carry it."

"But, Professor, she offered—"

"Very commendable. But she ought to have known better. Here—give it to me—now, if you will kindly step out of the way—"

Before he could proceed, he was halted by the arrival of Gargery. "This is for you, Professor. A messenger has just now delivered it."

"Well, don't stand there brandishing it at me," Emerson replied. "How do you expect me to take it when both my hands are holding a water can? Give it to Mrs. Emerson."

He entered the room, bade me a cheerful "Good evening, Peabody," and went on to the bathroom. A thump and a splash followed; Emerson emerged, brushing vaguely at the wet spots on his coat and trousers.

"Good evening, my dear Emerson," I replied.

Mrs. Watson had retreated (shaking her head, I am sure, over the professor's peculiar behavior). The housemaid, head averted in understandable embarrassment, sidled into the bathroom; and Gargery advanced toward me carrying a silver tray and looking very composed and dignified except for the grin he was unable to hide. It was only too clear that he, like so many others, had succumbed to Emerson's charismatic personality (which for some reason is more appreciated by servants and other members of the lower classes than by Emerson's peers).

"Thank you, Gargery," I said, taking the object that reposed genteelly on the silver salver. It was not a letter, as I had supposed, but a small parcel, wrapped, tied, and sealed.

Emerson threw himself into a chair next to mine and put his feet on the fender.

"Ah," he said, with a long sigh. "It is good to be home, Peabody. Especially without . . . that is to say, where are the children?"

I explained. Regrettably, Emerson was more amused than shocked at his son's most recent addition to his vocabulary. "Coprolite! Upon my word, Peabody, it could be worse. Other than that, my dear, did you have a pleasant day?"

"Part of it was pleasant," I replied. "And you, my dear Emerson? Where have you been so long?"

"I went for a long walk. Then I paid a call on Budge."

"Mr. Budge? Good heavens, Emerson, why? I can't remember your ever paying a social call on Budge."

"He seemed surprised too," said Emerson, with an evil smile. "Only imagine, Peabody, that bloody idiot—"

"Please, Emerson, watch your language." I indicated the door of the bathroom.

"Why the devil should I? Oh. Is that girl still there? What the . . . what is she doing?"

"Filling the bath, as she does every evening, Emerson. And mopping up after you. Never mind; what prompted you to call on Mr. Budge?"

"Well, I made him an offer," Emerson said, stretching till his muscles cracked. "To unwrap the mummy. *The* mummy."

"Unwrap . . . What the devil for?"

"Watch your language, Peabody," Emerson said, grinning. "The idea came to me while I was walking through . . . er . . . the park. Yes, Hyde Park. The incident at the Museum the other afternoon might have been much more serious. Public hysteria has reached such a pitch . . . By the way, did you know one of your journalist friends has already printed a story about the reincarnation of the priestly lover of the princess? I was crushed when I read it, for I had hoped to sell the idea for a large sum."

"Don't be facetious, Emerson. You are wandering from the subject."

"So I am," Emerson said agreeably. "Well, then, it seems to me it is high time we put an end to this nonsense, before someone is seriously injured. The Museum must suffer from such incidents; incompetently as it is managed, we don't want it to become an arena for riots or a stage for theatrical performances."

"I quite agree, Emerson. But how does the unwrapping of the mummy come into it?"

"Why, it is the most logical way of ending the absurd speculations. We will see what inscriptions, if any, are on the inside of the coffin; we will expose the unfortunate lady's withered hide and fleshless grin. You know, Peabody, that even a well-preserved mummy is distinctly unsightly. Romantic fantasies about beautiful princesses must shrivel—like the lady's own flesh—under the merciless glare of scientific truth. She may have abscessed teeth, Peabody. She may be . . . middle-aged! Could anything be more destructive of sentiment than a middle-aged, gray-haired woman with toothache?"

I put my feet on the fender next to Emerson's and reached for his hand. "Emerson, I have said it before and I will say it again—your academic acumen is exceeded only by your profound understanding of human nature. Brilliant, my dear—brilliant!"

Husbands, I have found, appreciate these little compliments. Emerson beamed from ear to ear and kissed my hand.

What I did not say, because I had better sense, was that I suspected his motives were not entirely altruistic. Emerson is not as passionate about mummies as I am about pyramids, but he does like them, and one of my fondest and earliest memories of him is the relish with which he went about unwrapping a mummy. (It is from Emerson, I hardly need say, that Ramses' fascination with mummies derives—carried, as is often the case with Ramses, to excess.)

"You might also take advantage of the opportunity to lecture on the subject of ancient Egyptian curses," I suggested. "And to point out that there was no such thing."

"Well, but that would not be strictly true, Peabody. You remember the text from the mastaba of Khentika: 'As for all men who shall enter this my tomb being impure, having eaten abominations . . .' How does it go on?"

"I cannot recall the exact words. Something about pouncing on him, as upon a bird, and being judged for it in the tribunal of the Great God. Hardly a death threat, Emerson, since the tribunal referred to was the one faced by all devout Egyptians *after* death. Besides, that text and others like it were directed against neglectful caretakers of the necropolis."

"Then there are the cursing texts written on bowls and scraps of pottery," Emerson mused. "'As for so-and-so, son of so-and-so, he shall die . . .' A classic example of sympathetic magic; when the bowl was smashed, the individual perished."

"You certainly might mention such cases," I agreed.

"I might," said Emerson gloomily, "if I were going to deliver a lecture and unwrap the mummy."

"Budge disapproved the scheme?"

"Oh, he thought it was an excellent idea."

"Then why—"

"Because, my dear Peabody, the damned—er—confounded bas—er—rascal is going to do it himself!"

"Oh, my dear," I said sympathetically. "After you looked forward so much . . . But how can he? After all, there is no sense in just unwinding yard upon yard of bandages unless one has enough knowledge of anatomy to make an examination of the remains themselves, and determining the sex, the age, and—er—and that sort of thing."

"He will have some flunky from the Royal College of Surgeons standing by," Emerson said, snapping his teeth together. "While he does all the talking and hypnotizes the audience into believing he knows what is going on."

"Perhaps he will change his mind, Emerson."

Emerson's lowering brows lifted and his cheery chuckle filled the room. "I know what you are thinking, Peabody, and I absolutely forbid it. You are not to call on Budge and try to persuade him to change his mind."

"I was only—"

"I know, my darling Peabody. You were thinking of me; and I cannot tell you how much your tender concern moves me. In fact, I believe Budge was having second thoughts. An odd thing occurred just before I left him."

"And what was that?"

Emerson settled himself more comfortably. "It was quite dramatic, my dear. Picture, if you will, Budge behind his desk, spouting smug nonsense as he always does. Your humble servant, walking briskly up and down the room—"

"Spouting criticism," I suggested.

"Carrying on a civil conversation," Emerson corrected. "Enter a servant carrying a packet. Budge reaches for that absurd paper knife of which he is so fond—the one he claims he found in a tomb at Assiut—and slits the wrappings. The color drains from his face—his voice fades into silence—he stares in horror at—at—"

"A severed human ear?" I suggested, entering into the spirit of the thing. "A mummified member?"

"Member?" Emerson repeated in surprise. "What particular organ of the human body did you have—"

"A hand or a foot, what else?"

"Oh. Well, it wasn't anything so grisly. Quite a fine antique, in fact—an ushebti. It was not the ushebti that frightened Budge, though. It was the accompanying message."

"What did the message say, Emerson?"

"I don't know. Budge refused to show it to me, or let me examine the ushebti. But he was unnerved, Peabody; he was decidedly unnerved. Though I confess he did not exhibit the violent signs of terror I have described."

He chuckled merrily as he spoke; but a spreading sense of chill horror prevented me from joining in his innocent amusement.

"Emerson," I began.

"Yes, Peabody?"

"Emerson . . . the packet Gargery brought . . ."

"Good Gad!" Emerson bounded to his feet. "Where is it, Peabody? What have you done with it? Curse it, I thought there was a familiar look to the thing!"

"It is there on the table beside you, Emerson."

"Oh." Emerson returned to his chair. Instead of ripping off the wrappings in his usual vigorous manner he sat quite still, turning the object over and over in his hands. "Yes, it looks the same," he remarked after a moment. "Wrapped in brown paper, addressed in block letters and black India ink, with a pen whose nib wants mending. And by a man of some education."

Anxious as I was to behold the dread contents of the deadly packet, I could not help being distracted by this sweeping pronouncement. "Now, Emerson, you are inventing that. Especially the bit about education. How can you possibly tell anything about the sender's education, or even gender?"

"The writing is masculine—bold, sprawling, forceful. As for the other—I have my methods, Peabody, it would take too long to explain them."

"What nonsense," I exclaimed indignantly.

"That appears to be all there is to learn from the external wrappings," Emerson continued. "Nevertheless, we will remove them carefully . . . so . . . in order to preserve them for future examination. Inside we find . . . Ha! Just as I suspected."

"What, Emerson, what?"

"A cardboard box."

I sank back into my chair. "Your attempt at humor is singularly misplaced, Emerson. I am in a positive fever of apprehension for you, and you make jokes."

"I beg your pardon, Peabody. Hmmmm. The box has nothing distinctive about it. Except . . ." He raised it to his nose. "A faint, lingering scent of tobacco. And good tobacco, too. From my pipe-smoking days I recall—"

"Emerson, if you don't open that box, I am going to scream."

"I have been thinking of taking up a pipe again," Emerson mused. "It is conducive to meditation. Peabody, you are exhibiting unbecoming impatience for someone who claims to be an investigator of crime. We must go about this slowly and methodically, overlooking no possible clue."

I snatched the box from his hand and wrenched off the lid.

A thick layer of cotton wool hid the contents, but not for long. Flinging it to the floor, I removed the object inside.

"A shawabty," I cried.

"Don't wave it around in that theatrical fashion," Emerson said coolly. "It is faience, and will break if you drop it."

The shawabty (or ushebti—Walter, among others, favored the latter reading) figures were quaint examples of the Egyptians' fanciful yet practical attitude toward the requirements of life after death. In order to explain their function, I believe I can do no better than to quote the spell inscribed on the little figurines (taken from Chapter VI of the so-called Book of the Dead). "Oh thou shawabty, if the Osiris Senmut [or whatever the name of the owner might be] is called on to do any work that has to be done in the Underworld—to cultivate the fields, to irrigate the desert, to carry sand to the East or the West—'Here am I! I will do it!' thou shalt say."

Shawabtys were made in a variety of materials, from stone and gilded wood to the paste-like faience, but they always imitated the mummified human form. Sometimes a tomb might contain dozens, even hundreds, of the little servant figures. This example was unusual, however, for it was that of a pharaoh wearing the *nemes* headdress and holding the two scepters. A line of hieroglyphs identified the owner, but I paid scant attention to them at the time.

"Was Budge's the same?" I asked.

"It appeared to be identical. But I can't say that it was, since I was given no opportunity to examine it." Emerson had taken the box from me. Now he extracted a scrap of paper covered with close-written signs. "Well, well, what a strange coincidence," he remarked, after a cursory glance. "We were just now speaking of this very thing. Here you are, Peabody, have a look."

A hideous premonition set my hands to trembling so that I could scarcely hold the paper. In a hollow voice I read the words aloud: "'As for any man who shall enter into this my tomb, I will pounce on him as on a bird—'"

"'Pounce' seems a bit playful and frivolous for a document of such portentousness," commented Emerson. "May I suggest 'fall upon' or 'seize—'"

"Oh, do be quiet, Emerson! There is worse to come. 'As for Emerson, Father of Curses—he shall die!'"

The echoes of that dire word had scarcely faded before they were followed by a harsh metallic clang, like that of a great cymbal. I started violently; Emerson began to chuckle; and the housemaid, carrying the empty water can (whose lid, hastily replaced, had produced the clanging sound) sidled crabwise through the room and exited.

"You needn't have shouted, Peabody," Emerson remarked. "You probably frightened the poor girl out of her wits."

"I forgot she was there," I admitted. "One does, doesn't one? A sad commentary on our perverse social system. How can you be so cool, Emerson? This is a direct threat—a threat of death—or worse—"

"There cannot be anything worse, Peabody," Emerson replied, with such sublime indifference to danger that I forbore to mention examples that would have proved him mistaken.

"Excuse me, Mama, excuse me, Papa—"

Ramses could not have appeared at a worse time. Such was the state of my nerves that I rounded on him with a loud cry. "Ramses, what are you doing out of your room? I told you—"

"Technically, I know, I am in violation of orders, Mama; however, I thought I might venture to emerge long enough to greet Papa, since I have not seen him since breakfast; and hearing what sounded very much like a death threat echo along the corridor—"

"You could not have heard it unless you were listening at the door," I snapped.

"Never mind, Peabody. Relax your rules for once." Emerson smiled fondly at his son, who had advanced tentatively into the room. He looked quite deceptively young and innocent in his long white nightgown with his little bare feet peeping out from under the hem and his grave dark eyes fixed on his father's face.

"Well," I said.

That was enough for Ramses, who trotted to Emerson's side and squatted on the floor beside him, in the Egyptian style. I hardly need add, I believe, that he was talking all the while.

"I trust, Mama, that my concern for Papa will excuse this apparent contempt for your commands, which under almost any other circumstances I would of course—"

"It is just nonsense, my boy," Emerson said, patting the tumbled black curls. "Another practical joke."

"If I might be allowed to examine—"

"You may as well show it to him, Emerson," I said resignedly. "He will go on talking until you do."

So Emerson handed over the ushebti and the message, and after giving the former a cursory glance and dismissing it with the comment "A fine example of its type," Ramses wrinkled his juvenile brow over the message. "Ha," he remarked after a brief interval, "the message appears to be a combination of two different texts, the first deriving, if memory serves me, from an Eighteenth Dynasty tomb at Thebes. The second, as I am sure I need not tell you, may be an adaptation of a so-called cursing text, written on pottery bowls or figurines which were then smashed—"

"You need not tell us," said Emerson.

"As for the orthography," Ramses went on, "the writer appears to have followed the rules Mr. Budge has laid down in his popular book on Egyptian grammar. In my opinion the use of the reed-leaf in spelling the proper name 'Emerson'—"

"For someone who is supposed to be filled with anxiety over your papa's safety, you are very cool," I said critically.

"Rest assured, Mama, that my concern is no less profound for being rigidly controlled. Hmmm. There is little more to be learned from the message except that it was written by a man of some education—"

"Oh, good Gad!" I exclaimed.

"—with a pen whose nib needed mending. In fact, Mama, the situation is not as grave as I feared; for if Mr. Budge also received such an ushebti, the malice of the writer is not concentrated solely upon Papa. I would be curious to know whether any other scholars or officials of the Museum received such a message."

"Exactly," Emerson said, taking advantage of Ramses' pause to draw breath. "I told you, Peabody, it is just another rude joke. These things feed on one another; a newspaper account may have inspired some other lunatic to join in the fun—"

"For if that is indeed the case, as I suspect—"

"Go to bed, Ramses," I said.

"Yes, Mama. Thank you for your indulgence in letting me reassure—"

"Now, Ramses."

After embracing his Papa and me, Ramses finally did as he was asked. It was not until after he had left the room that I realized he had taken the shawabty with him.

"Let him have it," Emerson said indulgently. "Poor little chap, he probably wants to perform some of his quaint chemical tests upon it. I say, Peabody, that was a good idea of his. I think I will just run out and call on Petrie and Quibell to ask if they received—"

"Not now, Emerson. Cook is holding dinner; you were very late, you know."

"In that case," Emerson said, "we had better not take the time to dress for dinner."

I hope that one day someone will make a study of the means whereby information is dispensed in households such as ours. Of course Ramses is a unique case; there are times when a superstitious person might well believe, as certain of our Egyptian workmen do believe, that he can hear through walls, and see through them too. Whether it was from Ramses, or from the maid who had been in the bathroom, or some other source, Gargery knew all about the shawabty and the threatening message, even before Emerson told him. He was kind enough to agree with Emerson that it might be advantageous to learn whether any other individuals had received such objects.

"If you would like to begin inquiries this evening, sir, I will see to it that any letters you might wish to write are delivered."

"Very good of you, Gargery," said Emerson.

"Not at all, sir."

After he had left the room to supervise the serving of the next course (an excellent Capon à la Godard), I addressed Emerson severely. "Really, Emerson, do you think it advisable to take Gargery into your confidence as you do? I am sure Evelyn won't like it if her butler joins in the conversation at the dinner table."

"Well, but Gargery is not like Wilkins; I can never get that fellow to say anything but 'I really could not say, sir.' Gargery made a useful suggestion. I wonder . . ."

"Yes, Emerson?"

"I wonder if he might have an extra pipe he could lend me. I could replace it tomorrow after the shops open."

After dinner we retired to the library to write the letters Gargery had suggested. But this was one task that was never to be completed. Scarcely had we settled ourselves with pen and paper—and a pipe, which Gargery had indeed been pleased to provide—than the butler reappeared.

"There is someone to see you, Professor—Mrs. Emerson."

"At this hour?" Emerson exclaimed, throwing his pen down. "What infernal presumption!"

"You were perfectly willing to send messengers to your friends at this hour," I reminded him. "Who is it, Gargery? Give me his card."

"He had no card, madam," said Gargery, with a sneer almost up to Wilkins' standard. "But he insists the matter is urgent. His name is O'Connell—"

"O'Connell? O'Connell?" Emerson's brows lowered. "Take Mr. O'Connell and . . . but you will require assistance, Gargery; you are, if you will excuse my saying so, on the weedy side. Fetch the largest of the footmen, request him to take Mr. O'Connell by his collar, and propel him—"

"No, wait, Emerson," I said; for Gargery's expression suggested that he was ready and willing to carry out any suggestion his idol might make. "Mr. O'Connell would not come here—and at such a late hour—unless he had pressing news. Should we not hear what he has to say?"

"A point, Peabody. I can always pitch him into the lily pond afterward, and have the satisfaction of doing it myself. Show the gentleman in, Gargery."

"Yes, sir." Gargery marched out. Emerson leaned forward, his eyes bright with anticipation—whether of the information O'Connell might bring, or the expectation of being able to perpetrate the described indignity upon his person, I would hesitate to say.

For once O'Connell showed no sign of the nervousness he usually displayed in Emerson's presence. He was so anxious to speak to us, he pushed past Gargery before the butler could announce him properly. Hat in hand, hair wildly askew, he cried, "There has been an arrest in the murder case. Mrs. Emerson—Professor—they have got the wrong man!"

EIGHT

I persuaded Mr. O'Connell to take a chair and join us in a whiskey and soda. "For," I explained, "although your dramatic announcement has certainly captured our full attention, I would appreciate a careful, ordered narrative, which you do not appear at present in a fit state to deliver."

I also hoped, by this little stratagem, to improve Emerson's relations with Kevin O'Connell. Once a man has taken refreshment in your home and a chair in your sitting room, you are less likely to pitch him into a pond.

Gargery served us and then retired. But I noticed he left the door open a crack.

Once Kevin had imbibed a quantity of whiskey, his reportorial instincts returned, and he told a coherent, if somewhat lurid, story.

The man who had been arrested was a member of London's Egyptian community, one Ahmet, who was distinguished from his numerous compatriots of the same name by the significant epithet of "the Louse." He described himself grandly as a merchant, but according to Kevin he was only a small trader, and an unsuccessful one at that, probably because he consumed much of his stock.

"Opium, hashish, and other popular commodities of that sort," Kevin said. "Oh, I admit he is a thoroughly unsavory character. He'll do anything for money, and when he is desperate for the drug, he would inform on his own mother. I've used him myself on occasion. But he is a pathetic little swine in his way, without the courage or physical strength to commit such a brutal murder."

"Then he will be freed in due course," Emerson grunted around the stem of his (Gargery's) pipe.

"The police have been under a great deal of pressure to solve the case since the riot at the Museum," Kevin insisted. "The trustees have pressed the Home Secretary, who has pressed the Commissioner, who has had his subordinates on the carpet; and that fool Cuff has selected Ahmet as the scapegoat. No one will come to his defense—"

"You are absolutely right, Kevin," I exclaimed. "The poor fellow is in great danger. I was not at all impressed with Inspector Cuff's acumen."

Stroking his well-modeled chin, as is his habit when deep in thought, Emerson was not so deep in thought as to miss this slip of the tongue. "What?" he shouted. "What did you say? When did you—"

"Never mind that now, Emerson. Mr. O'Connell is in the right. No uneducated, petty criminal planned this series of crimes."

"Humph," said Emerson. "Well, but—"

Kevin leaned forward. "You must intervene, Professor, in the interests of justice. The Metropolitan Police don't know the Egyptian character as you do.

Even those who have lived in Cairo have had little to do with the natives, they don't speak the language, they—"

"Yes, Emerson, yes," I cried. "It is our duty to assist the police in this matter. When I think of that poor chap under interrogation, being jostled and struck by large constables—"

"Oh, come, Peabody, the police don't torture suspects," Emerson growled. But he was disturbed; fingering the cleft in his chin, he went on, "What do you expect me to do? Surely, Mr. O'Connell, you don't expect me to visit an opium den—"

I finished the sentence. "—on the Sabbath. I appreciate your thoughtfulness, Emerson, for as I am well aware, such considerations do not weigh heavily with you. However, the Sabbath ends at midnight, and that hour, we know, is a good time to find such dens functioning, although, I have been assured, they are in operation at all hours, since to their wretched clients day and night are alike."

"Who said anything about opium dens?" Kevin stuttered.

"Peabody," Emerson bellowed, "I am not taking you to an opium den on the Sabbath or at any other time."

"Your syntax gives you away, Emerson," I replied, with a playful shake of my finger. "You do not deny that *you* mean to visit an opium den. You cannot suppose I would let you go alone to such a place? 'Whither thou goest I will go, and whither thou lodgest I will lodge; thy people shall be—'"

"Oh, do be quiet, Peabody! And don't quote Scripture to me!"

"Very well, if it disturbs you. A little more whiskey, my dear? I am sure Mr. O'Connell would like another glass."

I took it from the journalist's limp hand. "Do you mind my asking why you are talking about opium dens?" he asked weakly.

I took it upon myself to enlighten the young man, since Emerson had fallen into a kind of blank-faced stupor and was muttering to himself. Now and then a phrase was audible: "Lock her in a room? Absurd . . . she would find a way out, she always does . . . And the servants would suppose . . . oh, good Gad!"

"Surely, Kevin, you must see that an opium den is the most obvious place in which to begin our investigation. Ahmet is an opium trader and an opium eater. His friends (if he has any) and colleagues are likely to be found in establishments catering to the trade. I am not myself acquainted with those particular locations in London favored by Egyptians who indulge in opium—for birds of a feather, as the saying has it, tend to flock together, and so, one must suppose, do Egyptians and other groups of expatriates. However, Emerson's wide experience and acquaintance with a variety of . . . Emerson, I do wish you would stop mumbling. You distract me."

". . . bound and gagged . . . but I should never hear the end of *that* . . ."

"What was I saying, Mr. O'Connell?"

"You were explaining your reasons for—for visiting an opium den," said Kevin, struggling to control the nervous contractions of his lips.

"Oh yes, thank you. It is the Egyptian connection, you see. I have overlooked this aspect thus far, since the business seemed to me to have a distinctly European, not to say English, cast. Yet no one has seen the face of the false priest; what if he is not an Englishman but an Egyptian, better educated than some of his fellows, but not entirely free of the pagan superstitions that continue to flourish despite British educational efforts? We have encountered such phenomena in other cases. You remember, Emerson, the mudir who tried to prevent you from opening the Baskerville tomb?"

Lost in reverie, Emerson did not respond, but Kevin exclaimed, "Right enough. I remember him well. Your own workmen were so afraid of the supposed curse they refused to enter the tomb until Professor Emerson performed one of his famous exorcisms.[*] But I say, Mrs. E., if superstition is indeed the motive for the murder, it doesn't bode well for poor old Ahmet."

"I mentioned that only as one possibility among many," I said. "But it is one that ought to be investigated. My husband has friends and acquaintances in a number of peculiar places, you know. Being a singularly modest individual, he does not boast of his connections, but I would not be at all surprised to discover that he is familiar with the habitats of Egyptians residing here in—"

Emerson's eyes came back into focus. "Dismiss the idea, Peabody. We are not visiting any opium dens."

"I thought I would dress as a young man," I explained. "A woman would be more noticeable

_____

[*] *The Curse of the Pharaohs.*

in such an ambiance, and the convenience of trousers—"

Emerson looked me over, head to foot and back again. "Peabody," he said, "under no possible circumstance and in no conceivable costume could you pass for a man. The prominence of your—"

"One of the footmen must have something I could borrow," I mused. "Henry is about my height. Mr. O'Connell, you appear to have something caught in your throat. Sip your whiskey more slowly."

"I—er—swallowed the wrong way," Kevin said hoarsely. "Hem. That's better. Your scheme is brilliant, Mrs. E. I'm sure you can manage the—er—difficulty the professor mentioned, and in any case it will be dark. We will take care no one gets near enough to look at you closely."

"We," I repeated.

"Yes, ma'am—we. The professor may protest all he likes, but I know you, Mrs. E., and I know you will have your way. And whither you go, Mrs. Emerson, I will go."

"Oh dear," I said, with an apologetic glance at Emerson. "I am sorry! I should not have spoken so freely. I quite forgot, in my enthusiasm—"

"Never mind, Peabody," Emerson replied slowly. "Mr. O'Connell has us by . . . has the right of it. We can't prevent him from following us, so we may as well take him along. Another able-bodied man might be useful."

"Excellent," O'Connell exclaimed, his eyes shining. "Thank you, Professor. You won't regret it, I assure you."

"I am confident I won't," said Emerson. "But in

deference to Mrs. Emerson's sensibilities we must wait until midnight, so we may as well relax. Another whiskey, Mr. O'Connell?"

I would have expected a member of a profession noted for its cynicism to be more suspicious of Emerson's sudden amiability, but in Kevin's defense it must be said that when he puts himself out to be affable, no one is more affable than my dear husband. Subdued by chagrin at my unusual lack of reticence, I kept still and let Emerson do the talking. Admirable man! Not once, by word or glance, did he reproach me. Instead he exerted himself to win Kevin's confidence and lower his guard—with immediate success. Conversationally, almost negligently, he mentioned the threatening message he had received earlier.

Kevin fell on it like a fish on a worm. "I say, Professor, but that is . . . it opens up all sorts of possibilities, don't you think? For one thing, Ahmet was in police custody . . . no, that won't wash, for there is no way of knowing when the messages were dispatched, eh? On the other hand . . ." He rubbed his forehead. "Confound it, I have forgot what I was going to say."

"Take your time, Mr. O'Connell, take your time," said Emerson, with a benevolent smile. "We are in no hurry."

"Thank you, sir. I say, sir, but I do appreciate your confidence. I hope this is the beginning of a firm friendship, sir. I have always admired your . . . your . . ."

"Have another whiskey," said Emerson.

"Thank you, Emerson, old chap. Excellent

whishkey . . . Now I remember what I was about to say. These usherbis—shaberis—oh, hang it, never mind, you know what I mean. These li'l statues. If you and Mr. Budge got 'em, maybe some of the other chaps did too, eh?"

Emerson exclaimed, "There, you see, Peabody? I told you Mr. O'Connell was a sharp young fellow. We had begun to wonder the same thing, Mr. O'Connell, and were, in fact, about to send round to inquire. We got so far as to make out a list of possible recipients before your startling news distracted us."

"What a story," Kevin muttered, helping himself to the whiskey—for Emerson had placed the decanter handily at his elbow.

"Yes, indeed," said Emerson. "It is a pity there is not time enough to make the inquiries immediately. One would prefer to get the initial reactions of the recipients, before they have time to think it over, and perhaps refuse to talk to the press."

With some little difficulty Kevin extracted his watch from his waistcoat and squinted at it. "There is time," he declared. "Plenty of time. Yes. You won't be leaving until after midnight . . ."

"Mrs. Emerson's religious scruples forbid it," Emerson said gravely.

"Yes, quite. Very nice, too . . . I'll tell you what, my dear chap—you don't mind if I call you my dear chap?"

Emerson replied with the most malevolent grin I have ever seen on a human countenance, and with a slap on the back that almost propelled Kevin out of his chair. "Whatever you like, my boy."

"Good old Emerson," Kevin exclaimed. "You wait for me, eh? I'll—I'll just run off and do my errands and come back here. You wait for me, eh? I'll hurry, that's what I'll do. Eh?"

"Do that," Emerson replied. "Gargery, Mr. O'Connell is leaving; fetch his coat, if you please."

O'Connell had scarcely left the room when Emerson was on his feet. "Quick, Peabody."

"But Emerson," I exclaimed, scarcely able to contain my laughter, "my religious scruples—"

Emerson seized me by the wrist. "What religious scruples? What scruples? You have none, Peabody, and you know it."

"Not when duty and honor call," I replied—somewhat breathlessly, for Emerson was pulling me along at a great pace. "All lesser considerations must give way—Emerson, please, these cursed ruffles—are tripping me up—"

Scarcely pausing, Emerson swept me into his arms, ruffles and all, and ran up the stairs. Upon reaching our room, he set me on my feet with a thump. "Peabody," he said, holding me by the shoulders, "I am acceding to your absurd expectation only because the alternative is worse—to have you follow me in some ludicrous disguise. Which you would do, wouldn't you?"

"Certainly." I placed my arms around his neck. "And you wouldn't have it any other way."

"Quite right, my darling Peabody. Why do you suppose I love you so much?"

"Well," I said, lowering my eyelids, "I had thought perhaps—"

"Right again, Peabody." Emerson gave me a

hearty smack on the lips and then released me and began tearing off his coat. "Make haste, Peabody, or I'll leave you behind."

The ghostly gaslights glowed amid the fog as hand-in-hand we hastened through the darkness. Never, I venture to say, has there been a more suitable ambiance for eerie adventure than the reeking, murky, muddy streets of dear old London. I had trod the vile alleyways of Old Cairo after dark, and pursued a faceless shadow across desert wastes lit only by the distant stars; all experiences I would not have missed for the world, and this was another such. In addition to being extremely picturesque, fog has many advantages for those who wish to pass unseen. We had not gone a hundred feet from the house before we were invisible to anyone who might be watching the establishment.

Nevertheless, Emerson set a rapid pace until we reached the Strand, where we took a hansom cab. The streets near St. James's Square had been almost deserted, but as we proceeded eastward, a strange new world became apparent to my interested gaze.

Wharves line the north side of the Thames east of London Bridge. It was here that the cab stopped, and Emerson helped me out. I had noticed the strange look the cab driver gave Emerson, when the latter mentioned our destination; I understood it better now. Even at that hour and on that holy day, the wretched inhabitants of the East End were out in search of pleasure and forgetfulness, crawling rodentlike to the gin mills (and worse) in the vile alleyways. Into such a narrow passage Emerson led me. I was reminded of another such night in quite a different clime: the night we had wandered the alleys of the Khan el Khaleel, and found the body of the antiquities dealer hung like a sack of potatoes from the ceiling beam of his own shop.[*] The same foul stench and impenetrable darkness, the same unnameable liquids squelching underfoot. . . . If anything, the smells of London were richer and more spontaneous. I was filled with a flood of affectionate appreciation so abundant it would not be denied expression.

"Emerson," I whispered, "this may not be the most appropriate moment for such a statement, but I must tell you, my dear, that I am well aware that few men would demonstrate such confidence and respect for a wife as you are presently demonstrating in allowing me to share—"

Emerson squeezed my hand. "Do keep quiet, Peabody. Remember what I told you."

The warning had not been necessary, but it had been valid. My voice was low for a woman's, but it would never pass for that of a man; I had therefore agreed to let Emerson do whatever talking was necessary, and to refrain from comment.

A flight of stairs led down to a pitch-black entrance. After fumbling for a moment, Emerson found the latch, and the door swung open.

A single lamp near the door barely penetrated the gloom within. The room was narrow; how long it

The Mummy Case.

was I could not tell, for the far end was lost in murky darkness. Wooden bunks lined both walls. The occupants were visible only as fragments of bodies—a pallid, upturned face here, a limp dangling arm there. Like the eyes of crouching beasts the small red circles of burning opium in the bowls of the metal pipes brightened and dimmed, as the smokers inhaled the poison. There was a low murmur of sound—not conversation, but myriad mumbled monologues, broken now and then by a soft cry or high-pitched gasp of maniacal laughter.

In the narrow passageway between the rows of beds, about ten feet from the entrance, was a brazier filled with charcoal, whose reek blended with the fragrant smoke of the drug. It was tended—oh horror!—by a woman. She was no more than a huddle of rags as she crouched by the foul little fire. A filthy cloth was thrown over her head, like a travesty of the *tarhah* of fine muslin worn by Egyptian ladies. From beneath it wisps of coarse gray hair straggled down to conceal the face that had sunk upon her breast.

Emerson's notion of disguise runs heavily to beards. He was wearing the one he had worn at the Museum, but he had done nothing else to change his appearance, except to cover his head with a cap and wrinkle his oldest tweed coat by rolling it into a ball and stamping on it. The cap, borrowed from Gargery, was too small for him, and the breadth of his shoulders prohibited the acquisition of any other article of attire from one of the servants. In any case it would have been impossible for him to conceal that splendid physique or his mellow, resonant voice. His attempt to soften the last-mentioned characteristic resulted in a grotesque growl.

"Two pipes!"

The woman's head lifted sharply, and she drew a corner of the *tarhah* across the lower part of her face. The serpentine smoothness of her movements betrayed the falsity of her disguise, and the eyes that fixed themselves on Emerson were those of a woman in the prime of life—dark as a midnight sky, smoldering with suppressed fires. For she knew him—and he knew her. The shock of astonishment and of recognition that ran through his body was as palpable as a shudder.

A hiss of ironic laughter issued from the lips hidden by the *tarhah*. "Two pipes, effendi? For Emerson, Father of Curses, and his—his . . ."

Her head tilted on her long slender neck, as she leaned to one side in an effort to see me more clearly. Emerson pushed me behind him.

"Your tastes have changed since last we met, Emerson," she went on in a jeering voice. "You did not care for boys then."

"They will hear you," Emerson muttered, indicating the lax forms on the nearby beds.

"They are in Paradise; they hear only the murmurs of the houris. Tell me what you came for, and then go. This is no place for you or your . . ."

"I would speak with you. If not here, tell me where."

"So you have not forgotten Ayesha? Your words come as balm to my wounded and forsaken heart . . ." A burst of mocking laughter ended the sentence. Then she hissed, "Your face was not meant to conceal your thoughts, Emerson. I read them now as I used to do. You did not expect to find me here. What do you want? How dare you come here, flaunting your new lover and endangering me by your very presence?"

Needless to say, I was hanging on every word, and finding the conversation—to say the least—replete with provocative suggestions. Unfortunately at this most interesting point, Ayesha caught herself. What she heard or what she saw I never knew. With a supple, serpentine twist, she sprang to her feet and vanished into the smoky shadows at the back of the room.

"The devil," Emerson exclaimed. "Quick, Peabody!"

But the door through which she had passed was known only to her. Emerson was still kicking the wall and swearing when a flood of men swept down the stairs and into the room. The silver badges on their helmets glistened and the blast of police whistles rent the air.

The befuddled occupants of the couches were dragged up and hustled out. Most were too bewildered to protest; the few that did were roughly subdued. There was nothing for it but to submit and wait until a more propitious moment to explain our identities and demand our release, and I certainly did not need Emerson's reminder: "If you utter one word, Peabody, in English, Arabic, or any other language known to you, I will throttle you."

I forgave him the peremptory tone, for there was no time for discussion. (There were other things I might or might not forgive, once I had had leisure to consider them.) Though our hopes of gaining information had been foiled by the raid, we might yet learn something from our fellow prisoners if they believed we were prisoners like themselves, and if they were unaware of the fact that we understood their native tongue.

In the darkness and the confusion we went unremarked, especially since we were not (though I blush to say it) the only English persons present. After being pushed up the stairs, we were thrust into a waiting vehicle along with a dozen others. There was hardly room to stand, much less sit; after the horses had been whipped up, the wagon rattled violently over the cobblestones and only the press of bodies around us prevented us from being thrown to the floor. My dear Emerson had wrapped his arms around me, holding me close and sparing me the worst of the bumps, but he could do nothing to protect me from the aroma of opium, unwashed bodies, and other elements I hesitate to mention.

Except in its final stages, opium does not dull the senses of the user. The men around us had been shaken from their happy stupors; they were now fully capable of vocalization, and they indulged freely. Emerson kept trying to cover my ears with his hands. What with that handicap, and the general racket—the groans and curses within and the banging of the wagon wheels without—I was unable to make much sense of what was said; but one remark aroused considerable interest.

"Curse the unbelievers! It is because of them we are here; the police never would bother if they had not . . ."

But at that juncture the wagon came to an abrupt halt, and the speaker (whose adjectives I have edited out) was thrown off-balance and said no more.

Dragged from the vehicle as roughly as we had been thrust into it, we were escorted through a courtyard whose paving stones shone greasily in the light of the lamps flanking the door, and into a large, crowded room. It seemed very bright after the darkness outside; the flaring gas lamps played with merciless accuracy on the sickly faces and tattered rags of the prisoners. They were beating their breasts and wringing their hands and wailing in their high-pitched Egyptian fashion; the officers were cursing and shouting orders. It was a very Bedlam.

Emerson drew me within the protective circle of his arm. "Hang on, Peabody," he whispered. "I will announce my identity and we'll soon—"

He broke off with a faint cry; and for the first time, I saw the pallor of fear whiten my gallant Emerson's face. His eyes, fixed and glaring, had focused on the object that had shaken his courageous spirit—a camera.

How the journalists had got wind of the affair I did not know. I thought perhaps the police commissioners, desirous of public acclaim, had notified the press in advance. In any event, they were there in full measure, sharp-eyed as birds of prey.

"Oh, damnation," said Emerson hoarsely. "I will *not* announce my identity, Peabody. Not until I can find some way of doing so in private."

The police officers were arranging the prisoners in a rough line. Two of them approached us. In that motley and bedraggled throng, Emerson stood out like a lion among jackals, though his beard had come loose and was hanging at an angle. Even the constables recognized his quality. One nudged the other and they came to a stop, staring.

"Now keep cool and don't lose your temper, Peabody," Emerson muttered. "Er—Constable—"

"Ow, ain't it pretty," said the individual addressed—speaking not to Emerson but to his companion. "A touchin' sight to see this 'ere gent protectin' of 'is . . ."

He never said the word. Emerson's fist hit him cleanly on the chin and toppled him over.

"How dare you speak that way in the presence of a lady," Emerson roared. "Not only a lady, you villain, but my—my . . . oh, good Gad!"

A burst of illumination and a puff of black smoke prompted this final comment. Emerson's action had unfortunately captured that very degree of attention he had warned me to avoid.

I stepped forward and addressed the nearest policeman. "Please take me and this gentleman immediately to a private room. We must communicate with Inspector Cuff of Scotland Yard; I beg you will send someone to fetch him."

I daresay it was the unmistakable accents of cultivation and breeding in my voice, as much as the name of Inspector Cuff, that prevented the officer from laying rough hands on Emerson, who had assumed a posture of defense, while at the same time keeping a wary eye on the camera. The officer's arm fell to his side, and the others who were hastening to his assistance stopped in their tracks. I reached into my pocket. "My card," I said.

"What in the name of heaven possessed you to bring your calling cards on this expedition?" Emerson demanded.

We were seated side by side in the private room I had requested, a small windowless cubicle containing only a few chairs and a deal table. The air was heavy with the accumulated aromas of countless years of fear and despair, terror and grief. Emerson had lit his pipe, which added another dimension to the smell, but I did not deem it appropriate to protest.

"You forbade me to bring my knife, Emerson. I thought some eventuality might arise in which it would be useful to be able to prove our identity. As indeed it did."

"Why didn't you hand the rest of the cursed things around to the press?" Emerson inquired.

"As I have had occasion to mention in the past, my dear, sarcasm does not become you. Once you had struck the policeman in your inimitable and characteristic fashion, any hope of concealing our identity was gone. What was that word to which you objected so strongly? I didn't hear it."

"Never mind," Emerson growled.

I took off my cap, which no longer sufficed to keep my hair in place; I seemed to have lost quite a quantity of hairpins over the course of the evening, what with one thing and another. I smoothed the heavy locks as best I could and began to braid them.

"Who was that woman, Emerson?"

"Woman?" Emerson took a box of matches from his pocket. He struck a match and put the flame to the bowl of his pipe. "What woman?"

"She must have been very beautiful once upon a time."

"Mmmmm," said Emerson, striking another match.

"She knew you, Emerson."

"A good many people know me, Peabody." Emerson lit a third match.

"Your pipe is already lighted," I pointed out. "When did you know her, Emerson? And *how well*?"

The door opened. Emerson leaped to his feet and greeted the newcomer like a long-lost friend.

"Inspector Cuff, I presume? Sorry we had to knock you up. Greatly appreciate your coming at this hour."

"Control your enthusiasm, Emerson," I said coolly. "After all, we are here at this hour of the night, are we not? Inspector Cuff is only doing his duty."

"Quite right, ma'am." Cuff freed his hand from Emerson's grasp and blew on his reddened fingers. "I have long looked forward to meeting you, Professor. But I had hardly anticipated it would be under such—er—unusual circumstances."

"Humph," said Emerson. "I would be gratified to improve our acquaintance, Inspector, but not, as you say, under these circumstances. If you will be so good as to confirm our identities, I will just take Mrs. Emerson home to—that is, home."

"Why, Emerson," I exclaimed. "I am surprised, after all the lectures you have given me, to see you concealing information from the official police. The object of our expedition this evening, Inspector, as you may have surmised, was to obtain evidence that the unfortunate Egyptian you arrested is innocent of the crime. At least, that is to say, of the crime of murder; for I don't doubt that he is as unsavory a character as—"

"He is that, ma'am," the Inspector agreed, so affably that I could not resent his interrupting me. "But what makes you suppose he is innocent of the murder?"

"I don't suppose, I know. Tell him, Emerson."

"Tell him what, Peabody?" Emerson clawed at his chin. The beard came off in his hand; he scowled at it and thrust it into his pocket.

"What we overheard in the—I believe 'paddy wagon' is the cant term."

"Ah. With your permission, ma'am . . . ?" The Inspector pulled up a chair and sat down. He indicated another to my husband, but Emerson folded his arms, and stood mute. "Of course, you understand their language. Well, ma'am?"

"I heard very little," I admitted. "But the reference to the cursed heretics whose activities had stirred up the police and aroused the latter's unwelcome interest in their community, should be suggestive."

"Suggestive, indeed," said the Inspector politely. "No, ma'am, you needn't explain, I quite grasp all the implications. Have you anything to add, Professor?"

Emerson shook his head. He was not looking at the Inspector, but at me, and by comparison Medusa was a mere apprentice in the art of stony stares.

It was obvious to me that Emerson was concealing something. To my astonishment the Inspector, who ought to have developed equally keen instincts, failed to observe this, nor did he pursue the matter. "Most interesting, Professor and Mrs. Emerson. Rest assured your theory will be investigated to the best of my ability. And now, it is late, and you must be tired. I will have one of the constables fetch a hansom cab."

"I am not at all tired, Inspector. I want to discuss with you your reasons for placing Ahmet under arrest. It might be advisable for you to bring him here so that I can question him—"

"Good Gad, Peabody," Emerson began. But he could say no more; indignation choked him.

"You wouldn't want to wake the poor chap at this hour, would you, ma'am?" Inspector Cuff said. "I will be happy to make arrangements for you to interview the prisoner later—tomorrow, if you like."

And there I was forced to leave the matter. It is no wonder the world is in such wretched shape, with men running its affairs.

The Inspector considerately led us to a back exit, for, as he remarked, a number of journalists were still hanging around in the hope of interviewing us. Here we found a cab waiting, and after thanking the Inspector and assuring him I would call on him the following day, I allowed Emerson to help me into the cab. Once inside, he immediately rested his head against the wall and began to snore. Taking this as an indication that he was not inclined toward conversation, I did not disturb him.

On recalling the events of that interesting evening I confess to a certain sense of chagrin. Unbelievable as it may seem, I had been guilty of one or two minor errors in judgment. One of them was my display of excessive interest in the woman in the opium den. Jealousy is an emotion I abhor. It is an emotion I could never harbor in my breast, for my confidence in my husband is as boundless as my being. I was not jealous. Nevertheless, some people might have interpreted my questioning of Emerson in that light, and I was sorry to have given that impression. Besides, it is a capital error to attempt to browbeat a husband—especially a husband like Emerson—into a confession of guilt. I had, needless to say, every intention of discovering who the woman was and what her relationship to my husband had been; but there were other methods that would, I did not doubt, prove more effective.

The second error of that evening did not occur until we reached Chalfont House. I regret it even more bitterly, but I must say in my defense that it was one anyone might have made.

Emerson bundled me out of the cab and tossed the driver a coin. Fog shrouded the dripping trees and made the iron railings gleam as if freshly painted. Dawn was not far away, though it was to be seen more as a diminution of darkness than an increase of light. Nevertheless, neither darkness nor Emerson's attempt to hurry me could prevent me from observing the figure huddled by the gates.

"Oh, good Gad," I exclaimed. "Of all the . . . I cannot believe . . ."

Catching hold of a limp, dank fold of cloth, I pulled the crouching figure to its feet and propelled it through the gate, which Emerson had opened.

"Hurry and close the gate, Emerson," I exclaimed. "This is the last straw! Just wait till I get you inside, young man!"

"But, Peabody," Emerson began.

"You cannot excuse this, Emerson. I gave strict orders."

Gargery had been watching for us. He opened the door before I could knock, and fell back, eyes wide with consternation, as I pulled the dripping, squirming, filthy child into the hall.

He was not Ramses.

Even the muck that smeared his face could not blur features so distinct from those of my son. This child's nose was a mere button; the eyes that gleamed ferretlike between squinting lids were a pale, washed-out blue.

"Emerson," I said. "You will wake the whole house laughing so loudly. I see nothing amusing in the situation."

I started up the stairs. Emerson stayed behind in the hall; I heard the chink of coins—his inevitable panacea for social distress—and a muttered colloquy with Gargery, broken by infuriating gurgles of laughter. He soon caught me up, however, and put his arm round my shoulders.

"Off to bed, are you, Peabody? Good, good. You must be very tired. I believe I will just—"

"If you are going to look in on Ramses, I will accompany you. I will not believe that child is where he is supposed to be until I see it with my own eyes."

Ramses was where he was supposed to be, in the strict legal sense of the phrase, though he was not in his bed. His door was open and he stood on the threshold, his small bare toes just touching the sill. "Good evening, Mama, good evening, Papa," he began. "Hearing Papa's voice downstairs, I ventured to—"

"Go to bed, Ramses," I said.

"Yes, Mama. May I venture to ask—"

"No, you may not."

"Knowing of your destination," said Ramses, trying another tack, "I was in some concern for your safety. I trust you have taken no—"

"Oh, good Gad," I cried. "Does nothing escape your insatiable curiosity, Ramses?"

"Ssssh," said Emerson, putting his finger to his lips. "You will wake the children, Amelia. I don't doubt that every servant in the house has been gossiping about our expedition; didn't you observe Gargery lurking at the library door while we were talking with O'Connell? Since you are awake, Ramses, and understandably concerned, come downstairs and Papa will tell you all about it. I promised Gargery—"

"Ramses is confined to his room," I reminded Emerson. My voice was, as I hope it always is, quite calm.

"Ah, yes," said Emerson. "I had forgotten. In that case, I will ask Gargery to come up here. I promised him . . ."

I am the most tolerant of women, but to join my

husband, my son, and my butler in a discussion of our evening in an opium den and at Bow Street was really a bit too much. I went to bed, knowing full well that one of Emerson's reason for such uncouth conviviality was to avoid the questions he expected on a certain subject I had vowed not to mention again.

NINE

How long the discussion continued I cannot say;
but I know that the housemaids complained
next day of the strong smell of pipe smoke and beer
in Ramses' room, and I was obliged, in all fairness,
to clear him of the imputed accusation. When I
awoke, Emerson was at my side, sleeping as sweetly
as if he had nothing whatever on his conscience, and
smiling in a way that roused the direst suspicions.
He had taken care not to disturb me when he came
to bed.

Though I had slept only a few hours, I felt quite
fresh and full of ambition. Righteous indignation
has that effect on my character.

As I sat at breakfast looking through the morning post I was pleased to find letters from Evelyn
and from Rose. The latter elaborated on the recov-
ery of Bastet in terms that made plain the writer's
affection for that estimable animal, and reassured
me as to its health. Rose's conjectures concerning
the reasons for the cat's absence and subsequent
return need not be repeated here, for I have already touched upon them; and succeeding events

were to prove her—and me—quite correct. (Though no one has ever explained, to my satisfaction, why a feline of such outstanding intelligence should have been so retarded in this particularly interesting area.)

Evelyn's letter contained the usual amiable domestic news, but unfortunately she had seen the reports of the riot at the Museum, and her alarm and distress filled several pages of notepaper. She urged me to leave London at once; "for," as she wrote, "one cannot be sure what will happen when persons of unsound mind are involved, and you, my dearest Amelia, have an extraordinary propensity for attracting such persons."

I promised myself I must write her immediately to reassure her—not only about what she had read in the newspapers, but what she was about to read. I could only hope she and Walter did not take the *Morning Mirror*. Not that the unkempt individual in the photograph bore the slightest resemblance to my handsome husband. His ruffianly costume, his ferocious snarl, and the loosened false beard (whose position gave the impression that a small furry animal had seized him by the throat) would have rendered him unrecognizable, were it not for the fact that the caption underneath the photograph removed any possible misapprehensions on the part of the reader. ("Professor Radcliffe Emerson, the well-known Egyptologist, knocking down a constable at the Bow Street police station.") The accompanying text made a number of libelous allegations and did not fail to mention the establishment in which we had been found. (I could almost hear my dear Evelyn's cry of horror: "An opium den! Walter, what will they do next?")

Kevin's story in the *Daily Yell* made no reference to the Bow Street affair (for reasons which should be evident); but he made a nice, lurid yarn out of the Affair of the Sinister Statues, as he termed it. The shawabtys had been received by several other scholars, but, as might have been expected, Emerson was again the featured player.

Poor Evelyn. However, one would suppose that by now she ought to be getting used to it.

I directed the maid to take away the newspapers, for although I knew I could not prevent Emerson from seeing them, I hoped to postpone the painful moment until after he had enjoyed a quiet breakfast. I was barely in time; Mary Ann was leaving the room when Emerson entered, and greeted her with his customary affability. "Hullo, there, Susan. (He has great difficulty in remembering the names of the servants.) Are those by chance . . . Well, never mind, I haven't time to read them, I am in a great hurry this morning."

His greeting to me was equally cheerful—but he was careful to avoid meeting my eyes. "Good morning, good morning, my dear Peabody. What a splendid morning. (The fog was so thick one could not see as far as the park railings.) Good morning—er—Frank. (The footman's name was Henry.) What have we this morning? Kippers—no, I thank you, I loathe the creatures, they are all bones and pickle. Eggs and bacon, if you please, John. (The footman's name had not changed, it was still Henry.) I am in a great hurry this morning."

As he spoke he looked through his letters, ripping them apart and giving them a cursory glance before tossing them over his shoulder.

"Where are you off to in such a hurry, Emerson?" I inquired. "John—er—Henry—bring fresh toast. This is quite leathery."

"Why, to the Museum, of course," Emerson replied. "I must finish that manuscript, Peabody; here is another impertinent inquiry from the Press, wanting to know when they may expect to receive it. Curse their impudence!" And the communication from Oxford University Press followed the other letters to the floor.

It was as well I had determined to maintain dignified silence on all issues, for Emerson never gave me a chance to speak. "And how are the dear children this morning? You have visited them, I know; your maternal devotion is so—er—so . . . Don't you agree, Mrs. Waters?"

The housekeeper, who was waiting to discuss the day's domestic arrangements, nodded and smiled. "Yes, sir. The children are well, sir. Except that Master Ramses is still asleep; and although I am sorry to mention it, there is a peculiar smell of—"

"Er, hem, yes," said Emerson. "I know about that, Mrs. Watkins. It is quite all right."

"That reminds me," I said, addressing my remark to the housekeeper, "Miss Violet seems to me to have gained weight at an astonishing rate the past week. What has she been eating?"

"Everything," said the housekeeper briefly. "Her appetite is quite incredible, and I suspect she is buying sweets and tarts and the like whenever she goes out. Her papa must have given her a large amount of pocket money."

"That doesn't sound like my worthy brother-in-law," remarked Emerson.

I ignored the remark. "Tell the nurserymaid not to permit her to buy such things. Too many sweets are not good for her."

"I have told her, madam, but she is young and rather timid; and Miss Violet . . ."

"Yes, I know, Mrs. Watson. I will have a little talk with Miss Violet. And perhaps another nurserymaid? I have forgotten which it is, Kitty or Jane."

"Jane, madam. Kitty expressed some doubts as to her ability to handle the duties required."

"That was after she had met Miss Violet, I expect. Well, Mrs. Watson, try another of the maids. Were none of the applicants who responded to my advertisement suitable?"

"No, madam. I hired one young person to replace Jane; she had excellent references, from the Dowager—"

"Very well, Mrs. Watson. As usual, I leave it to you. Emerson—"

"I must be off," exclaimed Emerson, stuffing the rest of his slice of toast into his mouth. "Have a pleasant day, my dear. Have you any particular plans?"

I looked at him. My look was severe and unsmiling; but although I take care never to admit it to Emerson, for fear of making him vain, the sight of him seldom fails to soften my resentment. The keen blue eyes, now a trifle narrowed with anxiety, the firm lips, now wearing a tentative smile, the broad brow with its tumbled waves of black hair—every lineament of his face touches chords of tender memory.

"I am going to Scotland Yard, Emerson," I said quietly. "I wonder that you need to ask, since you heard me make the appointment with Inspector Cuff."

"I heard no such thing," Emerson cried indignantly. "But I might have known you would go. There is no use, I suppose, in asking you not to go? No. I thought not. Oh, curse it!"

He stamped out, with, I was pleased to observe, all his old vigor. I do not like to see Emerson subdued and apologetic; those little differences of opinion which add so much to the enjoyment of marriage lack their usual spice when he does not meet me on equal terms. (And I am bound to say that such occurrences are extremely rare.)

"Scotland Yard, Mrs. Emerson?" the housekeeper said uneasily. "I trust you have no complaints concerning any of the servants?"

How the dear innocent woman had managed to remain ignorant of our activities I cannot imagine. I hastened to reassure her. "No, Mrs. Watson, it is another matter entirely. I am about to interview a man wrongly accused of murder and free him from captivity."

"How—how nice, ma'am," said Mrs. Watson.

The fog was lifting by the time I reached New Scotland Yard. Inspector Cuff was delighted to see me.

"My dear Mrs. Emerson! I trust you suffered no ill effects from your adventure of last night?"

"No, thank you, I am in excellent health. You were expecting me, I suppose?"

"Oh yes, ma'am. In fact, in anticipation of your visit I had the suspect brought here from Bow Street."

"Suspect? He is under arrest for murder—"

"My dear Mrs. Emerson!" Cuff smiled angelically. "I don't know where you got your information. Perhaps your informant was guilty of a certain amount of dramatic exaggeration. We have simply asked Mr. Ahmet to assist us in our investigations. You know that according to the standards of British justice, every man is innocent until proven guilty."

"A very pretty speech, Inspector. Yet the fact remains that Mr. Ahmet is in police custody, and that you have yet to explain to me why you determined to detain him. What is your evidence? What, in your no doubt honest but unquestionably misguided opinion, was his motive for murdering Oldacre?"

"Perhaps you would prefer to speak with him and form your own opinions," Cuff said, with the greatest politeness imaginable. "This way, Mrs. Emerson, if you please."

A sturdy uniformed constable guarded the captive, but one glance assured me no such precaution was necessary. Ahmet had all the stigmata of the long-time user of drugs—the pasty, yellow face, the extreme emaciation, the tremulous hands and wandering look.

"*Salaam aleikhum, Ahmet il Kamleh*," I said. "Do you know me? I am Sitt Emerson, sometimes called Sitt Hakim; my lord (unfortunately, the Arabic word for 'husband' carries this connotation) is Emerson Effendi, Father of Curses."

He knew me. A dim spark of intelligence woke in

his eyes; he stumbled to his feet and made a deep, if wobbly, obeisance. "Peace be with you, honored Sitt."

"*U'aleikhum es-sâlam*," I replied. "*Warahmet Allâh wabarakâtu.* Though it does not seem likely, Ahmet, that you can expect mercy, even from the All-Merciful. What does the Holy Book, the Koran, say about the sin of murder?"

His eyes shifted. "I did not kill the effendi, Sitt. I was not there. My friends will say so."

It was a singularly unconvincing declaration of innocence. Nevertheless, I believed it. "But you know something you have not told, Ahmet. If you keep silence, you will be hanged for the murder. Save yourself. Confide in me."

He did not move or speak; but I caught a flickering sideways glance in the direction of the constable.

"He does not understand Arabic," I said.

"That," said Ahmet cynically, "is what they say—that they do not understand. But they set spies among us, Sitt Hakim. Some of them speak our tongue." He spat, suddenly and shockingly.

"Then I will send him away."

The constable objected, as one might have expected, but I soon overcame his scruples. "Do you suppose this miserable wreck of a man would dare threaten me, Constable? Aside from the fact that I am fully armed"—I flourished my parasol, to the visible alarm of both the constable and Ahmet—"he knows my husband, Emerson Effendi; he knows the fearful vengeance that would fall on his head and the heads of all his family should a single hair of mine be ruffled."

This threat was not lost upon Ahmet. His voluble and tremulous protestations (addressed, some of them, to the single barred window, as if he suspected Emerson might be hovering without, like a disembodied spirit) convinced the constable.

Once he had gone, I waved Ahmet to a chair. "Sit and be at ease, my friend. I mean you no harm; I have come to help you. Only answer my questions and you will be restored to your friends and your family."

This happy prospect obviously did not appeal to Ahmet. An expression of deep gloom spread over his unprepossessing features. "What is it you want to know, Sitt?"

I cleared my throat and leaned forward. "There is a certain woman—her name is Ayesha—who is sometimes to be found in the opium den on Sadwell Street. I want—I want to know . . ."

I caught myself in the nick of time. Had I, Amelia Peabody Emerson, been about to ask this wretched little creature whether my husband, the dreaded and dignified Father of Curses, was in the habit of visiting a low woman of the streets? In point of fact, I had. How degrading, and how despicable!

I had struck some kind of nerve, though not, thank Heaven, the one I feared. Ahmet eyed me warily. "Ayesha," he repeated. "It is not an uncommon name, Sitt, for Ayesha bint Abi Bekr was the honored wife of the Prophet, in whose arms he died—"

"I know that. And you know the woman I mean, Ahmet. Don't try to deny it. Who is she? She does not have the look of an eater of opium. Why does she go to that place?"

Ahmet shrugged. "She is the owner, Sitt."

"Of the opium establishment?"

"Of the building, Sitt."

"Good gracious." I pondered this bit of news. Incredible as it might sound, there was no reason why Ahmet should lie about it. "She is a wealthy woman, then—or at least, a woman who has money. Why does she dress in rags and sit with the wretched smokers of opium?"

Another shrug. "How should I know, Sitt? The ways of a woman are beyond understanding."

"Venture an opinion, my friend," I said, placing my parasol on the table between us.

But Ahmet insisted he never allowed himself to hold opinions. Considering the condition of his opium-soaked brain, one might have been inclined to believe him. Further questioning, however, elicited the reluctant admission that the Lady Ayesha did not live on the premises, but had her own house, elsewhere in London.

"Park Lane?" I repeated skeptically. "That is one of the best neighborhoods in London, my friend. A woman like that—the proprietress of an opium den—would not be rubbing shoulders with the aristocracy."

Ahmet produced a meaningful leer. "Rub shoulders, Sitt? That is not all she does."

Men can never resist the opportunity to make a vulgar joke. Almost as soon as the words were out of his mouth, a look of terror transformed his features and betrayed the fact that he had said more than he meant to say. He refused to elaborate, however, and I could not bring myself to insist. There are limits of common decency beyond which a lady cannot go, even when she is in pursuit of a murderer.

I was about to leave when I remembered I had not asked him about Mr. Oldacre. On this subject he was even less informative, insisting he did not know the man, had never heard of him, had never seen him, and had no opinion whatever about anything. I quoted the remark I had overheard in the paddy wagon. Ahmet rolled his eyes.

"They come," he murmured. "True believers and heretics, men and women, princes and beggars. Hashish and opium are the great levelers, Sitt, they give of their bounty to all Allah's creatures. Even a low, crawling insect like Ahmet . . . It has been so long—too long—since I dreamed . . . Find me opium, Sitt—and a pipe—only one . . . We will talk, and dream together . . ."

Whether he was wandering in his wits or only pretending to, he had found a good way of ending the discussion. I summoned the constable and left Ahmet to his conscience, such as it was; but not, of course, before I had offered him my protection and urged him to summon me at any hour of the day or night.

Cuff was waiting for me in the corridor. "Well?" he said.

"Why ask?" I retorted. "I observed the opening in the left wall, Inspector. Who was listening outside? Mr. Jones?"

The Inspector shook his head admiringly. "You are too sharp for me, Mrs. Emerson. Not Jones; I told you, he is on holiday. We have several officers who speak Arabic, though none as fluently as you.

Why were you so interested in the woman Aye-sha?"

I countered with another question. "What do you know about her, Inspector?"

"Nothing that would justify an official inquiry," Cuff replied. "I do beg, ma'am, that you will not approach that person. She is not a fit associate for a lady like yourself."

"I do not intend to invite her to dinner, Inspector," I said ironically. "However, she is obviously a person of influence in the Egyptian community, including the criminal part of it—for persons who own and operate opium dens can hardly be called pillars of society. I cannot understand why you are being so evasive. You should interrogate the woman immediately. And furthermore . . ."

We had descended the stairs to the lower floor. Here Cuff stopped, and, turning to face me, said earnestly, "Mrs. Emerson, I have the greatest respect for your character and your abilities. But insofar as the Department is concerned, you are a civilian and a lady—both of them attributes that make it impossible for me to take you into my confidence. Were I to do so without the explicit permission of my superiors I would risk reprimand, demotion, possibly even the loss of my position. I have spent thirty years in the police force. I hope shortly to retire, with my well-earned pension, to my little house in Dorking, where, following the example of my respected father and eminent grandfather, I will spend a peaceful old age cultivating my roses. It is truly beyond my powers—"

"Spare me the rest of the speech, Inspector," I cut

in. "I have heard it before—the same tired old excuses based on masculine arrogance and contempt for women. I don't blame you; you are no better and no worse than the rest of the men, and I have no doubt that your superiors are as blind and bigoted as you."

Cuff's sallow face took on a look of deep distress. Pressing his hand to his heart he began, "Mrs. Emerson, please believe me—"

"Oh, I believe your intentions are of the best. Forgive me if I became a trifle heated. I bear you no ill will. In fact, when I catch the real murderer I will hand him over to you. I want no credit save the satisfaction of doing my duty. Good day, Inspector."

Cuff was too moved to speak. He bowed deeply, and remained in that position as I left the building.

Waving my umbrella, I summoned a hansom cab. As it drove away I saw, entering Scotland Yard, a form that was strangely familiar; but before I could get a good look, it vanished within.

Emerson at Scotland Yard? Somehow I was not surprised.

Where to go next? The reader can hardly suppose I had any doubt about that. It was possible that Ahmet had invented a false address in order to get rid of me, but it was worth a try at any rate.

In recent years the fine old street bordering Hyde Park had undergone a transition from aristocratic elegance to pure ostentation. This change was due in large part to people like the Rothschilds and their great good friend, the Prince of Wales. Why His Royal Highness preferred the company of upstart millionaires to that of his peers was something of a mystery. Some claimed it was an inherent coarseness of character, or rather, an absence of the delicate sensibility one would like to find in a British monarch. But if that were the case, the inevitable question arose: Whence derived this deplorable tendency? Certainly not from his father, the primmest, properest prince of all time. As for Her Gracious Majesty his mother . . . she may have been stuffy, priggish, and somewhat inferior in intelligence, but vulgar? Never! (I give no credence whatever to the disgusting rumors concerning Her Majesty and a certain Mr. Brown. Admittedly her servants sometimes took advantage of her good nature in order to elevate themselves above their proper station. Brown had certainly done so, and her latest favorite, Abdul Karim, who called himself the Munshi, was almost as arrogant and unpopular. But that they were anything more than favored servants I would vehemently deny.)

As the hansom proceeded along Park Lane, I saw the opulent gray stone mansion owned by Leopold Rothschild, where, it was said, the Prince had often been entertained in the lavish style to which he had become only too accustomed. Not far away was the ostentatious outline of Aldford House, which had been completed, since I last was in London, by a South African diamond magnate. Another South African millionaire had the lease of Dudley House, and at Number 25 work was in progress on a structure which would, according to rumor, surpass all the others in expense and lavishness. The builder, one Barney Barnato, had been born a cockney in the slums of Whitechapel. To such had the dignity of Park Lane fallen, from dukes and earls to the nouveau riche. Perhaps Ayesha was not so out of place after all. She and Barney Barnato ought to get on well.

The cab stopped in front of a handsome old house not far from the corner of Park Lane and Upper Brook Street. A neat parlormaid answered my knock. She wore the usual black frock, crisp white apron, and ruffled cap, but her olive complexion and liquid black eyes betrayed her nationality. Evidently Ahmet was more reliable than I had expected.

I gave her my card. "Tell your mistress I would like to speak to her."

The maid's behavior made it all too evident that she was not accustomed to visitors of my sort. Overcoming her surprise, she took my card and invited me to step into the parlor while she went to see if "the lady" was in.

If I had not by then been certain I had found my quarry, the room into which I was shown might have made me wonder, for there was not a single object in it that might not have been found in the most up-to-date, well-furnished English parlor. In fact, a cynical person might wonder if it was not meant to be a caricature of an up-to-date, well-furnished English parlor. The walls were thickly covered with pictures and mirrors in gold frames so wide they dwarfed the space enclosed. One could scarcely see the carpet for the furniture: heavy carved sofas, plump upholstered chairs and hassocks, tables, tables, and still more tables—all chastely draped in heavy cloths that hid their "nether limbs," as prim ladies of the time were wont to say.

Before long the maid returned and indicated that I was to follow her. We ascended a staircase to the first floor and went along a carpeted corridor. She opened a door and waved me in.

It was like stepping from the nineteenth century to the fifteenth—crossing in a single stride the thousands of miles that separate London from Old Cairo.

Persian carpets covered the floor in careless profusion, layer on layer of them. Walls and ceiling were draped with gold brocade, even to the windows—if there were windows, for not a beam of light entered. The only illumination came from hanging lamps pierced in intricate patterns and suspended from chains so fine that the slightest movement of air set them swaying and sent golden specks of light darting through the gloom like falling stars, or the small fiery insects that inhabit the western continent.

I thought at first that no one was there; but after my eyes had adjusted to the dim light I made out a form, sitting still as any statue on a divan against the farther wall. Unconsciously my hands tightened on the handle of my parasol. I had no reason to fear attack, for I knew nothing that threatened her; but the atmosphere reminded me, painfully and vividly, of another such room in which I had recently spent several of the most uncomfortable hours of my life,* and the sweet-scented smoke from a low brazier beside the couch on which she reclined made my senses swim.

*Lion in the Valley.

But only for a moment. I remembered my mission; I remembered who I was, and what she was. By Eastern custom, the inferior waits to be addressed before speaking. I cleared my throat and addressed her.

"Good morning. I apologize for the intrusion. I am—"

"I know who you are." She gestured—a movement of exquisite grace. "Sit there."

It was not a chair she indicated, but a low hassock. Most Englishwomen, I daresay, would have found the position uncomfortable, if not actually impossible to attain. I promptly sat down and arranged my skirts neatly.

She was now only a few feet away, but I still could not make out her features clearly, for she wore the long burko, or face veil, suspended from a jeweled band around her brow. This veil is fashioned of white muslin or silk, and it is not ordinarily worn in the presence of other females. I could only assume Ayesha intended a subtle insult of some sort, but it was too subtle for me; I did not understand what she meant by it. Her veil was so fine it outlined the perfect oval of her face, the strongly modeled nose and firm chin. Her head was bare. The waving tresses that fell over her shoulders gleamed like black satin. Her garments were of the sort worn by highborn Egyptian ladies in the privacy of the harim—loose trousers of striped silk and a long vest clinging tightly to her upper body and arms. It left half the bosom bare, for she wore no shirt underneath. All the areas thus defined, or exposed, were quite admirable in outline and in texture; her skin shone like polished amber.

Her pose was negligent, even contemptuous. Leaning on one elbow, she raised her knee, and the silken garment slipped back, baring a limb as shapely as that of a nymph. The trousers—quite contrary to the usual custom—were slit from hip to ankle.

"How did you find me?" she asked.

She spoke English, with only a slight trace of accent. The ways of the East are subtle and cunning. The women especially, who are denied the right to speak out on almost any subject, have developed their own methods of expressing disdain. Her use of my language—for she must have known I spoke hers—was a means of asserting superiority, and the question itself implied much more than it actually said. (For the sake of my duller readers I will spell it out. By not asking why I had come, she confirmed that I had reason to do so. What that reason might have been, even a dull reader should realize.)

I was not inclined to ignore the challenge, or to betray Ahmet, who, I considered, was in enough trouble already. "You say you know me, Ayesha. Then you must also know I have ways of finding people. I saw you last night, and my keen eyes penetrated your disguise."

"Last night?" Her long neck curved, poised like that of a cobra about to strike. "At the . . . *Wahyât en-nebi!* It was you?"

"It was I," I said calmly. "Your eyes did not penetrate *my* disguise."

"Then he took you there. Or at least he allowed . . ."

A sudden burst of light made me shade my eyes. When I lowered my hand I saw she had lit an oil lamp. It had been placed so that the beams fell directly on my face, and then I knew why I had been told to take that particular seat.

She studied me in silence for what seemed like a long time. I remained motionless and let her look her fill. I knew what she saw—not rippling locks nor supple limbs nor features of exquisite beauty—but I had known before ever I went there that I could not fight her and win on that ground. I did not intend to try.

At last a soft, sibilant sound that might have been laughter or a hiss of contempt escaped her lips. "He took you there," she repeated thoughtfully. "I had heard . . . But I found it difficult to believe. So, Sitt Hakim, wife of the great Emerson Effendi—you have found me. You honor my poor house. What do you want from me, the lowest of low slaves?"

I ignored this as the irony it undoubtedly was, and proceeded with my little speech, which I had carefully planned in advance. "I want your help, Miss—er—Madam Ayesha, to catch a murderer. You are surely aware that one of your countrymen has been arrested under suspicion of killing Mr. Oldacre?"

"I know it," she acknowledged.

"And you are also aware that Ahmet is innocent."

"I do not know that. How should I know it?"

"Oh, come, my dear—that is, Madam Ayesha. Let us not fence with one another. We both know that the police, being mere men, are not overly intelligent. However, they cannot be so dull as to believe a miserable worm like Ahmet committed the crime. This is some trick of theirs. I have thought the matter over and I have come to the conclusion that the only reason why they would 'ask him to assist them in their inquiries,' as they express it, is because they suspect that some person—or several persons—in the Egyptian community is involved in the crime. Ahmet is a dupe, a decoy, or a potential informer."

She listened intently, her great dark eyes fixed on my face. When I paused, inviting her reply, she was slow to respond. Finally she muttered, "It is possible. But how does that concern me? I don't fear those bunglers at Scotland Yard. I have powerful friends—"

"I am sure you do. But friends are sometimes false, when danger or disgrace threatens. At the least the attentions of the police must disrupt your—er—business activities, as was the case last night. Now I am certain the killer is not an Egyptian, but an Englishman—"

"What? Why do you believe that?"

"You ask questions, but you do not answer them, sitt." I now spoke in Arabic. "I think you know more than you admit. How could you be ignorant of what is happening among your own people, wealthy and influential as you are?"

She sat up, crossing her legs, and rested her chin on her slender hand. "I am ignorant of that matter, at least. You won't believe me—"

"If you are speaking the truth, sitt, I respectfully suggest that you had better begin to make inquiries—for your own sake. Together we could accomplish a great deal. As women—and women of considerable ability, each in her own sphere—"

Her little hiss of laughter—for such I had decided

it must be—interrupted me. "You compare us, Sitt Hakim? You must want something very badly, to stoop to that."

"Not at all; I only give you what is your due. I am familiar with the customs of the East and I am well aware of the difficulties you had to overcome in order to attain wealth and independence—"

"You are mad! How could you know, how could you begin to imagine . . . Ah, I too am mad, to sit talking such nonsense!" She threw herself back against the cushions, her hands clenched.

I had said, or done, something that had destroyed the tenuous link of understanding that had begun to build between us. I could not think what it might have been. Unless . . .

"The Englishman," I repeated. "There is such a man, is there not? You know of him. Perhaps you know him. Do you walk in fear of this man? For if you do, Emerson and I will hide you in our shadows. Is he your lover? Love is a fragile flower, Sitt Ayesha. Men trample it underfoot when the cold breath of danger withers its petals."

"All men, sitt? Yours?" She spat the words.

"Really," I began, "you mistake my—"

"Mistake! You invent foolish tales about a murdering English lord—it is an entertaining story, Sitt Hakim, but that is not why you came. You came to ask me whether Emerson Effendi is faithless. Who can read your heart better than I?"

"A great many people, I should think," I said coolly. "Look at me, Ayesha. If you can read my heart—or my countenance, which is a more accessible guide—you will see that never for an instant would I doubt Emerson. We are as one, and ever will be."

"But I knew him once," she purred. "I knew the strength of those great arms of his, the touch of his lips, his caresses. Does he still . . ."

I hope and believe I did not, by look or movement, betray the sensations that gripped me—sensations that are no more worthy of repetition than the phrases Ayesha proceeded to employ, accompanying her words with graphic gestures of her slim brown hands and undulating body. Yet her desire to wound me proved her undoing; and (as the moralists so rightly remark) her spite fell back upon her own sleek head. In her excitement she gradually slithered forward till her face almost touched mine, and the light of the oil lamp illumined her features for the first time. Neither the translucent veil nor the thick layer of cosmetics she had applied could conceal the ragged wound that had slashed one smooth cheek to the bone, leaving a purple cicatrice.

Too late, she realized what she had done. She broke off with a gasp, and withdrew into the shadows.

For a moment I was unable to speak. Anger, disgust, and—yes—pity choked me. Conquering these emotions with my usual efficiency, I cleared my throat.

"You will excuse me if I decline to emulate your candor, madam. What passes between my husband and myself is a private matter. I can assure you, however, that I have nothing whatever to complain of on that score—or any other—and that Emerson shares my sentiments."

One of her hands shot out and seized me by the wrist, her long, polished nails digging painfully into the flesh. "Does nothing move you, you cold fish of an Englishwoman? What can I do to wound you? You are ice, you are stone! What magical powers do you have, to win such a man and hold him?"

"I cannot imagine," I admitted. "However, there are many qualities other than physical beauty that draw people of the opposite sex to one another and cement the bonds of matrimonial affection. One day you may be fortunate enough to discover that. I sincerely hope you do. Which brings me back to the subject of the English lord—"

"What English lord? There is no such man." She flung my hand away. "Leave me, Sitt Hakim. I cannot defeat you. I cannot even fight you on equal grounds, you possess weapons beyond my comprehension. Leave me."

"Very well." I rose to my feet—without her grace, perhaps, but without stumbling or straining. "I did not expect you would be willing to confide in me on my first visit."

"First—"

"Please bear in mind that I stand ready to assist you in any way possible. The life you lead cannot be good for you. You should consider retiring to the country. There is nothing more soothing to a wounded spirit than solitude and the contemplation of nature—"

Ayesha rolled over and buried her face in the cushions. Taking this as a sign that the conversation was at an end, I went to the door. "Remember what I have said. Send to me at any time."

"Sitt Hakim." She did not move; her voice was muffled and uneven.

"Yes?"

"You will know my messenger if he comes. But I do not promise he will come."

"Very good. I hope he will."

"Sitt Hakim?"

"Yes."

"Before last night I had not seen Emerson Effendi for many years. It was in Egypt I knew him. Not in England. He has never visited me here."

"Oh, indeed? Well, I expect he will be along shortly."

This time she did not call me back.

After retrieving my cloak from the maid I crossed Park Lane and found a seat in the park, facing the house I had just left. Would Emerson come? I was not certain he would. My parting shot had been designed by resentment and a desire to appear clever (for even I succumb to such failings of character at times, and considering the provocation, I felt that on the whole I had behaved very well).

I was sure it had been Emerson I saw entering Scotland Yard. Knowing I planned to go there, he had probably waited till he saw me leave. If he had waited a little longer I would not have noticed him, but that was so like Emerson; impatience was his greatest weakness.

Tit for tat, Professor Emerson, I thought. I too would wait awhile, to see if Emerson was following the same trail I had followed. But perhaps not for the same reasons . . .

I had not been there long before a cab drew up

and Emerson bounded out. As soon as he had entered the house I took the precaution of hailing another cab. Getting in, I told the driver to wait. Emerson was not inside five minutes. He emerged even more precipitously than he had entered and stood on the pavement looking suspiciously about. Obviously Ayesha had told him of my visit, and he feared I might be lurking nearby.

I told my cabman to drive on. Peering out the small, dirty window, I watched Emerson cross the road and begin prowling the park. He was engaged in an altercation with a lady about my size and shape, whose old-fashioned, shovel-shaped bonnet he had attempted to remove, when the cab turned the corner into Upper Brook Street, and I beheld no more.

It is impossible to express fully the emotions that mingled within me following the interview with Ayesha (especially in the pages of a journal which may one day be published, though not, of course, before a great deal of editing takes place). My brain was a seething caldron of speculation.

If Ayesha had spoken the truth, I had nothing with which to reproach Emerson. It would have been entirely unreasonable to hold him accountable for anything he did or said or felt or thought prior to the unforgettable moment when he committed himself to me, body and soul, heart and hand.

But had she spoken the truth? Poor ruined beauty, she had every reason to lie and none whatever to reassure me. I wondered if she had felt the same reluctant sympathy for me that I had felt for her. We had something in common in addition to Emerson (and I freely confess that however sensible my reasoning on that subject might be, my emotional response did me no credit). She was a strong woman who had overcome even greater handicaps than the ones I had faced. If my knowledge of physiognomy was not at fault, she had English or European blood. A half-caste—for such is the opprobrious term—carries a double burden, despised by her mother's people, unrecognized by her father's. Add to this the position of women in her world—even more opprobrious than that of women in "enlightened" England—and I could hardly blame her for using the only means possible to pull herself out of the degrading abyss of semislavery that would have been her fate had she followed the conventional career of an Egyptian female—premature marriage, incessant childbearing, boredom, misery, and early death.

She was a clever woman, but in her agitation she had made one little slip. How meaningful it might be remained to be seen, but it had certainly opened up new possibilities I meant to explore.

Upon reaching home I discovered I had missed Mr. O'Connell. He had stayed quite some time—"stamping up and down the drawing room and talking to himself," according to Gargery—before abandoning his quest, but he had left a note. Although it was addressed to me, some of the reproaches in it were obviously meant for Emerson.

"Well, really," I said, tossing the note aside. "I am

sorry to find Mr. O'Connell is such a poor sport. He has played worse tricks on me. All is fair in love, war, and journalism, Gargery."

"I took the liberty of saying something of the sort to Mr. O'Connell," said Gargery. "Though it was not put so nicely, madam. You and the professor do have such a striking way of putting things, madam, if you don't mind my saying so."

At teatime Emerson had not returned. After waiting an extra quarter-hour, I ordered tea to be brought in and told Mrs. Watson she might send the children down. Percy and Violet were the first to appear. Both looked very neat and tidy, though the buttons straining across Violet's back reminded me of the lecture I had meant to deliver. I proceeded to do so and informed her that from now on she was restricted to one biscuit or slice of cake at tea. Having gobbled the allowed amount and tried in vain to persuade me to change my mind, she retreated in sullen silence to a corner.

Percy had decided that in lieu of butterflies, which were in short supply in London, he would begin collecting beetles. He went on to tell me about it at great length, and I confess the advent of Ramses came as such a relief I welcomed him with more than my usual affection, despite the fact that he smelled strongly of some nasty chemical which had burned several holes through his trousers.

"I was performing tests on the ushebti, Mama," he explained, handing me that object. "I am convinced now that it is genuine. The ancient paste burns with a yellow flame, whereas the modern imitation—"

"I will take your word for it, Ramses," I replied. "I never doubted that the shawabty was genuine."

"Your instincts were quite correct, Mama," Ramses replied with ineffable condescension. "However, I felt it expedient to make the tests, since, as you probably know, royal ushebtis are in rather short supply, even in museums."

Percy laughed boyishly. "You are a funny chap, Ramses. Fancy knowing all that." He gave Ramses a playful nudge.

Seeing Ramses' elbow move, I said sharply, "Don't fight, boys. Ramses, come here and sit next to me. And give me the shawabty; I don't want it to be broken."

Ramses obeyed. I edged away from him, since the smell did not improve on closer acquaintance. "So it is a royal shawabty. I thought so, but did not read the inscription."

"Men-maat-Re Sethos Mer-en-Ptah," said Ramses. "It is an interesting coincidence, Mama. The name of Sethos is not unfamiliar to us."

"You are unfortunately correct, Ramses."

"There is no possibility, I presume, that we are once again matching wits with that unknown genius of crime, that master of disguise, the Master—"

"I certainly hope not, Ramses. And I advise you not to repeat that idea, or any of the phrases you have just used, to your dear papa."

"I would never do that, Mama, since I have observed that any such references enrage Papa to a point even beyond his normal expressions of irritability. I have never really understood why."

"Because Sethos escaped us, that is why," I said.

Ramses nodded gravely. "That possibility had occurred to me, but it does not fully account for the peculiar character of Papa's fury. To be sure, the fellow had the audacity to hold you prisoner, Mama, and Papa's attachment to you is so great he would naturally wish to wreak vengeance on anyone who threatened your life—"

"Quite right, Ramses. He would feel the same if you had been held prisoner."

"And yet," Ramses insisted, "there is an element, indescribable yet persistent, that eludes me. For instance, Mama, the letter Sethos left contained several inexplicable phrases. He seemed to be blaming you for the criminal acts he contemplates in future. The obvious conclusion is that there was something you might have done that would have turned him from his evil ways. But I cannot think what it might have been."

"You can't?" I let out a long breath of relief. "Well, thank goodness there are some things . . . Never mind, Ramses. We have seen the last of Sethos, I am certain of that. This business lacks his characteristic touch. And," I added, glancing at Percy, "I would prefer not to discuss the subject."

However, Percy was paying no attention to the conversation. He had taken something from his pocket and was examining it with a pleased smile. It was a handsome watch, which appeared to be of solid gold, and I was about to comment on the inappropriateness of a boy his age possessing such an object when something about it struck me as familiar.

"That looks like your watch, Ramses. The one Miss Debenham gave you."

Percy's smile broadened. "It is Ramses' watch, Aunt Amelia. Or rather, it was; he gave it to me. For my birthday."

Ramses' face was, if possible, even less expressive than usual. He had seemed delighted by the watch, which Enid Debenham (now Enid Fraser) had insisted on presenting to him, and which, needless to say, I had put away until the time when he would be old enough and careful enough to wear it. Apparently he had grown tired of it, or else his attachment to the young lady had waned after her marriage, of which Ramses had not approved.

"You should not have given away a present from a friend, Ramses," I said.

Percy immediately offered me the watch. "I didn't think of that, Aunt Amelia. I say, I am sorry. Here, Ramses must have it back."

"No, if he gave it to you, it is yours. It was a generous gesture. However, it is too valuable an object to be carried by a little boy. I will put it away and give it to your mama when she comes, to keep for you."

"Of course, Aunt Amelia. I meant to ask you to do that. I only wanted to wear it for a little while, because it is so handsome and because . . . because of its being my birthday."

Though his disappointment was obvious, he had behaved so well I felt sorry for him. "I didn't know it was your birthday, Percy. We must certainly do something to commemorate the occasion. Supposing we all celebrate, tomorrow. What would you like to do?"

Violet stirred. "If Percy has a cake and a lot of things to eat for tea, can I have two pieces of cake? Or three?"

"We will see," I replied curtly. "It is your brother's birthday, and it is his decision as to what we are going to do. Think about it, Percy, and let me know tomorrow morning."

Percy's lips quivered. "Oh, Aunt Amelia, you are so good and kind. Thank you, thank you. And you, too, Cousin Ramses—for the beautiful watch." He gave Ramses a friendly slap on the shoulder. Ramses gave him one back, and although it was still rather early, I sent everyone to his or her room.

I had decided to dress for dinner. Honesty compels me to admit that I came to that decision in order to annoy Emerson, who hates dressing for dinner. Accustomed as I was to the free and easy style we kept at home, I kept forgetting that most upper-class establishments follow strict schedules, which I sometimes think are designed more for the convenience of the staff than of the master. When I opened the door of my room, I surprised one of the maids, who was crouched on the hearth.

She let out a squeal of surprise and curled into a sort of ball. Before I could reassure her, Mrs. Watson hurried in. Mrs. Watson looked annoyed. She was annoyed with me, for coming upstairs early, but of course she could not say so, so she began scolding the maid.

"You ought to have finished with the fire by the time Mrs. Emerson came. Run down now and fetch the hot water."

The girl scuttled out. "There is no hurry, Mrs. Watson," I said. "I am early. Did the professor say when he would be back?"

"No, madam, but I am sure he will be here shortly, since he is always so considerate about telling me when he expects to be late for dinner. Shall I have them wait until he arrives before they bring up the hot water?"

Like so many other modern "conveniences," the device that had been installed in the expectation of its producing hot water was constantly breaking down, so Evelyn had returned to the good old-fashioned customs. I informed Mrs. Watson I would not wait. Then I sat down with my feet on the fender. It had begun to rain, and the evening was cool.

I had decided not to mention my visit with Ayesha, or indicate by the slightest alteration in my manner that such an event had occurred. Emerson must know I had been there. It was up to Emerson to introduce the subject.

If he had nothing on his conscience, he *would* introduce the subject. After all—I kept telling myself—he was not responsible to me for his actions before we met. I knew that never once, since that time, had his devotion faltered; aye, I knew it because my trust in him was total, and also because he had not had much opportunity. At least not when we were in Egypt. At least . . .

There were occasions when he and Abdullah had gone off together, purportedly to visit the latter's village near Cairo. Abdullah would not hesitate to lie for the man he admired above all others.

Ayesha had said Emerson had never visited her in

England. But she had not said when she came to England, and she had not struck me as an individual who would rather go to the stake than tell a lie. During the years we lived in Kent, before we resumed our excavations, Emerson was always going up to London for the day, or for several days at a time. He had been lecturing at University College and working at the Reading Room of the Museum. Neither of those activities need fill an entire day.

Startled out of my dismal thoughts by an odd grinding noise, I looked all around the room before I realized it came from me—specifically, from my teeth. I relaxed my jaws and reminded myself of the excellent resolutions I had formed. I would not insult my beloved and devoted spouse by hinting, even in the most oblique fashion, at such unjust suspicions. No. I would wait for him to raise the subject of Ayesha. It would be natural for him to do so. It would be unnatural if he did not. Thanks to Emerson's precipitate departure that morning, and his long absence from home, we had not had the opportunity to discuss the previous evening's adventure, and speculate, as was our pleasant custom, on various theories and solutions. It would be extremely odd, under the circumstances, if the name of Ayesha did not arise.

Emerson is under the fond delusion that he can tiptoe. He makes as much noise tiptoeing as he does walking normally, and I was aware of his approach long before he reached the door. He stood outside for quite a time. He was, I felt sure, planning what approach to take, and I waited with interest to see what it would be.

Flinging the door open, he came straight to my side and lifted me out of my chair into a fond embrace.

"You look lovely tonight, Peabody," he murmured. "That dress you are wearing . . . it must be new, it becomes you well."

"It is not a dress, it is a tea gown," I replied, as soon as I was able to speak. "The same tea gown I wore last night and on several previous occasions. I wear it because . . . Oh, Emerson! That is certainly one of the reasons, but . . . Emerson . . ."

It cost more effort than I can possibly describe to put an end to the demonstrations the design of the tea gown facilitated, but I was beginning to suspect Emerson's motives, and resentment strengthened my will. Retreating behind the chair in which I had been sitting, I said sternly, "I am about to dress for dinner, and so must you. I daresay the hot water is now tepid. If you don't hurry, it will be cold."

"I am not going to dress for dinner," said Emerson.

"Yes, you are."

"No, I am not."

"Well, then, perhaps I won't change either." The dawning delight on Emerson's face should have made me ashamed of myself, but I am sorry to say it did not. I went on, "You can wear that beautiful smoking jacket I bought in Cairo—the one you swore you would be seen in only if you were deceased and unable to protest."

"Hmmm," said Emerson. "Peabody, are you annoyed about something?"

"I? Annoyed? My dear Emerson, what an idea. And the little fez that goes with it."

"Oh, curse it, Peabody, must I? The cursed tassel keeps getting in my mouth."

Gargery admired the smoking jacket very much, which put Emerson in a slightly better frame of mind. He admired the fez even more; with a defiant look at me, Emerson plucked it from his head and presented it to the butler. "Now then, Peabody," he said, when Gargery had gone off with his prize, "no more of this sniping, eh? Be open with me. What is on your mind? Were the children unusually vicious today?"

"No more so than usual, Emerson, thank you for inquiring. Violet is sulking because I have restricted her consumption of sweets, but Ramses and Percy seem to be getting on better. Ramses has tested the shawabty and declares it is genuine."

"Well, I knew it was, Peabody."

"So did I, Emerson."

Emerson helped himself to Brussels sprouts. "I don't suppose you have heard from your estimable brother or his wife?"

"No, not yet."

"It is cursed peculiar, Peabody. You would think the woman would have the simple courtesy to write to thank you, and ask about her children."

"She is under a doctor's care, I believe. He may have forbidden it."

"And dear James is safely on the high seas, out of our reach," Emerson grumbled. "How you ever came to have such despicable relations—"

"At least they are not ashamed to show their faces," I retorted. "Though honesty compels me to confess that they probably should be. Do you realize, Emerson, that except for Walter I have not met a single connection of yours? Your mother did not even have the courtesy to attend our nuptials."

"Damned lucky for you she did not," Emerson replied, stabbing viciously at his mutton. "Excuse me, Peabody. I told you she cast me out years ago—"

"But you never told me why."

Emerson slammed his knife down on the table. "Why the devil are we talking about our families? You are fencing with me, Peabody."

"You were the one who raised the subject, Emerson."

"Peabody—my darling Peabody . . ." Emerson's voice dropped in pitch and took on a wheedling tone. "We don't need our cursed families. You and I and Ramses . . . all for one and one for all, eh? Now tell me what happened today."

"Let me see. Oh yes, I almost forgot. You missed Mr. O'Connell. As did I. He left a note."

"I know. I read it." Emerson's lips curved upward. "I don't know what he is complaining about, he beat all his competitors with his story about the curse-carrying ushebtis (even if he did spell the word wrong). Six others received them—Petrie, Griffith, the Director of the Museum—"

"I know that, Emerson. I read Mr. O'Connell's story too. But thanks to you, he missed a bigger story, and his employers may not be pleased with him."

"Serves him right. It will teach him not to over-indulge in spirits or trust Egyptologists bearing gifts."

"I certainly hope so, Emerson."

I applied myself to my Brussels sprouts. Emerson picked at his and watched me out of the corner of his eye.

"Would you care to discuss the case, Peabody?"

"Why, Emerson," I said, with a little laugh. "What has come over you? How often have you insisted that (a), there is no case, and (b), we should have nothing to do with it?"

"I said no such thing," Emerson exclaimed, with such sincerity that if I had not heard him with my own ears, I would have believed him. "At least . . . there is unquestionably a case of something—heaven only knows what—therefore I propose we discuss the matter. As for having nothing to do with it— who was kind enough to take you to an opium den last night, Peabody?"

"It was good of you, Emerson."

"Yes, Peabody, it was."

"But you only gave in because you knew I would go anyway."

"Hmph," said Emerson. "Well, do you want to talk about it or not?"

"Certainly, Emerson. Shall we retire to the library, or would you rather stay at the table so that Gargery can join in?"

The sarcasm was so subtle it passed clear over the head of Gargery, who beamed appreciatively. Emerson scowled. "The library, then. You don't mind, do you, Gargery?"

"Emerson," I said, between my teeth.

"Yes, Peabody. At once."

The change in his demeanor was appalling—no fire, no protest, only courteous acquiescence. It augured badly for the confidence I expected, but I did not abandon hope. If Emerson made a full confession and threw himself upon my mercy—or, even better, if he confessed all and told me it was none of my confounded business—then we could thrash the matter out and be rid of it. But the confidence must come from him, the fatal name must pass his lips first.

We settled ourselves before the fire.

"Well, Peabody," said Emerson. "Would you care to begin?"

"No, thank you, Emerson."

"Oh. Well, then . . . hmmm. We have thus far (for who knows what tomorrow will bring?) three different and apparently separate groups of individuals. First, those connected with the Museum—Oldacre and the night watchman, Wilson, Budge, and the scholars who received the ushebtis. Second, the—er—the Egyptian connection, as you termed it."

He paused, and I waited with beating heart to see whether he would elaborate. Instead he pretended to clear his throat and continued. "Third, the dissolute aristocrats. It behooves us, I believe, to discuss whether two of the three, or all of them, are connected in any way.

"The cursed aristocrats are obviously connected with the Museum, through the gift of the mummy and Lord St. John's professed interest in archaeology. They are also connected with the opium trade and possibly thereby with group two. But there are a good many opium dens in London, the majority being operated by Chinese or Indians. There is nothing to suggest that Lord Liverpool procures his opium from an Egyptian."

"Except for the remark we overheard about unbelievers," I said coolly.

"Englishmen patronize these vile dens. We saw several of them last night."

And that was not all we saw last night, I thought. Would he now . . .

He would not. "One cannot call the lunatic priest a fourth group, since there is only one of him. What is his connection with any of the aforementioned—or is he an extraneous factor altogether?"

I rose, with dignity, from the easy chair in which I was sitting. "I see no sense in continuing this discussion, Emerson. We have not enough information on which to base an opinion, much less a theory. I must get to work on my paper for the Society for the Preservation of the Monuments of Ancient Egypt."

"Oh," said Emerson. "You—you have nothing to add to what I have said, Peabody?"

"Nothing. And you have nothing more to con—to say?"

"Er . . . I think not."

"Then I will leave you to your manuscript, Emerson, and begin mine."

Emerson went meekly to his desk. He glanced at his manuscript. "Damnation!" he shouted.

"Is anything wrong, my dear?" I inquired.

"Wrong! Of all the . . . er, hmmmm." His effort

to smile distorted his features to an alarming extent. "Er, no, my dear. Nothing at all."

Reader, my heart sickened within me. The old Emerson would have stormed up and down the room, throwing pens at the wall and telling me in no certain terms what he thought of my confounded conceit in daring to revise his work. This new Emerson was a man I scarcely recognized—a man I despised. Only guilt, and the fear of being found out, could produce such abhorrent civility.

Emerson returned to his work. Muffled growls and the violent quivering of his broad shoulders continued to convey sentiments he dared not voice aloud. I could not concentrate on my paper, even though the date of my appearance was only a fortnight away. How could I think of the flooded burial chamber of the Black Pyramid without remembering some of the most exquisitely tender moments of my marriage, when Emerson and I vowed to perish in one another's arms (providing, of course, that we were unable to find a way out of the place where we had been entombed, which I fully expected we would and which indeed proved to be the case).

I believe my lips trembled uncontrollably—but briefly, for I mastered my emotion and vowed again that never would a word of inquiry or reproach sully lips that had never been pressed to those of another than my husband (though I had had one or two narrow escapes). I decided to distract myself by making a few notes of my own on the British Museum Case.

In the past I had had occasion to try several methods of organizing my ideas, but had not found them useful, probably because my brain works too swiftly to be easily organized. I decided to attempt a new technique, writing down first the questions that remained unanswered and next to each a possible means of approach. I therefore ruled a sheet of paper into two neat columns and headed one QUESTIONS and the other WHAT TO DO ABOUT THEM.

The first question, in chronological order, concerned the death of the night watchman, so I wrote:

1. "Who is Ayesha, and where and how did Emerson know her? Question Ayesha . . ."

The words were not the ones I had meant to write. I scratched them out.

Emerson looked up from his work. "Your pen needs mending, my dear."

"Thank you for mentioning it, Emerson."

I began again.

1. "Was the death of the night watchman the result of natural causes?" Next to it I wrote, "Request the Home Secretary to exhume the body?"

I put a question mark after it because I doubted the Home Secretary, who was, after all, only a man, would respond to such a sensible suggestion without more evidence of foul play than I was able to offer.

2. "What is the meaning, if any, of the peculiar scraps of odds and ends found near the body?"

The obvious course of action to pursue here was to ask Mr. Budge when the room had last been swept. The debris might have been the meaningless accumulation of days or weeks (or months, to judge by what I had seen of Budge's housekeeping).

3. "Were the splashes of dark liquid human blood?"

Inquire of Inspector Cuff? I meant to do so,

though I did not expect significant results. The inept police might not have noticed the dried liquid, and Inspector Cuff might not tell me the truth.

That seemed to take care of questions relating to the night watchman. I proceeded, therefore, to the next incident, the murder of Mr. Oldacre.

4. "Was he a user of drugs? And, if the answer was in the affirmative, was he an habitué of the opium den we had visited?"

Ask Inspector Cuff. And hope that for once he would give over smiling and bowing and answer a simple question.

Or—a useful thought!—ask Mr. Wilson. He had been acquainted with the dead man. Miss Minton, who seemed to know everything Mr. Wilson knew, was another possible source of information. In fact, since she was a woman, it behooved me to try her first, since I was more likely to get a sensible answer from her.

5. "Was he a blackmailer? Whom was he blackmailing, and for what offense?"

It was unlikely in the extreme that Inspector Cuff would answer those questions, even if he knew the answers. Again, Mr. Wilson and Miss Minton might respond to interrogation.

Now inspired and feeling the intellectual juices flowing freely, I dashed off question after question.

6. "Who is the lunatic in the leopard skin?" The obvious solution was to catch the scoundrel in the act, but that was not as easy as it seemed. Emerson had already tried and failed; after the riot at the Museum, the fellow might not show his face in public again. Lure him out into the open, then, and set

an ambush. But how? Nothing useful occurred to me at the moment, so I put that aside for the time being and went on to the next question.

7. "Who sent the shawabtys to Emerson and the rest? Was it the same lunatic?" There seemed no action I could take to learn the answer, but I was inclined to believe the answer was yes. Thus far the lunatic had committed no act of violence. The warning of the shawabtys had the same hallmark as his activities in the Museum—sinister in appearance and harmless in actuality. Like Ramses, I was more and more inclined to think the fellow was not a lunatic at all, but a man with a distorted sense of humor and the means to indulge it. As Ramses had said (curse the child) royal shawabtys were not easily procured.

The weight of the evidence, such as it was, seemed to point to Lord Liverpool or Lord St. John or one of their "set." Yet there are, thanks to the lawless looting of ancient Near Eastern sites by antiquities dealers and idle tourists, many private collections of antiquities in England. Or the "priest" might have taken them from the Museum. He seemed to know his way about, and because of the wretched organization of the place there were probably hundreds of forgotten objects in the dusty cellars and storage rooms. The priest's familiarity with ancient Egyptian suggested to me not a dilettante, but a scholar, yet I found it hard to believe any of my acquaintances could behave in such an extraordinary fashion. Young Mr. Wilson had been with us when the priest made one of his appearances. Petrie . . . Certainly not Petrie, the man had absolutely no sense of humor.

8. (I had just thought of this, so it was not in proper chronological order.) "Were there any circumstances surrounding the acquisition of the mummy that might account for what was happening?" Unlikely as it seemed, the question ought to be explored, in my opinion, and the obvious source was Lord Liverpool. He had invited me to visit him; why not take advantage of the invitation? And have a look, while I was there, for an empty case that might have contained ushebtis.

9. His lordship was a user of opium. "What opium den did he frequent? Were he and his friends the unbelievers mentioned by the man in the paddy wagon?"

With a firm hand I inscribed, under WHAT TO DO ABOUT IT, "Question Ayesha."

TEN

Poets are always running on about the benefits of sleep, which is reputed to be "a gentle thing, beloved from pole to pole," and which "knits up the ravelled sleeve of care," et cetera, ad infinitum. I myself have always regarded it as a frightful waste of time. There are so many other interesting things to do, it seems a pity to waste one third of the day in a state of unconsciousness. However, I woke the following morning refreshed and in a slightly more cheerful state of mind. Making out a neat list had cleared my head and suggested several useful lines of inquiry. I was mulling them over and trying to determine which to pursue first when Emerson rolled over and flung his arm around me.

He was still asleep. The movement had been instinctive, habitual, unconscious. Was that what our marriage had become? Nothing more to him than dull habit? A groan escaped my lips. Without daring to look at him, I slipped out of bed.

It was not until I had studied my list that I remembered I could do nothing that day. I had promised to take the children out in honor of Percy's birthday. I was not about to go back on my promise, for I pride myself on keeping my word, even to children, but it was a bitter blow. Dare I confess what thought lessened the pain? I am ashamed to do so, but I suppose I may as well. It was the knowledge that Emerson would hate it even more than I would.

However, I let him eat his breakfast first, for I am not a vicious person, even when provoked. He retreated immediately behind his newspaper and did not speak until Percy asked, "Uncle Radcliffe, sir— when should we be ready to leave?"

"Where are you going?" Emerson asked, peering over the paper.

I explained. "It is Percy's birthday, Emerson. I promised we would take the children on a little excursion, to celebrate."

Emerson's face fell. "You promised? But, Peabody—"

"They have seen none of the sights of London, Emerson. Even if this were not a special occasion, we ought to acquaint them with the historic and artistic monuments of the capital of their nation. Their education has been badly neglected this past week—"

"Hire a tutor," Emerson grunted.

"That is a subject I mean to raise with you, and one that requires much more consideration than a single careless suggestion. Your presence, Emerson, would make the adventure much easier, and more pleasurable, for all of us."

"Oh," said Emerson. "Well, in that case, Peabody . . . Where do they want to go?"

"To the British Museum," said Ramses promptly.

Watching Percy's expressive face, I said, "That might amuse you, Ramses, and I am sure it would please your papa, but Percy must choose, since it is his birthday. What have you decided, Percy?"

"I will go anywhere you think best, of course, Aunt Amelia. But if you don't mind . . . Papa took us to Madame Tussaud's last year, when we were in London, and oh, it was jolly! I do think Ramses would like it too if he has never been."

Emerson stared at his nephew. Then his face cleared and he chuckled. "He might at that. But what about your sister, my boy? Some of the exhibits—"

"We will avoid the Chamber of Horrors, naturally," I said. "The historical exhibitions are quite educational. Ramses spends far too much time brooding over his morbid hobbies; it will do him good to learn something of modern history."

"Something modern and cheerful, like the French Revolution," Emerson said. "Was not Madame forced by the revolutionary government to model the heads brought to her from the guillotine?"

"Yes, sir, even the head of the poor queen," said Percy eagerly. "Whom Madame had known well. Only fancy, sir, how horrid!"

"Dead," murmured Violet.

Despite the mournful thoughts that darkened my spirit I felt a stir of pride when I beheld our (temporarily enlarged) family assembled for its outing.

Emerson had consented to wear a frock coat and a stiff collar, though he complained that the latter chafed his jaw. No persuasion of mine could convince him to complete the elegance of the ensemble with a top hat; and I must confess that the pipe looked a trifle odd jutting out from between his strong white teeth. However, Emerson looks magnificent at any time and in any costume.

The boys were dressed alike, in sailor suits and caps. The contrast between them had never been more striking: Percy's fresh English complexion and smooth brown locks next to the unmanageable mop of ebony curls and tanned cheeks of Ramses. I am bound to admit the costume did not suit my son any more than it would have suited Emerson. He looked like a grave, miniature adult dressed in children's clothes. The sailor suit had, however, the advantage of being washable. That advantage, with Ramses, was considerable.

Violet was so swathed in ruffles it was difficult to be certain a child was inside them. The frills on her little bonnet had not been properly starched; they hung down and hid most of her face. Instead of a doll she was carrying a stuffed lamb, which I recognized as one which had been given to Ramses when he was three. It was in pristine condition, since he had never played with it. (I will never forget the expression on his face when, after contemplating it in silence for several minutes, he placed it neatly on the shelf and returned to his study of hieroglyphs.)

As we drove, I pointed out monuments of historic interest, and I was pleased to see that Ramses stared as eagerly as any other small boy. As we proceeded along Baker Street, toward the Portman Rooms where Madame's display was housed, he kept leaning out of the carriage as if looking for something, but when I asked what it was he only shook his head.

I confess I have never been able to understand the attraction of waxworks, however accurately they may preserve the features and forms of individuals. It is animation that gives interest to a countenance— the shifting eyes that betray guilt, the quivering lips of an accused suspect.

The historical tableaux were of interest, however, and I gave a little lecture on each of them. Particularly affecting was one that showed Her Majesty as a young girl of eighteen, her hair down upon the shoulders of her modest white nightgown, as the grave, bearded dignitaries knelt to kiss her little hand and hail her as Queen. (For she had, as the Reader may or may not know, been aroused from innocent sleep.) And what tender memories were evoked by the tableau depicting the massacre of the gallant Gordon! I had been in Egypt that year—my first visit to the land of my destiny, my first meeting with my destined spouse. I glanced at Emerson.

"What memories this tableau evokes, Emerson."

"Mmmph," said Emerson, chewing on the stem of his pipe.

The cream of the collection is unquestionably the series of French Revolutionary tableaux, and the severed heads modeled by Madame herself under the grisly conditions Percy had described. One can only imagine the horror with which the unhappy artist must have contemplated the pallid features of the King and Queen who had treated her so graciously. Yet history had avenged Marie Antoinette; next to hers, in a ghastly row, were the heads of her murderers: Fouquier-Tinville, Hébert, and Robespierre himself, carried in their turn to the prison atelier of Madame Tussaud. A particularly gruesome tableau, also modeled from life, showed the murdered Marat lying in his bath, with the hilt of the knife protruding from his side. (I am sure I need not remind the reader that the courageous assassin was a woman.)

The reader may well ask, however, why I consented to allow the children to view these dreadful scenes. The answer is simple: I did not. The viewing rooms were crowded, not only with people but with their voluminous garments, and a small child could easily conceal himself among the sweeping skirts and heavy coats. Ramses was the first to steal away. When his absence was noted, Percy was quick to suggest an explanation.

"I expect he has gone to see the Chamber of Horrors, Aunt Amelia. I will find him, shall I?"

Without waiting for an answer, he slid away.

"I will go after them, Emerson," I said. "Do you stay here with Violet—and show her the tableau of Her Gracious Majesty, Prince Albert, and their lovely children."

But Violet tugged at her uncle's hand. "I want to see the dead people, Uncle Radcliffe."

"Violet, my dear," I began.

"She has seen them before, Amelia," Emerson said, letting the little tyrant draw him away. "The bloodthirstiness of innocent children is a perfectly natural thing, you know; I have often observed it, and cannot understand why so-called modern authorities refuse to admit it."

I knew why Emerson was so agreeable. Like myself, he had often wondered whether his son's interest in mummies and ancient bones was a sign of some deep, dangerous mental disturbance. Finding the same quality in supposedly normal children like Percy and Violet reassured him.

"Well, I do not approve, Emerson, but if you insist, I must of course submit."

"Bah," said Emerson. "You want to see the Chamber of Horrors too."

The boys had immediately discovered the most gruesome of all the exhibits; their mutual antipathy for once in abeyance, they stood side by side contemplating the "Celebrated Murderers."

A recently added figure was that of Neill Cream, who had been hanged for administering strychnine, rightfully called the most agonizing of poisons, to a series of unfortunate fallen women. His crossed eyes and large ginger mustache, his bald head and sinister leer composed a countenance so hideous one wondered why any woman, fallen or upright, would accept any substance whatever from his hand.

"Come away from that, Ramses," I exclaimed.

Holding Violet by the hand, Emerson joined Percy before the effigy of Dr. Pritchard. This reprobate had betrayed not only his physician's calling but his marital commitments by subjecting his wife to the slow torture of poisoning with tartar emetic. (He had also polished off his mother-in-law, presumably because she had become suspicious of her daughter's unusual symptoms.) We must all agree that there is something extraordinarily vile about the crime of uxoricide; and Pritchard was surely one of the most cold-blooded hypocrites in the annals of crime, for he had not only shared his wife's bed throughout her illness, and held her in his arms as she perished, but he had also insisted that her coffin be opened so that he might embrace her for the last time.

"Surely," I remarked to Emerson, "there is no more infamous example of a Judas kiss than when that villain, his face wet with crocodile tears, pressed his lips to the cold lips of the woman he had foully slain, betraying the tenderest of all human ties."

It would have been difficult to disagree with this statement; but Emerson was in a perverse mood that day. "Pritchard had his points," he remarked. "I find it difficult to wholly despise a man who could make the remarkable claim that he had 'plucked the eaglets from their eyries in the deserts of Arabia, and hunted the Nubian lion in the prairies of North America.'"

"Emerson," I exclaimed. "I must protest your frivolous attitude. The children, Emerson—remember the children."

None of them was paying the least attention, in fact. Ramses had managed to wriggle away from me again, and was lost somewhere in the crowd. Percy had gone to gape at Charles Peace, and Violet sucked on the ear of the lamb and stared, with eyes as round as saucers, at the hypocritical smile on the face of the doctor.

Conceding the wisdom of my observation, Emerson collared Percy and took him and Violet to look at Marat in his bath while I went after Ramses. I was a trifle distracted at first, for Emerson's observations on Dr. Pritchard had taken me by surprise. Here was a man who professed the greatest indifference to crime, and the highest contempt for those who were intrigued by it, and who could yet quote an obscure reference (for I had not known it) by a well-known poisoner. Emerson must have studied the case; with how many others, I wondered, was he equally familiar? The hypocrisy of his attitude appalled me, and cast serious doubts on his veracity in other areas.

Finally I saw Ramses moving toward the exit. Next to the door, and partially blocking it, was an effigy I had not noticed before. It was that of a gentleman in formal morning attire; not one of Madame's more skillful creations, for the face was particularly stiff and masklike. Yet it was realistic enough to deceive at a casual glance, and I supposed it was meant as a joke, like the uniformed "guard" in one of the upper rooms who was often addressed by visitors in search of information before they realized they were inquiring of a wax figure.

Ramses spoke to the image, asking (I presumed) its pardon for passing in front of it. He may not have been surprised, but I certainly was, when the effigy suddenly seized him in its arms and carried him rapidly out of the room.

So astonishing was the metamorphosis that I was rooted to the spot. But only for a moment; careless of the cries of pain and protest from people I inadvertently jostled, I went in pursuit. I knew I dared not delay, not even to summon Emerson to my assistance. The masked miscreant was dressed like a gentleman, which would make observers hesitate to detain him (such is the snobbery of our society), and unless I moved even faster than he, he and his prey would be gone before I could catch him up.

His path was easy to follow, for it was marked by indignant conversation and a few fallen bodies. With equal disregard for courtesy I pushed my way to the exit. Quick as I had been, I had been too slow. When I emerged onto the pavement he was nowhere in sight.

I seized the arm of a passing ostler. "A gentleman carrying a little boy in his arms and running, or walking quickly. Which way did he go?"

The man only stared at me, but his companion, a female dressed in tawdry lace and dirty satin, replied, "That way, ma'am, toward the Gaiety Bar."

I was unfamiliar with the establishment she mentioned, but her pointing hand indicated the direction; with a nod of thanks I ran on. Scarcely had I turned the corner, however, when I beheld Ramses walking toward me. His cap was gone, he was smeared with dirt, and he was rubbing his tousled head.

I seized him. "Ramses! Thank heaven! Are you unharmed? How did you escape?"

"I did not escape," Ramses replied, his chagrin evident. "I was let go. He dropped me—on my head, to be precise—in an alley not far away from here. I pray, Mama, that this was not a diversion, to separate our group and wreak greater harm on another member of it; for it seems evident—"

It seemed evident that Ramses was not hurt, so I told him to be quiet, and led him as quickly as I could toward Baker Street. Already I could hear the penetrating voice of Emerson calling my name and that of Ramses in poignant alternation.

Even in his agitation he had not neglected his duty; he held Violet in one hand and Percy in the other. I hastened to his side. Then and only then did he loose his hold on his charges, and—neglectful even of his kidnapped heir—flung his strong arms around me.

"Peabody, I wish to the devil you wouldn't go off like that," he mumbled into my ear.

I realized he was unaware of the dire necessity that had prompted my disappearance. My hasty explanation caused the color to fade from his face and evoked several incoherent and profane exclamations. Not until after we had climbed into the carriage and were on the homeward path did he simmer down enough to make sense.

"Let us give thanks that nothing serious transpired," I said. "Perhaps it was a case of mistaken identity, or a peculiar joke."

Not that I believed either theory, but I preferred not to discuss the darker implications of the event until Emerson and I were alone. I might have known Ramses was not to be fobbed off with such an inane suggestion.

"It was not a case of mistaken identity," said Ramses. "The man knew who I was. And if it was meant as a joke, the individual's sense of humor is warped. Just before he pitched me away, he said, 'My regards to your papa, young Master Emerson. Tell him that the next time I come calling, it will be on him.' "

"Oh, sir," exclaimed Percy. "I say, how exciting!"

Whereupon Ramses turned and punched Percy in the stomach. To be strictly accurate, it was not in the stomach. Percy fell off the seat and doubled up with a shriek of anguish. Emerson seized his son by the collar. "Ramses! Where did you learn—"

"From you, Papa," Ramses gasped. "Last winter, when we were searching for Mama, who had been abducted by . . . It was when we broke into the house behind the khan, and the man with the large knife came at you, and you—"

"Oh," said Emerson. "Well, er, hmmmm. That was quite a different matter, Ramses. When one is defending oneself against a villainous criminal armed with a knife . . . er. Yes. Gentlemen settle their differences in quite another way, Ramses."

"Emerson," I exclaimed, assisting the groaning youth back onto the seat of the carriage, "how can you speak so coolly? Ramses struck the first blow; it was unprovoked, and—"

"And inept," said Emerson, frowning. "See here, Ramses; fold your thumb over your closed fingers—"

"Ramses," I said wearily, "you are confined to your room until further notice."

To my annoyance, Emerson refused to take the incident seriously. "Boys will fight, Peabody. You cannot change human nature. A few lessons in boxing might be an excellent idea. Hmmm, yes. Under my supervision, of course . . ."

In honor of Percy's birthday we had plum cake

for tea. Violet ate three pieces. I was too unnerved to prevent her from doing so.

My hopes of accomplishing something useful that day were not entirely disappointed. I managed to send several important letters and telegrams, and of course the attack on Ramses was not devoid of interest. When we went up to change for dinner, Emerson agreed without a murmur to assume his evening clothes, and my heart twisted painfully. But however I might deplore his reticence, all lesser grievances had been temporarily submerged. Faithless he might have been—faithless he might yet be. But when danger threatened him I found that my devotion was as strong as ever, and that anguished concern for his safety rose triumphant over all.

We were almost dressed, and the maid was emptying the bath, when I spoke.

"Are you . . . Will you . . . You will take care, Emerson, won't you?"

"Take care?" He turned from brushing his hair to consider me with surprise. "What for, Peabody?"

"For your life and safety, of course. That was another threat, Emerson."

"Ramses was the one who was carried off, Peabody."

"Ramses took no harm—except for a bump on his head, and that is too hard to be easily damaged. The threat was directed at you. Knowing how precious Ramses is to you—"

Emerson crossed the room in a few long strides

and clasped me to him. "There is one object even more precious to me than Ramses," he said hoarsely. "My darling Peabody . . ."

With what a pang I cannot describe I freed myself gently but firmly. "We are not alone, Emerson."

"Is that cursed—er—that girl here again?" Emerson exclaimed. "Curse it, hasn't she anything else to do? Come along, Peabody, we may as well go down. There is no privacy in this confounded mausoleum. How much longer must we stay here?"

"Until you finish your manuscript," I replied, taking his arm as we reached the stairs.

"Curse the cursed manuscript! I want you out of this, Peabody. I want you to take the children and go home to Kent."

"Oh, do you? And why is that, Emerson?"

"Curse it, Peabody, you know why. (Hullo, Gargery; how are you this evening?) I don't like the way this fellow's mind works. He won't attack me. No one attacks me. He will try to strike at me through those I love, and as I mentioned earlier, Peabody—"

"Yes, I have not forgotten. But you have never tried to hustle me out of danger before."

"Not true, Peabody, not true. I always try. I never succeed, but I always try."

"Excuse me, sir and madam." Gargery put a plate of soup before Emerson. "I know I ought not ask, but in view of the profound respect I feel for you both, I must inquire whether there is any imminent danger, and if so, what we servants can do to help."

So moved was I by Gargery's concern that I would never have wounded his feelings by reminding him that it was not his place to join in the conversation. Emerson was equally touched; eyes bright with emotion, he clapped the butler on the back.

"Very good of you to say so, Gargery. Mrs. Emerson and I appreciate it. You see, what happened . . ."

I finished my soup while Emerson told Gargery all about it. Gargery's eyes flashed. "Sir and madam, there is not a servant in the house that would not risk life and limb in your defense. Don't you worry, sir, we won't let this chap get to Mrs. Emerson. Here's an idea, sir; supposing Bob—he's the huskiest of the footmen, sir—supposing he goes along with Mrs. Emerson on her little errands and so on? I could find him a nice little revolver, sir—"

"No, no, no firearms," Emerson said, shaking his head. "I won't have them in the house; you know Master Ramses, he'd pepper himself or the crockery before you could say 'Jack Robinson.' Perhaps a stout cudgel—"

"Nonsense," I exclaimed angrily. "No one is going anywhere with me on any errands of any kind. Gargery, you may take away the soup and fetch the next course."

I had barely time to say to Emerson, "If you set a bodyguard on me, Emerson, I will never—" before Gargery was back, breathless and bubbling with ideas.

"Has it occurred to you, sir," he said, slamming a platter of turbot with lobster sauce down in front of me, "that this incident may be not directed against you personally? Like those ushbers—shabters—"

"That is a point I was about to make myself," said Emerson. "We agree, do we not, that the (temporary) abduction of Ramses was perpetrated by the same individual who sent the ushebtis?"

"I am of that opinion, sir," said Gargery judiciously.

I frowned at Gargery. "If I may be allowed to speak, at my own dinner table . . ."

"I beg your pardon, madam," said Gargery, retreating to the sideboard.

"Thank you, Gargery. I agree—if a woman's humble opinion is of any worth in the presence of two such great intellects—that the same person is responsible for both incidents." Gargery and Emerson exchanged glances. Emerson shrugged and rolled his eyes; I went on, "It would behoove us, I suggest, to find out whether the others who received the ushebtis had anything unusual happen to them."

Gargery remained discreetly silent. Emerson exclaimed with false heartiness, "An excellent suggestion, Peabody. I will go round and pay a few calls after dinner. Would you care to accompany me?"

"No, thank you, Emerson. You and Gargery have a good time."

At breakfast next morning I remarked to my husband, "You might have spared yourself the effort of paying calls, which you generally dislike, Emerson. It is all here in the *Morning Mirror*."

"What is?" Emerson snatched the newspaper. "Oh, good Gad. How did they find out about Ramses and Madame Tussaud's?"

"Whom did you mention it to, Emerson?"

Emerson frowned at the newspaper. "Budge and Petrie and Griffith and . . . not Pritchett, he was not at home. They claimed—as you have surely read—that nothing untoward occurred to them."

"Which would suggest that the unknown has decided to concentrate on you, Emerson."

"Not necessarily. Except for Budge, who would court publicity at his mother's funeral, the others might not want to mention anything so out-of-the-way. Especially Petrie—you know what a dull stick he is—"

"So you learned nothing from any of them?" We had not talked the night before; it was very late when Emerson came to bed, reeking of tobacco. I pretended to be asleep.

"Griffith let me have a look at his ushebti. It was the image of the one I received, Peabody. Someone, somewhere, is missing a rare and valuable set of antiquities. If they could be traced . . ."

"That would certainly be a useful clue," I agreed politely, remembering my little list (which was locked in a drawer of my desk for safety's sake). "No one knew of any such objects, I assume?"

"No. Which strongly suggests that they came from a private collection. Even Budge would notice their disappearance from the Museum."

"What about University College, Manchester, Birmingham—"

"I could certainly inquire."

"There is something else you might do," I said, taking the morning post from Mary Ann, who had just brought it in.

"And what is that, Peabody?"

"Most citizens would report to the police an attack such as was made on our son."

Emerson looked startled and stroked his chin. "I suppose they might. I wonder, Peabody, if we are becoming too accustomed to going it alone."

"Oh, no, Emerson; considering who we are and what we are, we are behaving quite logically. Here are your letters."

"Thank you." Emerson ripped through them in his usual vigorous style, remarking only, "Confounded Oxford Press," as he flung the communication away. "Perhaps I might drop by the Yard later," he said casually.

"What a good idea, Emerson."

"Would you care to go along?"

"I see no reason why both of us should go, Emerson."

"I would—I would enjoy your company, Peabody."

"Thank you, Emerson, that is very kind of you. However, I have other things to do."

"Oh?"

"Yes."

"How are you getting on with your paper?"

"Very well, thank you."

Emerson threw his napkin and his remaining letters onto the floor and jumped to his feet. His chair fell over with a crash. "Damnation," he shouted, and rushed out of the room.

"Try to be home for tea, Emerson," I called after him. "I expect a guest."

Emerson's footsteps stopped. He returned to the

door and looked in. "Who?" he asked apprehensively.

"Mr. Wilson. He has been kind enough to accept my invitation."

"Oh," said Emerson. "Oh, I see. I will be here, Peabody."

He had been relieved at my answer, I had no doubt of it. What name, I wondered, had he expected—and dreaded? That of Ayesha?

Having received no answer to the note I had sent Miss Minton, I decided to call on her personally. The article in the *Morning Mirror* made me suspect she was still away, for it did not carry her name; but I went anyway, since I wanted exercise. As I had hoped, brisk walking calmed me, but the visit was in vain; the landlady said she had not seen or heard from her tenant and had no idea when she would return.

I consulted my list. Miss Minton would have to wait. Mr. Wilson was arranged for. A (flatteringly) prompt reply to my letter to Lord Liverpool invited me to have luncheon with him next day, and view his collection. Under the heading WHAT TO DO ABOUT IT there remained three names: Budge (on his housekeeping methods), Inspector Cuff (on a variety of questions he would probably not answer), and one other.

I spent the next few hours sitting in Hyde Park opposite Number 4, Park Lane. I will never forget those hours, and I venture to believe that they were unique in my experience; for I, Amelia P. Emerson, continued for that long period in a state of indecision and vacillation! The anomaly is worthy of being recorded, I believe.

The weather was (for London) fine, and a number of people were in the park enjoying the flowers and (for London) sunshine. I did not expect, however, that I would pass unobserved. Anyone who sits on the same spot for over two hours, without drinking, eating, reading, or moving, is bound to attract attention; two constables and a kindly old lady stopped to inquire whether I required assistance, and a male person stopped for inquiries of another sort. If Ayesha took note of possible spies (which she of all persons had good reason to do), she must have seen me. Four times I made up my mind to cross the road and knock at her door. Four times I changed my mind.

She had no callers. I do not include various tradesmen, who of course went round to the back. One of these was a tall, muscular individual carrying a basket of fish and wearing a very voluminous black beard. I rose and hailed a hansom cab.

At precisely half past four I sat in another such cab outside a modest building on Half-Moon Street. At precisely thirty-four minutes past four Mr. Wilson came out of the house, glanced at the cab, saw it was taken, and walked to the corner, where he was successful in finding another conveyance. He was going to be early. That was unfortunate. I hoped Emerson would be there in time to receive him.

Telling the cab driver to wait, I applied the knocker to the door of Number 17. The door was answered by a comfortable motherly woman who hastily whisked off her apron when she saw me, and apologized.

"I thought you were the baker, madam. That dratted girl is never here to answer the door when I want her . . ."

Her efforts to assure me of her gentility were wasted. "I have come to see Mr. Wilson," I said, start-ing for the stairs. "His rooms are—?"

"First floor front, madam. But, madam, he has just gone out."

"Really? How vexatious." I consulted my watch. "He will be returning soon, I expect. I had an ap-pointment with him at half past four. I will wait."

She moved quickly to bar my path. "Excuse me, madam. Mr. Wilson is very particular about my let-ting people in unless he tells me in advance they are expected."

"Oh, what nonsense," I said impatiently. "Here—my card."

I had hoped not to have to give it, but there was no other way. The landlady took the card. "Mrs. Emerson?" Then her worried frown was replaced by a broad, delighted smile. "Mrs. Emerson! The lady who's been in all the newspapers?"

"Er—yes," I replied.

"But you're the one that digs up all the mummies and things in India—"

"Egypt."

"Yes, madam, Egypt. Oh, madam, it is a pleasure to meet you. How is your poor little boy?"

"My poor little . . . ? Thank you, he is quite well."

She detained me for longer than I would have liked, but I finally made my escape; and as I mounted the stairs I could not help smiling wryly as I realized it was not my respectable appearance that had gained me entry, but the notoriety I had deplored.

Mr. Wilson had a nice little set of rooms, probably the best in the house, to judge from their location. The sitting room overlooked the street; behind it was a neat little bedroom. Though pleasant and nicely furnished, they were not luxurious. A few antiquities were scattered about; except for a lovely little alabaster head of an anonymous queen—whose features bore a certain resemblance to those of Miss Minton—none were exceptional, and I could not tell if any were missing. The landlady apparently dusted regularly.

A further investigation, which I was loath to make, but which I felt to be necessary, indicated that Mr. Wilson's habits were as proper as his appearance. A tantalus on the sideboard held decanters of brandy and whiskey, and there were cigars in a box nearby, but I found no trace of drugs. Only one thing defeated me—a locked drawer in his desk, for which I could not find the key and which I was afraid to tamper with. One may easily invent an excuse for calling on a young man, but it is a little difficult to explain why one ventured to break into a locked drawer.

The whole business only took ten minutes, for I can move like lightning when I must. Descending the stairs, I called to the landlady—whom I could hear banging pots around in the kitchen—to tell her I would wait no longer, and then I made my escape before she could engage me in conversation again.

I was only forty minutes late. When he saw me, Gargery's face went pink with pleasure. "Oh, Mrs. Emerson, we were beginning to worry. The gentleman is here—"

"Yes, thank you," I said, handing him my parasol and coat. "I will go right in."

I don't know who was more relieved to see me, Emerson or Mr. Wilson. I knew why Emerson was relieved, and I guessed that Mr. Wilson was glad to be freed from the relentless quizzing on Egyptology Emerson had been giving him. After greetings, apologies, and (on Emerson's part) scowls had been exchanged, I said cheerfully, "I am late because I made a silly mistake, Mr. Wilson. Somehow I got the notion that I was having tea with you, instead of the other way round. I waited for you for half an hour before I realized I must have been in error. Wasn't that absurd?"

The only possible answer was "Yes, it certainly was," but since Mr. Wilson could not in courtesy make it, he mumbled and grinned foolishly.

"Humph," said Emerson, giving me a hard look. "Yes, it certainly was. You missed a very interesting discussion of the pottery of the early dynastic period at Quesir, Peabody. Mr. Wilson was there two years ago. However, he doesn't seem to remember—"

"I am sorry I missed it, Emerson. However, if

Mr. Wilson doesn't mind, I would like to speak of something else."

Mr. Wilson was quick to assure me he did not mind in the slightest.

"I don't apologize for introducing the subject, Mr. Wilson, for the matter is becoming so serious it demands action. I want you to tell me all you know about Mr. Oldacre."

I had expected I would have to explain—for most people waste time in unnecessary discussion of the obvious—but Mr. Wilson proved himself superior to most people. Leaning back in his chair, he smiled faintly. "I see. I am sorry to disappoint you, Mrs. Emerson, for I believe I understand your reasons for raising the subject, and I am in complete sympathy with them. But I knew Oldacre only slightly. He was not the sort of man who could ever be a close friend of mine. Perhaps if you were to ask me questions—"

"Excellent," I said crisply. "I like the way your mind works, Mr. Wilson. Was he a user of drugs?"

"Not to my knowledge," was the prompt response. "It would not surprise me to learn that he dabbled in them—it is the fashionable thing to do in some circles—but he showed none of the signs of the habitual user."

"You don't know, then, whether he visited an opium den?"

"He would hardly have invited me to accompany him to such a place," was the smiling answer.

"Who were his friends—his intimates?"

Wilson mentioned a few names, all of which were

unfamiliar to me, adding, "As I have said, I was not a close friend of his. I would be unlikely to know—"

"Yes, quite. What about Lord St. John?"

Wilson laughed. He was quite a nice-looking young fellow when he was at ease, as he was then; his teeth were white and even, and his features finely cut. "If his lordship had anything to do with Oldacre, it would not be as a friend. He has a keen sense of social position, does Lord St. John."

"No doubt you are right. Well, then, you have nothing to suggest? Bad habits, debts, gambling, women?"

Wilson looked a little startled. "As to women . . . I hardly like to mention the subject in the presence of a lady . . ."

"Ah, I understand. Fallen women, is that it?"

"Er—yes. Only the usual thing, you know . . ."

"Hmph," I said.

"Oh, quite, Mrs. Emerson. I myself would never . . . As for other habits—yes, he gambled; he was always bragging about being a guest at one exclusive club or another, and I know he often lost heavily—for he bragged about that too, as if it were something to be proud of. And I have seen him show the effects of overindulgence. But really, you know, it is no more than most young fellows do."

"How true—and how sad, that such things should be so common. Well, that is very disappointing, but it is not your fault, Mr. Wilson. Emerson, have you any questions to ask?"

"No," Emerson said shortly.

"Then we can return to the discussion of pre-dynastic pottery."

Mr. Wilson pulled his watch from his pocket, glanced at it, and jumped to his feet. "Dear me, I had no idea it was so late. I must be running along. I have to assist Mr. Budge with his lecture tonight—"

"Is it tonight?" I asked. "I had quite forgotten."

"Yes, he moved the date up, for some reason. He doesn't explain himself to me," Wilson added, with his attractive smile. "He tells me what I am to do and I do it. Tonight I am to assist him with the famous mummy. Perhaps I will see you there. Thank you, Mrs. Emerson—Professor—it has been most enjoyable—next time you must come to me."

"I will hold you to that," I said, giving his hand a hearty shake.

"You may count on it," said Mr. Wilson, smiling.

After he had taken his departure, Emerson growled, "Well, Peabody, curse you, I hope you are proud of yourself. You worried the devil out of me—"

"And Gargery," I said. "I am particularly sorry to have worried Gargery."

Emerson ground his teeth, but curiosity overcame his anger. "Did you find anything of interest in Mr. Wilson's rooms?"

"No."

"Would you tell me if you had?"

"Of course, Emerson. You would do the same for me, would you not?"

Emerson's eyes fell. Struggling to conquer my emotions, I said, "I will have cook put dinner up half an hour. You are planning to attend the lecture, I assume?"

"Yes. Will you come?"

I smothered a yawn. "I think not, Emerson. I am a trifle fatigued, and as you know, mummies hold little attraction for me. Run along and enjoy yourself."

Emerson started for the stairs. Then he stopped. "If you change your mind, Amelia, you won't be able to get in. This is not a lecture but a scientific demonstration; it is not open to the general public, and it is by invitation only."

"It is?" Curiosity was throttling me, but I would rather have died than admit it. "Well, you will tell me all about it when you get home."

I waited a full ten minutes after Emerson left before I rang for Gargery and asked him to order the carriage. Emerson had gone on foot; the Royal Society, where the demonstration was to be held, was at Somerset House, not far away.

I had my reasons for using the carriage, and they had nothing to do with the danger or the propriety of a lady walking alone through the darkened London streets. Emerson was up to something. He had not gone to Somerset House to hear Mr. Budge expound on the subject of mummification. He would not have crossed the room to hear Mr. Budge on the subject of mummification. He had, on an early occasion, explained to me why he felt it would be expedient to unwrap the mummy, but I had suspected even then that he had other motives he had not explained. Whatever these might be, I knew he did not want me to go. If he had, he would have forbidden me to attend.

There was another possibility, which I hated to contemplate, but for which I was prepared. Emerson might not mean to attend the lecture. He might go . . . elsewhere. If I did not see him at Somerset House, I would follow him, and . . . I was not sure what I would do. If my suspicions proved to be correct, I refused to be responsible for what I might do.

ELEVEN

The naïveté of the male sex never ceases to amaze me. I thought I knew why Budge had moved up the date of his lecture. He hoped thereby to avoid the attentions of the false priest, his last encounter with that individual having proved embarrassing in the extreme; and perhaps he also hoped to avoid the attentions of Emerson. This was, of course, a vain hope. Emerson was an acknowledged expert on the subject, and he was bound to hear of the changed date from someone, as indeed he had.

If Emerson had been managing the affair—as ought to have been the case—he would have made certain the "priest" did not have a previous engagement. He had not admitted it to me, but it required very little intelligence to deduce that that was one of his reasons for wanting to unwrap the mummy in public and with the greatest possible fanfare. Twice he had failed to capture the rascal; he would be all the more determined to succeed on a third attempt.

If I had not known better, I would have supposed Henry had driven me to the wrong address—Covent Garden on opening night, or a dinner party at a great mansion. Carriage after carriage drew up and discharged its occupants—men in evening dress, women resplendent in silks and jewels. Apparently Budge had invited every titled and prominent person in London to attend his performance. By doing so (vain creature that he was), he had of course negated his original purpose; but I suppose he did not suspect, as I did, that the false priest was quite possibly one of those very aristocrats whose favor he courted.

I made my way through the crowd. I never have any difficulty making my way through a crowd. Much of the credit must go to my ever-useful parasols, of which I possess a good number, in different styles and colors. The one I carried that evening was a formal parasol in rich black taffeta, which matched my evening dress and cloak. It (the parasol) had a silver handle and ruffles trimmed with lace. I particularly liked the ruffles. They gave the implement a giddy, frivolous appearance that masked its true function; for the shaft was of tempered steel and the point was rather sharp.

I had been amused by Emerson's solemn warning that I would not be able to get in without an invitation, for I did not suppose I would have any trouble. In fact, a functionary at the door tried to prevent me from entering, but he yielded to my imperious announcement of my identity, and to my parasol.

Whether Budge had been silly enough to invite the press I did not know, but it would not have mattered; they were certain to find out. Almost the first person I saw was Kevin O'Connell, who stood outside the door of the lecture hall busily scribbling in his pocketbook.

When he recognized me he made an abrupt movement, as if to retreat, but the ruffles reassured him. Remembering he had (or thought he had) some cause for offense, he drew himself up to his full height and looked down his nose at me.

"Good evening, Mrs. Emerson," he said distantly.

I gave him a friendly poke with the parasol. "Now, Kevin, don't sulk. The score is still not even; you have played more tricks on me than I have played on you, and you know perfectly well you would have done the same if you had been in our shoes."

"Hmph," said Kevin.

"You are looking very handsome this evening," I went on. "Evening clothes become you, especially with your Titian hair. Did you hire the suit?"

He tried to maintain his air of offended dignity, but it was not in his nature to hold a grudge. His eyes began to twinkle and his mouth to curve up. "And when were you last in Ireland, Mrs. E.? For it's clear that you have kissed the Blarney stone yourself. No, I did not hire the suit."

"I thought not. It fits you too well."

"Where is the professor? I trust he is not ill."

"No, you don't; you would love to see him prostrate and writhing with pain." Kevin grinned, and I went on, "I was detained. He should have come before me. You haven't seen him?"

"No. But I haven't laid eyes on Mr. Budge, either, and he must be here. I suppose he came in by a private entrance, as the professor may have done. I," said Kevin, with an air of profound disgust, "am taking note of the distinguished guests. This is degenerating into a blooming social event, Mrs. E.; they should have sent Lady Whatworth, who writes the court circular for *The Queen*. 'Tis sorry I am I ever got involved in it, at all, at all."

"Perhaps you miss your rival," I said slyly.

"She added a certain zest," Kevin acknowledged. "But I never expected she would stick; she's given it up, and run home to Granny. They are about to close the doors, Mrs. E. We had better go in."

"I will sit with you, if I may."

Kevin shot me a suspicious look. "What are you up to, Mrs. Emerson? Why aren't you with the professor?"

"Hurry, Kevin, or we won't find a seat."

The hall was filled to capacity. There was an aisle on either side and another running down the center, dividing the rows of chairs. Flaring gas jets illumined the raised stage, on which were several chairs, a long table, a lectern, and a pair of trestles. The press occupied a reserved section in the front left, the choice seats in the center being occupied by the most distinguished of the guests. Kevin's colleagues gallantly made room for me, and we had scarcely seated ourselves when two men carried the coffin onto the stage and placed it carefully on the trestles.

Budge was the next to appear. Taking one of the chairs on the stage, he crossed his legs in an affected manner and pretended to study the papers he had brought with him.

He was followed by several other gentlemen—Sir William Appleby, one of the trustees of the Museum, Mr. Alan Smythe-Jones, a member of the Royal Society, and a stout bald-headed man in evening clothes who I assumed must be the surgeon. There were no Egyptologists present, and Emerson did not appear.

After waiting for anticipation to rise to fever pitch, Budge rose and went to the podium. "My lords, ladies, and gentlemen," he began—and then launched into the same interminable lecture he had given before.

His listeners endured very little of this before showing signs of impatience. They had come to see a mummy being unwrapped; they were not interested in Herodotus or the Book of the Dead. Evidently a few lower-class persons had got past the custodians, for the first voice to be heard over the growing murmur of boredom was unmistakably cockney. "'Ere, chum, let's get the ol' girl's clothes off, eh?"

He was suppressed by his neighbors, but the next interruption was not so easily dealt with. Budge had just mentioned the "bath of liquid natron in which the body of the deceased was submerged for the regulation ninety days," when a voice shouted, "Arrant nonsense, Budge! Why don't you give over the podium to someone who knows what he is talking about?"

My heart, which had slowly been subsiding into my slippers (black patent leather, beaded with gold, steel, and gray and white pearl beads), gave a sudden bound. There was no mistaking that voice! He was present; he had not gone . . . elsewhere. My worst fears were, if not allayed, at least delayed.

A loud murmur of approval from the bored audience forced Budge to stop droning on. Adjusting his spectacles, he peered into the room. He knew who had spoken as well as I did, but he pretended not to.

"If I may continue," he began.

"No, you dunderhead, you may not," the same voice thundered; and Kevin, who had turned to stare, gave a chortle of delight. "It's the professor! Hurrah! This evening may not turn out to be a deadly bore after all."

From the opposite side of the room, about halfway back, a form arose. It was not the stalwart form of my errant but adored husband. It was that of a black-haired child, dressed, I was pained to observe, in an extremely dusty Eton jacket and crumpled collar. With a weird air of levitation this apparition rose briskly into the air. I observed he was perched on his father's shoulders.

Ramses—for indeed, as the reader must have surmised, it was he—called out, "With all due respect, Mr. Budge, you are mistaken. My own experiments have proved what I suspected from the first—"

Budge recovered himself. "Of all the . . . this is the most . . . Sit down, Professor! Be silent, young man! How dare you allow—"

"Let the nipper talk," cried a voice from the back of the room. A burst of approving laughter seconded the speaker, and Emerson made his way to the front of the room. Ramses, as I hardly need mention, was still talking. I could see his lips moving, but his words, and the frantic expostulations of Mr. Budge, were drowned by the laughter from the auditorium.

Beside me, Kevin gurgled with amusement as he made rapid notes.

Facing the audience, Emerson held up an admonishing hand. The noise subsided, and the voice of Ramses became audible. ". . . strong smell of putrefaction, the body tissues discolored and distended and of a pulpy or jellylike consistency. On the other hand, natron in its solid form, with high proportions of sodium carbonate and sodium bicarbonate, produced . . ."

Emerson's handsome face glowed with paternal pride as he listened to his son spouting this accurate but revolting information. I murmured, "Oh, good Gad," not knowing whether to laugh or give way to emotion of another kind. "Ssssh," said Kevin, scribbling frantically.

Budge must have known that nothing short of physical violence could silence Ramses, but his fury was so great I half expected he would rush at the absurd pair with fists flailing. It was not his intervention that ended Ramses' lecture, however. The demonstration was of quite another kind.

Emerson saw the newcomer before I did; he stiffened perceptibly, but before he could move, a piercing shriek from a woman in one of the back rows brought the audience to its feet. The fellow had come in through the main door and was, when I caught sight of him, running down the central aisle toward the stage.

But what was this? He was not in the aisle, he was on the stage . . . No, across the room . . . There were at least six of them, all in white robes and staring masks, all identical. With priests popping up all over the auditorium and running in all directions, the spectators went mad. Screaming and struggling, they fought to escape from the room.

Whatever Emerson had expected, he had not expected this. Lips set, brow furrowed, he swung Ramses off his shoulder and tucked him under one arm.

I had risen with the rest. Parasol poised, I stood firm among the milling journalists, who were trying to go several ways at once. Most of them overtopped me by a head or more; but Emerson's eyes went straight to me and a thrill ran through every limb as I saw the agony in those keen blue orbs, and beheld the painful struggle of opposing desires that held him motionless.

Kevin's arms went round my waist and lifted me off my feet. "Hang on, Mrs. E., I'll get you out of this," he cried.

I lost track of what was happening for a moment as Kevin made his way, not to the nearest exit from the room, which was blocked by fleeing spectators, but to a relatively clear space not far from the stage.

The stage itself was under siege. The masked forms had all converged on the coffin. To my bewildered eyes there seemed to be dozens of them, and the nightmarish effect of those multiplied images can scarcely be imagined. In the thick of the struggle stood Emerson. Only his massive head was visible, for he was entirely surrounded by fluttering, billowing folds of muslin. One grotesque figure reeled back, clutching his midsection, and I caught a glimpse of my heroic spouse striking out with all his might. Without the impediment of Ramses, whom he still held to his side, he might have prevailed. But there were too many for him; he fought alone, the respected guests and Budge having disappeared, I knew not where. He went down under a whirl of draperies and pounding fists. The trestles gave way. The coffin fell with a crash, spilling its grisly contents onto the floor, where it was trampled underfoot.

I pounded on Kevin's arm. "Let me go! Release me at once! I must go to him. Oh, good Gad, I fear the worst—"

Kevin's cheeks were flushed with excitement and his lips had stretched into a ferocious fighting smile. "Begorra!" he bellowed. "That's the spirit, Mrs. E. Let's get 'em, eh? Up the O'Connells!"

"And the Peabodys," I shrieked, brandishing my parasol.

"And the Peabodys! Here we go, then!"

Side by side we fought our way to the stage. In fact, it was not such a desperate struggle after all, for by that time cooler heads (of which there were a few) had prevailed and the tumult had quieted, assisted in no small measure by the presence of several sturdy men with the unmistakable stamp of plain-clothes detectives. The masqueraders had seen them too. By the time we reached the scene of battle, only one warrior was left—my husband. I do not count Ramses, who, pinned by the prostrate form of his mighty sire, was kicking frantically and rending the air with agitated inquiries.

Faced with a journalist's greatest dilemma— several things happening at once—Kevin was at first

uncertain whether to go in pursuit of the masqueraders, as most of his colleagues had done, or to interview Emerson. I would like to think that kindness
as well as journalistic instinct guided his decision.
He assisted Emerson to sit up, despite my protests;
for my medical training warned against such a precipitate move.

"You have a head injury, Emerson," I exclaimed,
pushing against his chest. "Remain prostrate until I
can ascertain—"

Emerson's vigorous response reassured me.
"Hands off, Peabody! Simply because a lot of poor
ignorant Egyptians, who have no other medical
assistance available, allow you to experiment on
them—Oh, curse it! Ramses! Where is Ramses?"

"Here, Papa." Ramses was understandably short
of breath, but otherwise unharmed save for a few
scrapes and bruises. He crawled to Emerson's side.
"I am unable to express in mere words my overpowering sensation of relief at hearing you—"

"Thank you, my son." Emerson pushed away the
dainty handkerchief with which I was endeavoring
to stanch the stream of blood that encrimsoned his
broad brow. "Peabody, if you don't stop that—"

"Here, Professor." Kevin proffered a huge white
kerchief. Emerson bound it around his brow and
rose to his feet.

One of the detectives approached him. "Excuse
me, Professor—"

Emerson fixed him with a furious glare. "Confound it, Orlick, how could you allow this to happen?
I don't suppose you laid hands on him—them—any
one of them?"

The big man shuffled his feet and looked sheepish. "No, sir. Sorry, sir. But you told us to look out for one man. There was only three of us, and the odds was two to one, sir, and then such a hullaballoo broke out . . ."

"Well, at least keep the cursed reporters away from me," Emerson exclaimed, swatting wildly at an undersized man in a brown wide-awake who was plucking at his elbow and bleating, "Professor, what were your sensations when you beheld . . ."

"Yes, sir." The officer removed the reporter. Emerson turned his fiery gaze upon Kevin O'Connell.

"I'll just be taking myself off, then," said the latter quickly. "No need to call the police—"

"You mistake me," Emerson said. "I was about to thank you. By Gad, young man, I do thank you! You sacrificed your chance of a story in order to protect Mrs. Emerson. I won't forget it, Mr. O'Connell. I am in your debt."

"And I," added Ramses. "Shake hands, Mr. O'Connell, and remember that if I am ever in a position to be of use to you, you may count on me."

Kevin struggled to suppress a smile as he looked down at the small but dignified form of Ramses, and took the hand the latter had extended. I would have warned him not to do so if I had been given a chance, but Kevin didn't seem to mind, though his fingers stuck to those of Ramses and were only detached with some difficulty. (I have no idea what the substance was; Ramses was frequently covered, in part or in whole, with something sticky.)

"You haven't lost by your gallantly," Emerson went

on. "I doubt that any of your colleagues succeeded in catching up with the masqueraders."

"Begorra, but it does smack of black magic," Kevin muttered, wiping his hand on his trousers. "All of them, vanished into thin air?"

"The trick is not so difficult," Emerson replied. "We kept overlooking the fact that the masks are flimsy affairs made of paste and paper. Hardened into a shell, they appear solid enough, but a blow with fist or foot would reduce them to scraps. It would take only a few seconds to remove the all-concealing robe, crush the mask underfoot, and mingle with the crowd."

"You were closer to them than anyone else," Kevin said. "And you are a keen observer. You saw nothing that would help to identify one of them?"

"I was otherwise occupied at the time," said Emerson caustically. "And it appears I failed to protect the mummy."

Turning, he surveyed the wreckage on the stage.

Madame Tussaud's had no exhibit more grisly. The wood of which the coffin had been constructed was thin, and dried by century upon century of heat. It had not broken, it had shattered—splintered. Fragments were strewn far and wide; one section of the broken face lay not far away, and the painted black eye seemed to stare right at me. But the worst part of the wreckage was that of the mummy itself. The linen bandages and the bones had suffered the same desiccation that had reduced the wood to a fragile shell. There were indescribable bits and pieces scattered far and wide, some still in the wrappings, some bared in all their brown nakedness. The skull had rolled and come to rest against the foot of a chair. It was covered with brown leathery skin, and the hair that clung to the withered scalp was a pale, reddish yellow.

"May the Lord protect us," Kevin muttered, staring. "An Irishman!"

"The color is due to henna," Ramses explained. "The original shade was white or gray."

"So here is your middle-aged woman, Emerson," I said. "Don't be disheartened; they did not succeed in seizing the mummy."

"They didn't want the cursed mummy," Emerson said. "They did succeed, Peabody. This is what they hoped to do."

"To destroy it? But why, Professor?"

Emerson glanced at Kevin's notebook. "Gratitude has its limits, O'Connell. You'll get no more from me tonight."

I congratulated myself on my foresight in bringing the carriage; it was waiting for us, and we did not have to waste time looking for a cab. Henry, the coachman, almost fell off the box when he saw us approaching, and he hastened to climb down and run to lend a strong arm to Emerson. For once Emerson did not disdain assistance. The blow had left him dizzy and unsteady on his feet.

When we reached the house, which we did in record time, thanks to Henry's inspired driving, I handed my wounded spouse over to Gargery and then knelt down by Ramses.

"I must go to Papa, Ramses. Tell me first if you are hurt, for if you need attention—"

"Papa is in greater need than I, for he took the

brunt of the attack while shielding me from random blows to the best of his ability, which, as you know—"

"Be brief, Ramses, I beg you." I felt of him as I spoke, searching for any sign of broken bones.

"Yes, Mama. The few scrapes and bruises I acquired came when Papa fell on me. They are superficial. I believe I can best serve you by going at once to my room and keeping out of the way, though natural affection insists that I hasten to Papa's side—"

"You were right the first time, Ramses." I rose and took his hand in mine. "I will come to you later, not only to tend your bruises but to reassure you about Papa. I am sure you need not worry; he is weakened by shock and loss of blood, but there appears to be nothing seriously wrong."

I omit Ramses' reply, which contained nothing of importance and continued until we parted at the top of the stairs.

My diagnosis proved to be correct, as it usually did. Natural affection had triumphed over my medical instincts and also over the dark suspicions that had haunted me. To see Emerson weakened and wounded, to smooth the thick dark hair away from the ugly gash in his scalp and wipe the blood from his brown cheek—and feel his lips brush my hand as I worked over him—is it any wonder that for a time I forgot all else except how dear he was to me? And is it any wonder Emerson groaned rather loudly and affected to feel fainter than he really did? We both enjoyed it a great deal, and after I had attended to my other patient and tucked him into his bed, Emerson and I settled down before the fire in a spirit of amity almost as complete as the one that had always united us.

"Now," I said, "explain to me (I can hardly blame you for refusing to do so in front of Kevin, since, as you put it so well, even gratitude has its limits) . . . explain to me, if you please, why the masked men did not want to steal the mummy."

"Gladly, Peabody." Emerson sipped at the brandy which I had strictly forbidden him to take. "I had a number of reasons for wanting to have a look inside that mummy case. I told you some of them; but I also hoped to draw the false priest out of hiding, for I did not suppose he would be able to resist attending the demonstration."

"You certainly succeeded in that," I said with a smile.

"Beyond my wildest dreams! Not one, but six of them! Curse it, Peabody, the fellow has imagination, I must give him that. The coup was brilliantly conceived and brilliantly executed. I did take the precaution of forcing—er—persuading Budge to change the date of his lecture without advance warning—"

"That was your idea, Emerson?"

"Yes. I am sure you understand my reasoning, Peabody."

"Of course, my dear. You expected the unknown would hear of the change of date, but would be forced to act in haste, without time for elaborate preparation. You knew, then, that he intended to destroy, not steal, the mummy?"

"No," Emerson admitted with unusual candor

(loss of blood, and brandy, having presumably lowered his guard). "I felt sure he would do something, and I had a glimmering of an idea—so faint and elusive and mad I couldn't admit it even to myself—that he might want to prevent anyone from opening the coffin."

"And what was your faint, elusive idea?"

"I said I couldn't admit it, Peabody. Even while I was battling those fiends, to keep them from the coffin, I thought they intended to make off with it. But when I saw the fragments . . . You saw them too, Peabody. What is the inevitable conclusion?"

He had been candid with me; I could do no less. "I don't know, Emerson," I murmured. "Tell me."

"Why, obviously, that the mummy had been disturbed and partially unwrapped already. Such a fall would have damaged it extensively; the bones would have been separated, and perhaps broken. But the contents would not have been so widely dispersed and so hideously shattered if the bones had not already been freed from the wrappings."

"Of course," I exclaimed. "Quite right, Emerson. I should have observed it myself, and no doubt I would have, had I not been so concerned about you. Mummies come in various states of disrepair, of course; but I well remember the difficulty you have had in detaching wrappings that were in many cases glued into a solid carapace by the resins applied to the body and the bandages."

"The condition you describe is more common in later mummies," Emerson replied. "But even in other periods, including the one to which this mummy belongs, the extensive amount of linen employed would pad the remains to some extent, so that even if the bones became disarticulated, they would remain within the bandages. There can be no doubt, Peabody; the mummy had been unwrapped. But when? And for what reason?"

It was like old times; sitting side by side before a dying fire, engaged in amiable and fascinating discourse. Musingly I replied, "The mummy might have been disturbed by tomb robbers in ancient times, and then rewrapped. Such cases are known. But you are inclined to suspect, as am I, that the disturbance was much more recent. Obviously this did not occur after the mummy was presented to the Museum. I will question Lord Liverpool tomorrow—"

"Tomorrow," Emerson repeated. "Have you an appointment, Peabody, or are you planning another of your little burglaries?"

His voice had the ominous purring undertone that indicated rising temper.

"Oh," I said, laughing lightly. "I forgot to mention it. Lord Liverpool has invited us to luncheon and to view his collection."

"When did he do that?"

I saw no reason to mention that I had made the first overture. "I received the letter this morning," I replied truthfully.

"This morning. Hmmm. Then it cannot be . . ." But he did not finish the sentence. Instead, he said in a more amiable voice, "Well done, Peabody. Knowing you, I suspect it was your idea, and not

Lord Liverpool's, but it is a good one. I only hope his lordship won't be too put out when he sees I am with you."

I am sure I need not explain to any sensible (that is, female) reader why I woke the following morning absolutely furious with Emerson. Such are the vacillations of the human heart; and I have observed that the farther one goes in one direction, the more violent the swing in the opposite direction will be. In the stress of emotion I had gone quite far the night before.

Emerson, on his part, was preoccupied and distant. At breakfast he hid behind a newspaper, ignoring the eager questions of Percy, who had heard (from Ramses, I assumed) about our most recent adventure. His reiterations of "I say, how exciting!" were a trifle irritating.

"What a handsome pocket knife," I said—for Percy had taken it from his pocket and was fingering it in a manner bound to arouse dire apprehensions in the mother of a male child. "Ramses has one very much like it. His papa gave it to him, on the condition that he must never whittle on the furniture."

"I would never do that, Aunt Amelia," Percy assured me. "My papa gave me this one. Isn't it splendid? See, it has three blades and a fishhook—"

"Very nice, Percy. No, Violet, you have already had two muffins, and that is one too many. Ramses . . ."

But for once Ramses was not doing anything he

should not have been doing. His bruises had blossomed into multicolored splendor overnight, and his face was almost as introspective as his father's.

"Yes, Mama?" said Ramses, with a start.

"Nothing. Emerson, is there anything of interest in the newspapers?"

"No facts we do not already know, Peabody. The *Standard* remarks that lawless outrages of that kind could never occur under a Conservative government, and the *Daily News* observes that it must have been a harmless prank committed by a few high-spirited young gentlemen."

"What a pity you weren't able to catch the fellow, Uncle Radcliffe," said Percy. "This is the second time you've let him get away, isn't it?"

His eyes were as wide and innocent as a baby's.

Mauldy Manor, the ancient seat of the Earls of Liverpool, is on the river near Richmond. I was looking forward to seeing it, since, by all accounts, it was a picturesque and venerable pile whose foundations were rumored to have been laid at the same time as the earliest structures of the Tower of London. Besides architectural distinction, it had the usual claims to historic fame; Charles II had lain concealed there for a night before escaping to Holland (hence the prevalence of the distinctive Stuart features in that area); Edward II had been tortured in one of the dungeons before being removed to Berkeley; and practically everyone connected in any way with the Wars of the Roses had laid siege to the place. (The Earls of Liverpool were notable for their facility in changing sides.) No collection of supernatural tales could be complete without references to Mauldy's proud repertoire: the White Lady, the Black Dog, the Headless Elizabethan Courtier, and the Ghostly Carriage, drawn by skeleton horses.

Emerson was resplendent in frock coat, silk hat, and dark trousers. He had assumed this costume without any urging from me, which made me wonder what he was up to. I had had a little difficulty deciding what to wear. The honor of the Emerson-Peabodys demanded my best frock and parasol, but the good sense of the latter suggested that a more practical costume might be advisable, should I find myself compelled to beat a hasty retreat or defend myself against attack. After all, his lordship was one of my suspects. I could not imagine why he should want to kill Oldacre, or do a number of the other things that had been done, but a suspect he was, nevertheless, and to venture into the ivy-encrusted and moldering recesses of his ancestral castle without my trusty belt might be foolish.

Emerson's decision to accompany me relieved me of my concern on that score and I decided on a frock my dressmaker had just finished. (I have not described my visits to her establishment, since such details are not worthy of inclusion in a journal devoted to scholarly and detective activities, but the Reader must recall that soon after arriving in London I made arrangements for a new wardrobe.) The ensemble, called a visiting dress, was of shell-pink moire with a black, wide belt of morocco leather, and black braid in military designs on the lapels and sleeves. A high collar framed the face with ruffles, and the matching hat was a mere pouf of satin ribbon, satin roses, and satin leaves. Just to be on the safe side, I carried my black-ruffled parasol instead of the matching pink one, whose frame was not quite so stout.

We kept up a rather faltering conversation during the drive. Emerson brooded. His hand was constantly at his chin, stroking it as was his wont when perplexed or troubled, and even my mention of predynastic pottery failed to inspire more than an abstracted mumble of agreement.

Not until we had left the city behind and were traveling through a belt of suburban villas did he rouse himself. "See here, Peabody," he began, in almost his old style, "what are you after? If we don't compare notes before we get there, we may find ourselves at cross-purposes; and in the past that has led us into some embarrassing, not to say dangerous, situations."

"I will be perfectly candid with you, Emerson," I began.

"Ha," said Emerson.

"I have nothing particular in mind."

Emerson worried his chin. "Knowing you as I do, Peabody, I am inclined to believe that statement. In fact, I cannot conceive what you might be looking for. A workshop, where an endless stream of papier-mâché masks are being manufactured?"

"I hardly suppose his lordship would be foolish enough to show me such a place—assuming, of course, that it exists. If there were any way you could keep him occupied while I had a little look round—"

"Put it out of your mind, Amelia. From what I have heard about Mauldy Manor, it would take ten men ten days to explore every crumbling nook and decayed cranny. And if the ushebtis came from his father's collection, he would not leave the empty display case with the label still affixed."

"Well, of course not, Emerson. We will simply have to have our wits about us and keep alert for any interesting development. I have hopes that— supposing his lordship to be the man we are after—he will let something slip in the course of conversation. I am a great believer in allowing people to talk freely and without interruption—"

"You?" said Emerson. "'The clever-tongued, whose speech fails not'?"

I had a feeling it would be a long time before I heard the last of that coincidentally appropriate quotation, but I felt obliged to point out that it had surely been no more than that. "He could not have known we would be in the audience that day, Emerson. Since Henutmehit was a priestess of Isis, the speech was probably designed to be directed to her."

"Hmph," said Emerson.

The sun beamed down upon the grassy pastures of Richmond, and all the loveliness of spring spread out before us—wildflowers in bloom, little lambs frolicking in the fields, birds swinging and singing on blossomy boughs. I could only begin to imagine what Mauldy Manor would look like on a night of fog and rain; for even in sunlight its crumbling towers suggested the worst excesses of Gothic romance, and

the veil of soft green vines that clung to the weath-
ered walls did not soften their grim outlines.

The house was a typical hodgepodge of architectural styles, one wing being of stone and another of
brick and timber in the Tudor manner. Only one
wing appeared to be inhabited, and it was to the
door of this, a relatively modern eighteenth-century
structure, that the carriage drive led. As we descended from the brougham, a servant emerged to
greet us and to direct the coachman around to the
back.

I have seen more prepossessing countenances
than that of the butler, but his manner was perfectly
correct as he took Emerson's hat and stick and tried
to take my parasol, which I of course did not allow.
He then showed us into a pretty drawing room
which had wide windows opening onto a stretch of
lawn and a rose garden, whose bushes were leafing
out, but which as yet bore no flowers.

My scheme for getting his lordship to talk would
have worked well, if he had anything pertinent to say.
I would scarcely have recognized him as the limp,
lethargic young man we had met at the Museum. He
still looked ill. The bloom of spurious health on his
cheeks was the bloom of cosmetics, and he was skel-
etally thin. But the animation with which he greeted
us, the vigor with which he sprang up from his chair,
the frenetic energy of his conversation—all this was
as different as night and day from that of his earlier
persona.

He introduced the other guests—our acquaintance, Lord St. John, and a young man named Barnes,
who was notable primarily for the prominence of his

teeth and who never spoke a complete sentence, though he nodded and smiled incessantly.

Lord St. John bowed over my hand. "How brave of you to venture out today, Mrs. Emerson. We were afraid you might be overcome by your dreadful experience last night."

I glanced at the newspapers on a nearby table—a little piece of untidiness that looked significantly out of place in an otherwise neatly ordered room.

"I take it you were unable to attend, Lord St. John."

"Unfortunately I did not learn in time of the change in the date," said his lordship smoothly. "I was otherwise engaged. But I don't know that I would have chosen to attend in any case. There is to me something distasteful and unaesthetic about exposing human remains in that fashion."

Lord Liverpool gave one of his high-pitched giggles. "What a stuffy old moralist you are becoming, Jack. It was for a good purpose, wasn't it, ma'am? Advancement of learning and all that sort of thing."

"That was the intention," I agreed. "As you have no doubt read in the newspapers, matters did not work out that way. It is a pity you were not there, gentlemen; you might have been able to assist my husband, who was unable—despite efforts that would have been impossible for most men—to protect the specimen."

"Ah, yes," murmured Lord St. John, glancing at the square of plaster that adorned Emerson's brow. "It is a great relief to your friends, Professor—among whom I hope we may count ourselves—to see you took no serious injury. I had intended to ask Mrs. Emerson about you."

"Very kind, I'm sure," said Emerson, settling himself squarely in the exact center of the sofa. "I don't suppose you expected to see me. I was not invited. But here I am."

"And we are delighted to see you," said Lord St. John.

The Earl giggled.

We were served an excellent luncheon, of which our host ate almost nothing, though he imbibed a considerable quantity of wine and talked constantly. A question of mine concerning the history of the house prompted his burst of volubility, and I was surprised to find the idle, uneducated young man so well informed and so intensely interested. His monologue continued through three courses, recounting tales I had heard and others I had not.

Queen Elizabeth had slept in the Great Bedchamber and had been entertained with a masque, a moonlight hunt, and the usual orations. The Headless Courtier was a souvenir of this visit; according to Lord Liverpool, he had been discovered by the then-Earl in the bedchamber of the queen, in the very act of forcing his attentions upon her. She had certainly screamed loudly enough—but not until after the Earl entered. Guilty or innocent, the would-be ravisher had gone to the block like a gentleman, without betraying his queen; so one could hardly blame him for venting his annoyance on the descendants of the man who had been the cause of his untimely demise.

"Shame on you, Ned," said Lord St. John, laughing. "That is not a fit story for a lady like Mrs. Emerson."

I assured him I was not at all offended. "I do not greatly admire Elizabeth. She seems to me to have exhibited all the ruthless cruelty of her Tudor ancestry, but in a typically female fashion. I have no doubt the poor headless gentleman was innocent—of that offense, at any rate."

"The solution to the mystery is beyond even your powers," said Lord St. John with a whimsical smile. "So long ago as that—"

"No mystery is insoluble, Lord St. John," I replied coolly. "It is simply a question of how much time and effort one is willing to spend."

Lord St. John raised his glass in mute capitulation. His slight, twisted smile might have been viewed by some as decidedly sinister.

As the Earl continued his narrative, I began to understand his mood. It was pride of lineage that inspired him; his eyes shone and his thin cheeks glowed with febrile color when he spoke of the long unbroken line of gallant men and handsome ladies who were his ancestors. (History has a kindly way of glossing over little faults like brigandage, slaughter, piracy, and assaults on women, especially when the perpetrators possess titles and landed estates.)

I did not remark on this, as I might ordinarily have done, for it was only too apparent that the miserable youth could not admit, even to himself, that he was the last of his line. Firmly, and yet with a strange air of defiance, he spoke of marrying, and of holding in his arms a son who would inherit his name and titles. A feeling akin to pain stole over me as I listened. This boy would never live to see his son. Even if he succeeded in begetting an heir, the child and its unhappy mother would be infected with the same disease that was slowly killing him. Lord St. John, who was across the table from me, seemed similarly affected; his face had lost its mocking smile, and when Liverpool mentioned a certain young lady as one who might be worthy of the honor of becoming the Countess of Liverpool, St. John bit his lip with such vigor that a line of crimson droplets sprang up.

It was not difficult for me to persuade Lord Liverpool to show us round the house, whose appointments and design I praised extravagantly, to his obvious pleasure. Only the eighteenth-century wing was in use; but the Queen's Bedchamber had been preserved in all its state, although the draperies hung in tatters and an agitated rustling betrayed the residence of mice in the mattress.

At the end of the Long Gallery in the Tudor wing—which was filled with paintings of dubious merit but undoubted age—I noticed a heavy door whose massive dark oak timbers and heavy hinges spoke of venerable antiquity. In my impetuous fashion I tried the handle. "It is locked," I exclaimed. "Are the treasure rooms and the dungeons there, your lordship? Will I see skeletons hanging from rusting chains, and horrid implements of torture?"

My little joke eluded Lord Liverpool. He stood

staring in apparent consternation; but Lord St. John burst into a peal of laughter.

"That would be quite to your taste, would it not, Mrs. Emerson? I fear the skeletons are in the closets, not in the dungeons. That door leads to the oldest part of the house, but it has been shut up for many years. You wouldn't want to go there. It is full of cobwebs, mice, even a few bats."

"Bats do not bother me in the slightest," I assured him. "The pyramids and tombs of Egypt are infested with the creatures and I am quite accustomed to them."

"Ah, but the rotted floors and fallen plaster would bother you," Lord St. John said. "Isn't that right, Ned?"

"Oh. Oh yes, quite right. Wouldn't want you spraining one of those pretty ankles, Mrs. Emerson. Er—hope you don't mind my saying that, Professor?"

"Not at all," Emerson purred. "Mrs. Emerson does have nicely turned ankles. I am gratified you should take notice of them, your lordship."

I hastily drew Emerson away.

He had said very little thus far, but he came into his own when we inspected the late Earl's collection of antiquities. Nothing aroused his passion so much as the wanton looting and dispersal of antiquities that had prevailed in the earlier period of Egyptian exploration and that was still going on, despite the efforts of the Antiquities Department to stop it.

"He ought to have been hanged," Emerson exclaimed, referring to the late Earl. "He and all his peers! Look at this, Peabody—Old Kingdom for a certainty, similar in style to the mastabas of Ti and Mereruka—stolen from God knows where—"

The object to which he referred in such vigorous terms was a limestone block covered with exquisite low relief. It depicted part of a scene of hunting in the marshes. The central figure was that of a cat with a fish in its mouth, rendered with a playful affection and detailed refinement that placed it high among the ranks of artistic masterpieces. The ancients trained these animals to assist them in the hunt. This one wore a collar, and its resemblance to the cat Bastet was astonishing—or perhaps not so astonishing, since she was a descendant of the same line. Perhaps a descendant of this very cat? An amusing and fascinating speculation . . .

His lordship was more entertained than offended by Emerson's criticism. "Yes, the old boy was a robber, all right. But see here, Professor, everybody did it."

Seeing that Emerson was about to make an angry remark, I intervened, for it was not in our best interests to annoy the young man. "It is certainly not Lord Liverpool's fault, Emerson. What a lovely piece! We brought a cat back with us from Egypt one year, your lordship; this is the very image of Bastet."

"Is that so, ma'am?"

"Ned," said Lord St. John in a flat expressionless voice, "is very fond of cats."

"Oh yes, yes. Love the little creatures. Stables are full of 'em," Lord Liverpool added somewhat vaguely.

There was nothing else in the collection to rival

the limestone relief, though of course Emerson fussed and fumed over every scarab. The Earl then indicated a door at the far end of the room.

"The poor old mummy's next-to-the-last resting place," he said with a grin. "Not much left there now she's gone; I mean to turn the room into a sitting room one day—after I marry."

I opened the door and looked in. "Ah, most interesting. It was from this chamber that cries and groans were heard on the night of the full moon, and bric-a-brac broke of its own accord."

Lord Liverpool laughed, throwing his head back. The tendons in his thin neck stood out like strings. "A fetching tale, wasn't it? The girl was let go—not by me, I don't deal with such things—by the housekeeper—said she was lazy. Can't blame the little baggage for making a few shillings off us."

I marked the unevenness of his speech, and the fading of the color in his face, and glanced at Emerson. He nodded slightly. After making a cursory tour of the room which, as his lordship had said, contained nothing of interest except a fine set of canopic jars, with the lids carved like the heads of the mortuary deities, we thanked him and took our leave.

An involuntary sigh escaped my lips as the carriage rolled smoothly down the graveled drive. "Tired, Peabody?" Emerson asked, tossing his hat onto the seat and loosening his cravat.

"Not so much physically tired as inexpressibly sad, Emerson. How oppressive is the atmosphere of that house!"

"Don't spout Gothic nonsense," Emerson grumbled. "The inhabited part of the house is bright, modern, well-kept . . . Peabody, I told you not to touch any of the furniture in the Elizabethan room; you have got soot or grease on your hands."

"It is oil, I believe," I remarked, wiping my fingers on my handkerchief. "But I was not speaking of the house, Emerson; I was referring to its owner. Whatever his failings, it is tragic to see a young man facing inevitable, imminent death."

"The disease has already attacked his brain," Emerson muttered. "You observed the characteristic excitability. He could have homicidal fits, Peabody."

"I did not get that impression, Emerson."

"Impressions don't count for a jot. You are softening toward the young rascal because he is ill, and because he says he likes cats."

"It is an engaging quality, Emerson."

"That depends," said Emerson darkly, "on *how* he likes them."

TWELVE

Henry stopped the carriage in front of the house to let us out before going on around to the mews. As we descended, Emerson turned and shook his fist. "Hi, there, you little rascal! Don't try that again; you'll break a leg."

"I trust you were not speaking to me," I remarked playfully.

Emerson gestured at a ragged urchin who was retreating at full speed. "Another of those street arabs. They will hang on to the backs of carriages and cabs; it's a dangerous trick."

The wretched child—who had now disappeared from sight—aroused uncomfortable memories. "We had better go up and see what Ramses has been doing."

"That was not Ramses, Amelia. How could it be?"

"I didn't say it was. I only said I wanted to see what Ramses has been up to."

When Gargery admitted us, he was so puffed up with news he could hardly wait to take our things before telling it. "You've had a number of callers, sir and madam. That journalist has been twice—"

"Mr. O'Connell?"

"I believe that is his name, madam," said Gargery, his nose in the air. "He seemed in a state of some agitation, and said he would return later."

"If he hopes to presume on my good nature," Emerson began angrily.

"He would not be so foolish, Emerson. Who else, Gargery?"

"A young gentleman from the Museum, madam. A Mr. Wilson. Here is his card. He also said he would call again later in the hope of finding you in. Then this letter was hand-delivered; it appears to be of some importance."

My heart gave a great leap. Ayesha had said I would know her messenger. Well, I had not been there to see him. The envelope was conventional enough, of heavy, expensive, cream-colored linen, bearing my name in a flowing (obviously female) hand.

I ripped it open, trying to appear casual and at the same time prevent Emerson (who was breathing heavily into my left ear) from seeing the contents. It was an invitation to tea on Thursday from a friend of Evelyn's.

"Curse it," I said involuntarily.

"Were you expecting some particular message?" Emerson inquired pointedly.

"Er—no, of course not. I wonder what Mr. O'Connell wants?"

Gargery had not finished. "Professor, someone called for you."

"Who was it?" Emerson asked.

"He left no name, Professor. But he seemed quite put out—rudely so—to find you were not at home."

The pronoun did not relieve me. A messenger from Ayesha could be male or female.

"Oh, did he," said Emerson, bristling. "What sort of person was this scoundrel?"

"An unmannerly, arrogant sort of scoundrel, sir," Gargery replied. "And a foreigner to boot. He had a pronounced accent—"

A stifled exclamation burst from my lips. Emerson gave me a curious look. "What sort of accent, Gargery?"

"I don't know, sir. He wore a turban, sir. I took him for an Indian."

"Do we know any Indians, Peabody?" Emerson asked.

"I don't think so, Emerson." But we knew a good many Egyptians; and they also wore the turban.

"He said he would call again," Gargery volunteered.

"Hmph," said Emerson. "Well, Amelia, it appears we are about to be deluged by visitors, curse them. If you want to speak with Ramses, you had better do it now."

"It is almost time for tea," I replied, glancing at the watch pinned to my lapel. "Tell them to bring it in, Gargery, and ask the children to come down."

Emerson went upstairs to change out of the despised frock coat, and I proceeded to the drawing room. I was looking through the afternoon post when the children entered, and after greeting them, I remarked to Percy, "It is strange we haven't heard anything from your mama, Percy. Not that I wish to alarm you—for I am sure there is no cause—but perhaps I ought to write to her. Have you the address?"

"No, Aunt Amelia, I haven't. It was somewhere in Bavaria," Percy added helpfully.

"I see. Hmmm. Ramses, would you mind sitting over there, across the room? I congratulate you on washing your face and your hands, but the aroma of chemicals that clings to your clothing . . . What experiments are you working on?"

"Just my usual experiments, Mama."

"Nasty," muttered Violet, reaching for a muffin.

Gargery appeared at the door. "Mr. O'Connor is here, madam."

"O'Connell," I corrected, knowing full well Gargery had deliberately mistaken the name. "Show him in, then. And tell the professor to hurry."

O'Connell came in with his usual rush, stuffing his cap into his pocket. "What is it now, Kevin?" I asked. "A murder, or another arrest, or what?"

"Nothing so bad as that, Mrs. E. At least I hope it is not." He took the chair I indicated and looked curiously at the children.

"No more muffins, Violet," I said sharply. "And don't pout, or Aunt Amelia will put you on bread and water for a few days. Go over there in the corner and play nicely with your doll."

"I don't want . . ." Violet began.

Percy patted her on her fat curls. "I will play spillikins with you, Violet. If you will excuse us, Aunt Amelia?"

"Quite the little gentleman," said Kevin, as the two went off hand in hand. "And how are you,

Master Ramses? No ill effects after last night, I hope?"

Fearing that Ramses would answer in detail—scratch by scratch and bruise by bruise—I answered for him. "None. Emerson's wound was not so serious as I feared. He should be here . . . Well, Gargery, where is the professor?"

Gargery, who, the Reader may have noted, was not inclined to suppress his feelings or his opinions, made no attempt to conceal his agitation. "He's gone off, Mrs. Emerson. With that Indian."

"What?" I half-rose from my chair. "With no explanation, no word—"

"All he said, madam, was that he was going out and would be back later, and not to worry. But, madam, I can't help worrying, not with all those heathens seemingly after the professor and you, and this fellow was such a haughty, high-handed chap . . ."

"Did you see where they went?" I inquired.

"He had a carriage waiting, madam. A nice turnout it was, with as fine a pair of matched grays as I've ever seen."

"Was there nothing distinctive about the carriage? No armorial bearings or crest?"

"No, madam. Just a plain black brougham—very handsome, and polished to a turn, madam. They drove off in the direction of Pall Mall—"

"Which means nothing," I muttered. Pall Mall leads to Hyde Park and Park Lane . . . and to a million other places.

"No, madam. They were off so fast I didn't have time to send anyone after them—and when I made so bold as to say to the professor that perhaps he ought to take Bob along, or one of the others, he gave a queer kind of laugh and said no one else had been included in the invitation, madam. He was looking . . . queer, madam."

"Afraid, Gargery?"

"Madam!"

"Of course not. Angry?"

"Well . . ."

"You said he laughed."

"But in a queer way, madam."

"Oh, do go away, Gargery," I exclaimed. "If you can't do better than that . . . Now, now, don't be hurt, I know you did your best and I am sure there is no need for concern."

"Thank you, madam," said Gargery mournfully.

After he had gone I looked at Ramses. "Do you know anything about this, Ramses?"

"No, Mama. Which is something of a blow to my pride, since I try always to be *au courant* when the safety of yourself or Papa is involved. One might of course speculate—"

"Do not speculate, Ramses."

"What is all this about, Mrs. E.?" Kevin asked curiously.

I had almost forgotten his presence until that moment. I ought not to have been so indiscreet; but I beg the Reader to say honestly whether she would not have done the same.

"Nothing, I suppose," I replied. "I ought to apologize, Mr. O'Connell, for this interruption prevented you from telling me why you came to see me."

Kevin cleared his throat, crossed his legs, uncrossed

them, and cleared his throat again. "I happened to be passing by—"

"Three times in one day? Dear me, Kevin, I have never seen you so ill at ease, not even when you broke into my house in Kent and knocked my butler down. What on earth can it be this time?"

"It is probably nothing," Kevin began, crossing his legs.

"Stop fidgeting and speak out. I will be the judge of whether it is important."

"Well . . . I wondered whether you had heard anything from Miss Minton."

"She is still at her grandmama's, I believe," I replied, wondering what had prompted the question. Some professional matter, I assumed.

Kevin uncrossed his knees and struck one of them with his clenched fist. "No, Mrs. E., she is not. No one has seen her or heard from her for almost a week."

"Impossible. How do you know she isn't there?"

"A friend—a person—a friend—wrote to her. A letter came back saying she was in London, and giving the address you know. But her landlady says she has not been there since Friday."

The door opened. "Mr. Wilson to see you, madam," Gargery announced.

"What the—what is he doing here?" Kevin demanded.

"I don't know. Perhaps he is paying a social call. Some people do that, you know. Ah, Mr. Wilson, how nice to see you. You know Mr. O'Connell, I believe."

Wilson nodded distantly at Kevin, who did not

respond with even that minimal show of courtesy. He took a chair.

"I stopped by to ask how you are feeling, after that dreadful business last night," he began. "And to inquire after the professor, who, I understand, was injured."

"That was kind of you. As you see, I am undamaged, and the professor is . . . The professor is well. I didn't see you there, Mr. Wilson."

"I was in the wings, so to speak," was the smiling reply.

"Well, I am glad you weren't hurt in the melee."

Wilson raised his hand to his brow and brushed his hair back, displaying a purpling bruise.

"I did encounter the priest—one of them. You see the result."

I made noises expressive of regret and concern. Then Kevin, whose fidgeting had assumed the proportions of an epileptic attack, sprang to his feet. "It's back to me job I must go," he announced, in the vilest brogue I had yet heard from him. "Wishing you good day, Mrs. Emerson—"

"No, sit down, Mr. O'Connell. I assure you I have not forgotten you or your inquiry. Let us ask Mr. Wilson if he knows anything, since he is a friend of Miss Minton's."

"Something about Miss Minton?" Wilson asked. "What is the trouble?"

"She has disappeared," I said gravely. "At least I hope it is not as serious as that; but apparently no one has laid eyes on her since Friday."

"She is visiting the Dowager Duchess, her grandmother," said Wilson.

His calm infuriated Kevin. "Begorra, but she is not. The old lady hasn't seen a hair of her, and neither has anyone else."

Wilson stiffened. "I fancy she would not like casual acquaintances speculating on her whereabouts," he said coldly. "She has many friends; a wealthy young lady like that—"

"Och, don't be more of a fool than you can help, man," cried O'Connell. "I only found it out lately, but you, being such a particular friend of hers, must have known—she hasn't a penny. The old Duchess is living on pride and pretense, keeping up appearances and subsisting on radishes and carrots she raises in the castle courtyard!"

Wilson was as surprised as I. His jaw dropped. "That—that is impossible," he sputtered. "She obtained her position on the *Mirror*—"

"Through her own abilities." Kevin spat the words between his teeth. He appeared to be on the verge of striking young Wilson, but I knew—for I know the human heart—that his anger was directed against himself. "There was influence, surely, the old lady trading on past friendships, but, but . . . May the devil curse my tongue and may it wither and drop out for the things I said! She's a poor wage earner, like meself, and where would she go—alone, with not a spare shilling in her little pockets, then . . ."

He shoved his clenched fists into his pockets and turned away.

Wilson had gone dead white. "But . . . if this is true . . ."

"It's true," said Kevin, without turning.

"But . . . but Mr. O'Connell is right . . . When one thinks of the dreadful things that can happen to a young woman like that . . . in this vile city . . ."

Dedicated student of human nature that I am, I had followed the dialogue with considerable interest. Poor Emerson, he would be so annoyed when he learned that the "cursed romantic interest" he deplored was a feature of this case . . . Poor Emerson indeed. If he had gone where I suspected he had gone, he would have cause to rue the day.

But this was not the time to yield to those emotions; I had another little matter to settle first. Both young men appeared desperately distressed and I did not want to prolong their anguish any longer than was absolutely necessary. On the other hand, I did not want to make a dogmatic pronouncement when there was a possibility, however slight, that I might be mistaken.

"I think I know where Miss Minton might be," I said.

Kevin whirled around. Wilson rose impetuously. In chorus they cried, "Where? What? Why—"

"I said I thought I knew. If I am correct (and I usually am), there is absolutely no cause for concern—on your parts, at least. As for Miss Minton herself . . . You had better run along now and let me pursue my investigation."

They were not to be got rid of so easily, but I quelled their questions and pleas with a firm hand. "Neither of you is in a position to demand that I betray Miss Minton's confidence. Were either of you married or affianced to her, I might admit such a claim, but you are not, and therefore I decline to answer. I promise I will send round to you (both of you) the moment I confirm my theory. The sooner you leave, the sooner I can begin to investigate."

I got them out the door, at any rate, and I did not wait to see whether they went any farther. I turned to Ramses, who had followed me into the hall.

"I have a feeling you share my suspicions, Ramses."

"Mine are not suspicions, Mama," said Ramses. "I am certain—"

"I see. I don't know whether to commend you for finally learning to hold your tongue, or punish you for not telling me at once."

"I only learned of it yesterday," Ramses explained. "She has been careful to keep out of the way; and the change in her appearance—"

"And the fact that people pay so little attention to the servants. Except your father . . . But he is strangely obtuse about such things, you recall how long Miss Debenham deceived him."

Gargery, who had been listening in bewildered silence, began, "May I ask, madam—"

"It will all be explained at the proper time, Gargery. Please return to the drawing room and tell the children to go to their rooms. I expect Violet has eaten every scrap of food on the tea table by now."

(And indeed, as it proved, she had.)

I found the housemaid in my room mending the fire. She rose to her feet with a murmured apology when I entered; face averted, she picked up the coal bucket and edged toward the door.

"The jig is up, Miss Minton," I said. "Drop that bucket instantly and turn around."

The bucket tipped, spilling coals onto the carpet. "Never mind that," I said, as she knelt to retrieve them. "Of all the contemptible, shameless tricks ever perpetrated on me by a member of the press (and I include Kevin O'Connell, who is no slouch at shamelessness), this is the worst. You never put my advertisement in the newspaper, did you?"

Slowly Miss Minton rose to her feet. In her black frock, ruffled apron, and neat cap, she made a pretty little maidservant, but I wondered how I could have been so dense, even with the attempts she had made to alter her features. It was more a change of expression—downcast eyes, drooping lips, and lowered chin—than of feature, and it made me realize how cruelly wide is the chasm between the social classes in our society.

After a moment her head came up and her shoulders straightened. She tried to look ashamed, but there was a wicked sparkle in her black eyes and a defiant set to her chin. "I'm glad you found me out," she said. "You have no idea how frustrating it has been! Once in, I could not get out. Your housekeeper, you will be glad to hear, watches over the female servants like a motherly hawk."

"Impertinent girl!" I exclaimed. "What! Not one word of apology or regret?"

"I do apologize. I cannot honestly say I regret what I did—except that I was unable to make good use of my opportunities. I had not a moment to myself; instead of writing the stories and seeing them appear under my name, I was forced to get the information out by whatever means I could, and let someone else take the credit."

"I see. So it was not a coincidence, then, that the police raided the opium den while the professor and I were there, and that the press had been notified in advance."

"That was my greatest success," said the shameless female proudly. "We were about to sit down to supper, in the servants' hall, when Gargery came rushing in, so excited by your talk of opium dens that he couldn't keep the news to himself. I pretended to have a headache and asked permission to step outside for a breath of air. I hoped, of course, to find someone who would take the note I had written to the editor of my newspaper. A little street arab was hanging about, and I paid him to carry my message. But I overheard a number of other things I was unable to act upon."

I tried to remember what Emerson and I had discussed when she was present; but again the abominable habit of treating servants like pieces of furniture got in my way. I had paid so little attention to her . . . One thing stood out, however, and if I had been in the habit of blushing, which I am not, I might have done so.

"I don't know what Emerson is going to say," I murmured.

Miss Minton's mischievous smile vanished. She clasped her hands. "Oh, must you tell the professor?"

"I don't see why I should not. Marriage, Miss Minton, necessitates straightforward and absolutely honest behavior between . . . But this is not the proper time for such a discussion. I must say, I am annoyed that you seem to care more for his opinion than for mine. Emerson does have that effect on susceptible females; he cannot help it . . . Sometimes he cannot help it."

"You don't understand." The rosy color in her cheeks deepened, but she met my eyes steadily. "Listening to the exchanges between you—being privileged to hear, if not actually to behold, the intercourse of two minds so utterly in harmony . . . Mrs. Emerson, it has given me a new idea altogether of what a man can be—of what a woman may expect he *should* be. His humor, his kindness, his strength and tender care . . ."

I was relieved to learn she had not actually beheld the intercourse of two such minds. The master thinks he commands the servant, but the servant knows—more than he should. Yet my righteous indignation lessened as I listened, and when her voice faltered and broke, I felt a deep, if unwilling, sympathy. It was clear to me now why she had stayed on after it became apparent her ruse had backfired. How well could I, of all women, understand the spell Emerson casts on a woman with the intelligence to appreciate him! And I rather suspected that in addition to appreciating his humor and his kindness, she had not been blind to his blue eyes and raven hair and his admirable musculature, of which she had probably seen a good deal more than she should.

It was she who broke the deep reverie into which we had both fallen, contemplating, I have no doubt, the same object. "I will go," she said. "I beg, madam, to give notice. Will half an hour be too long?"

"You may not leave your post, you are dismissed," I said. "And without a character. Take half an hour or an hour, but leave my house. I will make some explanation to Mrs. Watson."

"Yes, madam," she said, biting off each syllable. Well, I could hardly blame her for disliking me, who possessed (as she believed) all rights to the object of her adoration. I, who knew only too well the bitter pain of jealousy!

But as she started to go out the door I remembered what Kevin had told me. She had a room in London, but she might not have the money for cab fare or for food. I could not send the girl out of the house, at night, without a penny in her pocket. And there were other considerations.

"Wait," I said. "I have changed my mind. You will stay here tonight—still in your capacity of housemaid, of course. No, don't argue, I will admit no discussion. In the morning you may go where you like and do what you like. Unless, that is, you would prefer to let one of your admirers, who are probably pacing up and down in the square, take charge of you."

"What did you say?" She turned to stare. "Admirers? I have no—"

"Perhaps the word was ill advised. But there are certainly two young gentlemen anxiously awaiting the word I promised to give them—word of your safety, Miss Minton. It was cruel and thoughtless of you to leave your friends in doubt as to what had happened to you."

"I have no friends," she said wildly. "Only rivals. And there is no man I know whose protection I would accept."

Except one, I thought. And he would give it, too,

even after the treacherous trick you played on him. But not the sort of protection you would want, Miss Minton.

"Suit yourself," I said.

"I will leave first thing in the morning, madam. With your permission, madam." But she did not wait for permission, and she slammed the door in a fashion that would have made Mrs. Watson dismiss her on the spot.

After she had gone I began pacing briskly up and down the room, an exercise I find conducive to ratiocination. Accustomed as I am to dealing quickly and decisively with events as they occur, the startling developments of the past hour had taxed my resources to their limits.

I had suspected Mr. Wilson was in love with the young lady, but even my talents, which are particularly refined in that area, had been deceived by O'Connell's pretense of indifference. Yet—I consoled myself—perhaps he had only learned recently to love her, when fear for her safety awakened sensations slumbering deep in his breast. I could not be blamed for failing to perceive something he had not been aware of himself.

The additional complication of Miss Minton's *tendresse* for Emerson was of no importance. He did not reciprocate her feelings, and I would make certain he never did.

Of overpowering importance was the mystery of Emerson's strange caller. What possible message, what appeal or threat could have drawn him out of the house without so much as a word to me? One answer was painfully evident, but it might not be the right one. I hardly knew whether to hope I was wrong—for in that case my estimable spouse might be facing some unknown peril alone—or to hope I was right.

There was nothing I could do at the moment but wait until he returned. But what if he did not? What if the slow hours dragged by with no word? Knowing myself as I did, I knew I would not be able to sit for long with folded hands.

I would deal with that, I decided, when the time came. In the meantime, there were the two young men to be dealt with. I had promised to relieve their anxiety, and Amelia P. Emerson always keeps her word, even when her heart is elsewhere.

Gargery was in the hall, peering out the window. "It is too early to expect him back," I said, with mingled exasperation and sympathy. "He has been gone less than an hour. Open the door, Gargery, if you please."

He did as I asked, but reluctantly. "Madam, don't you go off and disappear, too. The professor would never forgive me—"

"I am only going across the street." For they were there, as I had expected they would be; O'Connell was pacing up and down, but Mr. Wilson stood motionless staring at the house.

"Please, madam, don't—"

I patted his arm. "You can stand in the door and watch me the entire time, Gargery. I only want to say a few words to those gentlemen; I will come straight back."

It was not necessary for me to cross the pavement.

As soon as I appeared, both hurried to the gate, and it was there that our conversation took place.

"My surmise was correct," I informed them. "Miss Minton is and has been perfectly safe."

"Your word on it, Mrs. E.?" Kevin asked.

"My word on it. Have I ever misled you, Mr. O'Connell?"

A little smile played around the corners of the young man's lips. "Well . . . I will believe you this time."

"But where is she?" Wilson demanded. "I must speak to her, make certain—"

"I am surprised to see you in such a state of agitation, Mr. Wilson." For indeed he was; he had neglected to remove his hat, which was tilted at a rakish angle, and his hands clutched the rusty iron bars in careless disregard of his elegant gray gloves.

"Forgive me," Wilson muttered. "I don't doubt your word, Mrs. Emerson—"

"You had better not. Miss Minton will be returning to her rooms tomorrow; you can see her then. Go home now, and sleep soundly in the knowledge that she is in no danger."

O'Connell had already turned away, hands in his pockets, shoulders hunched. "Put on your cap, Mr. O'Connell," I called. "The night air is damp."

He acknowledged the suggestion with a wave of his hand, but did not stop—or obey the order, at least not while he was within eyeshot. Mr. Wilson lingered to thank me and apologize again—and again. I cut short his raptures and ordered him to depart.

Instead of returning immediately to the house I remained at the gate. The night air was damp and permeated with the acrid smell of burning coal, but I am sure I need not tell the Reader why I lingered. If there is any among you who has not, on one occasion or another, stood by a window or at a door, watching with bated breath for a returning wanderer—whose heart has not quickened at the sight of every vehicle turning into the street, or any pedestrian whose form bears the slightest resemblance to the one awaited—who has not felt the sickening pain of disappointment when the vehicle passes without stopping and the form is that of another—then I heartily congratulate that individual on the tranquillity of his or her existence.

Gargery stood in the doorway, watching as intently as I. It was a futile exercise, and well I knew it; after a few moments I gave a deep sigh and started to turn.

The shrubbery beside the gate, now fully leaved, swayed as if in a sudden breeze. But there was no wind. The leaves on the bushes opposite hung limp and still. Something that might have been a giant snow white spider crawled out of the enclosing branches. It was not a spider; it was a hand, of leprous pallor and skeletal thinness. And it held a piece of paper.

The moment I took the paper the hand disappeared; a faint rustling sound, which would have been inaudible to anyone who was not straining her ears to hear it, faded into silence as the messenger retreated the same way he had come, crawling in reptilian fashion flat on the ground.

Ayesha had said I would know her messenger. It was hardly likely that anyone else would deliver a letter in such a distinctive fashion.

Gargery had not seen anything unusual. I felt sure he would have shouted or run to me if he had. Concealing the paper in the folds of my skirt, I hastened back to the house and went directly to the library.

The paper had been folded twice but not sealed. There was no superscription on the outside. On the inside was a single line of bizarre symbols.

My blurred vision took an unconscionably long time to focus. The symbols were, as I might have expected, those of hieroglyphic writing, but the signs were clumsily written, as though by someone only superficially acquainted with the graceful picture writing of ancient Egypt, and the spelling—if I may use that word to describe a language which is not primarily alphabetic—was appalling. I had to puzzle over it for some time before I deciphered it. The obelisk was unmistakable—there could be only one such in London—but no Egyptian would have used the phrase "the middle of the night" to refer, as I assumed this did, to midnight. There was only one other group of signs—the walking legs, used as determinatives for verbs descriptive of motion, and a single stroke.

"Come alone?" There could be no other meaning. It was the sort of unoriginal suggestion writers of anonymous messages were always making, especially to people they hoped to lure into a trap. An assignation at midnight, on the Embankment, made by a woman who had no cause to love me and every cause to feel otherwise, might well be such a trap.

I decided to arrive at the rendezvous at half past eleven. When one anticipates an ambush, it is strategically advantageous to be on the spot beforehand.

There are few times in my long and (I am happy to say) adventurous life I recall with less pleasure than that spring evening in London. Anticipation and apprehension warred within my breast, and never have the hours dragged so slowly. I dined alone—though to use that verb would be misleading, for Gargery, in a state of perturbation almost equal to my own, whisked the dishes on and off the table so rapidly I could not have eaten of them even if I had felt like eating, which I did not. When I passed through the hall to the stairs, I saw him at his post by the window. He had pulled the curtains back into a bunch and was creasing them horribly, but I did not have the heart to complain.

I hesitate to record the wild theories that barraged my brain. At one moment I was convinced that the rendezvous could only be a trap out of which I would have to fight my way. The next moment I decided Ayesha had after all admitted the bond between us—the sympathy of one oppressed female for another—and was about to give me the information I desired. There was a third possibility—that she had lured Emerson to her with a plea for help or an offer of . . . of some sort, and that he was being held against his will. Were that the case, the purpose of the meeting was to demand ransom. How I hoped and prayed it might be so!

After the slow passage of approximately a century of time (for so it felt), my musing was interrupted by a knock at the door.

"Who is it?" I called.

"It is I, Mama. May I come in?"

I realized I should have gone to say good night to him, and make sure he was where he was supposed to be. "Yes, Ramses, come in." Then I added, "I was about to come to you. There has been no word from your papa as yet, but I am not at all concerned about him."

Ramses closed the door carefully behind him and stood looking gravely at me. He was already in his nightgown and was, for Ramses, comparatively clean. I wondered if he was aware of the softening impression made on his mother by the angelic whiteness of his flowing gown and the touching sight of his little bare feet (he was supposed to be wearing slippers, but never mind that). The suspicion did not linger; surely not even Ramses could be so depraved as to employ appeals to the tenderest of maternal sentiments in order to allay maternal suspicion.

"I came to say good night, Mama, and to ask . . ." Ramses began.

"So I supposed. Give me a kiss, then, and go to bed. It is late."

"Yes, Mama." Ramses delivered the kiss, which I returned, but slipped away from the arm I had put around him. "I came to ask—"

"I told you, Ramses, your papa is still out. He will come up to kiss you good night when he returns; he always does."

"Yes, Mama. But that was not what I came to ask.

I am only too well aware of Papa's prolonged absence, since I have been listening—"

"You have, have you? What is it, then?"

"I wanted to ask for an advance on my allowance."

The idea of giving Ramses his pocket money on a regular basis had been Emerson's, and I must say it had worked well. The amount was ridiculously high, but, as Emerson pointed out, we were always buying him books and paper and pens and other academic necessities; being obliged to budget his needs would be a useful lesson in management, and would end in costing us no more than we would have given him anyway.

"What, have you spent last week's already? You told Miss Helen you had twelve shillings sixpence, and that was before your papa gave you—"

"I have had unusual expenses," Ramses explained.

"Your mummification experiments, I suppose," I said, grimacing. "Very well; Mama's pocketbook is on the bureau, take what you need."

"Thank you, Mama. And may I say that the confidence you demonstrate in my integrity touches the deepest wells of—"

"Very well, my son, very well." I glanced at my watch. A scant five minutes had passed since I last looked at it. Would the hands never move?

Ramses went straight to the door. "Good night, Mama."

"Good night, my son. Sleep—"

The door closed before I could finish. It was just as well; in my state of nervous excitability I could hardly bear to be in the same room with another person, much less carry on a conversation.

At last the interminable period of waiting was over and I prepared to leave. I had debated at length about what to wear. I decided to assume one of the costumes I had found so convenient on the dig in Egypt—full tweed trousers to the knee, with stout boots below, a loose shirt, and, under all, the new corset I had had specially made to order. Then I took my belt from the bureau and buckled it on; and the familiar clash and jangle of the useful implements attached to it filled me with a sense of confidence and valor. I much regretted the absence of my revolver. I had left it in the care of Abdullah, on account of Emerson's prejudice against having firearms around the house, and his claim that no such precaution was necessary in civilized England. If he had been there, I would have pointed out the fatuous folly of this assumption.

I was vaguely aware of sounds in the distance, but so loud was the beating of my fevered heart, I paid them little heed until the door of the bedroom burst open. How can I describe the sensations that filled every square inch of my anatomy to overflowing when I beheld . . . Emerson. That one word says it all. I cannot describe those sensations and will not attempt to.

After an interval which I will not attempt to describe either, Emerson held me off at arms' length and looked at me inquiringly. "Not that I don't appreciate your ardor, Peabody," he remarked, "but I am at somewhat of a loss to account for it. Has something happened?"

"Has something . . . has . . ." I put both hands in the middle of his chest and shoved as hard as I could. Emerson fell back against the door; his broad grin infuriated me even more. "How dare you ask me that?" I cried, clenching my fists. "How dare you leave this house without a word of explanation, and stay away for hours, missing your dinner and leaving me prostrate with anxiety—"

"That's more like it," remarked Emerson. Folding his arms, he watched me stride up and down, the jingling of my implements providing a musical accompaniment. After a moment he said, "And where were you off to, Peabody? For I presume you were not planning to retire fully dressed and armed to the teeth?"

I came to a sudden stop. How typical of a man, I thought bitterly, to stay away just long enough to rouse the direst of apprehensions—and then turn up in time to foil my plans. If he had stayed away five minutes longer, I would have been out of the house.

"I was going out to look for you," I murmured.

"Were you, Peabody?" He rushed to my side; he enfolded me in his arms. "My darling Peabody . . ."

Life, dear Reader, is sometimes ironic. The very embraces I had encouraged—and which I welcomed, needless to say, for their own sake—proved my undoing. For the cursed paper, which I had placed in my pocket (never mind which one) crackled under the pressure of Emerson's hand. My explanation had pleased and touched him, but it had not wholly allayed his doubts—for Emerson is neither stupid nor gullible. Before I could stop him he had plucked the message from its hiding place and was reading it.

"Whom is this from, Amelia?" he asked quietly.

"Don't you know, Emerson? Cannot you hazard a guess?"

"Not really. None of my acquaintances writes such vile Egyptian." He strove to speak lightly, but the ridges of muscle on his jaws and the quivering of that magnificent indented chin betrayed the struggle he made to keep from bellowing. I turned from him; his steely fingers caught my shoulders and whirled me round to face him.

"You were not going to look for me. How the devil could you? Where, in all this teeming rat cage of a city would you . . ."

"Where do you suppose? Where else? I would have begun my inquires there; fortunately she has saved me the trouble."

"She?" Emerson's grip relaxed. He gave me a look almost of awe. "How could you possibly have known . . ."

"I saw you enter her house, Emerson. Not once, but twice. I was in the park, watching, the second time; did you suppose that silly beard and a basket of fish could hide you from my eyes?"

"Fish!" Emerson exclaimed. "Fish? Fish . . ." Enlightenment dawned; the bunched muscles of cheek and jaw smoothed out, the lowered brows rose. "Ayesha! It is Ayesha of whom you are speaking. Is this note from her?"

"You mean there is another one?" I cried.

Emerson paid no attention. Now it was he who paced up and down uttering broken ejaculations. "Then she is ready to talk. But why would she . . . Midnight, she said. How very trite and conventional . . . Amelia! You weren't going to respond to this ingenuous invitation, were you? You couldn't be such a bumbling blockhead! Oh, curse it, but of course you could. You would!"

"I could, would, and am about to go," I replied, mastering my confusion and indignation. "And I must go at once."

Emerson stopped pacing. "It is a trap, Amelia."

"You can't be certain of that. But if it is, all the more reason why I should arrive early. The strategic advantage—"

"Don't lecture me, damn it!"

"Emerson, please!"

"Excuse me, Peabody." Emerson rubbed his chin. "She's right, of course," he muttered. "And there's no preventing her. Unless."

His eyes moved to my face; the look of calculation in them, and the (I am sure) involuntary flexing of his hands, made me step back a pace.

"Emerson, if you ever lay a hand on me—in the way of restraint, I mean—you will regret it to the end of your days."

"Oh, well, I know that, Peabody," Emerson said querulously. "There are times when I wonder whether it wouldn't be worth it; but when I think of the things you could do—or not do . . . Hadn't we better be going?"

"In a moment. What does that woman mean to you, Emerson? When did you know her? And—"

"Which woman?" Emerson asked, grinning. "Now, Peabody, don't lose your temper, we haven't time for that—or for explanations. I promise you you will get them, in due course—providing, of course, that we survive this evening's adventure, which seems at the moment highly problematic. Shall we take Gargery along, or . . . No, I can see by your expression that the idea does not strike you favorably. We two, then—side by side and back to back, as before."

How could I resist that appeal, or reject the strong brown hand that reached for mine?

Despite Emerson's promise of half a crown to the driver if he made all possible speed, we were later than I had hoped to be, and we were still arguing when the cab reached the foot of Savoy Street, next to Waterloo Bridge. (For this stratagem enabled me to approach the site of the rendezvous from the direction opposite to the one a watcher would expect.)

"She said to come alone," I repeated for the tenth time. "If she sees you are with me, she may not show her face."

Emerson had to admit the logic of this, but the solutions he proposed were either impractical or preposterous. It would have been impossible for him to pass for me, even in a muffling cloak and old-fashioned bonnet. He finally agreed (profanely) to the only sensible method—namely, that he should follow at a distance and try to find a place of concealment near the Needle.

I had persuaded him to forswear the beard. With his collar turned up and his cap pulled low over his forehead, he might pass as a casual vagabond, if the fog was as thick as I hoped it would be (though I have to admit he would never have deceived me, or any other woman whose keenness of vision was strengthened by affection). Unfortunately the night was clear, except for strands of mist that hung over the water.

We watched the cab turn and clatter off. Emerson took my hand.

"You have your parasol, Peabody?"

"As you see," I replied, brandishing it.

A quick and bruising embrace was his only answer. Wordlessly he gestured me to proceed.

From the bridge, which was almost overhead, the rumble and rattle of traffic reached my ears, mingled with the shrieks of locomotives approaching Waterloo Station on the other side of the river. Straight ahead of me stretched the Embankment, lit by incandescent gas globes. They were raised on wrought-iron pedestals and were approximately twenty yards apart; from where I stood they formed a shimmering necklace of light, shaped into a double strand by the reflection in the dark water.

I started walking, keeping as far away from the lights as possible. I was not the only person abroad; after one burly and unkempt male individual paused, with the obvious intention of addressing me, I turned my parasol into a walking stick and hobbled painfully along, feigning feeble old age. Above and to my right shone the glow of light from the busy streets; on my left was the rippling river; and straight ahead, dark against the starry sky, loomed the towering shape of that simplest and most impressive of manmade monuments—the obelisk that had once graced a temple in sunny Egypt. Now it stood beside an alien river, wreathed in chilly mist; and I thought how strange its ambiance would have seemed, had it been capable of sentient feeling.

But this was not the time for philosophical musing, fond as I am of that activity. I put my back against the fence enclosing the obelisk and stood waiting, every sense alert. The veil of curdled mist over the river had thickened and sent drifting tendrils ashore. A lamp some twenty yards away shone brightly on the pavement, but only its farthest fringes touched the side of the monument.

It had lacked thirty minutes to the designated hour when I left Emerson. Knowing how distorted one's sense of time can be under such conditions, I had resigned myself to what would seem a long wait; but I had scarcely taken up my position when a soft hiss made me turn my head sharply to my left.

She was muffled in dark garments. Only the pale glimmer of one hand, holding the draperies tight across her face, betrayed her presence.

"Good evening," I began.

Her hand darted out and covered my mouth. "Hush! Don't speak, listen. There is no time. Go quickly, before he comes."

I pulled the clinging feverish fingers from my lips. "You asked me—"

"Fool! He made me write that note. I hoped you would come before the time, so I could warn you, for I have . . . But never mind that, you must get away. I thought he wanted you for the ceremony, tomorrow night, and that would . . . But he has the other now, she will serve his purpose, and yet when I said good, I will not go to meet the Sitt Hakim, he . . . He means to kill you, there can be no other reason."

She thrust her face close to mine and hurled the incoherent phrases at me like missiles. Her hands pushed and plucked at me, reinforcing her urgent words. Her veil had fallen, and even in the gloom I could see what he had done to her after she tried to defy him.

"Come with me," I urged, trying to capture one of her frantic hands. "Why do you shield a man who threatens you, beats you? Tell me his name. I promise he will never—"

"You don't know him. You don't know what he can do. He has powers . . . Oh, you are a mad, cold Englishwoman, do you not fear death?"

"Not as you fear it," I said. "And yet you took the risk of warning me. Why?"

The fluttering hands quieted; for a moment they lay still upon my breast. "He loves you," she whispered. "Of all the men I knew, he alone . . . And you spoke to me that day in such words . . . Oh, this is madness! Will you go?"

"Not unless you come with me. I will not leave you to face him."

She looked into my eyes. I thought, I truly believed, I had persuaded her. Then her hands released their hold and she glided away.

Impulsively I started to follow; but reason prevailed, and I resumed my place. She had passed out of sight, behind the obelisk; in the darkness and the thickening mist she could easily elude me. If I went after her I might miss my true quarry—the killer himself. Once I had the villain in my power I would have no need of Ayesha, or she of me. (Though I had every intention of pressing my suggestion that she retire to the rural peace and domestic harmony so necessary to a nature like hers.)

A shriek rent the night! It was abruptly cut off, as if a rough hand had compressed the straining vocal cords. It had to be Ayesha who had screamed, it could be no other. Parasol raised, I rushed impetuously in the direction from which the sound had come.

Conceive of my amazement when the first person I saw was Emerson. To be honest, I had almost forgotten about him. He stood in the circle of light cast by the nearest gas globe, and he was staring across the pavement toward the gardens beyond. They lay in deep shadow, but I made out a shape that was neither shrub nor tree—a huge, monstrous shape, hardly human in outline.

"Wait, Peabody," Emerson shouted. "He has a pistol at her head!"

Now that he mentioned it, I saw that the dull gleam of metal was indeed that of a weapon, and deduced that the pale oval next to it must be Ayesha's face. Her black garments blended with the dark clothing of her assailant, who seemed to be wearing an opera cloak and silk hat. His face was completely concealed behind a tight-fitting cloth of the same somber hue.

"Curse it," I exclaimed. "Where are the confounded police? One would suppose—"

A flutter of dark movement and a whimper from Ayesha stopped me. It required no verbal command from the dastardly wretch to warn me that a loud noise or sudden movement would cause him to press the trigger.

Too late, I realized I should have looked before I leaped instead of rushing blindly to the rescue. If I had crept up behind him . . .

Then came another, more abrupt, shift in the shape of darkness. It was hard for me to make out what he was doing; but Ayesha knew. Another scream burst from her, mingling with the sound of a pistol shot. Emerson raised his hand to his head. An expression of profound astonishment crossed his face. Slowly he sank to the ground.

I could not, I dared not, go to him. Emerson might not be slain, only wounded; but the demise of my beloved spouse (not to mention myself) was certain if the killer kept hold of the pistol. Ayesha was struggling with him, clinging to his arm. I rushed to aid her.

The second shot was muffled by her body. She fell like a wounded bird, crumpling at his feet; and as he leveled the pistol to fire again, the shaft of my parasol came down on his forearm.

The pistol fell; the toe of my boot struck it and sent it spinning away into the shrubbery. Emerson was saved! But I was not in such good condition, for the unknown had seized me by the throat. The cruel grip shifted and tightened, cutting off the air to my lungs and the blood to my brain. His hands were gloved; my nails made no impression. I tried to claw at his face, but my arm fell back. My feet dangled, free of the ground. Darkness closed over me. I remember thinking that the confounded police were never around when you needed them . . .

Reader, it came like an answer to prayer—faint and seemingly far away, muted by the pounding of the blood in my deafened ears—the shrill shriek of a police whistle! The hands on my throat loosed their grip. I toppled helpless to the ground, landing on a soft, yielding surface; and as the sight came back to my fogged eyes I found myself staring straight into the dead face of Ayesha.

Shuddering, I scrambled to hands and knees, just in time to see a small dark form dart across the somewhat limited field of my vision. Someone shouted, "'Ere, you little devil, come back then—what the 'ell—Jack, go round the other way, 'ead 'im off . . . Wot's all this, then?"

Rescue had arrived, in the shape of two very large boots. I presumed a constable was attached to them, but I did not pause to investigate. Too weak to rise, I crawled straight to the motionless form of my husband, who lay face down on the graveled path. My strength came back to me when I touched him; frantically I turned him onto his back.

His eyes opened. They saw me. He lived! Thank Heaven, he lived!

"Peabody," he remarked, "this is becoming embarrassing."

THIRTEEN

It need not be supposed that I slept a wink that
night. Huddled by the dying fire or pacing the
length of the room; bending at frequent intervals
over the couch whereon reposed my wounded and
heroic husband, brushing the dark hair from his
brow, or listening in an agony of joyful relief to his
deep and sonorous respiration—so I passed the
hours before dawn. He slept soundly; I had taken
the precaution of adding a soupçon of laudanum to
his cup of tea, since I knew his restless spirit would
never take the repose his body required without it.

Often as I strove to quiet my mind, my thoughts
kept returning to the horrors of that memorable
evening. Images flashed onto the screen of my agitated brain with the vividness of nightmare: the
fixed, staring eyes of Ayesha, who had given her life
for us—one of us, at any rate; the blessed and beautiful scowl of my dear Emerson as he returned to
consciousness and discovered that once again his
quarry had escaped him; the round, red, bewildered
face of the constable who had pursued a thieving
little street arab into Victoria Gardens and found

himself confronting a dead body, a wounded man, and a woman who was in scarce better case, what with agitation and being half strangled . . .

My throat still ached, despite the prompt and efficient medical assistance that had been provided to me and to Emerson. But the pain of that was nothing to the mental anguish that filled me. I had erred. Yes, I—Amelia Peabody Emerson—had failed to pursue the rigorous and logical deductions that are essential to a criminal investigation.

There is some excuse for me, I believe. The events of that exhilarating day had followed one upon the next with such bewildering speed that I had never had the leisure to think them through. Yet I knew that was not the real reason for my failure. Jealousy had blurred my mind; mistrust had prevented me from following the path of reason. How true it is, as the Scripture says, that "jealousy is cruel as the grave; the coals thereof are coals of fire, which hath a most vehement flame."

Once again I hovered over Emerson and pressed my lips to his wounded brow. The physician had been forced to shave a patch of hair before bandaging the furrow that had creased his scalp. One of the glossy black locks reposed even now in my bosom, for I had picked it up from the (rather dirty) floor and vowed I would carry it always, to remind me how close I had come to losing something dearer than life itself. Never again would I doubt him. Never!

After repeating the gesture and the vow a number of times, I discovered I was calm enough to resume ratiocination. I began with Miss Minton's revelations. It was no coincidence that the police should have chosen that hour and that evening to visit that particular opium den. Miss Minton had got the message to a colleague; and he had notified the police. Had he warned them we would be there, or had he used some other device to persuade them to investigate? The more I thought about it, the more I was convinced that the second alternative was the right one. Our presence had gone unnoticed until Emerson announced it with his customary vim and vigor. The fact that the police had been so swift to respond to a suggestion, however cleverly worded, from a member of the press, strongly suggested that they had already been suspicious of Ayesha and her establishment.

The despicable Inspector Cuff had deceived me. He had never believed Ahmet was the murderer. He had put the man under arrest for two reasons: one, to arouse consternation and alarm among his associates, in the hope of provoking a careless move or injudicious statement; and two, because he expected that that well-known informer might disclose useful information under the pressure of police interrogation. What did Cuff know? I did not have the answer, but I was certain of one thing: if Cuff believed the man he was after was an Englishman and a member of the aristocracy, he would proceed with extreme caution. An accusation against such a man would have to be supported by the strongest possible evidence.

That Ayesha had known the truth was confirmed by her own words. "He" had ordered her to lure me into a trap. Her reluctance to carry out the mission of betrayal must have aroused his suspicions and caused him to fear she would betray him instead (as I am convinced she would eventually have done). He had therefore followed her; perhaps he had been close enough to hear her warn me.

The fact that he had been sufficiently alarmed to attack me was encouraging. Less encouraging was the fact that I had no idea what I had said or done to alarm him. Was it possible that my visit to Ayesha had been enough in itself? That did not seem likely. It was, surely, more likely that I had stumbled on some clue whose meaning I had overlooked.

Ayesha had let slip one word during our initial conversation that I had considered significant. She had spoken of an English "lord." I had never used that word. But on reconsideration I was inclined to wonder if it meant to her what it meant to me. As I have said, the Arabic word for "husband"—even the one for "man"—carries that degrading implication, and in the course of her earlier business dealings Ayesha must often have used it to flatter her clients. A man is always ready to believe he is truly the lord and master of all he surveys, especially any women he encounters.

Though it was still far from conclusive, the evidence all pointed in the same direction: namely, that the false priest and the murderer of Oldacre were one and the same, and that he was either Lord Liverpool or his demonic mentor. Both must be involved in the plot, along with others, for there had been at least six masked intruders at the lecture hall.

At this stage the ratiocinative process was broken by a muffled cry from Emerson. I flew to his side.

He had not awakened, but he moved restlessly, turning his head from side to side and groping with his hand. I listened with beating heart to the broken syllables that escaped his lips; and with inexpressible joy recognized them for the syllables of my name.

As soon as I lay down beside him and took his hand in mine, he grew quieter. One last murmur stirred the ambient air. "Curse it, Peabody," he whispered. I drew his dark head to my breast and was about to resume my train of thought when for some unaccountable reason I fell asleep.

Upon waking my first thought was of Emerson. A quick glance into the countenance so near my own reassured me; he was sleeping sweetly. I then heard again the sound that had roused me.

"Ramses," I whispered. "What are you doing there?"

Ramses' head appeared at the foot of the bed. "I was very quiet, Mama. I only wanted to know if you were awake."

"I am now, thank you. But your papa is still sleeping, so—"

Emerson's lips parted. "He is not sleeping."

"Your eyes are closed," I said.

They opened. "What the devil is the time?" Emerson asked.

I pulled myself to a sitting position. I had gone to sleep in my dressing gown, so that was all right. Ramses' round, interested eyes followed my every movement.

Emerson rolled over onto his back. "Urgh," he said. "What the devil is—"

"I don't know, Emerson, I cannot see the clock from here."

"It is ten minutes past two," said Ramses. "I trust you will forgive this intrusion, Mama and Papa, but having learned from Gargery of Papa's most recent brush with death, my anxiety prompted—"

"Two!" Emerson exclaimed. "In the afternoon? It must be, the sun is shining . . . good Gad, Peabody, why did you let me sleep so late?"

My efforts to restrain him were vain; he swung his feet to the floor and headed for the bathroom. After hesitating for a moment Ramses followed him. He liked watching his father shave. He had been strictly forbidden to touch any of Emerson's razors, after once almost cutting his throat while imitating that (in his case unnecessary) procedure.

After ringing the bell I followed them, to discover Ramses sitting on the commode while Emerson splashed cold water on his face. "That's better," he said cheerfully. "What a night, eh, Peabody?"

"It is not better. You have got the bandage wet. Emerson, how often must I tell you—"

Ramses spoke at the same time. "I presume, Papa, that your question refers to your latest encounter with the criminous masquerader. I would be most interested in learning what—"

Before either of us could finish, the bedroom door opened and a positive parade of servants entered— one of the maids carrying a tea tray, another with hot water, Mrs. Watson to supervise their activities, and Gargery . . . well, I knew why Gargery was there. He did not even pretend to have a reasonable excuse.

"How is the professor, madam?" he demanded.

"Fine, fine," Emerson shouted. "Good morning, Gargery. Who else is there? Mrs. Watson? Splendid. I shall want a very large breakfast, Mrs. Watson—or lunch—or whatever meal seems appropriate . . . as soon as possible, eh? Oh—excuse me—er—Susan—" He backed up, to allow the maid (Mary Ann) to put a pitcher of hot water on the table.

Behind Gargery I saw what appeared to be the entire household staff—four footmen, the cook, and three other maids, including the kitchenmaid, who was supposed never to show her face abovestairs. I said resignedly, "As you observe, Gargery—and the rest of you—Professor Emerson is himself again. I hope that now your minds are set at ease, you will return to your duties."

"Oh, Mrs. Emerson," the housekeeper exclaimed. "I am sorry—I don't know what has come over them, they don't usually behave like this—"

"It is quite all right, Mrs. Watson. I have seen it happen before. It is not your fault."

"I beg your pardon, madam," Gargery began.

"Yes, what is it?"

"With all respect, madam, they—and I—would like to inquire about yourself, madam. You sound a little hoarse, madam. Wouldn't you like me to send for the doctor, madam, to have a look at you?"

It took some time to reassure them, but at last they dispersed, after the cook had informed me she knew a fine remedy for sore throats, consisting in part of honey, horehound, and brandy, which she would concoct immediately. I closed the door and sank into a chair. For once, I felt quite incapable of speech.

It would have been impossible to carry on a conversation while Ramses was present anyway. So I sat quietly and drank tea—it hurt a little to swallow, but the hot liquid revived me wonderfully—and listened to the vigorous sounds of Emerson completing his toilette, assisted by admiring comments, questions, and suggestions from Ramses.

Eventually they emerged, arm in arm. Emerson kindly allowed me to change the bandage—it, and his hair, were both soaking wet. I then retired to tidy myself, while Emerson sat down and took Ramses on his knee, and started to tell him all about it.

My timing was excellent. When I came out of the bathroom, I heard Ramses say, "Just who was this unfortunate lady, Papa? And how did it happen that she was fatally injured during the struggle? I understand that you had been rendered unconscious and were as a result unaware of what occurred during the final moments, but from what you have said it is clear that the villain fired first at you and would no doubt have shot Mama next, for if I know Mama, and I am sure I do, she would never run away but would attack your assailant with the utmost energy, and indeed the bruises on her throat make it evident that she closed with him—and he with her—so to speak—"

"I understand what you mean, Ramses," said Emerson. He glanced at me. "Er—did you speak, Peabody?"

"No."

"And no wonder," Emerson exclaimed, putting Ramses aside and jumping to his feet. "My poor dear Peabody, your beautiful swanlike throat resembles a fragment of a Turner painting. It is turning all the colors of the sunset. Where is cook? She spoke of a remedy—"

Ramses trotted toward the bathroom, remarking, "Cold water, constantly applied—"

I caught hold of him. "No, thank you, Ramses, I appreciate your concern, but I don't need you dripping water all over me and the bathroom. Run along now, I want to get dressed."

"Yes, Mama. May I first inquire—"

"Later, Ramses."

Emerson offered to help me dress, but before there was time for anything to develop, Mrs. Watson appeared, to announce that luncheon was ready. Emerson glanced at his watch. "Hmmmmm, yes, time is getting on. Ready, are you, Peabody? Here, take my arm."

"There is first a little matter of buttoning me up the back," I replied. "Perhaps, Mrs. Watson, you would oblige?"

Emerson looked hurt. I pretended not to observe it.

Cook had most considerately prepared a cold luncheon, with a variety of aspics, jellies, and other smooth substances that slid down without discomfort. Emerson ate quickly—with any other man, I would say he gobbled his food—and kept sneaking surreptitious glances at his watch. For once his conversation was as bland and correct as any hostess could desire. "Lovely spring weather, isn't it, my dear? I am making excellent progress with my manuscript; did I remember to thank you, my dear Peabody, for your helpful suggestions? Have you heard from Evelyn and Walter lately? How are Raddie and Johnny and Willy and little Amelia?"

I replied in monosyllables; I was afraid to leave my mouth open too long for fear of what might come out of it. A rational person might suppose my anger and jealousy had been dispelled by the sad death of that unhappy woman who had loved "not wisely but too well"; but oh, Reader, jealousy is not rational. She had died to save him. The gun had been pointing at Emerson, not at her, when she seized the assassin's arm and clung, with the fierce strength of passion, to prevent him from administering the *coup de grace*. She had not struggled to escape, but only to turn the weapon away from the man she adored. Dead and martyred, she was a greater rival than she had been living.

A strangled sound escaped my lips. It might have been a sob; but I rather think it was a smothered cry of fury. Emerson looked anxiously at me. "You had better spend the rest of the day in bed, my dear. Have a nice rest—"

I crumpled my napkin and threw it on the floor. "So you can creep out of the house unbeknownst to me? Where are you going, Emerson? To make arrangements for a fitting funeral and a marble monument? To have the coffin opened, that you may kiss her lips for the last time? Who was that woman, Emerson? What did she mean to you?"

Emerson sat gripping the arms of his chair, eyes bulging and mouth ajar. Gargery's reaction was

more explosive; he dropped the platter he was holding, and the cook's beautiful three-layer jelly collapsed into a rainbow puddle.

"Oh, madam," he gasped.

"Wait a minute," Emerson said. "Peabody, you
take my breath away! You think I . . . You think
she . . . Was that why you . . . Upon my word, Peabody, I assumed you were joking."

"Joking! About a subject so serious as fidelity,
lifelong devotion, trust—"

"Now, just a bloody minute, Peabody," Emerson
exclaimed.

"Oh, madam!" Gargery advanced toward me, his
feet squelching in the ruins of the jelly. "Madam,
the professor would never—he could not—he is utterly devoted, body and soul—"

I took a deep breath. "Emerson," I said, quite
calmly, "I really do not think I can control myself
much longer. I am very fond of Gargery here, and I
appreciate his friendly interest in us, but—"

"Oh, quite, Peabody," said Emerson. "*Pas devant
les domestiques*, eh? At least not this time. Excuse us,
Gargery, there's a good chap. Don't worry, everything is quite all right."

He offered me his arm. I took it. We proceeded,
with measured pace and in perfect dignity, to the
drawing room.

The moment the door closed, Emerson picked me
up in his arms and carried me to the sofa.

"My darling Peabody—" he began.

"Caresses will not avail you in the present instance," I cried, struggling to free myself.

"Oh, no? Peabody, were you really jealous? Were

you? How good of you, my darling. I cannot remember when I have felt so highly complimented."

"Emerson, you are really . . . Emerson, don't do
that. I cannot think clearly when you . . ."

Emerson stopped what he was doing, and assisted
me to sit up. When I sat on his knee, my eyes were
on a level with his. Holding me by the shoulders, he
looked gravely at me. "Have you forgotten, Peabody, what happened last winter in Cairo?"

My eyes fell before his. "No, Emerson. I have not
forgotten."

"I will not insist I had greater cause than you to
feel the pangs of jealousy," Emerson continued seriously. "For that might start one of those amiable little
arguments of ours, which tend to go on and on without ever arriving at a conclusion. I will only repeat
the words you said to me shortly afterward. 'If the
years we have spent together,' you said, 'and the intensity of my devotion, have not convinced you that I
never have, never will, and never could love another,
no words of mine can change your opinion.' I beg to
remind you, Peabody, of that eloquent speech."

I hid my crimson face and trembling lips against
his breast and placed my arms around his neck.

A short time later, when we were sitting side by
side in mutual accord, I remarked, "All the same,
Emerson—and I hope you will take the question in
the spirit in which it is meant, as a simple request
for information—"

Emerson's arm tightened round my shoulders.
"You are incorrigible, Peabody! Not only am I willing to answer the question you are about to ask, I
insist on doing so.

"I don't know what Ayesha told you. She said you had been to visit her, and gave me her version of your conversation; but I place no more credence in that than you ought to place on the accuracy of what she said to you. What I am about to tell you is the simple truth—no more, no less.

"I knew her—yes, my dear Peabody, I admit it—I knew her in every sense of the word. It happened during my first visit to Egypt, not as an archaeologist but as a beardless boy just down from Oxford, and as naïve about the world as poor little Ramses. I do myself the credit, however, of claiming that I soon learned to loathe the way of life to which I was introduced by so-called friends. The degradation of those poor women horrified me. It made me think less of myself and of the men who had condemned them to a life of fawning slavery.

"It was Ayesha who really opened my eyes. She was not like the others. To see a woman like her— intelligent, beautiful, as capable as any man— reduced to such an existence only because she *was* a woman, beautiful, intelligent and capable . . . I believe I offered to take her away from it all, as the saying goes. She laughed at me. It was already too late for her.

"As in your case, my dear Peabody, that first trip to Egypt convinced me I had found my life's work and I threw myself into it with what you are pleased to call my enthusiastic exuberance. From time to time I encountered Ayesha, who was by then one of the most famous (and expensive) practitioners of her profession. A few years later she left Egypt. I heard from mutual acquaintances that she had gone to

Paris with a wealthy admirer, who gave her her own establishment. Her history thereafter was a sad one. Her protector was a man of violent temper. Whether she betrayed him or not I do not know; he claimed she had, and he cast her off, after giving her a beating that scarred her for life. She had saved her money, however, and later I heard that she had moved to London and set herself up in business. But—and this I swear by everything I hold dear, Peabody—I had not set eyes on her for years. I almost dropped in my tracks the other night when I recognized her."

"That is what she told me," I said softly. "Poor thing. Poor, poor woman."

"Peabody." Emerson took me by the chin and looked intently into my eyes. "Did you really offer to help her move to the country and find solace in the beauties of nature?"

"Why, yes. Even then I recognized her quality—Emerson, don't squeeze me so hard. I can't breathe."

"Peabody, Peabody! You are the thirteenth wonder of the world. Was there ever anyone like you?"

"We are all unique in the eyes of Heaven, Emerson," I replied, smoothing my tumbled hair. "But, Emerson—"

"Now what, Peabody?"

"I am thinking of what I said a little while ago—and a cruel, unkind statement it was—about a proper burial and a monument. It is the least we can do, Emerson, don't you agree? She did give her life for yours. Not that I am at all jealous now, and I don't blame you, because you cannot help it if women—"

"Wait a moment, Peabody. I am in full agreement with your suggestion, and I will see to it at once. But giving her life for mine? What nonsense is that?"

I felt he ought to know all that had transpired, so I told him what Ayesha had said, about being forced to lure me into a trap, and what I had said, trying to persuade her to accept our protection.

"I didn't overhear the conversation," he said soberly. "I was too far away, and concerned, besides, with keeping watch. I saw him coming, Peabody, but before I could move, she ran straight into his arms. And after that—"

"He shot you and you fell. Oh, Emerson, I will never forget that moment!"

It was some time before I could continue. Emerson listened without comment while I described what had happened. Then he said thoughtfully, "It will be a very handsome monument, Peabody. And before the stonemason starts work, I will see to it that her killer gets his just deserts. Confound it, Peabody, don't you see? It was not I she fought to save. It was you."

"My dear," I began.

"You are not what I would call a humble woman, Peabody, but you are singularly obtuse about some things. Think it through. I was already down—dead, for all she knew. Upon whom would that murderous weapon have turned next, Peabody? He came there to kill you, and she knew it. She took the risk of warning you, and at the end she fought to the death, not to save me, but to save you. You were the first woman in years—perhaps the first in all her life—to speak to her like an equal and to express concern for her well-being. Nothing in her life became her like the leaving of it."

He pressed me close to him and I felt his breast heave with a long sigh.

It was a touching moment, and I respected his sentiments, so I did not point out the flaws in his logic. If he chose to believe the poor soul had given her life for *mine*, let him enjoy the illusion; I knew better and would always cherish the memory of Ayesha because she had given her life for *his*.

After a moment of respectful silence I remarked, "Emerson, I have only one more question."

"That," said Emerson, "I find hard to believe. Well, my dear?"

"You say you never thought I could be jealous."

"Quite right, Peabody."

"Then why have you been acting so confoundedly peculiar?" I demanded. "If I ever saw guilt writ large upon a human countenance, it was writ upon yours. You have been painfully polite, disgustingly considerate—you never complained when I corrected your manuscript—"

Emerson gave me a hearty hug. "I said you were obtuse, Peabody. Don't you know what was worrying me? Have you not read the inscription on the ushebti?"

"Men-maat-Re Sethos . . . Emerson! Oh, Emerson, you were jealous too!"

"Madly, furiously, desperately," Emerson declared, squeezing me till my ribs creaked. "Well, curse it, Peabody, it is an odd coincidence, to find that abominable name cropping up again, in a criminal case . . . It is only a coincidence—isn't it?"

"Yes, Emerson, it must be. Shall I swear to you, as you were good enough to swear to me, that never—"

"No, Peabody. It is not necessary. I will never doubt you again."

"Oh, my dear Emerson!"

"My darling Peabody!"

After a considerable period of time had passed, I got off his knee and straightened my dress. "You are closer to the bellpull than I am, Emerson. Will you ring for Gargery? It is rather early, but I think we might have a little whiskey and soda, to calm our nerves."

"Splendid idea, Peabody," Emerson declared. "And then what do you say to another of our little competitions in crime? We have enough information now, I believe, to construct a theory or two. I've seen you do it with much less, my dear."

"Thank you, my dear Emerson," I replied, with considerable emotion. "I accept the challenge in the spirit in which it was offered, and in the spirit which always rules us in these situations: May the best person win, devil take the hindmost, and no fair cheating."

"Would you care to begin, my dear Peabody?"

"No, my dear Emerson, I yield to you."

"I expected you would," Emerson remarked. "Oh, there you are, Gargery. Bring the whiskey, if you please."

"And, Gargery," I added, "you will be glad to hear that everything is quite all right, just as the professor said."

"I can see that, madam," said Gargery, beaming. "Not that I ever doubted it would be."

"I tell you what, Peabody," said Emerson, after Gargery had brought the whiskey and departed, still beaming. "We might have Wilkins and Gargery trade places, eh? Wilkins would be much happier in a quiet, well-regulated household like this."

"It is worth considering," I agreed. "Now, Emerson, you were about to begin . . ."

"Yes." Emerson went to the desk and began rummaging around. "Where did I put that confounded . . . ah, here it is."

He handed me a sheet of paper. I glanced at it and burst out laughing.

"Oh, Emerson, how amusing! No, my dear, don't glower, I am not laughing at you, but at another coincidence. There is an almost identical list upstairs in the drawer of my desk."

"Is that so? Well, my dear Peabody, I have often said our minds are as one."

"We seem to agree on the major points," I mused, studying his list. "I see you mention the scraps of glass and paper found by the body of the night watchman. I confess I thought you would miss that, Emerson."

"Oh, you did, did you? What do you make of it, Peabody?"

"I haven't had an opportunity to speak to Mr. Budge," I replied. "My answer depends on how recently the room was swept."

"Oh." Emerson's brows lowered. "Oh, yes. I didn't think of that."

"There was nothing that might not have accumulated in the normal course of events, as a result of the untidy habits of the museum-visiting public."

"Humph," said Emerson, scowling.

"However," I went on, "there is confirmatory evidence of my tentative theory from another source."

"The unwrapped mummy," said Emerson.

"And the speech the priest delivered—the invocation to Isis."

"'Whose speech fails not,'" said Emerson, unable to repress a smile.

"Quite. I see we agree so far, Emerson. Do we also agree that the man we saw last night is not only the murderer of Ayesha but of Mr. Oldacre?"

"Certainly, Peabody. Is he also the false priest?"

"Yes and no, Emerson."

"Curse it, Peabody—"

"That is not the important question, Emerson. The killer is the man who sent the ushebtis and abducted Ramses. But who the devil—that is, who is he really? Which of our suspects is the mastermind behind all this?"

"That seems obvious," said Emerson.

"It does."

"Would you care—"

"Not just yet. We are still lacking one or two vital bits of evidence. Wasn't it you who said it is a capital error to theorize before one has all the facts?"

"No, it wasn't. What evidence do we lack?"

"Well—here is a question you omitted." Taking a pencil, I scribbled a few sentences and handed the paper to him.

Question: "Who is the man in the turban who called on Professor Emerson, and where did they go yesterday?" What to do about it: "Ask Professor Emerson."

Emerson crumpled the paper in his hand. "Confound it, Peabody—"

I held up a hand. "Wait, Emerson. I vowed this

evening never to admit a doubt of your devotion to enter my mind. I do not doubt it. But my dear Emerson, I made no promise about anything else. If you are concealing evidence from me—"

"Have a little more whiskey, Peabody."

"No, thank you, I don't believe I will."

"Then I will," Emerson muttered, suiting the action to the words. "Listen to me, Peabody. I am not concealing evidence. The individual to whom you referred knows nothing, and told me nothing, that would be of the slightest assistance in solving the case."

"Then why won't you tell me who he is and what he wanted?"

"Because he . . . because I . . . I gave my word, Peabody. I swore I would not tell a living soul of what transpired yesterday afternoon. Would you have me break my solemn oath?"

"Did the words 'forever' and 'never' appeal in that oath you took, Emerson?"

Emerson burst out laughing. "Yes, my dear Peabody. I seem to recall someone also using the phrase 'eternal silence.' People can be so cursed theatrical at times . . ." Then he sobered. "My dear, it appears we are facing a test of that utter confidence you just expressed. The test was not of my making, but there it is. Will you live up to your word and not try to make me break mine? For you know you could make me break it, Peabody. I can't resist you when you try."

"My dear Emerson, how can you possibly suppose I would do such a thing?"

Emerson took me in his arms.

For a moment we stood motionless. Emerson's chin rested on the top of my head. I could not see his face, and I would have given a great deal to be able to read his expression. He was planning something underhanded, I had not the least doubt of it.

In the silence I heard the faint chime of the clock in the hall. Emerson moved slightly. "It is almost time for tea," I said.

"Hmmm, yes. The day has flown by. I suppose we have to have those wretched . . . those children downstairs?"

"How unkind you are, Emerson."

"They are really very boring children, Peabody."

"I know. But we agreed to take them and do our best for them, and we must stick to our promise, Emerson."

Emerson's grasp tightened. "We have half an hour, Peabody. If we went upstairs directly . . . I could face the ordeal in a much better frame of mind after . . ."

I suppose I ought to have known better. But I defy any Reader to say she would have acted otherwise under the circumstances, which included a number of those little gestures to which I was susceptible under *all* circumstances and which were particularly poignant just then.

When we came out of the drawing room arm in arm I saw Gargery behind the curve of the stairs, grinning like the sentimental idiot he was; and then I saw no more of him, because Emerson swept me into his arms and ran up the stairs in, as I assumed, a burst of affectionate impatience. So impatient was he that he neglected to close the door, and I exclaimed, "Emerson, don't you think . . . a little privacy . . ."

"Oh, yes," said Emerson, breathing heavily. "One moment—"

Without going into improper details as to my position at the time, I will only say that I did not see the door close. I heard it, though. And then I heard another sound that affected me like a dash of icy water in the face. It was the sound of the key turning in the lock.

I bounded up from the bed. I was alone. I heard his footsteps retreating; he made no attempt to tiptoe. One touch of the knob confirmed what I already knew. He had locked me in.

I ran to the window and drew back the curtains. I was in time to see him leave the house. It was still bright daylight outside, though the shadows were lengthening. As he walked, with the rapid stride that could cover miles of desert terrain as quickly as another man might run, he shrugged into his coat. He was bareheaded. At the gate he turned for a moment and looked up at the window.

I doubt that he saw me, for the sun was directly opposite the house and when it was in that position it reflected blindingly from the front windows. But he knew I would be there. Raising his hand to his lips, he blew me a kiss. Then he broke into a run; within seconds he had vanished.

How long I remained at the window, prey to sensations I prefer not to recall, I cannot say; but it could not have been more than a minute before I heard the rattle of the key in the lock, and the voice of Gargery.

"Madam? Mrs. Emerson, are you there?"

"Where else would I be, you idiot?" I replied. "Unlock the door instantly."

"Yes, madam, of course. That is what the professor said I should do. But I don't understand . . ." The door opened. "I don't understand what is going on," Gargery continued. "He said the lock was jammed, and went to get tools, but why it should be locked at all, and you inside, and the professor outside—"

"'Outside' is the key word, Gargery, if you will excuse a vile pun. I don't suppose he mentioned where he was going?"

"To get tools, madam. He . . ." Gargery's jaw dropped. "Blimey!" he exclaimed. "'E 'asn't got away from us, 'as 'e?"

"'E certainly 'as," I replied, in considerable bitterness of spirit. "He fooled us very nicely, Gargery— both of us. Never mind—" For Gargery had begun pounding himself on the forehead with his clenched fist and was using expressions I had never heard him employ. "It was not your fault—and I apologize for calling you an idiot, Gargery. If you are, I am a greater one."

"Oh, madam." Gargery took a long, quivering breath and regained control of his speech. "I beg your pardon—I am afraid that in the 'eat—the heat—of the moment I forgot myself. There is no use going after him, I suppose?"

"No, he has made good his escape. We can only wait, and exhibit that fortitude for which English persons of both sexes and all social classes are famous. It is time for tea, Gargery. I will be down shortly."

"Yes, madam." Gargery drew himself up to his full height. "And may I say, madam—"

"No, Gargery, I would rather you did not. For my shell of calm is about to crack and I would prefer to express my sentiments in private."

Gargery went away.

Of course I did not break into hysterics or tears. That is not my habit. I was not even angry with Emerson. He was always complaining about his inability to prevent me from rushing headlong into danger, but that was only his little joke; never before had he made any real effort to stop me. He must be desperate to resort to a trick like this, which he knew would bring down vehement reproaches on his head. . . . Oh, my dear Emerson, I thought—my shell of calm breaking for an instant—only return, safe and sound, and I will never speak a word.

I forced myself to sit down and use my head instead of my heart. Naturally I had no intention of sitting idly by, waiting for Emerson to come back. I had no idea where he might have gone. However, from his guarded remarks earlier I knew he and I were on the same track, insofar as the solution of the murder case was concerned. Obviously he knew more than I—or thought he did. Surely, if I applied my intelligence to the matter, I ought to be able to arrive at the same conclusion he had reached—and, in due course of time, at the same place to which those conclusions had led him.

Something was nagging at my mind. I knew the

sensation well, for it had happened to me before—a sense of something seen or heard to which I had not paid proper attention at the time. Something overlooked or misunderstood . . . something of consummate importance. I sat down and pressed my hands over my eyes—not because they were damp with incipient tears, but in order to blot out external distractions. What could it have been? For long, agonized seconds I had dangled helplessly from the throttling hands of the killer, my face only inches from his. I had been somewhat distracted at the time, but might there not have been a clue—a scent or a sound or a sensation—to that villain's identity?

I felt I was on the right track, but before I could pursue my recollection, the prattle of childish voices without reminded me of another duty. If I did not get downstairs at once, Violet would eat all the biscuits.

She had consumed several before I arrived on the scene, so I put an end to that, and ordered them all to their places. "And what have you been doing today?" I asked pleasantly.

"We went to the park," said Percy. "I took my hoop and my butterfly net."

"There was a muffin man," murmured Violet. "A nice, nice muffin man."

"And did you catch any butterflies, Percy?" I inquired. I did not bother to ask whether Violet had caught any muffins; I felt sure she had. The child was swelling up like a toad.

"Yes, Aunt Amelia. Only a few Monarchs, but it was good exercise, you know, running after them."

"Yes, indeed," I replied encouragingly. "And you, Ramses—did you help Percy catch butterflies?"

"I wonder that you can ask, Mama, since you know my views on the needless murder of living creatures," Ramses replied in his stateliest manner. "If you will excuse my changing the subject—which is boring in the extreme—I would like to ask whether Papa has gone out? In his present weakened condition—"

"He has gone out," I replied somewhat sharply. "And no—I do not know where he has gone or when he will return. He is not accountable to you, Ramses—or to me—for his actions."

"Not in the legal sense," Ramses replied. "But the gentle urging of domestic affection implies a moral obligation, and I am surprised to find that Papa, who is as a rule most considerate of our concern—"

"Please, Ramses."

"Yes, Mama."

A brief silence followed. I moved the plate of biscuits out of Violet's reach and tried to think of something to say. I was not really in a fit state for idle conversation.

After a moment Percy coughed. "May I ask you something, Aunt Amelia?"

"Certainly, Percy. What is it?"

"Well, you see, I have been wondering . . . The matter has been on my mind for some time."

"If it is your mama you are worrying about," I began.

"No, it isn't that, Aunt. In fact, it isn't about any person, any person I know. What Ramses would call a theoretical question, I suppose."

"Well?" I said impatiently.

"Supposing," said Percy slowly, "supposing some-one knew that someone had done something. Something he wasn't supposed to do."

I wondered how I could ever have complained about Ramses' speech patterns. At least he knew more than fifty words, and could arrange them into a coherent sentence. Percy went on, even more slowly, "Something bad, Aunt Amelia. Really bad, I mean. Should the person—the person who knew about it—tell?"

"Tell whom?" I inquired.

"Oh . . . someone else."

I knew perfectly well what he was aiming at. He kept glancing sideways at Ramses, who returned his look with a concentrated glare of dislike.

"I believe I understand you, Percy," I said. "You are posing a hypothetical question on a moral issue. There is never a simple answer to such questions. It depends on a number of things. For example, on whether the first individual had been sworn to se-crecy, or had promised to keep silent. A Roman Catholic priest, hearing confession—"

"It wasn't like that, Aunt Amelia," said Percy.

"And also," I continued, "on how serious was the action in question. If it was only a harmless prank—"

"It was bad," said Percy—metaphorically licking his chops. "Very, very bad. Very, ver—"

Ramses rose up from the sofa and launched him-self at Percy's throat.

They fell to the floor in a tangle of limbs, taking a small table down with them and spilling the biscuits, which had been on the table, far and wide. Out of the corner of my eye I saw Violet pounce, like a cat on a mouse, but I could do nothing about her until I got the boys separated.

It was not as easy as I had expected. The first time I reached out, someone kicked me—I could not tell which it was. They rolled from side to side, arms and legs flailing; Percy was yelping and crying out, but Ramses fought in ominous silence; the only sounds I heard from him were grunts of pain and/or effort. Seizing the teapot, I took off the lid and threw the contents onto the combatants.

The water was no longer boiling, but it was hot enough to induce a momentary lull. I took advantage of it to pluck Ramses from the tangle and pull him to his feet.

Percy promptly rolled out of reach and got to his hands and knees. In comparing the two, I was interested to observe that Ramses, though slighter and shorter than his cousin, had managed to hold his own. Perhaps his father had given him those lessons in boxing after all. His nose was bleeding copiously—considering the size of the member, it was not surprising that Percy should have managed to strike it—his hair was standing straight up, and it appeared that Percy had bit him on the thumb. But Percy was in worse case. He too was bleeding, from a split lip, and his face was beginning to swell.

Having eaten all the biscuits, Violet was able to turn her mind to another matter. She darted at Ramses and pounded him with her fists. "Nasty, nasty, bad," she screamed. "Nasty!"

Maintaining my grip on Ramses—who made no attempt to retaliate, only shielding his face with his arms—I put my free hand over Violet's face and shoved. She flew backward onto the sofa with force enough to drive the breath out of her.

There was no need for me to ring the bell. The sounds of battle had brought Gargery, as well as Mrs. Watson, into the room. I turned Violet over to Mrs. Watson and Percy over to Gargery.

"Well, Ramses," I said.

"I am confined to my room," Ramses remarked, wiping his bloody nose on his sleeve.

"Yes." I plucked a few tea leaves out of his hair. "Do you require assistance in washing, changing, and tending your bruises?"

"No, thank you, I would prefer to deal with the matter myself. As you see, my nose has stopped bleeding. The application of cold water—"

"A great deal of cold water, I should think."

"Yes, Mama. At once." He started from the room. Then he stopped and turned. "One question, Mama, if I may."

"I will discuss this disgraceful incident with you at a later time, Ramses. At present I have other things on my mind."

"Yes, Mama. You refer, I suppose, to Papa's where-abouts, and I quite agree that that is a more urgent matter. However, I wanted to ask you about Miss Minton. She has gone."

"Yes, Ramses, I know. I sent her away. She left the house this morning."

"She left the house last night," said Ramses. "At least so I have been informed. And she left behind her clothing and other possessions."

"There is nothing strange about that, Ramses.

She had with her, I suppose, only those articles a housemaid might be expected to possess. No doubt she abandoned them as worthless reminders of an action of contemptible treachery."

"No doubt," said Ramses. "However, it seemed to me that you might wish to be informed—"

"And now you have informed me. Thank you. To your room, Ramses."

"Yes, Mama."

I stood pondering for a moment. Then I rang the bell. When Gargery answered, I said, "I want a letter delivered at once, Gargery. Give the footman money for cab fare, and tell him to make haste."

By the time the footman came, I had the note written. I instructed him to wait for an answer. Next I summoned Mrs. Watson and told her I would have dinner on a tray in my room, since the professor would not be there for dinner. The good kind woman approved of my having a nice rest and an early night after all I had been through.

I could make no definite plans until I received the answer to my message. If it was not the one I expected . . . well, then there was a fatal flaw in my theory, and I would have to revise it. But I did not see how I could be mistaken. Why, oh why had I ignored that one significant statement? Being half-strangled was no excuse for such negligence.

I forced myself to remain calm. There was no hurry. If I was right, and if I had correctly estimated the eccentricities of the man I was after, nothing of importance would happen for a good many hours. I took out my list and went through it again. It was too late now to finish my inquiries, but the list raised another question. To call, or not to call, upon the police?

After weighing the pros and cons, I decided upon a compromise. There was only one police officer who might—and I stress the word "might"—give credence to the admittedly bizarre solution I had arrived at. I could not fathom the behavior of Inspector Cuff; was he shrewd and secretive, or only very stupid? In either case I had to assume he suffered from the same unaccountable prejudice toward the female sex that afflicted most men, and that he would therefore strenuously object to my taking part in the evening's entertainment—even supposing he could be persuaded to participate himself. Cuff would have no compunctions about locking me in a cell, and keeping me there as long as he considered necessary.

Still, it seemed only fair to give him a chance to show his quality—and it was possible I might be in need of assistance if matters did not work out quite as I hoped. I sat down at my table and began to write. It proved to be a rather lengthy epistle, since I had to explain a lot of things in detail, in order to add verisimilitude to the narrative, and I had not finished when Gargery brought me the answer to my letter.

He waited while I read it, and then exclaimed, "Is it—I hope it is not bad news, madam."

"It was the answer I expected," I replied. "Thank you, Gargery."

Miss Minton had not returned to her lodging. Her landlady had not seen her or heard from her since the preceding Friday.

So that was settled. It was not likely that she had set off for Northumberland dressed like a housemaid and without luggage or money. It was even more unlikely that she would have accepted the protection of Kevin or Mr. Wilson. No; I knew where she was. It must be she to whom Ayesha had referred in that breathless and unfortunately neglected speech. "He" had her now, and I knew where he had taken her—to the ruined wing of Mauldy Manor, behind that massive door whose lock had been so recently repaired that traces of oil had transferred themselves to my fingers when I tried the latch.

FOURTEEN

I waited until the servants were at their dinner before I left the house. I did not trust Gargery; he might have been ordered by Emerson to prevent me from leaving. (Not that he would have succeeded, but I wanted to avoid argument.) I much regretted I had been unable to inquire of Gargery where I might purchase a little pistol. He seemed to know about such things. However, I had my tools and my parasol, and they should suffice.

Darkness had fallen, and I was pleased to see that the skies were overcast. Tendrils of fog curled languidly among the trees in the park; no doubt it would lift when we were out of London, but there might be a river mist. I sincerely hoped so.

The drive was a long one, and as the cab clattered through the busy streets, I went over my plans. I had left the letter for Inspector Cuff on the hall table, with directions that it was to be delivered immediately. I had my weapons. I had the strength of righteous indignation to support me—and the expectation that I would soon be in the presence of that being who was all in all to me.

I did wonder how the devil Emerson had figured it out. He had not heard Ayesha's speech, and I had not repeated the crucial sentence, since it had had no meaning to me at the time. How then did Emerson know that a ceremony of some sort was taking place that night? Perhaps he did not know. Perhaps he had gone there searching for the evidence he needed (as did I) to substantiate his theory. But to Mauldy Manor he had gone, I was as certain of that as if I had followed him there. It was the only logical place to find what was lacking in my reconstruction of the case.

It was less than two hours until midnight when I directed the cab driver to let me out, a safe distance from the gates of the manor. I suppose he cannot be blamed for thinking the worst; a solitary female swathed in a hooded black cloak, who demands to be put down on a country road not far from the habitation of a man whose reputation is not of the best, must expect to have her motives questioned. The driver's parting remark has no bearing on the present narrative.

Moon and stars were hidden under heavy clouds, and mist spread a blanket of white over the surface of the river. As I stole silently toward the gate, a lurid glow of red brightened the clouds, and a faint growl of thunder announced its presence. A storm was brewing.

Lighted windows in the lodge warned me from the gate. It would be locked at this hour—all the more so if the activities I expected were about to take place—and I did not want to be seen. I had to follow the wall for some distance before I found a place where I could get over it, with the help of a tall elm that overhung the top. The cursed cloak kept catching on thorns and branches, but I did not dare discard it. Underneath I wore the most subdued of my working costumes, and although its color was such as to blend with the shadows, my outline (as Emerson had often remarked) would have betrayed me for a woman.

By means of the lightning flashes, which increased in frequency and intensity as the storm rumbled closer, I made my way from tree to tree and shrub to shrub across the wide empty lawn. I had expected dogs, and was pleased to learn I had been mistaken, though it struck me as a little strange that a young bachelor would not have such animals around—as guards if not as pets. I remembered what Emerson had said about his lordship's fondness for cats, and a shudder of revulsion ran through me. Resolutely I fixed my mind on other things. I was prepared for the worst; there was no point in brooding over it beforehand.

The grounds were absolutely deserted, without a sign of man or beast. In fact, if I had not known better, I would have supposed Lord Liverpool was away from home. There were no lights in the inhabited wing of the house, except for a few on the uppermost floor, which must be the servants' quarters.

I had the plan of the place clearly in mind from my earlier visit. It was arranged like the letter E— the greater portion of the present house having been constructed during the reign of Elizabeth, whose monumental ego enjoyed such tributes and whose courtiers were wise enough to indulge her.

The modern wing must have replaced an earlier structure on the same spot; it was at one end, with the kitchens and other domestic offices occupying the center leg of the E, and the old wing at the other end.

I reached the moss-encrusted wall of the old wing without incident or alarm, and was congratulating myself on my good fortune when I received my first check. The structure, which had appeared from the outside to be on the verge of collapse, was not so vulnerable as I had hoped. Every window was boarded up; the boards were new, thick, and fixed with stout nails. I could not get so much as a fingernail into a crack. The door, on the short end of the wing, was as immovable as stone, and when I tried the handle the rust flaked off like a shower of dry raindrops.

I was about to try one of the other wings, hoping a window had been left unlatched (and fully prepared to break a pane if I had to) when I saw a faint glow of light, which appeared to emanate from the ground next to my feet. It faded almost at once, but it had given me the clue I needed. Someone had walked through a subterranean room carrying a lamp or lantern, betraying the existence of apertures which I might not otherwise have suspected— small windows at ground level, opening into the cellars.

At one time they had been closed with bars or grilles of iron, but the long passage of years had corroded the metal to a thin shell and I was able to wrench the remaining bars from their sockets. The apertures were so narrow only a child—or a small woman—could have passed through, which is probably why the bars had never been replaced.

I got through, though not without a struggle and some rather painful pressure on a certain portion of my anatomy which has inconvenienced me before. I went in feet-first, and lowered myself to the farthest extremity of my arms, but still could feel nothing but air under my stretching toes. The darkness was impenetrable, the moment one of considerable anxiety. How far below me was the floor? What, other than the presumed floor, might be there? If I fell heavily or knocked over some breakable object, the noise would announce my presence. Someone was in the house, I had seen the light.

There was no use worrying about it, so I let go my grip on the ledge and dropped—a few feet only, as it proved, but it felt like a greater distance. I landed with knees bent, and did not lose my balance.

The place was black as pitch and smelled like a grave. Risky as it was to strike a light—which was why I had not brought the dark lantern I normally wore attached to my belt—I dared not move until I knew what obstacles lay ahead. I took every possible precaution before I struck the match, shielding it with hand and body.

Almost instantly I put it out. I had seen enough—a narrow empty room, with walls and floor of stone smeared sickeningly with lichen and containing nothing except a few scraps of wood. On both side walls, dark openings gaped.

Which direction? I tried to remember the fleeting glimpse of light, and decided it had moved from right to left across the window. Surefooted in the darkness, and holding my tools to my side to prevent them from jingling, I followed the direction the lantern-holder had taken.

No sooner had I entered the next room than I saw light ahead. Proceeding with the utmost caution, I passed through a door that hung askew on broken hinges into a stony corridor as low-ceilinged and as dank as the room I had just left. The light was straight ahead; it came from an opening at the top of a flight of narrow stairs.

Wrapping my cloak tightly around me and pulling the hood low over my face, I went up the stairs. They did not creak underfoot; they were of stone, worn by the passage of centuries. At the top I paused and peered cautiously around the edge of the opening.

What I saw astonished me so that I straightened up and hit my head a smart blow on the low stone lintel of the archway.

Directly in front of me was a group of statuary, life-sized, and shaped of beautifully polished alabaster. I use the word "group" advisedly; I could not tell how many people were involved, so closely were they intertwined. There must have been at least three, for I made out five arms.

Good gracious, I thought to myself. I did not speak aloud, however, because I heard voices. The statuary group had been placed conveniently—for my purposes, at any rate—in front of the opening. I ventured a little farther out, into what proved to be a passageway running the whole length of the wing. To my right, only a few feet away, was the door leading into the front part of the house—the long base of the E. To my left the corridor stretched away till it ended in a heavy black curtain of what appeared to be velvet or plush. Boarded-up windows lined one wall; between them were paintings, statues, and other works of art (to use that term loosely) which carried out the same theme as that of the original statuary group I had seen. They had come from all parts of the world and from various centuries; the painting directly opposite the entrance to the cellar was an extraordinary composition, originating most probably in sixteenth-century India, which depicted a number of individuals in positions which are best not described, but which Ramses would undoubtedly have considered "uncomfortable, not to say impossible."

The function of this closed-off portion of the house was now quite apparent to me. It seemed unlikely, however, that it had been designed by the present Earl; no doubt a number of his ancestors had contributed to the décor and enjoyed the amenities, and he had remodeled it—in ways I had yet to ascertain, but which I rather thought I could anticipate—to suit his own purpose.

The voices I had heard came from an open doorway immediately to my left, and were accompanied by the gurgling of liquid and the chiming of crystal. The light-bearer I had seen must have been returning from the wine cellar.

Resting my hand on the polished shoulder of one of the individuals in the statuary group, I edged closer to the open door.

"There's plenty of time," said a voice that sounded familiar. "Have another glass."

"Or another bottle." The high-pitched giggle identified this speaker. "Dutch courage, eh, Frank?"

"I'm here, ain't I?" was the sullen response. "And the only one, too. Where are the others?"

"They declined the invitation," said Lord Liverpool, with another of his inane giggles. "Cold feet, cold hearts, cold all over, the bloody damned cowards!"

"Maybe they show good sense," muttered the other man—whom I had now identified as Mr. Barnes. "Call it off, Ned. There aren't enough of us—"

"Oh yes, there are." I was so close to the door I could hear him swallow. "I hired a few of the lads—you know the ones—to fill out the ranks."

Barnes let out a yelp of protest. "Damn it, Ned, why'd you do that? A group of louts like that—they'll spill their guts at the first sign of a truncheon—or blackmail you . . . This was supposed to be our own private entertainment—"

"Entertainment!" Lord Liverpool must have thrown his glass down; I heard the ringing shatter of fine crystal. "This is no game, Frank, not to me. It's life or death."

"But Ned—I know, old chap, I know what it means to you, but . . ."

"But he can't deliver what he promised—is that what you think? You don't believe in his powers, do you?"

"Do you?"

There was a moment of silence. Then the young Earl muttered, "I have to, Frank. I have to. I'll try anything, do anything . . ."

"All right, then. I'm with you, old fellow."

"Damn right you are," said the Earl with an ugly laugh. "Through thick and thin and every penny I own, eh? Don't think I don't know why you stick by me, Frank. I only had one friend; and he . . . Ah, don't look so sick. They'll never find us out. And what if they did? Do you suppose the old lady would let a vulgar policeman arrest her great-grandnephew, or her second cousin once removed? Buck up, Frank; finish the bottle and let's get to it."

The only reply from Barnes was a series of gurgles as he followed Lord Liverpool's advice.

Heeding the warning, I glided back into the shelter of the statuary group. The corridor was lit at intervals by oil lamps, and I was fairly sure that in my black cloak, and in the shadow, I would not be observed. In fact, neither man so much as glanced in my direction. Leaving the door open behind them, they walked down the corridor and passed behind the black curtain.

Both were masked and robed. I waited till they were out of sight before I emerged, and hearing no sound within the room they had left, entered it.

It was the strangest place, halfway between the robing room of a theater and the vestibule of a church or temple. Hanging from hooks along the wall were several of the white robes. The door of a tall cabinet, left carelessly ajar, displayed shelves filled with staring masks. There must have been a dozen of them. But it was the sight of the objects on a long table that brought me to a stop, with my heart pounding painfully against my ribs. They were also masks but not copies of the one with which I was so familiar. Heads of ibis and baboon, vulture's hooked beak and lion's snarl—the animal-headed gods of ancient Egypt, molded in papier-mâché and painted in bright colors.

I had almost forgotten that ghastly dream. But there were the animal heads, just as I had beheld them in nightmare . . . and nowhere else.

I dared not yield to the hideous speculations that assailed me. Here was my chance of passing unobserved into the very room where the others were gathering. But I had to move quickly, for there were several robes left and I did not know how many participants were yet to come. At any second I might be discovered.

I bundled my cloak into the cupboard and pulled one of the robes over my head. It was a good six inches too long, but that was all to the good, because it would hide my boots. The men had worn sandals, but the others I found, in the cupboard, were all too big for me. Besides, boots can be very useful in a scrimmage.

After examining the bits and pieces of ceremonial attire scattered among the masks on the table, I decided none was sturdy enough to serve as a weapon; maces, staffs and scepters were of thin wood or papier-mâché. It would have been madness to abandon my parasol, so I hooked it over my belt, under the robe, and held it in place with my elbow while I practiced walking. It was a little awkward, but I thought I could manage.

I was ready to go—except for one thing.

His lordship and Mr. Barnes had both worn the priest-mask. There were plenty of them left; Emerson's little jest about a workshop that produced them had not been so far off the mark. They would need a good number of the cursed things; no doubt the priest had destroyed the one he wore after each performance. My hand had actually touched one of the damnable objects when I had second thoughts.

My decision rested on such a fragile strand of evidence—a dream. But in that dream only the high priest had worn the mask with the human features. The others, acolytes and attendants, had worn the animal heads.

Well, I would soon find out whether I had made the right choice. I selected the lion mask—Sekhmet, goddess of love, and of war. It seemed appropriate.

The corridor was as still as death. With stiff, hieratic stride, I paced its length. It was lucky for me no one was watching, because once the parasol got between my limbs and almost tripped me, but I recovered in time. My vision was limited by the eye-holes of the mask, so I could only see straight ahead, and I was conscious of a nasty prickling sensation in the middle of my back.

I lifted the curtain and passed through. Before me was a door, its surface carved in low relief, and gilded. The depictions were most extraordinary.

The latch yielded to the pressure of my hand; in smooth silence the panel swung inward. I came to a sudden stop.

There before me was the very scene of my dream, and I stood, as I had huddled then, on a balcony overlooking a vast chamber.

It was not exactly the same, however. The door had swung shut behind me, and no one appeared to have observed my entrance, so I had a few moments to collect myself.

The room comprised two levels of the original structure; by removing the flooring and bracing the walls with pillars, they had opened up the entire space between the roof and the cellar floor. The walls had been covered, not with polished stone, but with tapestries and hangings. The statue was not twenty feet high, but life-sized, and the deity depicted was not the dignified Osiris. He has a number of names (Min is one of them), but he is easily recognizable by one outstanding characteristic.

The illumination was erratic and not particularly impressive—modern oil lamps, whose wicks all needed trimming, and fires flickering in open braziers raised on tall, rather wobbly tripods. There were half a dozen men present; all were robed and some were masked, but others had removed the headgear in order to puff at a cigar or cigarette. The prevailing mood was far from solemn. One fellow was sprawled on the altar, another had a bottle raised to his lips. Someone pointed at the statue and made a joke I refuse to repeat; a howl of rude laughter followed.

As I scanned the room I realized with a thrill of dismay that one of the masked men had seen me. His mask, which was that of the ibis headed Thoth, god of wisdom, looked squarely at me. He took a step toward the stairs that led to the balcony.

There was nothing for it but to brazen it out. If he became suspicious and raised the alarm I could never outrun him. More importantly, I had not yet accomplished what I came for. If the girl was a prisoner in this vile den, I could not abandon her.

I had never realized how difficult it would be to descend a flight of stairs with a parasol hooked to my belt. After a near-fatal stumble, I pushed it back out of the way, as a swordsman does with his long saber, and hoped no one would notice my odd appendage.

I reached the bottom of the stairs at last and breathed a sigh of relief. The ibis mask had turned away, and no one else seemed to be paying attention to me. I glided into a handy patch of shadow, with my back against the wall.

One loses track of time under such circumstances. I had no idea what hour it might be, nor how long I waited, trying not to listen to the disgusting language and jests of the others, before one of them tossed his cigarette on the floor and ground it out.

"'Ere we go, lads," he said cheerfully. "Don't let 'is loverly lordship see you slouchin' around so vulgar-like."

Masks were assumed, cigars tossed into the braziers. The man sprawled on the altar arose and straightened his robe.

Though I cannot truthfully say I was entirely comfortable, the shadow of supernatural terror had lifted from my mind. The reality was nothing like my dream, it was rather a Gilbertian parody of pagan ritual. And the parody continued; instead of a solemn procession, with flaring torches and grim chanting, the two men simply walked through a door under the balcony, and one of them burst out, "What the devil is this? Get rid of that bottle, you—

straighten the cloth on the altar—get into your places!"

I stifled a laugh. He sounded like a baritone Mrs. Watson, lecturing her subordinates for untidiness. What sort of ridiculous farce was this to be? Perhaps all I would have to do was unmask and give the lot of them a good scolding.

My amusement was short-lived. The men had shifted positions, following Lord Liverpool's orders; and I saw that ibis-headed Thoth was once again approaching me. I could not retreat without stepping directly into the pool of light from the lamp to my left.

He was a tall man. The mask added another inch or two; he towered over me. I fumbled for the handle of my parasol. But he did not speak, or make a threatening move; he stopped, at my side, and turned to face the altar.

The last vestiges of amusement left me as I watched his lordship. This was no parody to him. He was hideously, tragically in earnest. Raising his hands, he addressed the image; and the hairs on my neck lifted when I recognized the voice that had once hailed mighty Isis, powerful in the word of command.

Suddenly he shouted aloud. "He comes! He comes! The Great One comes!" and dropped to the ground in a profound obeisance. But he was not facing the god.

Masked, and robed in white, with the *sem* priest's leopard skin over his shoulders, he emerged from the shadows under the balcony.

I held my breath. This was the man. Not the

pathetic young Earl, who was his dupe and his aco-
lyte, who would (as he had said) do anything, and
try anything, that might cure him of his fatal illness. How vilely that creature had played on the
boy's fear of death—a boy already half-crazed by
the disease that had rotted the tissue of his brain.

The wretch had presence, there was no question
about it. Even the hardened hirelings responded,
watching in respectful silence the eerie exchange
between the young Earl and his mentor. They spoke
Egyptian—or, in Liverpool's case, attempted to
speak it. The other man's voice, though weirdly distorted by the mask, was slow and sure.

Then he turned toward the shadows from which
he had come and clapped his hands three times.

They came singing, in ululating and unharmoni-
ous voices. They were naked except for loincloths,
and the dark skin of their bodies gleamed like bronze.
The form that lay on the litter they carried was still,
swathed even to its face in white wrappings.

I could not have repressed the cry that felt as if it
would burst my straining lungs; but as I lunged forward, lips parting, an arm like steel encircled me
and a hand clamped over my mouth.

"For God's sake, Peabody, don't bellow!" hissed a
voice.

I believe I would have fallen to the ground had it
not been for the strong arm that held me. I pried his
fingers from my mouth. "Emerson," I whispered.
"Emerson . . ."

"Sssssssh," said Thoth, the ibis-headed.

The adjuration was unnecessary; joy, relief, rapture, and rising rage held me mute. But if it was not

Emerson on the litter, who was it? I knew the answer, even before the bearers lowered it gently onto the long altar and the *sem* priest slowly stripped the veils away.

A murmur of interest and appreciation arose as the poor girl's limp form was bared to the staring eyes of the men. Her costume was a surprisingly accurate adaptation of one an ancient Egyptian female might have worn, but it was not the elegant pleated linen robe of a high-born lady. This was the dress of a servant or peasant girl—a simple shift that ended just above her slim ankles and was suspended by broad straps that covered—more or less—her bosom.

Emerson had transferred his grip from my waist to my arm. Now he gave me a little shake. "Don't move, Peabody."

"But Emerson, they are going to—"

"No, they aren't. Hang on."

No one paid any attention to us; the greedy eyes were all fixed on Miss Minton. One tall, thin individual, wearing the mask of a baboon, began edging forward.

Lord Liverpool bent forward, studying the girl's face. Suddenly he stepped back. His hand went to his mask and lifted it off.

"I say," he exclaimed. "I know her. You told me—"

"She is the selected one," said the solemn voice of the *sem* priest. "The bride of the god."

"Yes, but—but . . . it's Durham's granddaughter, dash it all! You said she would be willing—"

"She is willing." The priest put an arm under Miss Minton's shoulders and raised her to a sitting position. "Wake, Margaret, bride of the god. Open your eyes and smile on your devotees."

Her long lashes fluttered bewitchingly; her languid lids lifted. A singularly silly smile spread across her face.

"Mmmmmmmm," she said agreeably. "Who are all you peculiar people?"

"Greet your lord and your lover, bride of the god," chanted the *sem* priest.

She could hardly keep her eyes open. "Lord and lover . . . oh, yes. How nice . . . Which one of you . . ."

"Damn it, the girl's been drugged," Liverpool shouted. "I can't . . . I won't . . . not to a lady, damn it!"

"I never intended you should," said the masked figure coolly. He let go of Miss Minton, who collapsed onto the pillow with a foolish giggle, and unfastened his leopard skin.

"What?" The Earl's jaw dropped. "You said—"

"The consummation of the divine marriage would cure you," replied the other man. "And so it will—my lord. Of your illness, and everything else that ails you."

Miss Minton raised her white arms. "Lord and lover," she murmured rapturously. "How absolutely splendid. My dear—my dear Radcliffe—"

"Thoth" started violently and let go my arm. "Damnation!" he cried.

His exclamation was drowned by a louder cry from Lord Liverpool. "Damn it, man, you go too far. I won't let you do this."

The other man stepped back. "Of all the cursed

nonsense . . . I never would have expected you to be so chicken-livered, Ned. Very well. Get out—all of you."

Several of the attendants had already discreetly drifted away, including Mr. Barnes. The Earl doubled up his fists. "She goes with me. I'll see her safe home."

"Like hell you will!" The priest reached into his robe.

Emerson started forward, but he was too late; the sound of a shot rang out, and the Earl staggered back, clutching his side. He dropped to his knees; it appeared for a dreadful moment that he was bowing before the god. Then he fell forward onto his face and lay still.

Emerson's headlong rush struck the killer and bowled him over before he could aim again. Only one of the masked attendants remained in the room—the tall, thin fellow wearing the baboon head. I dashed at him with my parasol raised, but before I could bring it down I was seized by a pair of sinewy bare arms, and a bare, sinewy hand wrested the weapon from my grasp. I had not overlooked the litter-bearers; I had realized they were present; but I had taken them for paid attendants, like the thugs hired by the Earl to fill out the necessary number of priests, and I had never expected they would risk themselves in a criminal struggle. Evidently I had been sadly in error.

Two more of them had collared the man in the baboon mask, and the third pair pounced on the combatants—or, I should say, the single combatant, for Emerson had dragged the *sem* priest to his feet and was about to administer a mighty blow to the midsection when he was grasped and pulled away. Before he could shake off his assailants, the killer snatched up the gun he had dropped and leveled it, not at Emerson, but at me.

"Everything seems to have gone wrong tonight," he remarked rather breathlessly. "You, there—the little one, whose robe badly needs to be shortened—I don't know how you happen to be present, Mrs. Emerson, but you are next on my list, and if your allies don't stop struggling I will shoot."

The back of his mask had been smashed when he fell; he had to hold it in place with one hand. Emerson's ibis-head was in tatters, and the priest laughed aloud when he looked at him.

"Time to unmask," he said with sinister gaiety. "Don't be shy, Mrs. Emerson, I'd know you anywhere. And the big fellow has to be the professor. I might have known he'd choose Thoth. The scholar of the pantheon . . . But who's the baboon?"

I removed the mask and threw it aside. So did Emerson. The baboon folded his arms and stood still; one of the Egyptians snatched off the mask.

"Inspector Cuff!" I cried.

"Good evening, Mrs. Emerson," said the Inspector politely.

"Well, this is certainly a ridiculous state of affairs," I remarked somewhat later. "I left a message for you, Inspector, explaining the situation and asking you to search Mauldy Manor if I had not returned by morning. But I suppose I cannot expect you to come to the rescue now. Didn't you even bring a brace of constables with you?"

"You don't understand, Mrs. Emerson," the Inspector replied sadly. "This is a very delicate matter—very delicate indeed. I am here without the permission or the knowledge of my superiors, and my little pension—"

"Oh, never mind. This is no time for excuses. We must bend all our efforts on escape."

"Any ideas?" inquired Emerson.

He was leaning against the wall, his arms folded. We were all leaning against the wall; there was nothing in the room to sit on. It was one of the bare stone-walled cells in the cellars, differing from the others only in the fact that it had a stout door, which was now closed and bolted.

"One or two," I replied.

"I hope they are better than the last one," Emerson said grumpily. "You said the bars on those windows were rusted through—"

"On the other windows they are. Someone has renewed these recently. I wonder how many unhappy prisoners have languished in this foul cell?"

Neither of them replied. I went on thoughtfully, "It is Miss Minton I am chiefly concerned about. We must hasten to make our escape and hope we are in time to save her."

"I wouldn't object to saving myself—and you, ma'am," said the Inspector. "And may I say how much I admire your composure?"

"Thank you. I have no great fear for our safety. If he had meant to kill us, he would have done it on the spot, instead of imprisoning us."

"Now that is just the sort of unfounded conclusion you are always jumping to, Peabody," Emerson exclaimed. "We make a fairly formidable trio; even though the odds were against us, we might have inflicted some damage on our friend the priest if he had tried to murder us then and there. Now he can exterminate us at his leisure, without risking his precious hide."

"But his options are limited, Emerson, you must confess. It is only in sensational novels that the villain floods the cellar room with water or poison gas. And he must know that the first person who comes in that door will be subject to violent attack."

Emerson began, "Starvation—"

"Takes a long time. Someone will certainly find us before that eventuates, even if we are unable to free ourselves, which I consider probable."

Another dismal silence fell. I was about to make a little joke about pessimism, and the necessity of keeping up one's spirits, when I became aware of an odd sensation. Something cold and slimy slid across my foot. There are very few dangers I cannot accept with equanimity; but I really do not like reptiles.

"Oh, Emerson, I am afraid there is a snake in here," I said.

"It is not a snake, Peabody," Emerson said in a strangled voice. "It is water. Curse it, Peabody, aren't we in enough trouble without you offering suggestions to a killer? Let him invent his own murder method."

"Now, Emerson, that is nonsense. This is only an unfortunate coincidence. Where do you suppose the water is coming from? Strike another match, will you?"

"They are almost gone, Peabody, and so are the pages from the inspector's pocketbook," Emerson replied calmly. "We used several when we first investigated the room and the window, if you remember. But I expect that pipe, which you insisted was a drainage pipe—"

"Yes, to be sure. Save the matches, then, Emerson."

The storm had passed and the moon was out; a faint ray illumined a narrow patch of floor, and as I watched I saw the ripple of water spread and deepen. It looked very pretty and silvery and harmless.

"I wonder how long it will take to fill the room," I mused.

"I don't care how long it will take to fill the room," Emerson replied furiously. "Here, Cuff, let me have another go at those bars. If you can raise me on your shoulders—"

"Keep calm, Emerson, I beg you," I said. "This is really rather an inefficient way of killing people, you know. The door, though quite tight, is not sealed shut, and when the water rises to window level it will run out—"

"Not as fast as it is running in," Emerson replied; and indeed he was probably correct, for already the icy water was over my ankles. "And since it comes from the river, there is quite a lot of it at his disposal."

"Yes, I expect so. In that case . . . Inspector, will you please turn your back?"

"I don't know what you intend to do, ma'am," said Cuff mildly, "but I assure you I cannot see a blooming thing. You could—er—disrobe in perfect propriety."

"That is what I am going to do," I replied. "So, your protestations notwithstanding, I would prefer that you turn your back. As a gesture, you understand."

Emerson splashed to my side. "Peabody, what the devil—you don't have another belt of tools under those trousers, by any chance?"

"No, Emerson, but I have something that may serve us just as well. The idea occurred to me after . . . after . . ."

"Don't be so tactful, Peabody," Emerson growled. "After that bas— . . . that fellow Sethos abducted you."

"Yes, quite. My belt and its accoutrements, are too conspicuous to be overlooked, so I thought perhaps . . . Emerson, please stop fumbling at me. You have your hand . . ."

"What the devil are you doing?" Emerson demanded.

"We are not alone, Emerson," I reminded him. "Here, hold this and keep it from getting wet. And this."

"Peabody, what is . . . good Gad! My dear, are you wearing a corset?"

"Emerson, please!"

"I thought you felt rather rigid this evening," Emerson exclaimed. "But you swore you would never wear the cursed things because—"

"I can't stand this," said Inspector Cuff suddenly.

"Mrs. Emerson, I respect and admire you more than any lady I have ever known, but if you don't tell me why you are—er—disrobing, I may lose my mind."

"It is very simple," I said. "Most women wear corsets; they are not regarded as potential weapons. But what, gentlemen, holds a corset in position?"

"Cursed if I know," said Emerson.

"Stays," muttered the inspector. "Narrow strips of whalebone—or steel!—sewed into pockets along the sides and back . . ."

"Like this one," I said, pressing it into Emerson's hand. "Be careful, my dear, it is quite sharp; I had it set into its own little scabbard, and very uncomfortable it was, I must say. And this one, which is serrated along one edge . . . Now you can have another go at those bars, Emerson."

"Incredible, Mrs. Emerson," gasped the inspector.

"Elementary, my dear Inspector Cuff. How do you know so much about corsets, if I may ask? Are you a married man?"

"No, ma'am, I am not. I have been a confirmed bachelor all my life. But by Heaven, Mrs. Emerson, you have shaken my belief in the advantages of the single life. If I could meet another such woman as you—"

"There is only one of her," Emerson said, in tones of intense satisfaction. "Just as well, I expect . . . Put your clothes back on, Peabody. Here we go, Cuff . . ."

It was all the Inspector could do to raise that mighty form, so as soon as I was dressed, I went to help. The water lapped at my calves as I stood with my back braced against the wall and Emerson's boot resting on my shoulder. The play of moonlight across the limpid liquid had a strange, hypnotic fascination . . .

Suddenly the moonlight was cut off. Emerson let out a sharp cry and started back. Our human pyramid swayed dangerously. My foot slipped and I sat down with a splash, as Cuff, cursing with more imagination than I would have credited him with, struggled to keep his balance.

"What the devil is going on?" I shouted.

"You won't believe it," said Emerson in a hollow voice.

Then another voice said calmly, "Good evening, Mama. Good evening, Papa. Good evening, sir. I do not know who you are, but in view of the fact that you share the incarceration of my dear parents, I can only assume you are an ally, or possibly . . ."

FIFTEEN

How long Ramses went on I cannot say. I was incapable of interrupting him, and I fancy Emerson felt the same. When next I took note of what was going on, another voice was speaking.

"Oh, sir, are you there? Oh, madam, are you all right? Don't worry, sir and madam, we'll have you out of there!"

I had started to stand up. I sat down again. "Gargery?"

"Yes, madam, I am here, at your service. Oh, madam—"

I made an effort. "Ramses," I said, rising slowly to my feet and observing, in passing, that the water was now almost to my knees. "Even if you remove the bars, your papa cannot get out that window; it is too narrow. You will have to go around through the house."

"I am afraid that is out of the question, Mama," said Ramses. "Papa, if you will please stand away from the window? We have chisels, sledgehammers, and other tools, but we cannot employ them while you—"

"Yes, my son," said Emerson. He got down—or Cuff collapsed, most probably the latter. In between the ear-shattering attacks on the narrow window and its surrounding, I inquired, "Why can't you come through the house, Ramses?"

Crash, thud. "It is on fire, Mama," said Ramses.

I had to wait till the next lull before pursuing the matter. "I take it, Ramses, that the miscreants have fled? For I cannot suppose they would allow you . . ."

Crash, thud, crash. "Now, Mama, Papa, and sir," said Ramses, "please withdraw to the farthest corner and crouch down with your backs turned. It is as I feared; we will never break through by this method. The walls are eight feet thick. Fortunately I brought along a little nitroglycerin—"

"Oh, good Gad," shrieked Inspector Cuff.

I thought for a minute the whole wall was going to collapse, but after the sound of the explosion had faded, and my ears had stopped ringing, and Emerson had lifted me up out of the water, I saw that it still stood, though the gap in it was large enough to have admitted a horse and carriage, much less Emerson. With Gargery's enthusiastic assistance we climbed out; and while Emerson anxiously inspected the inspector, who appeared to be in a condition of mild catatonia, I had leisure to examine my surroundings.

The far end of the wing, which included the temple, was ablaze. Flames spouted from the windows and soared from the roof. There was nothing to be done there, so I turned my attention to Ramses.

He had not had time to change clothes, I suppose. He was dressed as I had seen him once before, like a ragged, filthy little street urchin. One eye was half closed. I had not observed that Percy had hit his eye.

"Miss Minton," I said, keeping my priorities clearly in mind. "I don't suppose you—"

"We 'ave the young lady, madam," said Gargery. "She was in the carriage with the gentleman—well, I don't suppose I should call him a gent, madam, since according to Master Ramses here—"

"We," I repeated. "You and Ramses and—"

"Henry, and Tom, and Bob—all of the footmen, madam. And the other young gentleman."

Behind me I heard Emerson exclaim, "Come, come, Cuff, this is no way for a grown man to behave," followed by the sound of a sharp slap. It did the job; Cuff said weakly, "Thank you, Professor. I beg your pardon; I don't believe I have ever had an experience quite like . . . Now then. What's going on here, eh?"

I believe he was addressing Gargery, but of course it was Ramses who replied, and I must say he was as succinct as possible. "We arrived on the scene a few minutes ago, sir, just in time to intercept a carriage that was driving rather quickly toward the gate. Fearing that Mama (for at the time I was unaware Papa was also here) might be within, I ordered it stopped, which was successfully accomplished, though the gentleman inside fired a pistol, blowing a hole through Bob's cap and slightly wounding Henry in the left thumb. The gentleman was subdued after a brief struggle and I then discovered the lady inside was not Mama, but Miss Minton, who was in a state of what appeared to be mild inebriation, though further investigation (that is, smelling her breath) suggested that opium rather than alcohol—"

"And where are the occupants of the carriage now?" Emerson inquired.

"Just inside the gate, with Bob and Henry standing guard," Ramses replied. "The rest of us at once hastened to the house, for we had learned (thanks to the insistent questioning of Mr. Gargery here) that you were imprisoned in the cellar and that—if you will excuse a somewhat melodramatic turn of phrase—the water was rising rapidly. I heard Papa's voice—"

"Yes, all right, my boy, we know what happened after that," Cuff said. "And this person is—"

"Gargery, our butler," I said.

Cuff stared at Gargery, who was swinging a life preserver in one hand. "Butler," he repeated.

"Never mind that now," Emerson said impatiently. "While we stand here chatting the house is blazing like a torch. Shouldn't we send for the fire engines? And what about the servants? Better get them out, eh?"

"I doubt there is imminent danger, Papa," Ramses replied judiciously. "The fire is still a good distance from the main part of the house, and I hear cries and calls of alarm which would suggest the occupants have been alerted to the danger. But I will go and make certain."

He trotted off.

The fire was so bright it cast ghastly shadows across the clipped grass. The old wing would soon be a gutted shell; the windows had all burned out and flames soared like bright banners from every empty aperture. There was a dreadful beauty about the sight, and we stood watching in silence. Emerson's arm was around me, and Cuff had bowed his head.

"He was dead, Emerson. Wasn't he?"

"Yes, my dear." After a moment Emerson said in an odd voice, "A noble end, trying to save a helpless woman from a fate worse than death. Eh, Cuff?"

Cuff's head lifted sharply. He and Emerson exchanged a long look. "Quite right, sir," said Inspector Cuff. "And now, sir, and Mrs. Emerson, shall we go and take charge of the prisoner your son and your butler have kindly captured for us?"

By the time we reached the gate the household had been aroused and the grounds were alive with screaming maids in billowing white nightgowns, looking like a flock of chickens that had escaped from the henhouse. By the gate were two carriages. Our own brougham had been drawn across the drive in such a way as to block the passage of the other, a dark, closed carriage drawn by a pair of handsome black horses. I could not see Henry, but Bob, one of the younger footmen, stood rigidly at attention, as if guarding two people who were half-sitting, half-reclining on the grassy verge.

Miss Minton was swathed from neck to feet in some heavy dark fabric. Her loosened hair had tumbled down; it spread in a shining veil across the knees of the young man on whose lap her head rested. He had pressed both hands to his face, but I knew him, for the moonlight shone full upon his fiery red head.

"O'Connell!" I cried. "No! Not Kevin O'Connell—"

Emerson caught me by the shirttail, which I had neglected to tuck in. "I fancy he is part of the rescue force, Peabody. Surely you didn't think he—"

"Certainly not. Never for an instant." (But when the strangling hands had held me with careless strength, clean off the ground, I had been reminded of the ease with which Kevin had lifted me on the night of the riot at the Royal Academy. Few men could have done it—certainly not the frail young Earl.)

"Ha, ha," I said. "You will have your little joke, Emerson. The murderer is not Mr. O'Connell. He is—"

I stopped and looked expectantly at Emerson. He smiled. "Inside the carriage, Peabody."

And that is where he was, so tightly swathed with ropes, cravats, handkerchiefs, and scarves that he was no more capable of motion than the poor mummy he had desecrated. On the seat opposite sat Henry, with a cudgel in his hand. But there was no more fight left in the killer—Mr. Eustace Wilson.

After we had delivered the prisoner to Bow Street and seen him charged, Inspector Cuff declared he had a great deal of work to do, but Emerson insisted he accompany us back to Chalfont House. "You can take our statements there as conveniently and much more comfortably," he declared. "Confound it, Cuff, we have all had a hard night. We deserve a little rest and a celebration."

Fortunately we had been up very late the night

before, and slept late in consequence; after I had changed and removed the cursed corset, I felt quite fresh. We all gathered round the table in the servants' dining room, which was conveniently close to the kitchen, and where Gargery and the others would feel more at ease; and a merry party it was, with cold mutton and pickles and a nice apple tart, and a great quantity of things to drink. Ramses tried his usual trick when the wine was being poured, holding out a glass and hoping his papa would fill it before he noticed whose it was. Emerson did notice; but he laughed and splashed a scant inch of hock into the tumbler. "You deserve it, my son. Now, Peabody, don't frown; he must learn to drink his wine like a gentleman."

"He deserves it is right," declared Gargery, who had already had a glass of stout. "Wasn't for him, we wouldn't have come in time, sir and madam, for none of us knew where you'd gone off to."

"I suppose you were hanging on to the back of the cab," I said to Ramses.

"Yes, Mama, that is correct. I knew you would go out looking for Papa, so I changed my clothing and followed you. Greatly as I was tempted to stay with you and render whatever assistance I could, I knew that would not be sensible; so I stayed with the cab when it returned to London, and immediately enlisted the aid of Mr. Gargery and the others. Mr. O'Connell had been here inquiring about Miss Minton, so I took the liberty of sending for him as well."

Kevin, of course, made one of the party. In fact, the only people not at the table were Miss Minton, who was upstairs sleeping off her inadvertent debauch, and Mrs. Watson, who was watching over her, and who would, in any case, have found the proceedings not to her taste.

"I am sure your concern will touch Miss Minton deeply," I assured Kevin.

"She thought I was someone else," Kevin muttered, staring sadly into his glass of beer. "All the time I held her and rained kisses on her dear face . . . Och, I know a gentleman should not take advantage, but it was more than flesh and blood could bear, finding her so yielding and soft and sweet . . . She put her arms around my neck and smiled into my eyes, and called me . . . She called me . . ."

Emerson was as red as a mahogany bureau. I let him suffer for a while before I interrupted. "People who are delirious or suffering from the effects of drugs are quite unaware of what they are saying, Kevin. Nor do their mutterings have any significance whatever. It is up to you to win her affection, if that is what you want. You will be well on the way to doing it when I tell her of how you pummeled Mr. Wilson into unconsciousness, despite the revolver he fired at you, and with complete disregard for your own safety."

Emerson made a rumbling noise and scowled at me. "Enough of this sentimental nonsense," he declared. "We promised the Inspector a statement. He has his work to do, you know. He has no time to waste on romantic twaddle. Have a little more wine, Inspector."

"I don't mind if I do," Cuff remarked. "A very fine vintage, Professor; fruity and not too sweet, with just the proper touch of acidity. Hem."

"You see," Emerson explained, "Mrs. Emerson and I are in the habit of carrying on friendly little competitions when it comes to solving cases such as this. So I am going to let her begin the narrative. Tell the Inspector how you deduced the identity of the killer, Peabody."

There was a suspicious twitch at the corner of his mouth, which I chose to ignore. "Thank you, Emerson, I will be glad to begin. This has proved to be one of the strangest cases I—we—have ever investigated—a peculiar blend of vulgar crime and exotic trimmings, if I may put it that way."

"Put it any way you like, but get on with it," Emerson said.

"Let me begin at the beginning, then—with the death of the night watchman. By the way, Inspector, I think you may want to have the body exhumed. You will find, I believe, that the poor man died of an overdose of opium."

"What?" The Inspector stared at me. "But the medical examiner said—"

"The effects of an excessively large amount of opium resemble those of cerebral hemorrhage, Inspector. It affects the respiratory center in the medulla oblongata, and results in death from respiratory failure. The watchman had not taken opium before. He was given it as a treat—part of his payment for allowing the orgy—for so I must call it—to take place.

"That was the meaning of the strange debris found in the room where the body lay. Not only an orgy, but one with an ancient Egyptian theme—wreaths of flowers, wine in crystal glasses (not so appropriate, that, but common clay cups would not be good enough for those spoiled young men), and suitable costumes, including scepters and masks made of the ever-popular papier-mâché. It was the sort of bizarre, unseemly jest that would have appealed to these jaded men; and there was another purpose in the selection of that unlikely place, a darker and more sinister purpose, which I will discuss in due time.

"Obviously a number of people had to be bribed if such an event was to take place. Oldacre was one of them; he was always toadying to the rich and would have given his mean little soul to be a member of such a group. The night watchman in charge of that part of the museum was paid a large sum, and invited to participate, as a means of ensuring his silence. His death was an accident; none of them anticipated the opium would kill him. When they realized he was dead, their first thought was to conceal what had taken place. They gathered up the bottles and glasses and the wreaths of flowers, leaving the body where it lay. The women . . . I fancy Ayesha supplied them. They were no danger, they would not dare speak out against such noble gentlemen.

"Oldacre was another matter. It wasn't only money he wanted; he wanted to be one of them, an intimate—a guest at their clubs, and in their homes. His death was in itself the clue to the identity of his killer; for which of those young aristocrats had real cause to fear him? The truth might have caused a scandal, but they were used to scandals, they had seen plenty of them.

"Eustace Wilson, on the other hand, stood to lose everything if the truth came out. He would never find another position in archaeology; and if he was arrested and disgraced, he would also lose his hold on the young man he was methodically milking of his fortune."

The Inspector looked doubtful. "That's all well and good, Mrs. Emerson, and now that the case is solved, your reasoning makes excellent sense; but I didn't see it that way at the time. Those who suffer from—from his lordship's disease are sometimes subject to violent rages. Being threatened by a contemptible creature like Oldacre might well have induced such a homicidal rage."

Emerson coughed. He no longer attempted to conceal his smile.

"If you will allow me to continue, Inspector," I said coldly, "you will find that my assumption concerning the death of Oldacre was confirmed by other evidence."

"I beg your pardon, ma'am," said the Inspector.

"I had felt all along that the man we wanted was no dilettante, but an individual who had been trained in Egyptology. His costume was authentic in every meaningful detail, and the quotations he chose were too obscure and too apt to be readily discovered by a casual student of the subject. The paper found in Oldacre's dead hand contained an invented message, not a quotation—and that was an even stronger indication of expertise in the language, for it is easier to copy a text than compose a new one. The errors of orthography and grammar in that message were of the sort that would be made, not by an amateur, but by a student—particularly by a student of Mr. Budge's.

"Oldacre was one of Budge's subordinates. It was barely conceivable (for in the investigation of crime, Ramses and gentlemen, one must consider all possibilities, however unlikely) that he had written the message himself, for purposes unknown, and that its application to his death was purely coincidental. However, Oldacre was dead when the ushebtis and their messages were delivered. Heaven knows there are many of Budge's students wandering around the world—too many, some might say. But the only other one closely connected with the case was Mr. Eustace Wilson. He knew Oldacre, and I do not doubt that the acquaintance was closer than he led me to believe.

"What threw me off the track for a time was the involvement of Lord Liverpool and his friend, Lord St. John. In fact, the Earl's hideous disease was the ultimate cause of the entire business. There is no cure for it. Death is certain. When people face death, they will try any purported cure, however bizarre and senseless. What have they got to lose? I confess that the full truth did not dawn on me until we discovered, on the night of the affair at the Royal Society, that the mummy had been unwrapped.

"The wrappings must have been removed while the mummy was still at Mauldy Manor. Certainly the Museum authorities had never authorized such an act, so it must have been done by the former Earl or his son, who succeeded him as Lord Liverpool. But why would either do such a thing? The late Earl was a collector pure and simple, not an amateur student of Egyptology. His son had even less interest in the subject. Moreover, if innocent though inept scientific curiosity had prompted the unwrapping, there would not have been such a desperate need to conceal its having been done. What other possible reason could there be for exposing a mummy?"

Emerson's lips parted. He was in a quizzical mood that evening, and I thought it wiser not to allow him to offer a suggestion, so I hastened on.

"As early as the twelfth century, there is a record of a physician prescribing ground-up mummy as medicine. Four centuries later, mummy was a standard drug, to be found in apothecaries' shops throughout Europe. Large quantities of mummies were imported for that purpose, and when the supply dwindled, unscrupulous persons manufactured them, from fresh cadavers.

"One would suppose that in this modern age, the advancement of science and reason would have destroyed this superstition, but in fact there are still shops in London and, I am told, in Paris and in New York, where powdered mummy can be purchased. Ignorance never dies, Ramses and gentlemen; and when it is combined with desperation, we can hardly wonder that the young Earl was ready to believe that the revolting substance, drawn from an unimpeachably genuine source, and combined with solemn rituals and prayers, might assist his desperate need.

"Like Oldacre, Wilson met the Earl through Lord St. John, who does have a dilettante's interest in archaeology, and who also possesses a perverse sense of humor. They were all involved in the original scheme. Why should Lord St. John not participate if it comforted his friend and allowed him to mock the conventions he despised? At first the rituals and concomitant orgies took place at Mauldy Manor; it is no wonder the housemaids heard strange noises from the room in question at various times. Then the Earl's father discovered what was going on. He was no saint, but these perversions appalled him; he presented the violated mummy to the British Museum and forbade further experiments. Shortly thereafter he died; and although it probably can never be proved, I suspect the hunting accident was no accident. It would be interesting to obtain a list of the guests who were present on that occasion.

"I also suspect that Oldacre was not one of the original members of the conspiracy. He may have discovered what was happening in the dignified halls of the Museum and was then, perforce, allowed to join the group. Not content with a subordinate role, he demanded greater power and a share of the money Wilson was squeezing from Lord Liverpool. So Wilson killed him. He considered himself quite safe, did the gentle Mr. Wilson, until Emerson and I entered the case. He knew our reputations, and feared (quite correctly, as it proved) that we would see through his scheme. It was my discovery of Ayesha's involvement that brought matters to a head. As Emerson once pointed out, most opium dens are managed by Indians or Chinese; it was not mere happenchance that Lord Liverpool procured his supply of the drug from this particular establishment. He was introduced to it and to Ayesha by Wilson, who had worked in

Egypt, and had connections in the Egyptian community here.

"By this time Wilson faced another dangerous dilemma. The Earl was dying; the grim, though lucrative charade could not be continued much longer. In the beginning, Lord St. John had been a willing participant in the scheme; they all took turns playing the *sem* priest, which is why that mysterious individual's behavior confused us so—on one occasion hesitant and unsure of his role, on another confident and cool. As time went on St. John came to despise Wilson, and to resent his power over Liverpool; but by then he was helpless to interfere. Liverpool would brook no criticism of the man he hoped would save his life, and after the murder of Oldacre convinced St. John that the 'harmless' game had turned to deadly earnest, he could not expose the plot without involving his friend in a nasty scandal, even a possible accusation of murder. Yet St. John was a potential threat to Wilson, and the Earl himself was becoming increasingly undependable, as the disease strengthened its hold on his decaying body. If he decided the treatment was a failure, and turned on his would be savior, exposure was equally certain.

"Wilson decided to kill two birds with one stone— silence the Earl before he became a danger, and provide the police with the murderer for whom they were searching. He forced Ayesha to lead me into a trap; unlike the other hieroglyphic inscriptions we had seen, this message was so clumsy and inept it would have been taken for the product of someone relatively ignorant of the language. Wilson intended to use me in the ceremony we interrupted this evening. He planned to dismiss all the witnesses and dispatch both me and Liverpool, in such a way as to leave no doubt that the Earl had killed me and then himself—or, perhaps, that we had killed one another. I can think of a number of ways in which it could have been arranged—"

"I am sure you could, ma'am," said the Inspector respectfully. "But it was Miss Minton, not you—"

I waved my hand negligently. "A minor change in the cast of the play, Inspector. Miss Minton's role in all this was a very curious one. I fancy Wilson planned to marry her. To say he loved her would be a perversion of that noble word, but that is how he probably would have described it. Yet he resented her casual, contemptuous treatment of him, and when he learned she was penniless, he found it hard to conceal his outrage and disbelief. The insane egotism that had prompted his delusion (for I hardly need say that a lady like Miss Minton would never have consented to become his wife) now persuaded him that she had deceived and betrayed him, and made him determine to gain revenge. He discovered that same evening that she was here in this house. She had to be; otherwise I could not have ascertained so quickly that she was unharmed. I erred—I frankly admit it—by telling him, but I tried to protect the girl by insisting she remain here until morning. I had no idea she would dare disobey ME. In fact, she was in such a state of anger and chagrin that she determined to leave the house at once; and Wilson, who had been waiting outside in the hope of finding a means of communicating with her, had no difficulty in persuading her to accompany him. No doubt she expected him to escort her to her lodging, but once in the hansom cab she was at his mercy. It is not without reason that young ladies are warned against those dangerous vehicles!"

I had proceeded thus far without interruption from Emerson or Ramses, and all at once it struck me that this was so unusual as to merit inquiry. Emerson was smirking in a manner that made me want to shake him, and Ramses . . .

"That child is intoxicated," I exclaimed. "Emerson, how could you!"

Emerson was just in time to prevent Ramses from sliding quietly off his chair onto the floor. The boy's eyes were closed, and he did not stir when his father lifted him into his arms.

"He isn't drunk, Amelia, he is tired," said Emerson indignantly. "The little lad has had a busy night."

"Busy night, indeed. Busy week would be more like it. I don't suppose he has been in his bed more than . . . Take him up and tuck him in, Bob. And pray don't forget to take off those ghastly garments, and wash him, and—"

Emerson gave Ramses into the waiting arms of the footman, remarking, "Be gentle, Bob."

"Yes, sir. I will, sir."

"Now, then," I said, when Bob and his sleeping charge had departed, "it is getting late and we should all think of retiring. But first, Inspector, you owe me an explanation. I hope you aren't going to claim you followed the same train of deductive reasoning that led me to the solution of the crime?"

"Oh, no, ma'am," said the Inspector, blinking. "Such a train of reasoning would be quite beyond me. No; I am sorry to admit it was the dull, boring routine of police investigation that led me into quite the wrong conclusion. We make use of informers—"

"Ahmet," I exclaimed. "That wretched little spy! He told me nothing!"

"Well, ma'am, perhaps you did not ask the right questions," said Inspector Cuff mildly. "We took Ahmet into custody for his own protection. Knowing the reputations of the young gentlemen, I already had some suspicions of them, and after prolonged questioning—no, ma'am, not bullying, just questioning—Ahmet admitted Lord Liverpool was one of Ayesha's customers. Not in the opium den itself; she had rooms upstairs reserved for more distinguished visitors. Then later, when the professor—"

"Good Gad, only look at the time," Emerson exclaimed, taking his watch from his pocket. "I don't like to be inhospitable, Inspector—Mr. O'Connell—Gargery—"

A murmur of agreement interrupted the list, and the Inspector rose to his feet. "Yes, sir, you are quite right. I must be getting along. With profound thanks, Professor and ma'am—"

We said good night to the Inspector in the hall, and then proceeded upstairs. I looked in on Ramses and found him sound asleep; the parts of him that showed were relatively clean. I had my suspicions about the rest, but I decided not to disturb him. Returning to my room, I found Emerson lying on the bed. He was not asleep, however, and as soon as I closed the door he rose with his customary alacrity and began to assist me in preparing for repose, remarking that it would be thoughtless to disturb one of the maids at that hour.

"Emerson," I said.

"Yes, Peabody? Curse these buttons . . ."

"You interrupted the inspector just as he was about to explain how you had assisted him in his investigations."

"Did I, Peabody? Ah, there we go . . ."

A button bounced on the floor. "How did you assist him, Emerson? For if you are going to tell me you knew Eustace Wilson was the ringleader—"

"Did you know, Peabody?"

"Did I not explain my reasoning, Emerson?"

"Yes, Peabody, you did, and most ingeniously, too. However, the expression on your face when you saw Wilson in the carriage—"

"You could not have seen my expression, Emerson. My back was to you."

Emerson kicked a garment out of the way and wrapped both arms around me. "You thought it was Lord St. John. Oh, come, Peabody; I'll confess if you will."

"You too, Emerson?"

"Everything pointed to him, Peabody. The eminence grise, the Machiavellian mentor, the power behind the throne—"

"He was almost too perfect," I said regretfully. "He had been a soldier, hardened to slaughter and the spilling of blood; he is intelligent, cynical, quick-thinking . . ."

"Corrupt and dissipated," said Emerson, snapping his teeth together.

"Yes; but I fancy he had honestly sickened of the life that had brought his friend to such a hideous doom. He told me he had, but naturally I was somewhat skeptical of his claims of newfound virtue. I fear his manner is unfortunate; one tends to find double entendres and hidden meanings in everything he says. At any rate, he was not present this evening, and I sincerely hope he will find the good woman he purports to be seeking, and that she may assist him in attaining peace of mind and a virtuous life."

"There is nothing like the influence of a good woman," Emerson agreed solemnly. "Now, then, Peabody, why don't we—"

"With all my heart, Emerson."

After a prolonged interval Emerson raised his head and said somewhat breathlessly, "That was excellent, Peabody, and I intend to continue in the same vein almost at once; but first, would you care to admit you were mistaken about—"

"I see no reason to continue the discussion, Emerson."

"Mmmmmm," said Emerson. "Well, Peabody, I must confess your arguments are extremely persuasive."

A gray, rainy dawn was breaking before we fell asleep, and the same gloomy light met my eyes when I opened them some hours later. The house was quiet and peaceful; there was no sign of Ramses, at the foot of the bed, or at the door; and I lay in sleepy content for a time, engaged in philosophical meditation. There is nothing more soothing, I believe, than the consciousness of duty accomplished and dangers overcome. Another murderer had been safely delivered into the arms of the law, and I could now turn my attention to a little problem that had been perplexing me for several days. It had to do—inevitably—with Ramses. However, before I could concentrate on the matter, Emerson awoke, and the ensuing distractions, of the sort in which he is peculiarly gifted, turned my attention in another direction.

As a result it was quite late in the afternoon before we finally emerged from our room. Owing to the inclement weather, the skies outside were quite dark and all the lamps had been lighted. As we proceeded arm in arm along the corridor, Emerson remarked, "I presume you will insist on having tea, Peabody."

"Have you any objections, Emerson?"

"Well, yes, confound it, I do; and you know what they are, Peabody."

"I assure you, my dear, that I am about to turn my attention to the problem."

"Very well, my dear Peabody, I will leave it to you. But I warn you, I can't stand it much longer. I need peace and quiet if I am to finish that confounded manuscript—"

Before he could continue, a horrendous shriek reverberated through the house. It came from the direction of the children's rooms.

"Curse it," Emerson exclaimed. "What now? That child has the most piercing voice of any female I have ever heard. What will she be like in ten years, after her lungs have expanded? I tell you, Peabody—"

"That was not Violet, Emerson," I said. "If you will be quiet a minute . . ." Sure enough, another scream confirmed my hypothesis; it had come, I felt certain, from a female older than Violet. "One of the maids, I believe," I continued. "Perhaps we had better go and see what is wrong."

We met the maid in question—Mary Ann it was—in the hallway. She had both hands over her face, and ran full-tilt into Emerson, who politely caught her and propped her against the wall before proceeding on his way. "No use asking her," he remarked. "She appears to be in quite a state of agitation. I suppose that was Ramses' room from which she emerged?"

"That would be a safe assumption even if I had not seen her come out the door," I replied. "She must have gone to call him to tea and found . . . What, one wonders?"

We were soon to learn. The door was open. Somehow I was not surprised to find Ramses was not alone. He and Percy stood confronting one another across the table on which Ramses' mummies were arranged. Their faces presented an interesting contrast in color, for Percy was flushed and livid with anger, and Ramses was as pale as I had ever seen him. Owing to the natural darkness of his complexion and his deep tan, his cheeks had turned an odd shade of milky brown. On the table between them was what appeared to be a new specimen—

very new indeed, for it was covered with gore that ran freely from its wounds.

The carcass was that of a rat. With their long, obscenely naked tails and sharp teeth, rats are not the loveliest of God's creatures; but they are nevertheless God's creatures. The mutilations inflicted on this one were of a sort that could only have been perpetrated, not by claws of cat or fangs of dog, but by a sharp knife held in a human hand. Worst of all, the faintest pulsation of the flayed body showed that the wretched thing still lived, though mercifully it was incapable of feeling pain.

Emerson was at my side, as he always was when danger or difficulty threatened. He carried the thing away; I did not look to see what he did, and after a moment he said quietly, "It is dead, Peabody."

"Thank you, my dear Emerson."

I looked at the two boys. Percy was biting his lip and his eyes were luminous with tears he strove to hold back. The countenance of "Ramses" Walter Peabody Emerson was its usual enigmatic mask; but my keen maternal eyes caught a flicker of emotion in his black eyes. Apprehension, I thought.

"Who did this?" I asked.

There was no answer. I had not expected one. I turned my gaze upon Percy. He stiffened. Hands behind his back, lips tight, he met my eyes without blinking. "Did you do it, Percy?" I asked.

"No, Aunt Amelia."

"Then, if you did not, the culprit must have been Ramses. Was it Ramses, Percy?"

Percy might have stood for a portrait of Gallant Young England Facing the Enemy. He lifted his chin and straightened his shoulders. "I cannot answer you, Aunt Amelia. I owe you the love and duty of a son, but there are some things even more important to an English gentleman."

"I see. Very well, Percy. You are excused. Please go to your room and stay there until I come."

"Yes, Aunt Amelia." He marched out.

By contrast to his cousin, Ramses made a poor showing. His narrow shoulders were hunched as if in expectation of a blow, and his eyes would not meet mine.

I held out my arms.

"Ramses, I owe you a profound apology. Come here to me."

Emotion overcomes me when I recall that moment, and draws a veil over the tender scene that ensued. Emerson was frankly sniffing and rubbing his eyes with his sleeve (he never has a handkerchief). Ramses sat between us on the bed; his father's arm was around him and he was—of course—talking. I interrupted him.

"You need not explain, Ramses, I understand everything now. Is it not fascinating, Emerson, to see how events that appear quite comprehensible at the outset can take on quite the opposite interpretation after a slight change in one's perspective? But who could have supposed that a boy of Percy's age could be so sly?"

"That," said Emerson, "is the pernicious public school training. The poor little brutes have to learn such tricks in order to survive. If I have said it once—"

"You have said it a hundred times," I agreed.

"However, Percy finally overextended himself with this last accusation. Ramses' list of misdemeanors is quite extensive, in scope as in number; there are few things I would believe him incapable of doing. But to deliberately torture and mutilate an animal . . . I would as soon believe the sun would rise in the west, or that you, my dear Emerson, would deceive me."

"Er—hmmm," said Emerson.

"Thank you, Mama," said Ramses. "Words fail me when I attempt—"

But I knew they did not, so I again interrupted. "My suspicions of Percy and his sister arose only recently and were confirmed by my reconsideration of early events. From the very beginning—the incident of the cricket ball in the midriff—yes, Ramses, I know you tried to tell me that a player of Percy's skill might well have been able to direct the ball in the desired direction . . . Unfortunately, I have been preoccupied with matters of life and death and had not the time to consider the problem carefully. I suppose Violet told you that Miss Helen had given permission for you to ride her bicycle? Yes; Violet was a willing participant in the scheme and did her share of pushing and tripping and fibbing. Er . . . Ramses, your demonstrations of affection touch me deeply, but perhaps you might postpone further embraces until after you have washed. What is that substance on my skirt? It cannot be blood, it is too sticky . . . Well, never mind. I will make it up to you, Ramses, I promise. What would you like?"

"I would like to be allowed to pound Percy," said Ramses.

His father chuckled affectionately. "No doubt, my boy, no doubt. A most commendable and comprehensible desire. I too would like . . . But it can't be done, Ramses."

"I will rid us of the young man as soon as possible," I promised. "And Violet as well. You may take that as understood, Ramses. Something further is required, I believe. A little treat, or present . . ."

Ramses' black eyes flashed. "May I have my disguises back, Mama?"

In fact, he had done very well without them. The shortness of his stature limited him, but the role of the street arab had served him admirably on a number of occasions, and the diabolical cunning that had prompted him to bribe a genuine specimen of the breed to distract me, so I would be less suspicious in future, left me torn between admiration and horror. The only other part he had attempted was that of the little golden-tressed girl; after I took away the first wig, he fashioned another out of the hair of Violet's doll. But this, as he was the first to admit, was more limiting. "I have never fully appreciated the disadvantages, not only of being female in this present society, but of being well-to-do," he explained in his pedantic manner. "The only way I could get about as a girl was to attach myself to some adult, and that was not satisfactory, for the adult in question, unless extremely preoccupied, very often was the first to notice I was unattended, and would inquire what had happened to my nurse. I also considered disguising myself as a dwarf or midget, but concluded I would attract an undesirable amount of attention in that role."

From the first Percy, ably abetted by Violet, had set out to get Ramses in trouble. It may seem incredible that there are individuals whose chief pleasure in life is making someone else suffer; but the annals of crime, not to mention the ordinary history of the human race, contain too many examples for the conclusion to be doubted. Initially Ramses had found himself unable to deal with these machinations; he was used to murderers and thieves, but he had never encountered anyone like Percy before. His attempts to explain himself only seemed to make matters worse, and although he was wise enough not to say so, I could see he felt I had been a trifle too quick to assume he was at fault. I had to agree; but I would like to point out that Ramses' past history tended to confirm such an assumption. Percy had early on discovered that Ramses was creeping out of the house without permission and in disguise; Ramses had been forced (as he put it) to resort to bribery in order to keep his cousins silent. Percy had stripped him of all his pocket money and most of his valuables, including the watch and the knife, and then, having decided the cupboard was bare, had prepared his last trick.

I gave myself the satisfaction of returning Percy and Violet to their mama. She had been in Birmingham the whole time. That was just another example of my brother James's penuriousness, for if he had not been too miserly to send his wife abroad, it would have taken me longer to discover the plot. I found her squatting like a toad in her house; she had dismissed all the servants except for a single over-worked housemaid, and when I forced my way past this poor creature I discovered Elizabeth in the drawing room with a novel and a box of chocolates. The sight of me caused her to choke on the one she had just popped into her mouth, and I had to smack her on the back several times before her color returned to normal.

"But what the devil was the point of it all?" Emerson demanded upon my return. "Just to save a few sovereigns on their food and care?"

"No doubt James would consider that worth the effort," I replied in disgust. "But there was more to it than that, Emerson; Elizabeth frankly admitted it when I demanded the truth, she is even stupider than James and has less gumption. It was those newspaper stories that spoke of Ramses' frail health and danger-ous exploits. Percy was supposed to worm his way into our affections, so that if anything should happen to Ramses, we would make Percy our heir."

Emerson turned bright crimson. "What? What? Curse the murderous little—"

"No, no, Emerson, I don't believe for a moment that Percy was a precocious killer. Though some of the tricks he played might well have had fatal results . . . He was only supposed to be engaging and adorable and lovable."

"A role quite beyond his powers," Emerson grunted.

"But James has not enough imagination to realize that, Emerson. He felt it was worth a try, at any rate."

Emerson thought it over. "Then it is Mr. O'Connell

we have to thank for those ghastly children being foisted upon us," he said in an ominous voice. "It was he who wrote that story—"

What a pity, I thought; just when Kevin and Emerson had been getting on so well. I decided this was not the time to tell Emerson about my hopes for the young people. There was no real barrier to separate them; she was an aristocrat, but poor as a church mouse; he earned a salary sufficient to support a wife in respectable style, and I had always suspected his antecedents were more distinguished than he let on. He spoke quite good English when he was not trying to behave like a stage Irishman, and the suit of evening clothes—which he had admitted he owned— had been cut by an excellent tailor. It looked very promising, and I felt sure that by the time the wedding took place, Emerson would have got over his annoyance and might even agree to give the bride away.

I was in the library, scribbling busily away at my paper on the Black Pyramid, and meditating (for when the subject is one with which I am thoroughly at home I can easily think of two or more things at once) on the tranquillity of family life. One never truly appreciates one's happiness until after one has lost it and then seen it restored; I had never fully appreciated Ramses until I met Percy. The house was blissfully quiet. Emerson was at the Museum; Ramses was in his room, mummifying a rat or manufacturing dynamite, or doing something of the sort. How peaceful it all was, and how devoutly I thanked Heaven for my manifold blessings!

There was only one little thing. I did not mention it to Heaven, since I fully expected I would be able to deal with it unaided, but at the moment I was not quite certain how to proceed. I had told Emerson I would never do anything to make him break a solemn promise—nor would I. But there had to be some other way of ascertaining the identity of that mysterious man in the turban . . . He must be an Egyptian. An ally, or enemy, or business rival, or lover, of poor Ayesha's? Ahmet the Louse had been restored to his friends and his relations, but I knew how to reach him; he or some other of the opium addicts who had been poor unfortunate Ayesha's clients must know . . .

The library door burst open with the impetuosity that marks my beloved spouse. I greeted him with a smile; he greeted me with a fervent embrace. "Hullo, Peabody. How is the paper coming along?"

"Very well, my dear."

"Good. Then you can take a few minutes' respite from your labors."

"Certainly, my dear Emerson."

He threw himself down on the sofa and indicated the seat next to him. I took it, and studied him with considerable curiosity. He seemed in excessively high spirits; his whole body was bubbling with laughter that now and again escaped his smiling lips in a cheery chuckle. His eyes sparkled and his cheeks were handsomely flushed.

"What do you say to a whiskey and soda, Peabody?"

"My dear, not at this hour. It is too early."

"Well, I must do something to celebrate." He pursed his lips and blew out his breath in a long whistle. "What a narrow escape! I really feared for a time . . ."

"What is it, Emerson? Have you finished your manuscript?"

"Oh, that. Something much more important, Peabody. I tell you, I have narrowly escaped a horrible fate. Aren't you going to ask me what it was?"

An inkling of the truth had begun to dawn. I smiled demurely. "Why, no, Emerson, not if it is something you have sworn never to tell. 'Eternal silence' was, I believe—"

"Peabody, you can sometimes be very annoying. You are supposed to nag and scold and bully me into speaking."

"Consider it done, Emerson."

Emerson burst out laughing. "Thank you. Let me see, how can I put this . . . Peabody, would you like to be the wife of Sir Radcliffe Emerson, Knight?"

"Why, no, Emerson, that would not suit me at all," I replied calmly. "To be addressed as Lady Emerson—"

Emerson interrupted me with a hearty kiss. "I thought you would feel that way. So I declined. I was forced, however, to accept a small token of esteem."

He handed me a little velvet box. Inside was an emerald of astonishing size and clarity, set in a ring and encircled with small diamonds.

"My dear, how vulgar," I said, examining it. "How could she possibly suppose you would wear such a thing? She is a rather common little woman, I know, but—"

"Curse you, Peabody," Emerson shouted. "You knew all along, didn't you? That night, when I came back from Windsor, and you accused me of seeing another woman, but you put it in such a way that I wasn't sure whether you meant Ayesha or . . . Peabody, you ought to be ashamed of yourself!"

If I had been the arrogant, conniving female some people believe me to be, I would have let him preserve his delusion, for it certainly gave me credit for almost superhuman omniscience. Instead I laughed and laid my head against his shoulder.

"No, Emerson, I did not have the least idea. Not until this moment. But when you spoke of being knighted—well, there is only one individual in England who can bestow that honor. So the mysterious Indian was her intimate servant, the Munshi?"

"Quite right." Emerson's good humor was restored; he likes me to admit I was wrong, and he likes even more to have me put my head on his shoulder. "She summoned me, Peabody, after it was apparent that young Liverpool was deeply involved in an affair which might well end in a charge of murder. It was Cuff who gathered the evidence against him; and now perhaps you can forgive the good Inspector for concealing some of the facts, even after the case had been officially concluded. Like me, he was sworn to secrecy. Unlike me, he stands to lose a great deal if he breaks his word."

"It is not your fault, my dear. I nagged and bullied and scolded you."

"Quite right." Emerson grinned. "Since I have

succumbed to your underhanded wiles and cruel threats I may as well tell you the rest of it; for in telling you, my dearest Peabody, I confide only in the better half of myself, and I know you will consider yourself bound by the same oath."

"Naturally, my dearest Emerson. And may I say how much I admire the Jesuitical subtlety of your reasoning? It is worthy of Ramses at his best."

"Thank you, my dear. You mustn't blame yourself for failing to follow Cuff's deductions, since he had information you did not—to wit, a long dossier on the activities of Liverpool and his set. He knew Oldacre was one of them, and he also knew they were habitués of Ayesha's establishment. Being fully aware of Liverpool's illness and its symptoms, he came to the logical conclusion that Liverpool was a prime suspect in the murder case. But when he took his suspicions to his superiors he met with precisely the response experience had told him to expect: consternation and skepticism."

"And yet Cuff persisted? What a courageous thing to do."

"Well, not exactly," Emerson replied. "This country does suffer from a repellent infatuation with aristocracy; but to the eternal credit of British justice let it be said that neither rank nor title can save a man from the consequences of a criminal act. Cuff was told to proceed, but in strictest secrecy and alone, until he had obtained indisputable evidence of guilt. Naturally Her Majesty had to be told—warned—that Liverpool was in danger. She has, among other weaknesses less amiable, a sincere attachment to those related to her by blood;

consideration for her feelings had spared the young man on a number of earlier occasions.

"When I went to see Cuff on Monday last, after our visit to the opium den, I of course knew nothing of this, nor did he confide in me at that time. I wanted . . . Er, hem. I felt I ought . . ."

"You wanted Ayesha's address," I said calmly. "Never mind, Emerson. The past is buried in the grave of that unhappy woman. We will not refer to it again."

"Hmph," said Emerson. "Well, as it turned out, Cuff and I had a little discussion about the case, and afterwards he did me the honor of mentioning my name to Her Majesty. She sent for me and asked for my help in proving the young man innocent. She was in deep distress; for, though he had been guilty of a few indiscretions in the past (as the naïve lady put it) she could not believe a member of her family could commit such a vile crime."

"She is worse than naïve, she is rather stupid if she believes that," I remarked. "I can think of several instances—"

"As can I, Peabody. However, her request was confounded flattering, and since I felt the Earl was too much of a weakling, mentally and physically, to plan such a scheme, I promised I would do my best.

"From then on Cuff and I worked together. It was Cuff who learned of the bizarre ceremony planned for that fateful night. One of the Egyptian thugs hired for the occasion had participated in other such events, and he bragged of it to a lady-friend, who told another friend, who told another— who was one of Cuff's informants. I committed an unforgivable act of treachery, my darling Peabody, when I locked you in our room that day; but I was in a deuced uncomfortable dilemma, between the demands of Cuff and the Crown for absolute secrecy, and my suspicion that something damnable was likely to occur in that den of iniquity. And yet, do you know, Peabody, somehow I wasn't surprised to see you come stumbling down those stairs. I might have known your brilliant, incisive mind would solve the puzzle."

"All's well that ends well," I said cheerfully. "So you saw her again today, and she gave you the emerald as a token of appreciation?"

"Better than a knighthood." Emerson chuckled. "I will have the ring cut down for you, Peabody."

"Thank you, my dear Emerson. I accept, since I cannot imagine you flaunting emeralds on your person."

"And also," said Emerson fiercely, "because the credit is as much yours as mine. You know, Peabody, I never speak ill of a woman, and she is elderly, and deserving of respect on that account at least, but . . . but . . . She really is so confounded dull, Peabody! She thinks herself capable of ruling an empire, but denigrates all other women. Even you, my dear. I told her we always worked together, but she . . ."

"Never mind, Emerson. Your righteous indignation on my behalf, and that of all women, means far more to me than any token from that source. And, my dear, you were able to assure her that the young man was—was—"

"Hmph," said Emerson. "It is difficult to find an appropriate word, is it not? Hardly innocent . . . but he was innocent of murder, Peabody. And at the end he proved himself worthy of his lineage and his name. I saw nothing wrong in glossing over a few of the more unsavory details."

"And you were quite right, Emerson."

"I am glad you agree, Peabody, because if you didn't you would tell me so in no uncertain terms. Now then—what about that whiskey and soda?"